OFFICE *INTRIGUE*

Office Intrigue, Book 1

D1267996

By Nicole Edwards

The Alluring Indulgence Series
Kaleb
Zane
Travis
Holidays with the Walker Brothers
Ethan
Braydon
Sawyer
Brendon

The Austin Arrows Series
Rush
Kaufman

The Bad Boys of Sports Series
Bad Reputation
Bad Business

The Caine Cousins Series
Hard to Hold
Hard to Handle

The Club Destiny Series
Conviction
Temptation
Addicted
Seduction
Infatuation
Captivated
Devotion
Perception
Entrusted
Adored
Distraction

The Coyote Ridge Series
Curtis
Jared

The Dead Heat Ranch Series
Boots Optional
Betting on Grace
Overnight Love

By Nicole Edwards (cont.)

The Devil's Bend Series

Chasing Dreams
Vanishing Dreams

The Devil's Playground Series

Without Regret
Without Restraint

The Office Intrigue Series

Office Intrigue
Intrigued Out of the Office
Their Rebellious Submissive

The Pier 70 Series

Reckless
Fearless
Speechless
Harmless

The Sniper 1 Security Series

Wait for Morning
Never Say Never
Tomorrow's Too Late

The Southern Boy Mafia Series

Beautifully Brutal
Beautifully Loyal

Standalone Novels

A Million Tiny Pieces
Inked on Paper

Writing as Timberlyn Scott

Unhinged
Unraveling
Chaos

Naughty Holiday Editions

2015
2016

OFFICE INTRIGUE

Office Intrigue Duet, Book 1

NICOLE EDWARDS

Nicole Edwards Limited
PO Box 806
Hutto, Texas 78634
NicoleEdwardsLimited.com

Office Intrigue – An Office Intrigue Duet Novel is a work of fiction. Names, characters, businesses, places, events and incidents either are the products of the author's imagination or used in a fictitious manner. Any resemblance to actual persons, living or dead, or actual events is purely coincidental.

Cover Image: © Wander Aguiar | wanderbookclub.com
Model: Olivia Korte @ Brisebois Agency
Cover Background Image: © kantver | 123rf.com

Cover Design: © Nicole Edwards Limited
Editing: Blue Otter Editing | www.BlueOtterEditing.com
ISBN (ebook): 978-1-939786-84-5
ISBN (print): 978-1-939786-83-8

BDSM Romance
Mature Audience

DEDICATION

To my beast

ONE

BEEP-BA-BEEP.

"Son of a bitch."

It should be a crime to have to get up before six o'clock in the morning.

"Eight more minutes is all you get," I mumbled into my pillow, talking to myself as I smacked the snooze button on my phone.

Beep-ba-beep.

Eight minutes was not nearly long enough. It felt more like two.

And, okay, fine, it was safe to say I wasn't a morning person, but this was one of those rare days when it was necessary that I got up at the ass-crack of dawn. The worst time of the day as far as I was concerned. But it was a necessary evil, because unlike...*nobody*...I didn't crawl out of bed looking like a supermodel. That shit didn't really happen. To anyone.

I rolled onto my stomach and kicked the comforter off my bed and onto the floor. Getting rid of my warm cocoon was the only way to ensure I wouldn't snuggle down again and ignore the annoying *beep-ba-beep* that was supposed to be a signal to get my happy ass out of bed.

Of course, I still closed my eyes. That's what snooze buttons were for, right?

•

Beep-ba-beep.

"Craaaaaap!" I was jarred awake by that annoying sound once again, but this time procrastination was not my friend.

Before I could screw myself out of any more prep time, my feet hit the floor and my tired ass was vertical. I made a big production out of yawning and stretching as I marched groggily to the bathroom. Through the haze of sleep, I flipped on the shower before stripping off my pajama pants and tank top, leaving them on the floor to pick up later. It wasn't that I was a complete slob…okay, that was a lie, I was a complete slob. Especially when it came to laundry. Good thing I rarely had people over to my apartment.

During my shower, I had a moment of clarity as my hands drifted downward, soaping every inch of skin. It was time for me to schedule another waxing appointment. This realization did not make me happy. How could it? What sane woman enjoyed having her pubic hair brutally ripped from her nether region? Maybe there were people who were into that sort of torture, but I wasn't one of them.

However, it was a necessity. A woman had to be prepared for the day she ran into the man who would rock her world and tip her otherwise unsteady existence right on its axis.

Not that I was looking, of course. I had far better things to do than wait for Mr. Right Now to pop into my life and make anything tip or spin.

Okay, another lie.

I was on a roll today.

It was too early and I hadn't had coffee. That was my excuse.

When I was done in the shower, I cut the water off. One towel was used to dry my face, then went on my hair; the other was for drying me from neck to toe.

There.

The biggest portion of my morning routine was taken care of and that only cost me…

Thirty-four minutes.

"Shit, shit, shit."

I stared at myself in the mirror. Even I knew I should've had a little more energy. After all, I had a job interview in less than two hours, which meant I should've been darting around like it was the first day of school.

Unfortunately, mornings did not contain the fuel necessary to light a fire under my ass.

That meant I had to rush through my makeup, but first brushing my teeth was critical. If my dentist wasn't always on my ass about it, I would've skipped flossing, but I had to listen to my mother bitch about enough already. I didn't need to get a lecture about good dental hygiene, too.

"See, Mom?" I offered a toothy grin to my reflection. "All shiny and clean."

Once that was done, it was time to put my face on. I had to look good. It was a requirement. Admittedly, my resume wasn't exactly noteworthy, so it was imperative that I looked the part of a professional woman. How did the saying go? Fake it until you make it?

The makeup only took a few minutes, then on to drying my hair, which took a good twenty more thanks to the fact that I had so much of it. Then the flat iron to make the long strands shiny and straight. Finally, on to my clothes. A cute yet conservative black skirt and a white silk camisole paired with a charming yet uber-conservative blazer was the winner. Then I grabbed the best black heels I owned—a sexy little pair of Kate Spades that I couldn't live without when I saw them—and slipped them on my feet.

I was finally ready.

For coffee.

Clearly, I spent too much time on my morning ritual, but hey, I was twenty-four years old and jobless. The interview I had that day was going to be the last of many, I hoped. I'd only been on eight in the past two weeks, none of which had panned out, but I had high expectations for this one. It was one of the most prestigious PR firms in the city and they were looking for a secretary. Which I thought was the same thing as a receptionist, right? Different term, same job? At least I hoped so because I exceled at that, truly. I mean, I was born to talk on the phone, so yeah, I figured if nothing else, I had a damn good shot.

And maybe you were wondering why I didn't tell you what city I was in. Truth was, it didn't matter. If I did tell you, you might know it and that would take some of the intrigue out of my story. So, we'll keep that a secret as well as the name of the PR firm. After all, you might know that one too.

Back to getting ready.

I tossed my lip gloss into my clutch and grabbed my car key and cell phone before stopping in the kitchen.

The apartment I lived in wasn't very big. Nothing more than six hundred square feet, but it was in a good area of town, clean, and relatively inexpensive. And by relatively, I meant that I could afford it back when I had a job three weeks ago. If this didn't pan out, it was no longer going to be inexpensive. It was going to be available for the next tenant.

But I couldn't worry about that now because I had somewhere to be and not a lot of time to get there.

After pulling up my texting app on my phone, I shot a quick message to my friend Kristen.

Luci: *Heading to my interview. Wish me luck.*

When the coffeemaker brewed the single cup, I tossed in a little Equal and a few drops of creamer before popping a lid on the travel mug and heading for the door. As soon as I grabbed the knob, my phone buzzed.

Kristen: *You've got this one in the bag.*

I didn't know about all that, but I was grateful to my friend. She was the one who'd gotten me this interview and it couldn't have come at a better time.

If I was lucky, I'd make it on time and they would hire me. If I wasn't lucky, I'd be moving in with my parents.

•

Traffic was a bitch, and I could only hope that this place validated parking because I couldn't imagine how much it was going to cost. Since I valeted, I figured it wouldn't be cheap, but hey. It was that or be late, and like I said, I needed this job if I planned to have a roof over my head and food in my belly. I wasn't a huge fan of ramen noodles, and let's face it, moving back in with my folks wasn't an option.

"May I help you, miss?"

My eyes cut over to see an older man squinting at me from his spot behind a long counter. He had one eyebrow, bushy and solid white, and it was currently hovering close to what used to be his hairline.

"I'm good, thank you!" My heels clicked loudly on the marble floors as I dashed toward the elevator.

I knew exactly what I was looking for and the sign by the elevator said I needed to head to the thirty-second floor. I punched the button for the elevator, then adjusted my blazer and tugged on my skirt. It was a little shorter than I remembered it being, but there was nothing I could do about it at that point. It was an interview, so I'd likely be sitting down for it. Plus, I was wearing underwear, so it wasn't like I was indecent.

The elevator finally arrived, and at that point, I was beginning to sweat. I had two minutes and if this wasn't the expressway up to the thirty-second floor, I probably wouldn't make it. The lift was empty, so I stepped inside and hit the thirty-two, making it light up, then turned and checked myself in the mirrors.

"Not bad," I said to my reflection as I smoothed my hand over my hair, then swiped around my lips with one finger while another fanned my lashes to de-clump the mascara and *poof.* I was ready.

Another deep breath and then the elevator dinged, signaling my arrival.

I squared my shoulders, planted a brilliant smile on my face, then stepped off into a plush lobby and noticed...

Nothing.

Seriously. Not a soul.

It was empty.

Like ghost-town empty.

The lights weren't even on, which was slightly disconcerting. I quickly located the switch on the wall and made my way over. A second later, the room lit up like the surface of the sun. Okay, maybe not that bright, but at least it was no longer giving me an eerie feeling.

I strolled over to the desk, where I assumed a receptionist (fancier name for a secretary, I was pretty sure) should sit. If all went well, that was going to be my desk. As for it being empty, it sort of made sense because the job position was currently open. But it would soon be filled. By me!

I was optimistic, I wouldn't lie.

Sure, I had some reasons to be. One, Kristen had recommended me for this position, and considering her clout, I felt confident her word went a long way. And two, my resume had plenty of receptionist experience. Provided they could overlook the fact that I'd held twelve jobs in the past three years, I should be a shoo-in. Although I hadn't been let go from any of my previous jobs, I knew it didn't bode well that I hopped from one place to the next. In my defense, I was still searching for something to make me happy, not quite finding it anywhere.

As for being qualified, I couldn't tell you because this particular job posting didn't have any requirements. It actually said: REQUIREMENTS TO BE PROVIDED AT TIME OF INTERVIEW.

Now, I knew that sounded a little odd, but like I said, my friend suggested I apply. Plus, this was a prestigious PR firm with a great reputation. I seriously doubted they were up to anything nefarious.

As I stood in the lobby, I wasn't sure what to do next.

Did I slip down the hall and peek into offices until I found someone?

Did I take a seat and wait for someone to come to me?

I'd never had this happen before.

So, I asked myself: If I worked at an esteemed PR firm and I was looking to hire a secretary, wouldn't I want someone who had ambition? A problem solver? Someone who could think on the fly?

Straightening my spine and adjusting my blazer, I decided that, yes, that was exactly what I would want. So, that was exactly what I'd be.

But before I did that, I figured I could check out the outer sanctum. The single glass desk held a phone and a calendar. Was it a blotter? I thought that's what they called it. Not that it mattered. I doubted there would be a vocabulary test. And if there was, it wasn't like I was a dummy.

To my right, there were three charcoal leather couches that were positioned in a U, facing the reception desk. A glass table that matched the desk sat in the center on a plush gray rug decorated with neon-colored geometric shapes. The walls were painted a light gray, decorated with metal geometric shapes that, yes, matched the patterns on the rug. Very artsy.

On the wall behind me, closest to the elevator, was a small counter—light gray cabinets, dark gray granite—with a fancy coffeemaker and little else. On my left was an opaque-glass wall that ran the length of the area and continued down what appeared to be a hallway. It was fairly bright behind the wall, likely from the windows, but there were no shadows, which made me believe there were no people working back there.

I guessed that was the way I should go.

Just when I started toward the hallway, the elevator dinged and I spun around, waiting to see who the newcomer might be.

When the doors opened, I found myself staring. Hard.

Four imposing figures stepped out, two at a time, all wearing suits. Not the cheap kind either. These were likely Armani or Gucci or possibly Tom Ford and definitely tailored.

The well-dressed men seemed to be deep in discussion, not one of them noticing me. It gave me a few seconds to take them all in, and let me just say, since this was going to be my job (there was that optimism again), I was going to be one happy girl getting to see these yummy treats every day.

There were two brunettes, a blond, and one who was shiny bald. Their skin tones ranged from pale to a sexy, rich chocolate color. If I had to venture a guess about their ages, I would've said from mid to late thirties. Their heights ranged from probably right at six feet to several inches taller. Then again, I was totally guessing about that. I wasn't a good judge of height. Being that I was five two without shoes, everyone was tall to me.

"Oh, uh," the blond said, coming to an abrupt halt when he peered up at me. His eyes darted to the reception desk, then back to me.

I couldn't tell if he was disappointed to find me standing there or if he'd expected someone else to be with me. Rather than allow the awkward silence to continue, I greeted the men, trying on my best receptionist voice. "I'm Luciana Wagner. I've got an interview this morning."

The blond looked at the brunettes, who—now that I got a good look at them—appeared to be identical twins. Probably close to six and a half feet tall, the two men had a rugged appeal that was heightened by the fact that they wore those expensive suits. Double yum.

Neither of them said anything. It was the dark-skinned, bald gentleman with the glowing brown eyes—*swoon!*—who stepped forward and held out his hand. He was long and lean, probably the smallest of the four men, but still impressively built. The slow smile that tilted his lips distracted me momentarily. Long enough that I didn't notice right off the way his iridescent golden eyes had trailed from my breasts to my Kate Spades, then back up to meet my eyes.

"Nice to meet you, Luciana Wagner. I'm Benjamin Snowden. You can call me Ben."

I smiled, transfixed by his killer grin and perfect white teeth. My mother would've loved his teeth.

Keeping my tone polite, I replied with, "You can call me Luci." But what I was thinking was, "You can call me anything you'd like, just as long as you call me."

Rein it in, Luci.

"And these are my partners," Ben noted, turning toward the others but not releasing my hand. He pointed to the blond. "Justin Parker." His hand swiveled over to the twins. "Landon and Langston Moore."

"Very nice to meet you all." With a smile on my face, I reached out and shook each man's hand once Ben released me. I kept my grip firm but feminine. I didn't want them to think I was trying to overpower them or anything.

That, of course, got me to thinking about being overpowered by them. Don't ask me why.

And suddenly, the room had heated about fifteen degrees.

Should've nixed the blazer.

TWO

"IF YOU WOULD FOLLOW US, we'll set you up in the conference room," Justin said, his voice deep but clear, with an authoritative ring to it. I didn't detect an accent of any kind.

I met his smoldering blue eyes and nodded.

Turned out, I only ended up following Justin while the other three pulled up the rear. They resumed their conversation from the elevator, which, from what I could tell, was a rundown of their meetings for the day. I briefly wondered whose calendar the interview was on.

Justin stopped at a tall glass door, inserted a key to unlock it, then pushed it open. He allowed me to precede him, so I stepped into the room.

I was right about the windows. They ran the length of the room—floor to ceiling—and didn't have blinds to obstruct the view. The *awesome* view, I might add. The conference table that sat in the center and filled about three quarters of the space looked to hold roughly fifty people on a good day. I'd never seen anything like it. It was very modern with an opaque-glass top that appeared to be several inches thick. The chairs were black leather, all executive style. I had to wonder how many clients they had in there at a time. That seemed like a lot to me.

"A few times a year, we fly all of our managers in for meetings," Justin informed me, apparently reading my mind.

A lot of employees, then. I nodded and tucked that information away for later use.

Landon—I could tell the difference because he was wearing glasses and his twin was not—pulled out a chair and I mumbled my thanks as I slipped into it, careful to keep my skirt from riding up too far. As it was, I was baring quite a bit of thigh and the last thing I wanted was for them to think that I'd done it on purpose.

"Can we get you anything? Coffee? Tea? Water?" Langston offered. Now, he *did* have an accent, a sexy twang that hinted at his down-home roots. It wasn't local, I knew that much.

"I'm good, thank you." I felt as though I should've been offering them something, but I refrained. I would save that for my first day on the job. And no, I wasn't talking about offering up my body. Although...

"Would you mind giving us a few minutes?" Justin requested.

"No, not at all." I kept my tone sweet, meeting each of their eyes in turn.

I watched as all four men then walked out of the room.

"D-*ay*-um, Kristen. Where have you been hiding these guys?" I whispered to myself, then quickly jerked my gaze up to the corners of the room.

I was wondering if they had surveillance cameras. *And yep, lookie there.* They did. Several, in fact. Which meant I should probably stop ogling and undoubtedly stop muttering to myself.

Keeping my back straight and my hands tucked into my lap, I continued my perusal of the room. Aside from the ginormous table, there were three couches in this room also. These were black leather with neatly squared cushions, set in the same U formation as those in the lobby. Rather than facing a desk, though, they were positioned in front of a projection screen on the wall. Seemed like a good place to go through presentations to me.

Unlike the lobby, where the tiled floors were a dark gray rectangle in an offset pattern, the floors in here were big, oversized squares, neatly aligned and gleaming white.

Black, white, and chrome seemed to be the theme in this room.

It seemed a little sterile to me. On the other hand, it was professional. If it were mine, I would've decorated it with a few bright-colored floral decorations. Something to draw the eye and give a little life to the place.

Several minutes passed and I fought the urge to fidget, hyperaware of the cameras. I wanted to make a good impression, not look like I was ready to bolt at a moment's notice.

When the door opened again, Ben was the one who stepped inside. His smile was still firmly on his face, and I was still transfixed by it. He carried himself like a man who was comfortable in his own skin. The smile came across as warm and friendly, which instantly put me at ease.

"Are you sure I can't get you anything?" His voice was deep and it suited him nicely. No accent either.

Unless you're on the menu, then no.

"I'm sure. But thank you." I effectively ignored my inner hussy.

His charcoal suit highlighted his dark skin and looked spectacular on him. I could only imagine how nice his butt looked in those slacks without the jacket. Not that I was looking.

Fine, I *had* looked, but my attempt hadn't been successful.

He nodded, then took the seat directly across from me and placed a manila folder on the table.

Crap.

I didn't bring an extra copy of my resume. I knew I had forgotten something that morning.

Ben opened the folder and relief hit me like a tsunami. The first sheet was a copy of my resume. I was happy to see it for two reasons. One, it proved they were expecting me. And two, I forgot the extra one.

"Why don't you start by telling me a little about yourself, Luci."

Smoothing my hands over my skirt, I forced myself to maintain eye contact while making a concerted effort not to look constipated. Although I should've been a pro at these things by now, interviews weren't my forte. I got nervous, I sweated in places I shouldn't sweat, and I had a hard time speaking. Put me in front of a super-hot guy and it got doubly worse.

"As you can see by my resume, I have a significant amount of reception experience," I said, keeping my voice even, cheerful.

Ben's smile widened. "How about a little about you first. I'm more than aware of your work experience."

"Oh." That took me somewhat by surprise. "Like what? I mean, what would you like to know?"

"What are your hobbies? Where did you grow up? Those types of things."

Although his voice sounded professional, there was something in his eyes that said he would prefer to know my bra size. Then again, I could've been imagining that because I wanted to show him my bra so he could find the size himself.

Wait.

No I didn't.

I was no hussy.

Not like you could put a handsome man in a suit in front of me and my hormones took the reins.

Okay, they did.

That probably had a lot to do with the fact that I was single and the only orgasms I'd had in the past, oh, I don't know, two years had been from my trusty vibrator. Well, to be honest, it had been *two* vibrators. I wore the first one out completely. I had always had a powerful sex drive, but I was quite adept at sating my own urges. Porn and my vibrator were my two best friends, I wasn't ashamed to admit it.

Shit.

I was mentally off topic and now Ben was staring at me, his honey-gold eyes reflecting what I could only assume was amusement. If he knew what was going on in my head, I'm not sure he'd be smiling.

I took a deep breath, let it out.

What were my hobbies? Probably shouldn't tell him about porn and my vibrator.

So, that meant I had to go with the growing up part.

"I grew up not far from here," I told him. "My mother's a dentist, my stepfather's a firefighter—he adopted me when I was six—my real father died when I was three and I don't really remember him. I have no siblings, and they wouldn't let me have a pet growing up, but now I live in an apartment, still don't have a pet because I don't have time for one, but that was up until three weeks ago, anyway." Yes, I was a rambling mess. "Technically, right now I have plenty of time since I don't have a job, but that's not to say I don't want one, because I definitely do—a job, not a pet—and as you can see, I've got a ton of reception experience."

This time Ben laughed, a dark, rich sound that dripped with sexiness and made me grateful I'd worn panties.

I replayed what I'd just said in my head and realized I sounded like a total moron.

Great.

Ben leaned forward, closed the folder, then got to his feet. Shit.

Did I seriously just blow the entire interview with one ridiculously long run-on sentence? Well, *two* ridiculously long run-on sentences, to be fair. I had taken a breath in there somewhere. I think.

"Is the interview over?" I asked when he stepped away from the chair.

"Certainly not." His face was expressionless, his eyes assessing me again. "I'm going to have Mr. Parker come in. Then Langston and Landon. After they've all asked you a few questions, we'll convene and let you know."

"Oh." Okay then. I briefly wondered why he referred to one of his colleagues as mister but referred to the other two by their first names.

"It's been a pleasure to meet you, Luci."

"Thank you." When he shook my hand, this time I was reluctant to let go, but I forced my fingers to release his as he once again smiled down on me.

My brain suddenly conjured up an image of me on my knees and...

Oh.

My.
God.
I'd completely lost my mind.

•

By the time Mr. Parker—Justin—strolled into the conference room, I had managed to battle back the blush that heated my face when Ben was on his way out. I knew this because I had glanced at myself in the reflection of the table and it appeared I was as pale as I had been when I walked in the office.

Not that that would be the case once Mr. Parker began talking, but at least I got a clean slate to start from.

He didn't remain standing for long, so I only had a few seconds to take in the dark blue suit that emphasized his navy-blue eyes. He was taller and broader in the chest than Ben was, narrower in the hips as well, but I couldn't confirm on the butt because he, too, was wearing a jacket.

"I see you've held a multitude of jobs over the years."

"That's true," I agreed.

"Was there one that held your interest more than the others?"

I thought about that for a moment, then shook my head. "No, Mr. Parker, not that I can recall."

"Please, call me Justin."

Okay then.

"So, Luci, tell me a little about your experience at"—he opened the folder and skimmed the extensive list of companies I'd worked for—"um…Super Cuts?"

I smiled because this was the easy part. "I worked there for about three months as a receptionist back when I was just out of college. I answered phones and scheduled appointments. Sometimes they had me sweep the floor if I had nothing else to do."

Did I say *easy*?

I really meant lame because now that I heard myself, I was no longer wondering why no one was hiring me. Any idiot could work as a receptionist at Super Cuts if they were solely responsible for answering the phone and sweeping the floor. Sheesh.

Yes, Justin. I'm an idiot. But I take orders well.

I forced my mind not to wander because I felt Justin's eyes on me and I didn't want to imagine him ordering me to go to my knees.

Fuck.

I was completely out of control.

Someone shoot me now.

Before I could think of anything else to add, Justin leaned forward, closed the folder, then got to his feet.

Son of a bitch.

I was on a roll this morning.

Although Ben had assured me I would be meeting with all four of them, I wasn't sure that was the case any longer. After all, I *had* heard myself. I made eye contact with the handsome Justin and asked, "Is the interview over?"

"Not yet, no. I'm going to send Landon and Langston in. Once they've run through their questions, we'll meet and then let you know."

Okay, good. So that was still the plan. I felt a little better. Granted, this interview was a bit strange what with the lack of questions or details, but I figured I couldn't complain. They hadn't booted me out yet.

"Thank you for meeting with me." I shook his hand when he offered.

"My pleasure." He pivoted, then slipped out of the room.

"Okay, Luci. Time to make like Stella and get your groove on." I was no longer worried about the cameras overhearing me talking to myself. Wasn't like I could look more like an idiot than I already had.

I glanced over at the counter, noticing the bottles of water. Glass bottles. Fancy ones. The kind no one really drank, but they set out so they looked like they had class and money.

Not that I was doubting that these guys had either, but…

The door opened and I turned to see Landon and Langston coming in. Their suits were a conservative black, shirts a crisp white. Landon's tie was a deep burgundy while Langston's was a shimmering royal blue. They looked nice, professional. Sexy.

Langston grabbed one of the glass bottles of water and unscrewed the top before taking a sip, disproving my theory that they were only for show.

Landon sat down in the chair across from me and Langston perched his hip on the cabinet behind him. Both men seemed to be observing me intensely. I fought the urge to squirm under the scrutiny of their gazes. It wasn't easy, especially when my eyes met Langston's. There was something about that man, something that made me think of smoking-hot sex.

Finally, Landon spoke. "What makes you think you're qualified for this position?"

He had the type of deep, raspy voice that single women wanted to hear whispering in their ear moments before they were rocketed into the ether riding the waves of an intense orgasm.

Yep. Flip me over. I'm done.

Landon's dark eyebrow lifted and I realized he was waiting for me to speak.

"Well…" I smiled, then my mouth ran away from me when I blurted, "I'm not sure how to answer that since I haven't the faintest clue what the requirements are."

"If you don't know the requirements, why'd you apply for the job?" His voice rang with amusement. And sex. Mostly sex.

Damn it.

That wasn't him, that was me.

I didn't want to tell them that I applied because my friend told me I should. That didn't seem very responsible. It wasn't like I was expecting to get it simply because I knew Kristen either. Sure, we'd become good friends over the past two years, but I certainly wasn't trying to ride her coattails. Then again, I wasn't above latching on and taking a short ride if it meant steady employment. Hell, the idea of having to live with my parents was enough to have my desperation ratcheting up a notch or twenty.

I kept the smile on my face. "Because I'm quite aware of the reputation of this company and I felt I would be a good fit here. I'm a hard worker, speak well with clients, and I'm looking for something to broaden my horizons."

"Very nice answer," Landon stated at the same time Langston muttered, "Good girl," from his spot near the wall, his hazel eyes pinned on me.

There was something about the way he said that. Something that made me want to continue to have him praising me in the future. Like I said, I was losing my mind. But hey, I'd already dug a deep enough hole to hide in; what was the point in trying to climb out now?

Unlike Ben and Justin, Landon didn't open the folder. "Tell me how you know Kristen Morrow."

Okay, so they evidently knew how I'd heard about the job, and I had to assume that they knew her as well since they were the only ones who'd asked about her. "She's a friend of mine," I admitted. "We met at yoga class a couple of years ago. We hang out from time to time."

My answer seemed to placate them.

"I noticed you have a degree in accounting." Landon's eyes scanned my face as he spoke.

"That's true, I do."

I'd been told to never provide additional information that they didn't require because it overshadowed the interview and if they weren't in need of an accountant, what did it matter anyway?

"Are you interested in the secretary position, Luci?" Langston asked.

"Yes, sir. I'm actually interested in *any* position."

Jeezus. Did I really just say that?

There was a flash of something in Langston's eyes that instantly had me crossing my legs a little tighter, a welcome ache taking up residence between my thighs. Well, it would've been a welcome ache if I weren't in a job interview. And if I had my trusty second vibrator handy.

"We work Monday through Friday," Landon told me. "You'd be required to be here from seven thirty to five thirty. An hour for lunch. We shut the office down at one on Fridays, but we do require one Saturday a month. My partners and I don't arrive until closer to eight. One or more of us is often traveling, so it would be critical that you be able to manage your time and your duties with little instruction from us."

I nodded. I could handle those hours and those requirements, despite the fact that I'd be getting up at the ass-crack of dawn every day.

"We each have extensive teams who work remotely. Rarely will you see anyone else in the office. However, we are a client-facing business, so the dress code is professional. What you're wearing is certainly appropriate."

"With one exception," Langston noted.

My gaze shot to his face as I waited for him to elaborate.

"Your skirts should be no shorter than the tips of your fingers when your arms are hanging at your sides. Anything shorter would be considered indecent and grounds for…discipline."

I had no idea why the word discipline coming from that delectable mouth sounded so naughty, but it did.

"Yes, sir. Fingertip length."

"Otherwise, your attire is appropriate," he concluded.

Still, that meant I would have to go shopping because this was the extent of my professional wardrobe. I hadn't been required to dress up at Super Cuts or Home Depot or Target. When I'd done a brief stint as a receptionist at my mother's dental office, she insisted I wear scrubs. Those few weeks I had tried my hand at waitressing a couple of years back, Hooters had supplied the uniform.

But I had this. Fashion was totally my thing.

"Are you available to start immediately?" Landon inquired, once again taking control of the interview.

"Yes, sir. I am."

His response was a gravelly grunt that sounded like approval.

Now that I was used to it, I didn't panic when Landon got to his feet, this time grabbing the folder.

"If you'll excuse us for a few minutes, I'd like to discuss with my partners."

"Sure you don't want some water?" Langston offered.

"I'm sure." It was a lie. My mouth was parched, but I was too nervous to drink anything.

"We'll be back in a minute," Landon noted, then disappeared into the hallway, his twin following him.

I kept my eyes on them, which was the only reason I saw Langston wink at me.

That or he had something in his eye.

When the door closed, I stared at it for a minute, replaying that scene over in my head.

Yep. Definitely a wink.

It got warm again.

I'm too young for hot flashes, right?

I tried to relax, but it was nearly impossible.

Waiting was the worst part. Although, I realized, most of the interviews I'd been on had ended with a follow-up call to let me know I wasn't selected for the position, so there hadn't been a lot of waiting. From what I could tell, they were planning to give me the news before I left the building.

So, was that a good thing? Or bad? Face-to-face rejection seemed like it would be significantly more uncomfortable than over the phone.

I didn't have time to think about that before all four men stepped back into the conference room. They were intimidating on their own. Together they were a force to be reckoned with. And it was hard not to stare.

Ben moved over to me first and I jerked my gaze to his face.

"Luci, we'd like to offer you the job if you're interested. Here's the information on the position," he said, handing me a small sheet of paper, which listed out the salary information. "It also comes with full benefits, vacation, et cetera."

I nodded, smiling as I looked back up at him. "Yes, sir. I'm definitely interested."

"Good." He clasped my hand and helped me to my feet. "We'd like for you to start immediately. Will tomorrow morning work for you?"

"Absolutely."

"We'll expect you here at seven thirty."

I nodded again.

The next thing I knew, the four men were leading me back toward the elevator.

It wasn't until I was on my way down to the first floor that I realized I never did find out what the requirements were.

THREE

BOSS MEETING

LANGSTON

"OKAY, NOW THAT WE'VE OFFICIALLY hired her, tell me your thoughts," Justin prompted when we sat down in the conference room not two minutes after the elevator doors closed behind Luci.

Truthfully, I would've preferred to get coffee before we had this discussion.

"Before we get to that," Landon interrupted, "where's Jordan?"

"He had an appointment this morning," Ben confirmed. "Didn't say where, but I also didn't ask. Said he'd be in around eleven."

Landon frowned. "Didn't look great that we had no one in the office when she arrived."

It was obvious my twin wasn't impressed by the way we'd greeted our new employee, and I could understand his point. Good thing she'd decided to accept the job. Landon might've been the most laid-back of the four of us—well, except maybe Ben—but he was a stickler for etiquette. And he was right, we had failed in that regard.

Again, coffee would've been good right about now.

Justin nodded. "I agree. However, it's not like we had anyone to fill in for him."

Okay, so Justin had a good point, too. Sort of.

"And what? We're too good to come in early or answer the phones?" Landon huffed. "I woulda volunteered if I'd known."

Yeah. Not me. I didn't have the patience to man the front desk. Nor the desire.

We'd been down a secretary for the past week and a half. Getting someone in wasn't as easy as it looked. For one, we were looking for someone specific, someone who could manage the office, maintain a certain amount of decorum, not provide a lot of drama, and be open to future possibilities. Not to mention, get along with our remote employees and give our CPA guidance as needed.

To be fair, we had interviewed both men and women, although we weren't looking to hire a man. Not for this position anyway.

Needless to say, it had been hit or miss thus far and every time we seemed to find someone we all four agreed on, she was out the door within a couple of weeks tops. Apparently, we were rather intimidating, or so I'd heard.

But enough was enough. I was tired of talking about the empty office or who was willing to do what. So I decided to push things along since coffee was my first order of business.

"She came with a great recommendation from Kristen," I told them, leaning back in my chair and regarding my partners. It was far too early to be having this conversation—or any, for that matter—but even I couldn't think of a better time. The girl would be starting in the morning and it was pertinent that we were on the same page when it came to what she'd be doing.

"I'll admit," Landon began, "she didn't look at all like what I expected her to."

Unlike my brother, I hadn't had any expectations. Five feet two inches with light blue eyes, long, dark hair with a massive amount of highlights, and a heart-shaped ass were all good as far as I was concerned.

"Good or bad?" Justin's eyes held the question his lips spoke.

We all turned to Landon. "For one, she's younger than I thought she'd be."

Justin peered down at the notebook in his hand. "Her application says she's twenty-four."

I frowned. "I thought we weren't allowed to ask questions like that."

"It asks for date of birth." Justin's tone was defensive.

"She certainly caught my attention." We all knew what Ben was referring to.

Although we ran a respectable, multimillion-dollar business, there was no denying that we had a few idiosyncrasies. For example, we lived and breathed Dominance and submission. It wasn't merely a fetish, D/s was a lifestyle choice for each of us.

On top of that, we were all looking to find a woman we could...share. Perhaps it wasn't politically correct according to a lot of people, but it was what it was. I certainly wasn't about to apologize for it and I doubted my partners would either. And considering we spent the majority of our time in the office, we were looking for someone we could interact with in that particular setting. On more than a business level.

Not that we were solely willing to hire based on that. We had several positions we could fill and should the right person stumble upon us, we weren't opposed to finding them a spot.

"According to Kristen," Landon said, "she's a natural submissive."

"I got that just by talking to her," Ben noted.

Hell, I got it just by *looking* at her.

"Me, too," Justin confirmed. "How long has Kristen known her?"

"A couple of years," Landon supplied.

"Are they close?" Ben asked.

I sighed heavily. "I'm sorry, but we didn't interrogate Kristen about her friend. She mentioned that she knew someone who was right up our alley and she just so happened to be single *and* looking for a job. It seemed appropriate to have her nudge the girl in our direction."

Justin glanced between the three of us. "As with the others, we're going to have to give it some time, get to know her a little. Feel her out before we take the next steps."

"First and foremost," I said, drawing all eyes to me, "she has to be able to handle the responsibilities. Unlike the last woman you hired"—I glared over at Justin—"who didn't know how to properly answer a telephone."

"Or the one before that," Landon added, "who didn't know what email was."

"Regardless of our intentions," I continued, "we need someone who's competent in the office. I'm not willing to take anything less."

Justin rolled his eyes. "Point taken."

"Did anyone bother to ask her why she left her previous jobs?" Ben questioned. "Because she has an extensive list."

That she did.

I looked at each man in turn. No one said anything. Appeared as though we'd all been too tongue-tied to really find out the pertinent information. Not that anyone could blame us. Personally, I'd been quite taken by the girl. She was probably the most stunning woman I'd laid eyes on in a really long time. And yes, she had a sweet innocence about her that I'd instantly homed in on. I'd known as soon as I saw her that she would fit in here perfectly.

"Well, I found it interesting that she didn't ask about the job requirements," Landon said, smirking.

Ben grinned. "No, she definitely did not."

I cleared my throat and moved to get to my feet. "Well, I say we give her a month, see how she does. We'll reconvene after she's been here for a week to discuss where we're at. Unless something comes up that needs to be discussed before then."

Justin stood. "I'm good with that."

Ben and Landon both agreed.

Finally, we were going to get down to real business.

Coffee.

I needed caffeine before I dealt with anything else today.

Unfortunately, since we still lacked a secretary, I would have to make it myself.

FOUR

AFTER THE MOST UNCONVENTIONAL INTERVIEW I'd been on to date, I headed for the one place that would soothe my anxiety. The mall was my home away from home. Granted, I spent most of my time not buying anything because extra spending money was one of those fictional things I only read about in books, but still. It was nice to be back.

When I parked, I shot a quick text to Kristen, letting her know they had offered me the position and that I started tomorrow. She responded with a smiley face emoji and asked me to meet her for drinks tonight. I automatically agreed, excited to find out how she knew these men.

Unfortunately, that was the easy part. Now I had one thing left to do before I went inside.

I pulled up my contact list and hit the call button.

"I got the job!" I told my mother, cell phone pressed to my ear.

"What job is this?" she asked, her tone calm, casual. Slightly uninterested.

I was excited; she was not. The story of my life.

"The one at the PR firm."

"What will you be doing?"

"Receptionist." Or secretary, as they'd called it. Whatever.

I could only hope she didn't ask for details, because I didn't know what it entailed. I assumed I'd be doing the standard receptionist/secretarial duties such as answering phones, scheduling appointments, making coffee. That sort of thing. I didn't think they'd have me sweeping floors, which was a plus.

"Well, good for you," she said, the inflection of her voice never changing, which pretty much translated to, *If that's the best you can do, then I hope you're happy.*

Considering I'd gone to college on their dime but had yet to do anything with the accounting degree I'd earned, I sort of understood my mother's disappointment. Then again, I couldn't remember the last time I'd done something that truly pleased the woman.

And now I know what you're thinking. *An accounting degree and you're taking a job as a secretary?* I know, I know. But to be honest, I freaking hated accounting. My mother encouraged me to do it and...well, let's just say I tended to do what my mother wanted because arguing with her was a big waste of time. No matter what, she always got the last word in, which generally left me feeling about as tall as the four-inch heels on my shoes.

Nonetheless, she wasn't happy that I wasn't crunching numbers somewhere, but I wouldn't be happy crunching numbers, so it was a double-edged sword and I was the type to err on the side of my own happiness. Maybe it made me selfish, but so what.

"Would it be possible to borrow some money?" I threw the question out there because that was the reason I had called and my mother knew I wasn't one to beat around the bush. "I need to get some new clothes. It's a business-professional environment. I'm a little short on funds at the moment."

My mother sighed.

"Please. I'll pay you back, I promise." Trust me, at my age, it was really hard for me to beg my parents for money, but when it was necessary, I could suck it up.

Another dramatic sigh.

I waited.

I could hear her brain working over the phone. She was probably trying to figure out when the last time I paid her back was. Hopefully she wouldn't think on that too hard, because I couldn't even remember.

"Use the credit card," she finally said. "But keep it to a respectable amount, Luciana."

"Of course." I loved when she said that, because her definition of respectable and mine were entirely different. I couldn't be faulted for that. "Thank you, Mommy. Love you!"

My mother's sharp inhale reflected the shock my declaration gave her. "Good-bye, Luci."

If I had to guess, I would say she had said she loved me fewer times than I'd paid her back in the past five years. But whatever. I was grateful she was loaning me money.

Sometimes it paid to be an only child.

I disconnected the call, shut off the engine, then climbed out of my car, straightening my skirt once again.

I was already at the mall, but I did have the decency to call her before I went inside. It wasn't like I didn't know what the answer would be, but in the event my mother wanted to hassle me about it, I wasn't going to fight with her. Granted, I hadn't come up with a plan B, so it was a damn good thing she was so predictable.

"Business professional," I told myself as I stepped into one of my favorite places in the entire world.

What you're wearing is certainly appropriate.

Yep, I could still recall Landon's words.

Personally, I took that to mean they didn't have an issue with short skirts, provided they weren't shorter than the tips of my fingers. Granted, I had short arms, so I didn't think that would be a problem.

And since I tended to favor skirts, I figured that was the best way to go. After all, they accentuated my best asset. My legs.

I would admit, I had great legs. Sure, I was short, but thanks to yoga, I managed to keep my body toned. And skirts accentuated my legs while also concealing my larger-than-it-should-be rump. Hence the reason I had decided short skirts were the key to a functional yet professional wardrobe.

Three hours later, as I was walking out to my car, I wished I had worn more sensible shoes. Nevertheless, I still considered it a successful trip despite the fact that my toes were screaming at me.

I managed to select sexy yet professional items that could be mixed and matched to come up with multiple outfits and I didn't go ridiculously overboard. I think my mother would be proud, if, you know, that was her thing. Of course, I'd also picked out some sexy new kitten heels plus a pair of boots that I couldn't resist, but she wouldn't see the charge for a little while, which gave me time to get my first paycheck.

Now it was time for a mani-pedi and then off to have a few drinks with Kristen. I was sure she'd understand that I had to make it an early night.

After all, I needed to get my beauty sleep.

Tomorrow was going to be a big day.

•

I met Kristen at a bar close to my apartment. It was a little hole in the wall that we came to every now and then. Nothing fancy, but it was cozy and the owner/bartender was nice.

"Where's Tim?" I glanced around, noticing her boyfriend was absent.

Kristen grinned. "He had something he needed to work on."

"Well, that means we can dish about boys."

"Boys?" Her dark eyebrows rose.

"It appears you've been holding out on me," I prompted when Jerry delivered our drinks.

I went with my usual Sex on the Beach while Kristen had a glass of red wine. Granted, from time to time, I mixed it up and asked for a Blow Job, but only because I knew it embarrassed Jerry.

"Holding out on you?" She had a serious twinkle in her eye. One that told me she knew exactly what I was referring to.

I took a sip of my drink. "So, I show up at this fancy office building downtown only to find out no one was there. I was just about to start searching when four ridiculously hot guys stepped off the elevator. Imagine my surprise when I realized they worked there."

Her expression didn't change.

"You didn't happen to mention that you were friends with four of the hottest men in town."

Kristen chuckled. "I wouldn't necessarily call us friends."

"No?"

"We just…run in the same circles."

"What does that even mean?" I probed, leaning in closer. "Are you members of some sort of club or something?"

"Or something."

I huffed. "You're always so tight-lipped." I raised my hand to the bartender. "Hey, Jer. Could you bring her the bottle of wine and a straw? There's some information I need and I think I'll have to ply her with alcohol first."

Of course, Jerry didn't hear me because he was at the far end of the bar, but I got my point across.

"They obviously knew that I knew you," I admitted. "Landon asked me specifically how."

Kristen smiled and she looked like an angel. So sweet, so innocent.

Yeah, right.

"I told him about you," she finally admitted. "He mentioned he had a position open at his office and I immediately thought of you."

"Me? Why me?"

She lifted her glass to her lips. "Because you're my friend and you're looking for a job." She smiled. "I told them you'd be a good fit for the firm."

"Well, I sure hope you're right." I stirred my drink with the skinny straw.

"I am. You'll do fine. Plus, I happen to know they liked you."

My head jerked toward her. "How do you know that?"

"I talked to Landon."

Holy crap. So, she was more than merely an acquaintance if she had already spoken with him.

"What? Did he call you and tell you about it?"

Kristen shook her head. "Not exactly. We had…a meeting this afternoon."

I chuckled. "Right. For this club you're in?"

"Actually, yes."

I wasn't sure if I should believe her. I couldn't tell if she was just messing with me or not. I decided not to goad her into more details because, truthfully, I didn't want to know. They had offered me the position and now it was my turn to prove myself. Kristen might've put in a good word, but I wanted them to keep me based on merit, not loyalty to one of their friends.

"Fine. Whatever." I giggled. "But they are hot. All four of them. I'm not sure how I'm going to keep from spontaneously combusting when they're around."

"Oh, I'm sure you'll figure out how to…adapt."

Maybe.

Hopefully.

I guess we'd soon find out.

FIVE

I WOULD ADMIT, I WAS proud of myself.

It was 7:25 a.m. when I stepped out of the elevator the following morning. My first day on the job and I had arrived five minutes early. Not too shabby. Hopefully, that would go in the extra minutes bank and offset the day I came in five minutes late, because, let's face it, it was bound to happen. My snooze button and I had a good thing going and I wasn't looking to break up anytime soon.

Not that it mattered, I realized as I glanced around the lobby.

The lights were once again off. Since I was familiar with the place now, I headed over, hit the switch, and brought the room to life.

With a confident air, I waltzed over to the desk, set my purse on it, then turned toward the coffeemaker. Before I could get three steps away, the elevator dinged and I peered over, plastering a huge smile on my face.

"Ah, crap," the man in the elevator muttered as he stepped off, swiping at his shirt and the apparent coffee stain he now had. His gaze instantly lifted as though he sensed me. A smile formed quickly and his eyes twinkled. "Good morning, doll. You must be Luciana."

"Luci," I corrected, still smiling.

This guy looked to be about my age. Certainly closer to twenty than thirty. I didn't suspect he was an additional partner that I hadn't met yesterday. He didn't have the same imposing demeanor that the other men had. Plus, he was wearing a pair of khaki pants and a pink polo shirt instead of a suit.

He wiped his hand on a napkin he was holding as he moved toward me. *Pranced* would probably be a better way to describe it.

"So nice to meet you, honey." He held out his hand. "I'm Jordan. The receptionist."

I shook his hand, but my smile faltered.

Wait.

What?

He was the receptionist?

Then who was I?

When he released my hand, he moved to the desk and set his load down. A cup of coffee, croissant, and car keys. His blue eyes moved up to the clock on the wall.

"Thank goodness. One minute to spare. And you already got the lights, so technically, I'm ahead of schedule."

I tried not to frown, but I was working really hard to figure out what was going on here.

Jordan spun to face me, a huge grin plastered on his expressive features. His blond hair was styled perfectly. Not that sexy, mussed look that a lot of guys went for either. His was brushed to the side and he had bangs hanging over his forehead. His face was clean shaven, his eyebrows groomed better than mine, and not a single hair out of place. He was...pretty.

"Congratulations on the new job," he said kindly.

"Uh...thank you?"

"Did they show you your office?"

"My what?" I was confused.

"God, you're cute. I can totally see why they hired you." He chuckled, then took my hand. "You're just lucky I'm gay or I'd be all up on you right now. However, my man would so not be into that, so you're safe."

I laughed. Couldn't help myself.

"I'm loving the outfit, by the way. Very sexy yet professional. They're going to love you."

I was completely overwhelmed by Jordan. He was cute, in a little-brother sort of way. Considering he wasn't taller than me when I was wearing heels, he almost felt like he was my little brother.

I liked him instantly.

Plus, his smile was infectious.

"Come on," he said, tugging my hand. "Let's get you situated. The bosses'll be here any minute."

I snatched my purse from the desk—apparently *his* desk, not mine—and allowed him to drag me down the hall. My heels clicked on the tile, which sounded overly loud in the otherwise silent space.

"This is the main conference room," he noted as he released my hand to insert a key in the lock. It was the room I'd had my interview in. He turned it until it clicked, then pulled the key out.

We were once again in motion, moving to more doors on the opposite side of the hall.

"Restrooms are here; however, there are private restrooms in the back as well." He did the same with both doors, men and women. We moved to the next door. "This is the break room." Another lock was disengaged.

All the locked doors explained why the elevator stopped on this floor without needing a key.

Jordan paused momentarily so I could peek inside. The break room was as stylish as the rest of the place, with a stainless-steel refrigerator and several glass-topped tables with chairs neatly arranged around them. There was a coffeemaker and a tray full of snacks on the counter.

The second I turned back, Jordan was once again tugging my hand.

We came to a set of heavy, opaque-glass doors that had the name of the firm engraved on them. Once he unlocked them, Jordan pushed one open easily.

"Back here are the bosses' offices." He didn't stop when we passed the first closed door, or the second.

I could see farther down that there were two additional doors and I could only assume those were offices too. Instead, Jordan took a right, down a wide hallway lined with gleaming white filing cabinets that split the four rooms right down the middle. There was no door here.

"This, doll, is *your* office."

Technically, I didn't think it could be called an office because it didn't have a door. However, it did have an incredible view behind the glass-topped desk. There was a tall building directly across that blocked a portion of the view; however, to the right and left of the building, I could see almost all of downtown. The space was probably the size of my entire apartment, with a few potted plants, as well as four doors that faced my new desk.

Based on the layout on the opposite side, I could only assume those four doors led to their individual offices. Interesting layout, two exits for each room.

"You've got a phone, but it won't ring unless I direct a call to you. It works to call out, though. Just dial nine to get an outside line. And if you need me, I'm one on the speed dial."

Before I knew what was happening, Jordan offered a chipper wave. "See you in a bit. Gotta get back up front so the bosses don't get mad." He lowered his voice a little. "I had to take off yesterday morning, and I know how they are when I ask for time off."

I wanted to ask how they were, but I didn't. I didn't intend to take any time off for a little while, so it really didn't matter.

"You might want to get coffee started," he said in a singsong voice, tilting his chin toward a counter similar to the one in the lobby. "They all four drink it."

I nodded.

I could do that.

"Ta-ta for now." Jordan turned and scurried down the hall without a backward glance.

Setting my purse on my desk, I peered around, taking it all in again. It was a beautiful space. One I certainly didn't expect in an office building. Bright, airy, very modern with high-end fixtures. That seemed to be a theme here.

I managed to pull myself together long enough to go to the coffeemaker. Within minutes I had it brewing into the stainless-steel carafe and I had nothing else to do. I was tempted to wander around, give myself a personal tour, but decided against it. According to Jordan, the bosses would be coming in soon and I didn't want to be caught snooping.

Instead, I moved to the window and stared out.

This was definitely a place I could get used to.

•

"Good morning, Luci," a deep voice sounded from behind me a short time later.

I pivoted to see Ben walking my way, looking just as handsome as he had yesterday. Today he was sporting a light gray suit. His tie was what I would call salmon, but to some it would simply be a pinkish-orange. Whatever the color, it did nice things to his dark complexion.

"Good morning, Ben," I greeted cheerfully.

"I see Jordan showed you to your office."

"He did."

I stood there, unsure what I was supposed to do. I had yet to sit down, feeling slightly uncomfortable without anyone being here.

Ben moved to the door closest to the windows on my left. I mentally noted where his office was and tried to tie it back on the opposite side. I was wondering if that other door was their way of sneaking out or in. It seemed strange to me, but I vowed I would eventually figure it out.

"Come in," he said with a wave. "I'll give you a tour of my office."

With a smile, I ran my hands down my skirt and followed.

I was momentarily speechless when I stepped inside the room.

This was no ordinary office. Not like any that I'd seen anyway. For one, it was ridiculously large, far more space than a single person should need to handle their business during the day. Or at least to me it was. It was bright and airy like the rest of the place, but it was wholly masculine at the same time. More like an upscale apartment than an office. Thick, charcoal-gray carpet covered the floor, and two long, black leather couches sat on the far side of the room, facing one another.

Off-centered on the left side of the spacious room was an oversized gunmetal-gray desk with a charcoal glass top. It was positioned to face the windows, which overlooked the city. On the wall behind the desk, there were matching metal bookshelves, but they weren't filled with books. They were decorated with various framed certificates and what I could only assume were glass awards. To my left was the wall of windows, along with three black leather armchairs sitting directly in front of the desk.

It was a very nice office, and it seemed to suit Ben perfectly. At least what I knew about him anyway. Which, come to think of it, I didn't really know much of anything at all.

"I'm usually the first one here." Ben shot me a smile as he set his briefcase on the floor beside his desk before removing his suit jacket and placing it on a hanger. "Mr. Parker comes in early, too, but this morning he's meeting with a client. Won't arrive until closer to ten."

I wanted to ask him why he referred to Justin as Mr. Parker, but I saved that question for a later date.

After hanging his jacket in a small closet beside another door, Ben turned to face me and I gave him my full attention.

His eyes perused me from head to toe, then back again. It seemed every spot on my body that his gaze touched warmed a couple of degrees. I could only hope he approved of the outfit. I'd chosen a black, white, and gray sweater with a belted, short, gray pleated skirt, paired with black tights and my favorite lace-up, high-heeled boots. The boots gave me additional height and the tights helped to accentuate my legs, making them look longer than they were.

Based on Ben's lengthy stare, he approved.

When his golden gaze lifted to mine again, he smiled. "You look very nice today."

"Thank you." I had the overwhelming urge to put my hands behind my back and thrust out my chest to show that I did have boobs. They weren't big by any stretch of the imagination, but I thought they could be considered perky.

Not that I would. Thrust out my chest, that was.

This was my job.

Ben was my boss.

And that would've been inappropriate.

"Ben? You here already?"

I turned as Landon stepped into the room, his eyes zeroing in on me instantly.

"Good mornin', Luci."

Have I mentioned that I loved his twang? Well, I did. It was sexy in that *save-a-horse-ride-a-cowboy* sort of way.

"Good morning, Landon," I greeted.

His smile was warm when he met my eyes. "You can tell us apart?"

I nodded. "But probably not if you weren't wearing the glasses."

"I'll keep that in mind."

As the two men stood there, I felt the need to ask a pressing question. "So, um, who will I be working for?"

I glanced between Landon and Ben.

Ben was the one to answer. "We'll be sharing you."

The way he said that sent a ribbon of warmth curling low in my belly. I seriously doubted he meant it in a sexual way, but could you imagine? Being shared by the four hotties? Yum.

Apparently, the session with my vibrator last night hadn't taken the edge off.

"Okay, then," I said in agreement. "I shall be shared." I smiled.

I noticed a look that passed between Ben and Landon, but neither man said anything else on that subject.

"Come on, I'll show you my office," Landon said before looking at Ben. "I'd like to talk to you when you get a minute."

Ben nodded. "Sure. Come see me when you're finished with Luci."

There was a sexy smirk that curled the corner of Landon's succulent mouth, but I pretended not to notice. Okay, clarification: my body didn't pretend, but my brain did.

I followed Landon past my desk, to the first door on the opposite side of the hallway that led to my space. I took him in from head to toe and briefly wondered if it was casual Friday. In an effort not to check out Landon's superior ass, which happened to be hugged by a pair of distressed jeans today, I peered around the room the instant I stepped inside.

Landon's office was more along the rustic lines and slightly smaller than Ben's. It didn't have any windows in the space, so that could've easily made it feel smaller. There was a huge raw wood desk in the center of the room with matching bookshelves behind it. Unlike Ben's, there were books on Landon's shelves. Lots of books, all by various authors.

"Are these people you represent?" I asked, waving my hand toward the shelves at the back of the room.

I had done my homework after I got home from the bar last night. As tired as I was, my brain wouldn't shut down and thanks to Kristen's vague responses to all of my questions, my curiosity had been piqued. Wanting to know as much as possible about the company I would be working for, I'd pulled up the website and studied the information detailed on all four of my bosses.

"They are." Landon shifted, leaning one hip on his desk.

I continued to take it all in, noting the two brown leather sofas near the wall on the right, the three matching chairs in front of the desk. Swiveling my head to the other side of the room, I noticed another sofa, this one facing a large flat-panel television mounted on the wall. Looked as though Landon spent a lot of time in his office.

Realizing I hadn't said anything for at least a couple of minutes, I turned back to Landon. "Is there anything I can get you? A cup of coffee?" I motioned toward my office space. "I made some."

"That would be great. Thank you."

"How do you take it?" I thought I deserved credit for thinking that far ahead.

"Black."

Well, that was easy.

With a quick smile, I made my way back to the coffeemaker, pausing momentarily. I glanced over at Ben's office, noticing the door was still open. Figuring I should offer him some as well, I headed over and peeked inside. "Can I get you a cup of coffee, sir?"

"That would be great, Luci."

I proceeded to ask him how he took it, willed myself to remember the details as I nodded, before returning to do my first of what I hoped to be many tasks for these men.

SIX

THE MORNING FLEW BY, WHICH surprised me since I walked in here with absolutely nothing to do. That quickly changed once I delivered coffee to Ben and Landon. Both men then proceeded to give me instructions on what they needed.

After he gave me a brief overview of their computer system, Ben had me calling two companies who'd been entertaining the notion of hiring the firm. It was merely a follow-up to let them know Mr. Snowden looked forward to working with them.

Turned out, Ben represented mostly tech companies within the state, Justin's accounts consisted of new product developers all over the nation and he traveled a lot, and Landon and Langston focused solely on the publishing industry, which involved mostly telecommunication and video conferencing since their clients were all over the world.

I also learned that though they appeared to be a four-man operation, they did have a significant number of people who worked for them, ranging from people who managed the accounts to those who managed the people.

It didn't take long to realize that they were a diverse group and their clients were, as well. My first lesson came when it became apparent that I had to handle the phone calls differently. When Landon asked me to follow up with two of his authors, nailing down their publishing schedule and getting details on an upcoming signing, I found that I was talking to their account managers, who were employed by the firm. When contacting Ben's clients, I was dealing mostly with marketing managers within that specific company directly.

The phone on my desk rang and I grabbed the receiver, putting an extra note of cheer in my greeting.

"Hey, doll," Jordan replied. "Would you like to go downstairs and grab a bite with me? There's a fantastic sandwich shop in the main lobby."

"I…uh…I thought they closed down the office at one on Fridays?"

"Usually, yes. But since today's your first day, they opted to keep regular hours. And since I missed yesterday morning, I wasn't about to argue. So, you hungry?"

I peered up at the closed doors in front of me. I wasn't sure when I was supposed to take lunch. Aside from the few phone calls they had delegated, I hadn't had much conversation with anyone. I had yet to see Justin at all, and Langston had come in already on the phone.

Without instruction from my bosses, I didn't know what to say to Jordan.

He obviously sensed my concern because he kept talking. "They'll be taking lunch right at one. Unless they have lunch meetings scheduled or they're out of town, they always go out together and they're back in an hour."

As though they heard Jordan, all four doors opened and all four men walked out.

Hmm. Now I knew what the other door was for. It appeared Justin had snuck in at some point.

Ben looked over and nodded. "We're heading out to lunch. You're welcome to go out if you'd like."

"Thank you," I told him as the four men headed down the hall. Speaking to Jordan, I said, "Sure, I'd love to go down with you."

"Come on, girlie. Let's get a move on then."

Grabbing my purse, I headed toward the front. By the time I got to Jordan's desk, the lobby was empty except for him. He bypassed me quickly and I noticed he was locking the doors that led back to the offices.

"How's the morning so far?" he asked as we waited for the elevator to arrive.

"Good. Busy."

"It'll be that way. The girl before you—Andrea—she said it became too much for her to handle. That's why she left. And the girl before *her*—Debbie—couldn't seem to get along with Justin for whatever reason."

The elevator arrived and we stepped inside.

"To tell you the truth," he continued, "I think she got upset that Justin didn't hit on her."

"Really?" I turned to face Jordan, my curiosity piqued by the gossip. "Did the others?"

His golden eyebrow arched. "I think they were interested."

There was a distinct note in Jordan's tone. As though I was missing something, but I wasn't sure what it was. Almost as though it was expected that all four men were to be interested at the same time. And by *interested* I could only assume he meant...sexually? Maybe? Hell, I had no idea because it sounded strange even as I thought it.

"Do they not hire men?" That seemed the most pertinent question.

"Of course they do." His smile was wide. "I'm the best thing that's happened to them, don't you know?"

I laughed. How could I not? I truly liked Jordan.

"I mean for the secretary position."

"Not since I've been here. Although there have been some men who apply, but they tend to hire them and send them out into the field."

"Oh."

"Have they gone over the job requirements with you yet?"

I shook my head. "I figure they'll assign me tasks as they go along." That seemed to be the way things were working so far.

"They usually don't go over the full requirements until after two weeks. I think they want to ensure you'll stick around."

"Well, I can tell you, I have no intentions of going anywhere." Considering the amount of money they were willing to pay, along with the benefits, it would be hard to get me to walk away. And though I hadn't done much, I liked the feel of the office environment. My four bosses seemed relatively laid-back for the most part.

Except for Langston. That man intimidated me. But not necessarily in a bad way.

"Good." Jordan took my arm and steered me out of the elevator when it arrived in the main lobby. "It'll be nice for one of their girls to hang around for a while. So, what's your pleasure?" he asked the second we stepped into the bustling sandwich shop. "I'm pretty simple. Turkey and cheddar for me."

I didn't even bother glancing at the menu. "Uh…roast beef and Swiss. On wheat. And spicy mustard."

"I'm betting you're a riot at Starbucks," he said with a chuckle.

After we ordered and paid and our sandwiches were prepared, I followed Jordan to a table against the wall. I wasn't surprised to see that the small restaurant was packed. From what I could tell, it was the only one in the building, which was quite convenient for those who worked nearby.

"How long have you worked here?" I asked, opening my baked Lay's.

Jordan was unwrapping his sandwich when he smiled at me. "Eighteen months and let me tell you, it's been a ride."

"Really? You like working here?"

"Considering they leave me alone most of the time, sure. I get to interact with the clients, talk on the phone all day, play on the Internet when I'm bored, and they pay me to do all that…" He grinned sheepishly. "Yeah, I love it."

I wanted to ask Jordan to give me some insight into the bosses, but I didn't. I liked Jordan and all, but I needed to get to know him a little before I started prying. He might've been the kind to run to the bosses and tell them I was asking questions, for all I knew. I didn't want to look like a nosy Nancy. Not yet, anyway.

"You don't get bored?" As of right now, I was worried that I wasn't going to have enough to do. And yes, the morning had passed quickly, but unless someone wanted coffee this afternoon, I wasn't really sure what I would have on my agenda.

"Never. The pace here is fast. In fact, they work long hours. Sometimes late into the night."

"Does their secretary?"

"Sometimes. But they always ask first. A couple of them didn't want to, but some of them have. To be honest, I think the reason they've had to work late was because their secretary couldn't handle her share of the workload."

I made a mental note of that. I would not let these guys down.

Continuing with the small talk, I asked, "How many secretaries have they had?"

"About one every other month," Jordan said around a mouthful. "Although they've had to go a few weeks without one from time to time. The longest was a girl who stayed for seven weeks, but they eventually had to let her go."

One every two months? Wow.

That was a lot.

"Do you know why they don't keep them?"

He shook his head. "I think they haven't found anyone who can keep up with the fast pace. I don't think it's been personal. Then again, most of them didn't hang out with me since we're separated ninety-nine percent of the time. A couple were really snobbish. I think they rubbed the bosses the wrong way, too."

For whatever reason, that statement had me conjuring up some pretty dirty images of rubbing the bosses. Only I'd be doing it the *right* way.

And there went my inner hussy, clearly tired of being caged. I had to get laid sometime soon or who knew what I might do.

Sheesh.

•

The phone on my desk rang right at three o'clock. It was coming from inside, so I grabbed the receiver before it rang a second time.

"Luci, when you get a minute, can you please come in here?" Justin's voice was rich and sexy as it seemed to caress me through the phone.

Yep. I was in some serious trouble here.

Shaking myself out of my sex-hazed stupor, I answered with, "Yes, sir."

Hanging up the phone, I started toward his office door, then paused. I went back to my desk, grabbed a notepad and pen, then returned. Tapping twice, I waited until he called me inside.

"It's open."

I pushed open the door and offered him a shy smile.

"Please, have a seat," he urged, nodding toward one of the three chairs across from his desk.

Moving slowly, I glanced around, admiring every square inch of Justin's office. I had yet to be in here, so I felt the need to take it all in.

His desk was more traditional, a dark mahogany, probably eight feet wide or so. Very sturdy. For whatever reason, it had me thinking about being laid out on top of it, legs spread...

Shit.

I shook off the thought and took a deep breath as I moved to the chair and eased down into it. It was the same rich color as the desk, and there were two matching ones on either side of it. Like Ben's and Landon's offices, Justin's also had sofas. Two, which were set up the same as Ben's, facing each other with tables on each end. There were no windows in this room; however, there was a television on the wall and bookshelves, too. His held various products. I figured they were samples from his clients.

Something on the far right caught my eye and I squinted to see what it was.

A wave of heat engulfed me from head to toe, embarrassment making my face flush as I did a double take. There on the shelf was what looked a lot like a glass dildo. I quickly scanned a few of the other items, noticing that, yes, they were...sex toys.

Okay, so maybe *that* was the reason my hormones seemed to be on a pendulum. Back and forth, as though gravity-driven and picking up speed over time. Perhaps the sexual energy was ghosting through the building, turning me into a fiend.

Justin leaned back in his chair, crossed one ankle over the opposite knee, and regarded me silently.

It made me want to fidget, but I managed to keep my hands still and my knees from bouncing.

"How're things going so far?" he inquired.

I clicked my pen over and over, then stopped myself suddenly because *that* was annoying. "Good. I really like it here."

"What're you happy about so far?"

I hadn't expected an interrogation, so I had to think about that for a second. "I like the fast pace. Time seems to fly by. And I like talking to the managers and their team members, getting to know them."

Justin nodded. "I talked to Ben and Landon. They said you're doing great."

That pleased me and I couldn't hide the pride from my face.

Justin's eyes traveled a little lower, then back up. That was when I decided the man had bedroom eyes. Dark, seductive, the kind you wanted a man to pin on you when he had you laid out before him, naked and willing.

Shit.

I was beginning to wonder if they were pumping something in through the air conditioning. I mean, sure, I had a strong sex drive, but this was getting ridiculous.

"If you don't mind me asking, how old are you?" I blurted, immediately realizing how personal that was.

Justin merely smiled. "Thirty-seven."

"Oh, wow. You look much younger than that. I mean, not that you're old." My hand shot up and smacked over my mouth. "I'm so sorry," I mumbled, then withdrew my hand and repeated my apology before adding, "That was completely uncalled for."

He laughed. "It's all right. I get that sometimes." His eyes traveled over my face. "And how old are you, Luci?"

"Twenty-four." I figured he already knew that since I had to put my birthdate on the application I had filled out online.

"Are you married?" he inquired.

Shaking my head, I said, "God, no."

He seemed pleased by the answer. "Dating anyone?"

I shook my head again. "I'm not big on the relationship thing," I admitted. "I haven't technically had a date in about two years. I was seeing a guy in college—his name was Thomas—but that didn't work out."

I had no idea why I was telling this man so much about me, but I couldn't seem to shut up.

"You?" I questioned.

This sounded far too much like a first date conversation. Certainly not a conversation appropriate for my first day on the job.

Justin shook his head. "Never married, no. Not *dating* anyone." His lips curled up in a sexy grin. "However, it hasn't been two years."

No, I couldn't imagine it had.

I noticed he put emphasis on the word *dating*, however, I wasn't sure what that meant. Was he seeing someone? Maybe they didn't call it dating. Friends with benefits?

I glanced back toward the wall, then dropped my eyes to my lap when I noticed a thick black dildo. "Are any of the others? You know, married?"

Shit.

Someone should gag me now and put an end to this insanity.

"No. Landon and Langston have never been married. Ben was married back in his early twenties. Didn't work out. And no, they're not dating anyone at the moment either."

I nodded, a little surprised that Justin would offer up that information so easily.

"Do you live close?" Justin asked.

I shrugged. "Not too far. About twenty minutes on a good day. You?"

"I've got a house about an hour from here," he stated. "But I have an apartment here in the city for the nights I don't want to drive that far. We all do, actually. I tend to spend more time at the apartment these days."

"That must be nice."

His smile was a little wicked if I wasn't mistaken. "Very. Plus, it's in this building, so that makes it convenient."

"I'd say so."

We stared at one another for what felt like an interminably long time before finally Justin cleared his throat and sat up straight. "Well, that's all I had. Just wanted to check in. Make sure things are going well."

"They are," I said quickly, then got to my feet. "Very well."

"Good to hear."

I turned toward the door.

"And Luci?"

I peered at him over my shoulder, noticing the way his eyes were glued to my legs. "Hmm?"

He lifted his gaze to meet mine. "If you need anything, anything at all, just let me know."

"Yes, sir."

Once again, there was a flare of heat in his eyes, but I didn't get to see it long because I slipped out the door, terrified of what might possibly come out of my mouth next.

SEVEN

IT WAS ALMOST FIVE AND I was about to get up to ask if anyone needed me to do anything when Langston stuck his head out of his office door. I instantly glanced in his direction and he crooked his finger, inviting me to join him.

With a fluttery feeling in my belly, I got to my feet, smoothed out my skirt, then headed to his office. It took everything in me not to skip.

Clearly I needed something to do.

"Yes, sir?"

"Come in. Have a seat." He motioned toward the chairs in front of his desk.

I noticed the way his eyes slipped down to my legs. It looked almost as though he was gauging the length of my skirt. In an effort to show him that I had heeded his warning, I let my arms dangle listlessly at my sides, proving my skirt was as long as my fingertips. Barely.

His gaze shot up to mine and I realized he caught on to what I was doing. The smirk that curled his lips was rather sexy.

Quickly looking away, I tried to play it off. It wasn't hard to do because I was curious as to what made this man tick and I figured his office would probably give me a little insight. I had only caught a glimpse of this room earlier in the day, and now that I was here, I couldn't keep from checking it out.

I was pretty sure his office was bigger than all the others. The floor-to-ceiling windows that lined the entire right wall offered a fabulous view of downtown, without the interruption of the building I could see out my window.

The furniture was rustic, like Landon's. Almost all raw wood and brown leather. There were some wrought iron decorations adorning the walls and a couple of pictures. The floor was dark hardwood with several rugs laid out beneath the furniture. His desk was large and he was sitting behind it, staring at me.

Not only staring. He was waiting.

"I'm sorry," I muttered as I took a seat, placing my hands in my lap. "You have a very nice office."

"Thank you." He leaned back, resting his arms on the armrests as he regarded me. "I take it you've had a chance to talk to everyone today?"

"I have." I smiled. "It's been a good day."

"And you've learned the system? Understand how the calendar works? Got your email set up?"

"Yes, sir. Ben's been very helpful, walking me through everything and answering all my questions. But I'm good with software applications, and I know my way around a computer, so it's not too difficult."

He nodded. "Glad to hear it."

Langston regarded me for a long time, making my insides quiver. There was something about him that was distinctly different than the others. For one, he always seemed to be assessing. As though he was playing things out in his head. Unlike Landon and Ben, he wasn't quick to smile and he didn't speak much. Not to me, at least. I'd heard him on the phone, so I knew he didn't have an issue talking. And when he did, he was eloquent, if not a little demanding. It just seemed he was standoffish with me.

But it wasn't just that. It was in the way he looked at me. As though he wanted to tie me up and have his wicked way with me.

Then again, sex-deprived woman that I was, it could've very well just been my imagination.

I felt as though he was waiting for me to ask questions, so I came up with one. "Is there anything I can do for you? Something that I haven't been taught yet?"

"Not at the moment, but I'll be sure to let you know if somethin' comes up."

"Yes, sir."

"Do you read, Luci? For entertainment?"

"A little," I admitted. "I've enjoyed romantic suspense."

Langston turned and grabbed something from one of the shelves behind him. He turned back and pushed a paperback book across his desk. "Not romantic suspense, but I think you'll enjoy it. It's a new release from one of my clients. I'd be interested in your take on it if you don't mind."

I leaned forward and pulled the book closer, admiring the cover. It was sexy, with the image of a woman on her knees, staring up at a handsome dark-haired man, who was shirtless. I glanced at the title: *His Name Is Sir.*

Picking up the book, I smiled at him. "I'd be honored to read it."

He nodded again, still watching me intently. "Thank you, Luci."

"Yes, sir."

For some strange reason, my legs weren't as steady as I'd hoped they would be, but I managed to stand without falling over. I felt a nervous flutter in my belly as I walked out. I wasn't sure if Langston was watching me, but I could practically feel his eyes trailing down my backside.

And the worst part…

I liked it.

•

At five thirty, I packed up my things, making sure to grab the paperback Langston had loaned me before leaving for the day. Landon had already left, Ben was in Justin's office with the door closed, and Langston was on the phone, so I didn't say anything before slipping down the hall.

Jordan was flipping off the lights when I met him by the elevator.

"Well, you made it through the first day." His smile was as bright as it had been that morning.

"I did."

His eyes dropped to the book in my hand and I realized I was holding it with the cover facing out.

"Ooh. What do we have here? You smutty girl, you."

Heat traveled up my chest and engulfed my face. "Langston asked me to read it."

His grin widened. "I just bet he did."

It was hard to look him in the eye. "Have you read any of the authors they represent?"

"I have, actually. A few of them, in fact. There're a couple who write gay romance." He lifted an eyebrow. "Let's just say, I don't mind the sexy times."

I chuckled, feeling my cheeks heat. I would likely have to get over this embarrassment in order to work here. Especially since it appeared Justin represented the sex toy industry.

We were still waiting for the elevator when I felt the presence of someone behind me. I turned to see Langston heading toward us, his eyes perusing me from head to toe.

Jordan smiled. "Good evening, Mr. Moore."

"Good evening, Mr. Jenkins."

Jordan spun back around and winked at me.

There was a sudden charge in the air, one that hadn't been there before Langston arrived. I wondered if either of them felt it or if it was simply me and my overactive imagination.

When the elevator doors finally opened, Jordan motioned for me to go before him. There were three other people in the elevator already, so it was a smidge crowded. I managed to shift to the side, but then Langston joined us. He moved me so that I was in front of him, the warmth of him against my back.

It took everything in me not to sigh in contentment as I felt him standing there. I had the strange urge to lean into him. As it was, his scent was intoxicating. Spicy and rich, yet not overpowering. The type of aroma that made a woman want to sniff the air like a dog and follow the trail.

On the descent to the main floor, one more person got on, and at that point, I really was pressed almost completely against the sexy man at my back. I could tell Langston was keeping an appropriate distance between us.

I was pretty sure the elevator was moving at a normal speed, but for me it felt as though it was gliding down through molasses, taking its own sweet time.

Finally, the number above the door flashed one and the bell dinged.

On the main floor, several people flooded out before Langston nudged me forward with his hand at the small of my back. My eyes shot up to his face momentarily and he looked down at me. His expression was so intense I inhaled sharply.

He offered me a short nod. "I'm lookin' forward to seein' you on Monday, Luci."

"You, too, sir." And yes, I sounded breathless, but I couldn't help it. I was sure I would ridicule myself for it later, but in that moment, it simply happened.

Langston winked, then strode out of the building with a confidence I rarely saw on many people.

"Oh, yum," Jordan whispered as he came to stand beside me. "He is truly delicious."

I jerked my attention over to him, hoping he didn't see the pure lust in my eyes.

Jordan chuckled. "You get used to him. He's intimidating, sure, but he's always nice. At least to me."

We headed for the main doors.

"I'll see you on Monday, Luci. Have a good night." With a quick wave, Jordan took off down the sidewalk. I assumed that meant he lived nearby.

I was surprised to find my car was waiting for me out front. I fumbled for my purse, wondering how much was an appropriate tip. Jordan had mentioned that parking was free—one of our topics at lunch—but I wasn't sure if that pertained to a tip or not.

"Have a wonderful evening, Miss Wagner," the valet said formally, handing over my keys.

I managed to retrieve my wallet, but before I could get it open, the man shook his head. "No tip necessary. It's all taken care of."

Taking my keys, I watched him as I moved toward my car.

I was so lost in this new world I'd found myself in, but I was loving every second.

The only thing that could've been better…

Tomorrow wouldn't be Saturday.

•

"So, how was it?" Kristen asked when she called shortly after I got home.

"It was great." Even I noticed there was a little too much enthusiasm in my tone.

"I knew you'd say that. I'm so happy. They're really good guys, Luce. You're going to love working there."

"Yeah, yeah, yeah. I'm just waiting for them to become a little less hot," I said as I grabbed a bottle of water out of the refrigerator. "It's not easy being immersed in all that…sex appeal."

Kristen chuckled. "You'll get used to it, I'm sure. Just consider it a perk of the job."

There was a muffled sound and I realized Kristen had covered the phone.

"Okay, yeah. I'll be right there. Hey, Luce. I've gotta run. I just wanted to check in with you."

"You wanna grab drinks tomorrow night?" I offered.

"Sorry. No can do. I'm working all weekend. Maybe sometime next week."

"Absolutely."

The call disconnected and I stared at the phone, then shrugged my shoulders.

I missed hanging out with Kristen. Last night at the bar was the first time we'd been able to hang out in quite some time. Although we generally made it to yoga several times a week, it had been a while since I'd really spent any time with her other than when we were all hot and sweaty. She was always so busy with her job. Evidently, being a sous chef at a renowned restaurant took up a lot of free time.

As I reached for the remote to turn on the television, my gaze fell upon the paperback sitting on the coffee table. I bypassed the TV clicker and grabbed the book before snuggling into the cushions.

"So, tell me, TJ Arlington, just what sort of dirty, wicked stuff am I going to find in your book?"

I didn't even bother with the book description, launching right into chapter one.

By the time I was turning the page to chapter three, I was enthralled with what was transpiring between the heroine and the sexy dominating man she'd just met. By the time I was on chapter five, I was suddenly grateful tomorrow was Saturday.

Looked as though I'd found a way to pass the time.

EIGHT

BOSS MEETING

JUSTIN

"LUCI'S BEEN HERE FOR TWO weeks as of tomorrow," I prompted when Landon finally joined us in my office.

"Technically, she's been here two weeks as of Friday," Langston corrected. "She interviewed two weeks ago tomorrow."

The man was a stickler for accuracy and sometimes it irked the shit out of me. Today, I decided I could let it go. It was a few minutes before six and the four of us were the only ones still there. Luci and Jordan had left for the day and I figured it was as good a time as any to get a status update on how well our girl was doing.

Our girl.

Yes, I knew how that sounded, but I couldn't help myself. For two weeks, I'd watched her pretty face brighten up the entire office. I loved to hear her laugh, enjoyed watching her smile. I even laughed when she attempted to tell jokes. Which was not her forte, by the way. But it was cute, nonetheless.

"She's catching on quickly," Ben said, reclining. "She hasn't asked a single question twice."

"Remember the one who asked you to type up notes for her?" Landon chuckled.

Ben groaned. "She was serious. When I told her I wouldn't, she told me she couldn't work here because we weren't providing the tools necessary to do the job."

Oh, Lord. I remembered that woman. I'd been hesitant to hire her, but Landon and Ben had encouraged me to fall in line. Needless to say, I had enjoyed my *I told you so* moment.

"Thankfully, Luci's not that demanding," Ben added. "I've caught her taking notes on things she's worried she won't remember. I'm rather impressed."

"I've received several emails from my managers," Landon offered. "They're extremely happy with her. According to them, she's more than willing to help them out. Which is more than we can say for the last couple who've stayed longer than a week."

That was true. For whatever reason, until Luci, we had yet to find many secretaries who could mesh well with the managers in the field. There had been one, but she had flirted ruthlessly, making a couple of them uncomfortable. Most of the women we had hired seemed to think that their only job was supporting the four of us. And in a way, that was true; however, in order to support us, they had to support those who worked for us, too.

"Are we ready to present the requirements?" Langston asked, always the one to get right down to business.

I instantly shook my head. "Although I sense she's taken a liking to us, I'm not ready to do that just yet. I want her to get more comfortable here. Less chance of freaking her out."

"She's extremely flirtatious," Ben said, crossing one ankle over the opposite knee. I could tell he was regarding me, likely trying to figure out how I felt about the girl. "But not in an overly aggressive way."

"I don't think there's anything aggressive about that girl," Langston said.

I nodded my head while I unabashedly admired Ben, making sure he saw me doing it. Ben and I had been getting closer as the days passed. For about a year now, we'd begun openly seeing one another outside of the club. Initially, I'd kept all of our interactions in public for fear I would get too close to him.

However, I hadn't been lying when I told Luci that I wasn't dating anyone. That wasn't the right word for what Ben and I had going on. Not in my opinion, anyway.

Regardless, I'd gotten close to him. It was one of those things, I figured. It was going to happen, no matter how hard I tried to do the opposite. And I was getting too damned old to pretend otherwise.

"I noticed that," Landon added, his crude gaze darting from one man to another. "And she shows no favoritism."

"Which is a plus," Langston tacked on.

I knew Langston had a thing for Luci. I'd known it the moment I saw him look at her. There was something distinctly innocent about her and that was exactly what Langston was looking for. He and Landon both. They wanted a submissive who they could share permanently. The same as Ben and me. Although I was Ben's Dom, my pup was a switch and he was looking for a submissive that we could both top, while still giving me the freedom to top him whenever I felt like it.

The truth was, Landon, Langston, Ben, and I wanted someone we could share in the office. A woman we could get to know on a more intimate level yet still maintain a certain sense of professionalism.

Although Luci seemed like the perfect candidate for that position, I feared we were all going to want more from her. I saw the way Landon looked at her, too. He was enthralled, but I couldn't very well blame him.

"What I want to know is where she comes up with these outfits," Landon said, chuckling. "The girl makes me hard just looking at her."

I smiled. I knew the feeling well.

"I like that she rarely wears pants," Ben said, his perfect teeth flashing as he grinned. "It definitely spurs my imagination."

We were unquestionably getting off topic here, so I decided to bring it back around. "I think we continue on the way that we are. If any issues arise, we'll discuss them one off. However, we'll move forward as we have been. At the one-month mark, or close to, we'll implement the Monday meetings and see where it goes from there."

My three partners all agreed.

And it had me wondering just how long we would continue to be in agreement.

Luciana Wagner was a woman I didn't think any of us were prepared for.

Didn't mean we weren't going to see where it led.

NINE

"IS IT JUST ME, OR do you appear to be running out of the building?" Jordan teased when I made my way to the elevator right at five thirty on Thursday.

I smiled as he joined me. "I don't run. Ever."

"Not in those heels," he teased.

I laughed. "No, not ever. It would likely take a zombie apocalypse to get me to jog, much less run."

We were both chuckling when someone cleared their throat behind us. I peered over my shoulder to see Landon making his way toward us. Apparently, he was heading out, too.

Funny, for the past couple of weeks, it seemed that at least one of my bosses left at the same time I did.

"What about now?" Jordan chuckled, his voice low enough I heard him.

I cut my eyes to his face and widened them, silently urging him to be quiet.

"So, what's the big rush tonight?" he continued, as though I hadn't willed him to shut up.

I sighed. "I…I kinda have a date."

"Oh, do tell." It was as though my words supercharged his excitement and his eyes sparkled.

"Nothing fancy. There's this guy in my yoga class. He's asked me out at least three times. I finally gave in."

"How romantic." His tone said he thought it was quite the opposite.

"I didn't want to. But he's relentless. I figured I'd say yes to shut him up. We agreed to meet at a restaurant near the yoga studio. Super casual."

Jordan's gaze slid over me as the door to the elevator opened. "Are you wearing that?"

He didn't sound as though that was a bad thing.

"Actually, yes. It was either this or yoga pants."

My newfound friend chuckled. "Going all out, are you?"

I honestly didn't want to be going on this date, but Will—the guy in my class—wouldn't stop pestering me about it. He was a nice guy and all, even kind of cute, but certainly not my type. For one, I wasn't the only one he'd hit on. However, it was possible I was the only one who had accepted.

"I'm trying not to be rude," I told him, shifting over so that Landon could stand beside me. "I figure we'll have dinner, and he'll realize I'm totally not his type."

"But what if you are?" Jordan's eyes were wide.

"Trust me, I'm not. He just doesn't do it for me."

"So," Jordan's voice was a little softer. "What *does* do it for you?"

I giggled shyly, then my eyes flew up to Landon's face.

He does it for me.

Oh, thank God I didn't say that out loud.

However, based on the gleam in Landon's pretty eyes, I think he read my mind. A small smirk tilted his sexy mouth and I had to look away.

"Not into the bendy types, huh?" Jordan asked, continuing to carry the conversation.

"It's not that," I admitted, fighting the urge to look up at Landon. "I prefer guys who are a little more…sure of themselves but not stuck up. Will looks down his nose when he talks to people. Total turnoff."

"I know exactly what you mean."

"When he asked me out, he actually told me what he wanted me to do." I lowered my voice to imitate him. "'So, Luci, I'm going to ask you out and you're going to say yes, then we'll have a good time.'" I shivered because it still made me a little queasy.

"Seriously?" Jordan barked a laugh.

"Yes. Exactly like that. Not in the way a girl wants to hear. I mean, I could totally get behind a dominant man, but this… It was just icky." Not at all the way it was depicted in books.

I had absolutely no idea why I was sharing all this information with Jordan. Then again, he and I had established a friendship in the two weeks I'd been working there. On the other hand, perhaps my inner hussy was doing it for Landon's benefit.

Whatever the reason, I was grateful when the elevator reached the main floor.

"Well, have fun on the date," Jordan said as we stepped out of the elevator together. "I look forward to getting the details in the morning."

"I hope you like tragic endings," I said playfully.

Although I really wasn't joking.

•

I met Will at a small café near the yoga studio right at six. Okay, maybe a few minutes after, but I'd done the best I could considering the traffic. He was waiting out front for me when I arrived, pacing back and forth as though he didn't think I would make it.

I walked right up to him. "Will?"

He smiled, eyeing me from head to toe in a way that sort of creeped me out. "You look…breathtaking."

Now, I knew it was a line because I hadn't bothered to change clothes from work. After the long day, I felt a little frumpy. I hadn't even bothered to freshen up my makeup. However, I probably looked significantly better than if I'd been wearing my sweaty yoga clothes.

"Thank you." I glanced at the door.

Will stepped back and motioned for me to go ahead. It only took a second for me to realize he wasn't going to open the door for me, so I did it myself, then headed inside. Being that it was Thursday night, the place wasn't packed, so it was easy to find a table, which Will did, by moving in front of me and leading the way.

I usually enjoyed this place because they had great food and it always smelled like chocolate pie, which happened to be one of my vices. Unfortunately, whatever cologne Will was wearing overpowered any other smell in the room. It was enough to make my sinuses throb, but I pretended not to notice. Granted, a couple of other patrons glanced our way as Will's scent wafted by them. Apparently, they couldn't pretend the way that I could.

"How was work?" he asked when he flopped into a booth in the back.

I took my seat more eloquently. "Good. I'm just getting ramped up."

"Oh?" He looked confused. "New job?"

I nodded. "I've been there for two weeks."

"Wow. So, *really* new." He sounded as though that was a problem.

Will picked up a menu for himself from the small holder on the table. He didn't offer me one, so I reached for one after, although I already knew what I wanted.

"So, what is it that you do?" he inquired as his eyes scanned the menu.

I spoke to my menu as well. "I'm a secretary." I already knew he was going to be disappointed by that.

"But your outfit…"

I glanced down at myself. I wasn't sure what was wrong with my outfit. I was wearing a long-sleeve black silk blouse and a black skirt, which rested just above my knees. My heels were red because I'd wanted a splash of color. More than once I'd noticed my new bosses eyeing my shoes. I was pretty sure they liked them.

I lifted my gaze back to his. "Is there something wrong with my outfit?"

He shook his head. "No. It's just…"

Lifting one eyebrow, I waited for him to continue.

"I just thought you…"

"I what?"

"You had a higher-level position."

I smiled to myself and dropped my eyes to the menu. Apparently being a secretary was beneath this guy. Lord only knew what he'd think if I told him I had worked at various retailers in the past few years. The guy would probably have a coronary if he knew I'd worked at Hooters. Totally beneath him.

Now, it wasn't as though I hadn't known that Will was shallow. However, I *had* grossly underestimated how much.

"So, what is it that *you* do?" I already knew, but I figured what the hell. Might as well have a little fun.

"I'm a lawyer."

"Oh, really?" I pretended to be intrigued by the notion. "They make good money, huh?"

His eyes narrowed. It was what he'd expected me to say, obviously. As a secretary, I couldn't possibly make enough to support myself, nor could I enjoy being financially independent without raking in the dough. That was exactly the way this guy would think.

The waitress walked up and we both placed our orders. He went first, ordering a BLT while I opted for a salad. Water for both. Fast and easy.

"And you say you've only been with… What company did you say you worked for?" he probed.

I smiled. "I didn't, but it's a PR firm downtown."

That seemed to pique his interest. "Which one?"

I rattled off the name as though it didn't really matter.

Will leaned back and regarded me for a moment. I had no idea what he knew about the company, nor did I really care. I knew there'd been something I wasn't attracted to about him, and within the first few minutes of our dinner conversation, he had reminded me of what that was.

I wasn't good enough for this guy. Not working as a secretary. Had I mentioned my accounting degree, he might've shown a little interest, but the truth was, I didn't want him to. I had given in because he wouldn't let it go and now at least he would turn his attention elsewhere.

"So, what type of law do you practice?" I asked because the silence was getting to be too much.

"Family law."

"Oh, well, that must be fun."

"I enjoy it. I'll soon make junior partner, so I'm well on my way."

To what, I had no freaking clue. Again...I didn't care either.

Fortunately for both of us, our food was delivered and it gave each of us a valid excuse to ignore the other.

This was the very reason I hated dating. Rarely did I find a man who intrigued me enough to make it past a first date. Perhaps that made me the shallow one, but I needed some sort of stimulating conversation or, at the very least, some sort of physical attraction. I found neither with Will.

My mind drifted back to my four bosses. Now, those were men who could easily hold my interest for a night. Or a week. It was rare that a man could walk around and radiate sex appeal without even trying; however, the four of them did it effortlessly. And when they spoke... Those men were the types who spoke when they had something to say and they did it very well. People listened.

I thought about Landon and Langston. About how this dinner would've been very different had they been here. For one, they wouldn't have looked down on me because I was a secretary. In the two weeks I'd been there, they hadn't treated me any differently than they did each other. Or Jordan, for that matter. We worked there, they worked there, and we coexisted nicely.

While I picked at my salad, I noticed Will was checking his phone. He had done it several times in the past few minutes. It was beyond obvious that he was ready to bolt. Then again, so was I. The only reason I was still there was because I would likely see him at the yoga studio and I didn't want things to be awkward between us.

I probably should've told Kristen about my date. No doubt she would've called me just to give me an out. But I'd been hopeful that this would at least be enjoyable. Unfortunately, along with being shallow, the man was a shitty conversationalist.

Suddenly, Will punched a button on his phone and held it up to his ear. I chuckled to myself. There was no one on the other end of that call, but apparently, not only did he think I was beneath him, he also thought I was stupid.

"Yes, this is Will. Did you need something?"

He paused, as though someone was talking. The screen had already gone dark against his ear, but he clearly didn't notice.

For effect, he glanced at his watch. "Sure. I could..." He paused again, his eyes darting to me briefly. He tried to pull off an apologetic look, but it merely made him look like the douchebag he was. "Yeah. I can be back at the office in ten minutes. Does that work?" He paused. "Absolutely. I'm on my way."

I waited patiently until he put an end to his fake phone call.

"Oh, shucks," I said diligently. "You have to go? That's such a shame."

"Yeah, well...when work calls..."

"Oh, I know. Well, I don't know. I'm just a secretary, but I get it."

He offered a polite smile, then reached for his wallet.

"Oh, no," I snapped, holding up my hand. "I've got it. After all, I'm sticking around for some pie." Might as well make the best of it, right?

"Okay, then," he said warily.

Right. Like I bought the fact that he was saddened not to have to pay for dinner.

"I'll see you around," I told him, returning my attention to my salad.

Considering it was far more interesting than he was.

•

The following morning, Jordan and I penciled in lunch so we could dish about my shitty date. I was looking forward to having someone to talk to about it. It was a funny story, at least to me.

I spent the morning doing my usual, continuing to learn my way around the office, getting to know a few of the team members by interacting with them via email, and spending a lot of time by myself.

It was shortly before one when Landon's door opened and he stepped out.

Smiling up at him, I offered a pleasant, "Good afternoon."

The heat of his gaze warmed me as he approached my desk, propping himself on the edge. It was such a flirty thing to do, but I thought nothing of it.

"So...how was the date last night?"

I felt my cheeks heat, remembering the conversation I'd had with Jordan in the elevator.

"It was wonderful," I said, making sure he heard my sarcasm. "We talked and talked and..." I shook my head. "Wait. No. We didn't talk." I grinned wide. "But he did fake a phone call to get out of it. And since he thought I was beneath him because I'm just a lowly secretary while he's going to potentially make junior partner at his law firm, I offered to pay for dinner. He let me. So, I enjoyed a piece of chocolate pie by myself. All in all, it was great."

Landon laughed. "You paid for dinner?"

"I did. I insisted. And by *insist*, I mean, I said I'd get it and he said okay. Luckily for me, we went to a cute little diner, so I tipped more than the meal cost."

"You spend a lot of time paying for dinner?" he asked and I understood the fishing expedition for what it was.

"No. I don't date usually. But Will was pretty persistent. Apparently, my wardrobe made him believe I had more money than I do. He's very superficial," I said sweetly. "Which, now that I think about it, is probably why he's still single."

"That or he's letting his dates pay for their own meals."

"True."

Langston's door opened, then Justin's. Landon got to his feet, obviously prepared to head out to lunch. Ben's door then opened, too. They all started toward the front, but Landon turned around to face me.

"One of these days a real man will take you out to dinner." He flashed a sexy grin. "And I assure you, I won't let you pay."

With that, he spun around and left.

My eyes were wide as I stared at the empty hallway, replaying his comment over and over and over in my head.

Had he said what I thought he'd said?

I won't let you pay.

Yes, yes he had.

Swoon!

TEN

ANOTHER WEEK HAD PASSED AND I felt as though I was making significant progress in learning my new role within the company. I was able to answer questions now without always having to seek input from one of my bosses. It made me feel good. More so when one of them acknowledged me, which they did often. Usually with a flirty smile.

And now that it was closing in on one o'clock, I was getting ready to head out for the weekend. I liked the leaving-early-on-Friday thing. It made for a longer weekend, which I was no longer dreading since I'd been introduced to the world of fictional romantic BDSM, thanks to Langston's authors. It was a world unlike anything I'd ever known existed. I'd fallen head over heels for the Dominants and submissives who fell in love in a rather unique, albeit complicated, way. In fact, I looked forward to reading every day, something I hadn't done in quite some time.

However, I didn't have the opportunity to read at work, so I did my best not to think about it. But when it was only a few minutes from time to leave, I got myself prepared to be immersed into that sexy new world.

Langston's door opened and I glanced up to see him walking toward me. He was a few minutes early for their daily one o'clock lunch.

"We'd very much like you to join us for lunch today," he said, his tone dark and rich and oh-so-sexy.

It wasn't phrased as a question, but then again, nothing he said usually was. The man was very direct, and usually ridiculously blunt.

Landon's door opened before I could answer Langston. He moved toward me. A second later, both men stood in front of my desk, peering down at me.

"You can leave directly after," Landon added, as though he'd been there when Langston asked the question.

I wondered if these two had that twin thing. The whole mind-reading thing that some of them did, knowing what the other was thinking before they said it. Or even what the other was feeling when they weren't together.

Ben's and Justin's doors then opened. Justin glanced over at me, his blond eyebrow lifting slightly, as though he, too, was waiting for my response.

"I'd love to join you," I told them as I grabbed my purse from the bottom drawer and then got to my feet.

"I'm going to ask Jordan to join us," Ben said before heading down the hallway.

I briefly wondered if this was something they did often. I felt a little better knowing Jordan would be going with us. Although I liked my bosses, I was still rather nervous around them. I figured that was due to their hotness factor.

Both Landon and Langston waited for me to walk past them before they fell into step, each one putting a hand at the small of my back. I felt as though I was being ushered out of the building. Although, the feeling wasn't unpleasant by any means.

When we reached the elevators, Jordan was standing there, talking animatedly with Ben. Justin's gaze cut over to me and I saw a small smile on his lips.

"Is this something you do often?" I asked Langston directly, trying to hide the fact that I was on the verge of freaking out.

Sure, I understood that it was just lunch, a regular meal that normal people had every day. But with my bosses? Definitely nerve-racking.

The elevator arrived and I was steered inside.

"Every couple of months," Langston admitted as we all turned to face the elevator doors.

That made me curious. If the previous secretaries hadn't lasted that long, had they ever taken them out to lunch? I'd have to remember to ask Jordan about it.

The ride down was relatively quiet except for the normal sounds of the elevator. I could hear my heart beating rapidly, knew my breaths probably were a little too rushed. I couldn't help it; I was edgy.

When we stepped out onto the main floor, Landon and Langston were replaced by Ben and Justin behind me. They took up the same position, guiding me with their hands as we all headed toward the front doors. My heels clicked loudly, but it was an unexpectedly sexy sound being that I was the only female surrounded by these uber-hot men.

I was surprised when there wasn't a vehicle out front to pick us up.

"It's a short walk," Ben said softly. "Just about a block."

I nodded, silently wishing I had worn more comfortable shoes. The heels I had on were the tallest that I owned, but I had tons of practice, so it wasn't that I was uncomfortable walking in them. It was merely the fact that they weren't made to carry me long distances.

We arrived at a steakhouse around the corner, a fancy little place with white linen tablecloths and crystal vases full of decorative flowers on every table.

Jordan got the door, holding it open while my four bosses allowed me to walk inside first. Landon moved toward the hostess, giving her his name. Apparently, they had reservations. And based on the warm smile on the woman's face, they weren't strangers to this place.

The next fifteen minutes or so were the most uncomfortable while we all ordered drinks and then figured out what to eat. My four bosses ordered Glenlivet, a single malt scotch that I knew wasn't cheap. Not wanting to be completely left out, I ordered red wine and Jordan opted for sweet tea. When the waitress finally got our food order down, I was already on my second glass as we were left to our own devices.

"So, I hear you've been reading some of Langston's authors," Landon prompted, his eyes fixed on my face.

I felt heat rush up my neck. I took another gulp of wine, then nodded. "I have."

"And what do you think?" I could tell he was genuinely curious, as were the rest of them.

I opted to go for honest. "It's interesting. I didn't even know stuff like that existed."

No one said anything, so I wondered if maybe it didn't really exist. Perhaps it was truly fictional. I mean, I had read *The Hunger Games* and I knew that wasn't real.

"Which book did you read?" Ben inquired.

"*His Name Is Sir.*" I watched him to see what his response was. He didn't give anything away.

"You started her out slow," Justin said, chuckling.

Slow? They considered a woman being spanked in a dungeon slow? Or was he being facetious?

I focused on repositioning my napkin in my lap. Being that I was seated between Landon and Langston while directly across from Ben, I wasn't in a position to talk to Jordan, who was the only real friend I had at the table. Which had me wondering whether they'd done that on purpose.

"I'll get her worked up to the more intense stuff soon enough," Langston said, giving me a sideways smirk.

I wanted to tell him I was already progressing, but I kept that tidbit to myself.

"It's officially been three weeks," Justin stated, his voice drawing my attention to him.

I smiled. "It has been."

"And you haven't run screaming from the building," Ben noted with a smirk, obviously sensing my discomfort.

"Not yet," I teased, dropping my gaze to the table.

Landon laughed. "I promise, it'll only get better from here."

I was pretty sure there was an innuendo in that statement. My eyes darted over to Jordan as though he might be able to save me. Unfortunately, he was chuckling and his expression gave nothing away. Something told me they'd all set me up here.

Thank God for the wine. A little liquid courage was just what the doctor ordered.

I figured I had two choices. One, I could sit around and blush like a schoolgirl and make this rare occasion weird for everyone. Or two, I could participate in my own special way and let them know that I wasn't intimidated.

Granted, I *was* intimidated. However, that didn't mean I couldn't play with the big dogs.

"Do you have big plans for her one-month mark?" Jordan asked.

He had a knowing smile on his face and it was then I realized there was some sort of inside joke that I wasn't privy to. I waited, but no one said anything. However, Landon did chuckle, which told me all I needed to know.

Then the table fell silent once more and I felt the tension rising. I had to do something to get these guys talking. Fortunately, our salads arrived a few minutes later. I wasn't all that hungry, but the third glass of wine was definitely going a long way to ease some of my tension.

"Well, since you managed to get me here," I told them, keeping a smile firmly in place as I set my fork down, "maybe now would be a good time to play a game."

"A game?" Langston leaned back and regarded me coolly.

"Yes." I made eye contact with each of them. "A way to get to know each other?"

"What did you have in mind?" Justin seemed oddly curious.

"It's simple, really. It's called Never Have I Ever."

"And how do we play this game?" Justin queried, his eyes flashing with amusement.

I glanced at Jordan and noticed his subtle nod. He knew how to play this game.

"All right. We'll play the simple version. Typically, each one of us would come up with something outrageous that we've never done before. Everyone holds up five fingers. If you've done the outrageous thing that's mentioned, you'll lower one finger. And so on and so forth. Since we're playing the condensed version, the person with the most fingers still up after the questions are asked will be the winner."

Jordan chuckled. "I think, to make this interesting, we should let Luci ask all the questions."

"Me?" I frowned.

"I think it's safe to say you're the one who's done the least outrageous things." He shrugged. "Otherwise, this could last a while."

I glanced from one man to the next. They all seemed to be on board with Jordan's twist, so I figured what the hell.

"All right." I made eye contact with Justin. "But just to be sure, we're off the clock, correct?"

Landon nodded. "Correct."

"And you realize I've had three glasses of wine?"

"Duly noted," Langston said.

"So, anything goes?"

Langston's smile was wicked. "Anything goes."

Taking a sip of wine, I ran through a million things I wanted to know about these men. Although I figured they'd all done some crazy things, there had to be a few they hadn't done.

"Okay, I'll go easy on you the first time. Never have I ever...had sex in the office."

My gaze dropped to each man's fingers and I knew I looked a little shocked when every one of them put down one finger.

"You've *all* had sex at the office?"

My four bosses all glanced over at Jordan.

"What?" He shrugged and I could see his cheeks turning a brilliant shade of red.

"I don't even want to know," Justin said, his attention returning to me.

"All right, then." This was going to be harder than I thought. I grinned as my next question came to me. "Never have I ever...had sex at the office while one of the six people at this table was present."

Jordan was the only person who didn't lower a finger.

My mouth gaped open and I stared at each man in turn.

Admittedly, I was getting a little hot and bothered by the topic. I have no idea why, but the notion of having sex with one of my bosses in the office, while the others were there…yeah, that did it for me in major ways.

Not that I could tell any of them that.

I took another drink of my wine and noticed all four of my bosses were smirking at one another.

"Fine. Never have I ever…had sex in a moving vehicle."

All five of them lowered a finger.

"Holy crap."

Landon chuckled. "Is it just me or does it seem that our feisty little secretary has sex on the brain?"

"That and she's slightly prudish if she's never done any of these things," Jordan teased.

Okay, that time I did blush.

And I realized, it was probably time to call a halt to the game. Only, I couldn't really do that because it would make me look like a chicken. Which meant I had to come up with at least two more.

Sighing, I took another sip of my wine. At this rate, I was going to need another bottle.

"Hmm." I glanced at Landon, then Justin, then Ben. "I know. Never have I ever…had sex with one of the people at this table."

Jordan, Landon, and Langston kept their fingers up while Ben and Justin each lowered one.

I smiled at Ben and Justin because that simple response had answered so many questions I'd had. Although, I still wasn't certain why Ben referred to Justin as Mr. Parker. Or why Justin had said he wasn't dating anyone.

"One more, Luci," Justin urged.

"Right." This last one was going to get me into trouble, I knew it. But I decided to ask it anyway. "Never have I ever…*wanted* to have sex with someone at this table."

And fine, that didn't pertain to me because I certainly wanted to have sex with not one but four people at the table, but I liked the illusion it offered, although I was sure they all saw right through me.

Four fingers lowered. Those fingers belonged to my four bosses.

I smiled at Jordan. "Clearly you're the winner."

"Clearly," he said cheekily.

Although I had learned a lot more about my bosses than I ever thought I'd want to know, I couldn't shake the feeling that something significant had transpired here today.

And I couldn't help but wonder what it might lead to.

Or when.

ELEVEN

ONE MONTH AND FOUR DAYS since I was hired, my routine had become ingrained in me and I found that I looked forward to getting out of bed every morning. The hardest part had been finding what I wanted to wear each day. It turned into a game almost. It seemed the more flirtatious my outfit, the more the bosses talked to me.

Of course, that spurred me on and I did my best to keep my outfits professional yet fun. Of course, I never once gave anything away. My skirts were always a respectable length and I never revealed too much cleavage—then again, I didn't *have* much to reveal in the first place. It wasn't as though I was trying to get myself fired, but I was having a good time. I liked the flirtatiousness of my bosses. It kept things enjoyable in the office.

Which was the very reason I went for a sassy little off-white skirt, a lightweight chocolate-brown sweater, and a pair of cowboy boots today. As November progressed, the weather was quickly turning colder, but it was one of those outfits that was good for almost any season. Paired with a suede jacket, it made the perfect fall outfit.

I pulled my hair back away from my face—which people said made me look a lot younger than I was—curled the ends, and went very subtle with my makeup.

The extra time I spent making my selection and putting on my face proved to be worth it when Landon and Langston arrived together that morning. Both men stopped in front of my desk and spent a good ten minutes chatting about my weekend. Well, technically, Landon chatted and Langston merely listened, but they were both present and accounted for and that was all that mattered to me. Unfortunately, I didn't get to regale them with stories of debauchery and intrigue. I didn't do anything over the weekend besides sleep in, watch Netflix, and consume two more of TJ Arlington's wickedly delicious books.

Now that I thought about it, perhaps that was the reason I looked forward to coming into work every morning. Although I had thought my social life was picking up, turned out I was wrong. Sure, I chatted with Kristen a few times a week, mostly after our yoga class, but she'd been extremely busy with work and I had been left to my own devices. Since I did very little in my free time, with the exception of yoga, I wasn't around many people to make new friends. The most enjoyable days were those I spent at the office with the four men—five including Jordan—who had become pretty important to me.

Not only had they treated me kindly, they'd also started entrusting me with more things to do. They had yet to tell me what my job requirements were—although Jordan had said they'd do that at week two, it didn't happen—but I wasn't sitting around waiting to be told. Every afternoon, I visited each man's office, spoke to them for a few minutes before heading out for the day. That was the highlight of my afternoons, no doubt about it.

And during those interactions, I'd learned a few things about each of them.

Like Justin had originally stated, Ben was divorced. He had turned forty this year, and I'd learned that his birthday was the weekend after I'd been hired. He lived in an apartment in the building, having decided the commute was much easier when he didn't have to go anywhere. He had a master's degree and a highly respected reputation within the industry, and in his spare time, he enjoyed going to a club. He hadn't told me which one, but by the way he talked about it, I sensed that it was a place he attended frequently.

Justin traveled a lot, and he admitted that was something that he enjoyed. Meeting new people, spending time building relationships with his employees and his clients was very important to him. He never spoke about women in his life, so I assumed he still wasn't *dating* anyone. Although I was pretty sure he had something going on with Ben, but they clearly didn't call it dating for whatever reason.

Landon and Langston were thirty-four, but they'd been in the industry longer than Justin and Ben. Both shared an apartment within the building, but they lived on a ranch on the outskirts of town for the majority of their time. From what I could tell, they were very close, doing a lot of activities together.

As for their personalities, they were each uniquely different. Ben was outgoing and willing to answer any question that I had. Justin was middle of the pack, I'd say. He was often serious, but not in a harsh way. And then there was Landon... He was the funny one, constantly saying something to make me laugh. The guy was smoking-hot, down-to-earth, and drew me in like a moth to a flame. I was infatuated with that man.

Of course, his twin was just as charming.

Langston Moore had captured my attention. He was sexy, smart, and demanding in a way that I'd never experienced before. He didn't smile all that often, but when he did, it was truly a gift to see. In fact, I'd superimposed him as the dominating hero in the romance novels I was reading on more than one occasion.

"We'd like to have a meeting at ten," Justin informed me when he peeked out of his office shortly after nine. "Every Monday morning, in fact. In the back conference room."

I nodded.

"If you could make sure to have coffee ready, that'd be great."

"Yes, sir."

Justin's blue eyes flared, a small smile tilting his beautiful mouth before he disappeared from his doorway.

Wanting to ensure I got it all right, I immediately made my way up front to Jordan's desk. "Justin said I'm to prepare for a meeting in the back conference room." I peered over to the room I was interviewed in. "I take it he's not talking about that one."

Jordan's smile was as bright as the turquoise polo he was wearing today.

"Nope." He instantly shot to his feet. "I'll show you."

He quickly punched something into the phone, tucked an earpiece into his ear, then grabbed my hand and led me back down the hallway. When we passed the large conference room, he waved his hand at it. "That's the conference room they use for clients and staff meetings when they bring in their managers."

Made sense.

We stepped through the glass doors, but rather than veer off to my office, Jordan kept going. That was the first time I noticed there was another door at the very end, offset in the wall, which made it blend in.

"*This* is the back conference room."

Jordan opened the door and tugged me inside.

Like the front conference room, one wall was completely made up of windows. And just like most of the client-facing space, whoever designed this room was clearly going for the modern flare. Although the front conference room was bright due to the lack of shades covering the windows, this one was dark, making it far more intimate. Or it was until Jordan punched a button on the wall and the shades began to lift slowly.

"Always be sure to lift the shades unless they tell you otherwise. If they want to go through a presentation, they'll ask to keep them closed."

There were no conference tables in this room. Only five large leather chairs in a circle, surrounding a round table that was only about knee high. It was a casual setting, as though they spent a lot of time chatting in here. The furniture sat on a plush, charcoal-gray rug that covered the gleaming white tile. On the wall across from the seating area was a giant flat-panel television.

"It's very informal in here." Jordan motioned toward the left of the room. "The coffee bar is over there." His hand dropped lower. "And a wine refrigerator on the floor. They like to celebrate their big deals."

Good to know.

Jordan stood suddenly and held up a finger before tapping his ear. It took a second for me to realize he was greeting a caller, which meant he must have forwarded the phones to his earpiece? I wasn't sure how all that worked.

While he spoke coolly and professionally, I watched. Before I could ask any questions, he waved quickly, then disappeared out of the room, continuing to have a conversation with someone on the other end of the call.

"Okay," I said to myself as I stared around the room. "I should get the coffee ready."

As I did, several questions blasted me all at once and I wished Jordan was still there so I could speak them aloud.

Would they want me to leave so they could have their meeting?

Would they want me to stay in here? To serve coffee?

Or would they want me to stay and take notes?

Should I get something to write with or bring my laptop?

Crap.

I hadn't the slightest clue how this could get so complicated, but it seemed I was getting flustered. Obviously more so than I thought, because the next thing I knew, Ben and Justin were stepping into the room and I'd clearly lost track of time.

Ben made his way over to me—or rather the coffee bar— immediately. He gifted me with a sexy grin, flashing his pearly whites, before pouring a cup and adding two Sweet 'n Lows. That was how he took his coffee. No creamer.

When he stepped back, I found myself in his way and he suddenly brushed up against me. It caused me to automatically suck in a breath. One, I didn't expect it. Two, I didn't realize exactly how big the man was until right then. I'd always considered him the smallest of the four, but he made me feel incredibly tiny. And three, he smelled so freaking good it was hard not to want to inhale when he was around.

"Excuse me," he whispered softly, his warm hand sliding down my arm.

Was that...? Was he...?

It felt almost too casual a move for my boss to make on me, but maybe I had imagined it. After all, I was a little light-headed from the initial physical contact.

Justin was the next one to pass me and he, too, touched my arm. A frisson of heat speared my core as I tried to process what had just happened. Before I could get my bearings, Landon and Langston were there, practically sandwiching me between them as one got coffee, then the other. They took theirs black, so it didn't take but a second. Still, their proximity had me trying not to breathe. Or pass out.

When Langston's hand brushed my hip, my eyes flew up to his face. Way up. He flashed a rare grin and a quick wink and I was suddenly confused about where I was.

Maybe I was still at home, in my bed. This was a dream, right? Had to be. I mean, I did have a pretty nice fantasy on Saturday night that involved four sexy men and my vibrator. Well, the vibrator wasn't *in* the fantasy. It was the cure for the fantasy.

Surely that was the case. I was still asleep and that was the only reason all four of my bosses had casually touched me, inciting sparks beneath my skin.

I subtly reached up and pinched myself.

Ouch.

Okay, not dreaming.

When all four men took a seat, I turned toward the exit. Since they had a meeting, maybe I could go into the bathroom and...

"We'd like you to stay," Justin said, halting my progress toward the door.

I spun around and faced them, my short skirt flaring out and a cool wash of air hitting my upper thighs. At least one, if not all of them, noticed the move and I found four pairs of eyes drifting south, then quickly back up.

"Should I...um...get my laptop?"

Ben shook his head. "No need. But feel free to get some coffee if you'd like."

I swallowed hard.

I didn't want coffee, but I needed a minute to compose myself.

So coffee it was.

TWELVE

"EVERY MONDAY, GOING FORWARD, WE'LL have a standing meeting. You can add it to our calendars. We'll use this time to discuss the events of the previous week, as well as what's on the horizon," Justin explained, speaking directly to me.

"We'll want you to join us," Ben added.

That made perfect sense, so I offered a smile with a respectful, "Yes, sir."

His glowing eyes darkened and I realized that anytime I said *sir*, these men seemed to get off on it. It made me want to use that phrase all day, every day. And I'd given that some serious thought as well. Especially after I read the book Langston had let me borrow. *His Name Is Sir* had been an enlightening tale of wickedly delicious sex. I'd devoured every word, finding myself far more interested in a lifestyle I knew absolutely nothing about. It had spurred me to read more, so not only had I continued to read TJ Arlington's books, but I had discreetly found the names of other authors Langston represented and purposely sought their work on my iPad. Let's just say, not only was I intrigued but my vibrator had gotten plenty of use these past few weeks.

Hussy.

"To kick the meeting off, I'd like to discuss Luci's recent homework assignment," Langston said, his eyes locking on my face.

I frowned, trying to figure out what he was referring to.

"The reading assignment?" he clarified.

Ah. Right. We had briefly touched on it during lunch, but it didn't surprise me that he wanted to go into depth. He had warned me ahead of time, after all.

"Were you able to finish the book?" His tone was cool, almost aloof.

I nodded. "Yes, sir. I did."

"This is TJ Arlington's book, yes?" Justin inquired.

"Yes," Landon noted, his smile sexy.

"Interesting introduction," Justin stated.

"Have you read any more of his work?" Ben probed, clearly as curious about my thoughts as the others.

I felt a blush creep up my neck. "I have."

Ben seemed pleased by that response. "You enjoy them?"

"I do."

"I prefer you to be more detailed in your answer." Langston's matter-of-fact tone had my eyes darting over to him.

I hadn't realized there was going to be a book report. It took me a moment to think back on that book. I'd read others since and I wanted to ensure I gave as little away as possible.

"Did the book get you hot and bothered?" Landon asked.

I should've been surprised by the blunt question, but I wasn't. However, I would've expected it more from Langston or Justin, but they were all direct in their own way.

Figuring I wasn't going to get out of this, I forced a smile. "I did, actually. As I mentioned before, the topic is one I have no experience with, but I liked it. I noticed there was a lot of...sex." Considering I'd played Never Have I Ever with these men, talking about sex shouldn't have been difficult, yet it was.

"What was your favorite part of the book?" Langston questioned.

Swallowing hard, I let my gaze drop to my lap. "I liked the scene at the end." My face heated as I thought about it. "When she was in his office and he tied her to the St. Andrew's cross. She was naked. And he continued to work, enjoying the view."

As soon as the words were out of my mouth, I couldn't believe I'd said them.

"I enjoyed that scene as well," Ben said, drawing my gaze to his.

"That was a particularly interesting one," Justin added. "I think his next one is going to cross some serious boundaries, though."

"That's his goal." Langston smirked.

I would have to seek that one out because I liked the idea of crossing boundaries.

"Now, if we're finished with that topic, I want to discuss the upcoming managers' meeting," Justin prompted.

I was grateful that we were moving on.

"We hold a meeting once a quarter," Ben explained for my benefit, "for which we fly in all of our managers to discuss financials, prospects, and upcoming events."

Landon spoke next. "It's usually a three- or four-day event, which requires a tremendous amount of planning." He held my stare. "This quarter, we'd like for you to set it up, plan it out, and host the event in its entirety."

Holy shit.

That was an enormous task, but not one that I would shy away from.

"I'd be honored," I admitted, scribbling down the key words I'd heard thus far. "Is there a specific week you'd like this to take place?"

"The second week in December," Justin stated. "That'll give you five weeks for planning. Trust me when I say, that's not a long time. However, it's doable."

I nodded, then glanced between them. "Should I go to one of you with questions? Or will I need to meet with each of you separately?"

Justin was the one to answer. "More than likely, you'll be spending time with each of us. It's the only time that our teams come together, and due to the differences in their accounts, we have to be cognizant of their time and the conferences we'll plan."

I continued to jot down the information.

"Before the week's out, we'll give you as much information as we can to get you started. But today, we thought we'd go over your job requirements," Landon said, his tone deep, his eyes…God, they looked almost hungry.

Finally!

Keeping my expression neutral, I placed my pen flat on my notebook, setting them on the table and retrieving my coffee cup as I gave him my full attention. "I'm ready when you are."

His eyes flared, too.

"How's the workload been thus far?" Ben inquired.

I placed my hands in my lap and crossed my legs, discreetly looking to see which man was watching me. Turned out, all four of them noticed the move but only three sets of eyes quickly lifted to my face. Langston's eyes never left my face, his countenance cool.

"It's been good," I said. "I've spent a fair amount of time getting to know your team members, talking to them at length during our phone conversations." I didn't tell them that it was a good way for me to pass some of the time.

"Do you feel as though you have a decent workload?" Ben inquired.

I nodded. "Most of the time, I can keep myself busy. But if you have more things you would like me to do, besides the quarterly meeting..." I licked my lips and chose my words carefully. "I'm available for anything."

"Anything?" Langston asked, his eyes boring into me.

"*Any*thing," I repeated.

And I honestly couldn't believe I went there. Openly propositioning a boss was grounds for termination, I would think. But truthfully, I needed to know what was going on here. Every day I got the sense that one or more of them was flirting with me. And it was almost as though they were waiting for me to take the bait.

Now, could I really sleep with my boss?

Maybe.

I just wasn't sure which one I would pick.

"Could you possibly elaborate on the other things you're willin' to do?" Landon suggested.

That was easy. "You know, picking up lunch, contacting your team members, getting updates on upcoming events, coordinating travel." I licked my lips again. "And I would still have time for filing, getting coffee, or even dictation."

Yep, I went there.

"*Dic*tation?" There was a definite catch in Landon's voice that time.

"Yes, sir," I replied sweetly, meeting his gaze head on.
"Would you be willing to do *dic*tation for more than one
of us?" Ben asked directly.

I considered this for a moment, almost positive there was
an underlying sexual vibe to this conversation. After all, Ben did
enunciate the *dic* part of *dictation* rather thickly as well.

"Or all of us?" Landon asked.

"At the same time?" Justin added.

Yep. No way did I miss it that time.

While all four men watched me intently, I honestly
considered what I was getting myself into. I mean, if I was
misunderstanding, then there was a big possibility I would lose my
job. This could be construed as sexual harassment on my part,
right? However, if I *wasn't* misunderstanding and my four bosses
would like to...share me, then I had to consider what happened
from this point forward.

Keep in mind, I'd been reading a lot these past few weeks.
Thanks to the authors Langston represented, I'd learned quite a
few interesting things about sexual preferences. So, it didn't seem
like a farfetched conclusion.

I guess they could tell me in the job requirements.

"Before you answer that," Ben said, "I think you should
understand a few things."

"Yes, sir," I said simply because I knew they liked to hear
it.

"We're very demanding," Langston stated.

I nodded.

"And we require discretion," Ben supplied.

"Sometimes long hours," Justin included.

I peered over at Landon, waiting for his remark.

"I concur with all of those. And add that we're
very...hands-on."

I swallowed hard as I thought about their hands on me.
My pussy lit up like a Fourth of July fireworks show, my clit
pulsing.

"I understand." I met each of their eyes as I added, "and
I'm more than willing."

A round of exhales erupted, but no one moved.

"Would you be willing to...*interview* for this portion of the job requirements?" Langston asked directly.

"Interview?" I wasn't sure what he meant.

"Something a little more hands-on."

I didn't even hesitate. "I would, sir."

"You understand there's no increase in pay," Ben stated.

I kept my expression neutral and my tone smooth. "I wouldn't want there to be." After all, I wasn't a whore. I certainly wasn't going to ask to get paid for any...extracurricular activities. "I'm all about going above and beyond, and as far as I'm concerned, you pay me quite nicely as your secretary."

My body was on fire and if something didn't happen in the next few minutes, honestly, I was going to have to consider bringing my vibrator to work going forward.

All four men glanced between themselves and I watched intently, waiting.

"Would you please stand up?" Langston requested when it seemed they'd come to whatever conclusion they wanted to come to.

Placing my coffee cup on the table in front of me, I got to my feet.

"Over here," he instructed, pointing to the spot directly in front of him.

As I sidestepped the table, Langston got to his feet and pushed his chair back. I came to a stop directly in front of him and peered up into his face. He was so tall it required me to tilt my head back, but it certainly wasn't a hardship. From this close, I could see the green and gold striations in his hazel eyes, the sexy scruff along his jaw. And I could smell the spice of his cologne.

I wasn't sure what I expected him to do, but when he cupped my neck with both of his big hands and tilted my head back farther, I felt a little lost. And when his mouth descended on mine, slowly, gently...

I sighed.

Yep. I did.

Because holy smokes, the man's lips were utter perfection.

Langston applied exactly the right amount of pressure to prove that he was in control without being overbearing. His tongue licked its way into my mouth confidently. His smooth, warm lips melded to mine and I heard the soft rumble vibrating in his chest, which I took to mean he liked kissing me, too.

I was completely lost to his kiss, so it took a second to process the additional hands on me. On my hips to be exact. When Langston pulled back, our eyes met and held for several long seconds. I could've sworn I saw something there, something that urged me to give in to whatever demands he had.

However, before I could process what was transpiring between us, I found myself being turned until I was facing the equally sexy Landon. He gave me that wickedly mischievous grin of his, and if my panties hadn't already been wet, they certainly would've been from that sexy smirk.

"My turn," he whispered before pulling me into him.

Landon was as gentle as his twin but a little less demanding. Not completely lax. Just enough that I knew I would enjoy my time with him, but I would never be in control where he was concerned.

So we're clear, I was okay with that. *Very* okay with that.

A soft moan escaped me when Landon tugged me against him, his hands cupping my ass and squeezing gently, his erection pressing intimately against my belly. I wasn't ready for the kiss to be over, but the next hands on me were more insistent, and they were urging me to turn around.

I pulled back from Landon's luscious mouth and he offered a seductive grin. Then I was turned so that I was facing…

Ben.

I couldn't deny that I'd wanted to know what his full lips felt like since the second I saw him.

He didn't make me wait.

He was shorter than the others, but still tall enough that I had to tilt my head back to see his face. But that didn't matter when he leaned in and that delicious mouth covered mine. His lips were warm and far softer than I anticipated. His hands were still on my hips, practically spanning my entire pelvis with his thumbs brushing against my pelvic bone.

This time I moaned louder, leaning into him and placing my hand on his chest because I desperately wanted to know what was underneath that suit.

Of course, I didn't get to do much searching because Ben pulled back, his eyes meeting mine. There was something dark and hungry lurking beneath that sexy exterior and I was desperate for Ben to unleash it on me.

But then Justin reached for my hand and pulled me toward him. His eyes searched my face for long seconds before he, too, kissed me.

He was the most intense, I could tell. And it was obvious he was all about control. Not necessarily controlling me, but more so keeping himself in check. Yet his kiss was delivered with such delicate care I was ready and willing to submit to anything he asked of me.

The kiss ended when Justin growled low in his throat, pulling back slowly.

I wasn't sure what to do at that point, so I remained standing. I realized the others had once again taken their seats. Justin turned me around so that I was facing them, his hard chest at my back, his hands coming around and sliding up my thighs.

I sucked in air as I leaned back against him. I could feel the proof of his desire against my lower back.

"We're going to implement some rules," Justin said, his voice loud enough to carry to the others. "Is that okay with you?"

At that moment, I was pretty sure anything was okay with me.

But I didn't say that.

I simply nodded.

THIRTEEN

"FIRST RULE," JUSTIN SAID AS he slid his hands higher on my thighs just beneath the hem of my skirt. "Everyone in this room will provide current test results for sexually transmitted diseases."

This was a little shocking, I must admit, but I was completely on board with that plan. I mean, this was already unconventional on every level, so why wouldn't we take the necessary precautions up front? Safety was key.

"Second rule. Once clean test results are provided, condoms are optional for intercourse. Vaginal and anal."

The second part caught my attention and caused my breath to catch. I'd never had anal sex. Not that I was opposed to it. I'd admit that I had experimented with a couple of boyfriends, but we never got to the full penetration point. Usually just a finger, once a very slim vibrator. The thought of being fucked in the ass… Well, truthfully, it wasn't a horrible thought.

"Third rule." Justin's hands slid higher, lifting my skirt as he went.

Someone cleared their throat.

I was too focused on the warm hands gliding up my legs to think about anything else. Cool air caressed my lower lips when Justin pulled my panties to the side to reveal my freshly waxed pussy. Thank goodness I'd kept that appointment on Saturday. I'd known one day that pain would pay off. Today was that day.

"Hold your skirt up," Justin commanded softly in my ear. "And don't let it drop."

I fumbled to get the fabric in my fingers, then clutched it tightly, holding it above my hips.

"You will be required to be on birth control," Justin continued.

It required effort, but I kept my eyes open, watching as Landon's gaze centered on my nether region. I could tell he was affected by the way his chest rose and fell. Not to mention the sizeable tent in his slacks. I cut my gaze to Langston. He looked completely unfazed. However, I could see the heat in his eyes, the interest. He was good at maintaining control of himself and it turned me on.

"Are you good with that?" Justin nipped my ear.

What was the question again?

Oh, right. Birth control.

"Of course. I'm on the pill now," I explained although I wasn't sure anyone understood me thanks to the breathy moan that accompanied my words when Justin's finger caressed my clit.

"Fourth rule."

He continued to stroke my clit, applying minimal pressure, but it was enough to make my knees weaken and my thighs tremble.

I nodded, encouraging him to continue with the rules. Or fingering me. Either one. I didn't care.

"No sexual intercourse with anyone outside of this room." Justin's head lifted from beside mine. "For the duration of our agreement. And that goes for *everyone* in this room."

A round of "agree" came from the other three. I, however, could only nod because Justin had slipped one thick finger inside me.

"God, you're tight."

I whimpered.

"I fucking love that you're waxed smooth." His thumb brushed over my skin. "I can't wait to sink my cock into this sweet, hot pussy."

I trembled, completely turned on by the coarse words and the sexy tone of his voice. I wanted that, too, more than I could even explain. However, I knew that wasn't going to happen today because of all the rules and the required tests. But that didn't stop me from imagining the four of them fucking me into oblivion.

"Justin…please…" I was grinding my pelvis against his hand without shame, attempting to get him to fuck me deeper. One finger wasn't enough. It was merely a tease.

"You want me to make you come?"

"Yes, sir," I whispered, hoping that would do the trick.

"I fucking love when you say that," he groaned against my ear.

His head lifted again, but his finger didn't stop moving inside me.

"Anyone object to me being the first to make her come?"

No one said anything, so I could only assume they were all in agreement. I hoped they were, because I couldn't stand much more.

He slipped another finger inside me and began to move faster. I was moaning in earnest now, not caring that there were three other sets of eyes watching as Justin fingered me closer and closer to orgasm. In fact, knowing that they were watching made it that much hotter.

I couldn't help but watch Landon and Langston, who were directly in front of me. I even glanced over at Ben and I noticed he was grinding his palm against his cock through his slacks. What I wouldn't have given to see him jack off right in front of me, knowing that I was the one who was making him come.

Justin shifted, his left hand slipping behind my left knee. He lifted my leg, spreading me open for their viewing pleasure as he continued to drive two fingers into my pussy.

I was reduced to nothing more than sensation and a variety of grunts and groans as I let my climax build, growing in intensity until I couldn't contain it any longer. When I came, I cried out Justin's name over and over, my fingernails digging into his forearm as I held on for dear life.

"Very, very nice, princess," he whispered, his words rough against my ear.

I realized he was holding me up, which I was grateful for, because I would've been a puddle on the floor without his strength keeping me upright.

When Justin lowered my leg, his fingers slipping from my body, I inhaled deeply, trying to catch my breath and gain my bearings. His hand traveled upward, his arm brushing over my breasts until his fingers were hovering by my lips. I knew what he wanted, so I opened my mouth, allowing him to slide his fingers over my bottom lip. My tongue darted over them before I sucked both digits into my mouth, licking them clean.

Honestly, that was a wanton move that wasn't normal for me. I'd never once tasted myself on a lover's fingers or any other body part, for that matter. But for some reason, these men brought out the wildcat lurking underneath.

"Remember, test results ASAP," Ben stated gruffly as he got to his feet.

I thought he was leaving, but he shocked me when he leaned down and kissed me hard, his tongue thrusting into my mouth and dragging another whimper from me.

"I'm looking forward to working more closely with you," he stated firmly when he pulled back. "And Luci?"

"Hmm?"

"You might as well forget panties. They won't be necessary going forward."

I met his glowing gaze. "Yes, sir."

"Good girl."

The praise made my body hum.

I was surprised to see that I was once again standing on my own, my skirt no longer pulled up, and my panties had been righted. When Ben left the room, Landon got to his feet. I waited patiently, unsure what I should do now. When he came over and kissed me roughly, I could tell that he had enjoyed the show.

"Thank you for that," Landon said softly, his lips brushing over mine. "I enjoyed it immensely."

I swallowed hard and nodded.

Justin then stepped in front of me, cupping my face gently. "I'm definitely eager for more."

"Me, too." No way could I deny it. I didn't even care that it made me look like a hussy.

"If you need anything," Justin continued, "you let me know."

"Yes, sir," I replied softly, leaning into him when he pressed his mouth to mine.

"I'll be gone for the next few days, but I look forward to seeing you on Friday morning."

I smiled. "I'll add your trip to the calendar."

Then Justin left and I was alone with Langston. My heart rate spiked when he got to his feet and prowled closer. This man had captivated me from the beginning. He and Landon both. Perhaps it was due to the fact that they looked identical but were so different.

While Landon was more of an open book, Langston was so hard to read, but there was something about him that made me want to know more, to discover every nuance of his being. I wanted to listen to his voice when he spoke, wanted to do whatever was necessary to put a smile on his face.

His hands returned to my neck, the same way they had earlier, his thumbs brushing under my chin.

"You're so *fucking* beautiful." His tone was deep, gruff, with an edge to it, as though he didn't want to find me beautiful. "You make me want things I know I shouldn't want."

His words hit somewhere in the middle of my chest cavity. I wasn't sure why that was, but it happened. And as I stood there, my breaths back to normal, I had to wonder if I was getting in over my head.

Enjoying the pleasures of the flesh—times four—was one thing.

Letting my heart get involved was something else entirely.

Somehow, I was going to have to find a way to keep that silly organ out of the picture. Otherwise, I wasn't sure how I'd survive this.

"I hope you understand what you're gettin' yourself into."

"Yes, sir," I answered, my eyes locked with his. "I do." I licked my lips. "And I'm...eager."

"That's my girl."

Oh, yeah.

I was definitely going to have to have a talk with my heart. The damn thing was already starting to get jumpy.

As soon as I got back to my desk, I pulled out my cell phone and called to make an appointment with my ob-gyn. Thankfully, they had a cancellation that afternoon, which meant I didn't have to wait. As it was, they said it would take a few days to get the test results back, which meant I wouldn't have them until Friday at the earliest.

Since Ben seemed to be the one directing me most of the time, I shot him an email to let him know I needed to leave a little early. His response was, "Perfect."

When Jordan invited me to lunch, I declined because I didn't want to miss any more hours than I had to. He said he understood and surprised me by bringing me back a roast beef and Swiss sandwich.

"So, chickadee, where is it you're sneaking off to this afternoon?"

"Doctor's appointment," I told him around a bite of my sandwich.

"Took a little longer than I thought," he said.

Staring at him, I waited to see if he would expound on that statement. I had the sneaking suspicion that this wasn't the first time this had happened. Considering he'd already told me that they'd gone through one secretary every other month for the eighteen months he'd been here, I had to believe that Jordan had caught on to what was going on here.

The question was, did I want to confirm that I'd fallen prey to these men as well? I mean, I was happy about it. No, amend that. I was ecstatic. The things that went on in this office intrigued me. I needed to know more, to experience it for myself.

Sure, you're probably wondering what would make a woman consider taking on four men at one time.

Well, the answer was simple.

I fucking wanted to.

I couldn't deny that I felt some sort of attraction to each of them. They were unique men who had managed to endear me to them in a very short time. I wanted to see where it went. Plus, I was single, as were they. We were going to be discreet. Why the hell shouldn't I explore my sexuality, find out what they could offer me? Did it make me a slut? Maybe.

Did I care?

Not a bit.

We wouldn't be hurting anyone by doing this and that was the only thing that mattered. Safe and consensual was the name of the game. I read that in one of the books, by the way.

So, if you thought about it that way, wouldn't you want to jump on the train and ride it out, too?

If your answer was no, then perhaps you don't want to find out what comes next.

Then again, since you get to live vicariously through me, why the hell not?

FOURTEEN

BOSS MEETING

LANDON

CONSIDERING JUSTIN WOULD BE OUT of town for the remainder of the week, I scheduled some time for the four of us to discuss the outcome from that morning's meeting. Not wanting to draw attention to it, I waited until Luci left for the day before they joined me in my office.

There was no reason to call out the fact that it had gone better than we'd expected. That was a given. It had been quite an eventful meeting and I was sure I wasn't the only one who was eager to see where things went.

"I still want us to take things slow with Luci," Langston stated after I poured the four of us a drink. "She's sweetly naïve and I don't want her to think we're only out for one thing. She's the best damn secretary we've had."

"Agreed." Justin was studying his glass and I could tell he had something on his mind.

"Do you have concerns?" I asked him directly.

His gaze lifted, jumping over each of us. "I think we're going to get more than we bargained for." He didn't sound happy about that admission.

"How so?" Langston asked.

"She's obviously eager," Justin clarified.

"Okay. I'm not sure how that's a bad thing." I was more than happy with how things had turned out that morning. Watching Justin finger Luci in the meeting, watching her come apart in his arms... I couldn't have asked for a better outcome. Well, other than the fact I'd wanted to instruct her to drop to her knees and take my cock in her mouth. That would've been the *best* outcome, but I wasn't disappointed.

"The question is how we're gonna handle it." Langston took a sip of his scotch.

"Do we take turns?" Ben asked.

Justin turned directly to Ben. "In this instance, you will not play with Luci without express direction from me."

Admittedly, I was a little surprised by Justin's response. In the past few months, it seemed he'd grown more possessive of Ben. The man was a Dom, after all. And Ben was his submissive. It didn't matter that Ben was a switch. Anyone with eyes could see that Ben was submissive only to Justin.

Ben nodded. "Understood, Mr. Parker. And I wouldn't want it any other way."

Justin seemed content with Ben's answer.

"There are four of us," Langston said, "and one of her. I think it's safe to say we're gonna have to go easy on her in the beginning."

Well, that was a given. As it was, I wanted to fuck her three times a day. Multiply that by four and we would quickly break the girl.

"Definitely," I agreed. "Luci told me she hasn't dated in a while. Except for some douchebag who walked out on her and made her pay for dinner. Which, I can only assume, means she hasn't had sex in a while either."

"He made her pay for dinner?" Langston glowered. "What a dick."

Justin's eyes darkened. "I'm under that impression as well. She's not the type for casual sex."

Langston continued to frown. "Then why the fuck did we enter into this agreement with her? I thought the whole point was to be casual."

Justin's reaction was a little heated. "Like that's going to happen." He looked at me, then back to Langston. "Can you honestly tell me that you two aren't eager to see where this goes with her?"

I didn't respond. As an unspoken rule, I tended to follow Langston's lead when it came to the submissives we took. He knew I was looking for more, but I knew he wasn't. My brother had been burned early on and he wasn't eager to do it again. Hence the reason he tended to only play with submissives at the club. For at least five years, I hadn't known him to have dated anyone or to have taken a sub for longer than a couple of weeks at the most.

In the same sense, I saw the way he looked at Luci. He was as captivated as the rest of us.

"Are there any additional rules?" Ben asked. "Between the four of us?"

That was the question of the hour. The truth was, we hadn't yet found a woman who was eager to be shared between the four of us. There had been two women before Luci who had agreed. Each had quickly let us know that she had feelings for one of us and had thought by agreeing that she would be able to pick and choose.

That certainly wasn't the case. It wasn't what we wanted.

The overall objective was to pleasure Luci as only the four of us could. And maybe that was the difference. They might not admit it, but I knew we'd never found a woman who we wanted to dote on the way we did her.

There was something about Luci that intrigued us all. Now we simply had to figure out how to make this work without causing unnecessary issues.

"For the time being, I think we need to keep the interactions within the office." As Justin spoke, his eyes darted from one man to another. I could tell he was watching us for a reaction.

"I'm not completely on board with that," Langston countered. "For the most part, yes. However, should we choose to pursue her outside the office, I think it's only fair that we inform one another."

Justin frowned. "You're going after her, aren't you?"

"Absolutely not," my twin argued. "I think it's safe to say she won't be able to meet all of our needs here. For instance"—Langston glanced at me—"when we take her together."

I nodded. "He's right. There will be times when we want to double-team her. I think it's only fair to her that we show her the respect she deserves. I don't think fucking her on the desk is going to be appropriate all the time."

Justin seemed to relent, his nod subtle.

"Again, we simply need to discuss it beforehand," Langston repeated.

"Fine." Justin looked between Langston and me. "I'm out of town quite a bit, so, should I instruct my pup to interact with her, I'd appreciate if one of you could assist."

"Assist how?" Langston didn't sound fond of that directive.

"Watching."

Langston and I both nodded. That wouldn't be a hardship. One of the reasons we'd opted for this sort of environment was because we were all naturally voyeurs. The idea of watching Luci get fucked by one of my partners was quite stimulating.

"Anything else?" I prompted.

Justin got to his feet. "No." His gaze slammed into Langston's. "That doesn't mean we won't implement other rules as we go along."

"You have nothing to worry about," Langston assured him. "This is what we've all wanted. I say we take it one day at a time."

"And most importantly," I added, "we remember this is about Luci. The whole point is to bring her as much pleasure as possible, to introduce her to a world she doesn't even know exists. Our personal needs are secondary to that."

Justin's gaze met mine. "As long as we all abide by that."

With that, he turned and walked out, Ben following close behind.

I glanced over at Langston and sighed.

It always sounded good in theory.

Now, the question was, could we pull it off without Luci getting hurt?

No matter what we all said we wanted, underneath it all, I think there was still one thing no one was considering.

We each had developed feelings for this girl in the short time we'd known her. Which meant we needed to find a way to set those aside and enjoy the ride.

FIFTEEN

WALKING INTO THE OFFICE THE following Monday morning, I found that I'd lost every ounce of the nerve I had mustered up last week. When I stepped off the elevator onto the thirty-second floor, I was more anxious than I'd been the day of my interview, yet I still managed to make it to work on time. I even managed to get coffee brewing and get organized for the day before Ben arrived exactly at eight o'clock.

"Did you schedule the morning meeting?" he asked as he passed by on his way to his office. His eyes lingered on me for an extra second or two.

"Yes, sir. I did. Standing meeting at ten o'clock every Monday." Even as I spoke, I could feel my hands trembling.

"Good girl."

A nervous flutter started in my belly and radiated outward, making my fingers tingle. I didn't know exactly what they planned to do in the morning meeting, but I had a feeling we were going to dig deeper into last week's topic.

Ben disappeared into his office and I was left watching the hallway, waiting for the others to arrive.

After last Monday's meeting, I had been surprised to find that things had returned to business as usual. Any meetings they scheduled with me had been in regard to work. No other sexual advances were made and it had left me feeling on edge. I think they knew that and that was the overall plan.

It also had me looking forward to today's meeting. Even if I wasn't as confident as I had been, I was still interested to see what they had in store for me.

The phone started to ring about eight twenty and it didn't seem to stop until shortly before ten. At that point, I'd seen Landon and Langston arrive, both men giving me a brief nod as they passed by. Justin was the only one who had yet to show up and part of me was disappointed that he wasn't there.

At nine forty-five, I decided to head to the back conference room to get the coffee prepared. And a couple minutes shy of the hour, all four men walked in. They were all dressed impeccably, each man wearing a suit and looking like they'd spent the morning on the *GQ* set.

Admittedly, my heart skipped a beat when I saw that Justin had arrived.

"All clear." Justin held a single file folder and handed it over to me as he made his way to the coffeepot.

I opened it to see there were five sheets of paper inside.

Test results.

A blush stole over my face as I realized what this meant.

I had emailed my results to Justin on Friday when I received them. He hadn't responded, which had left me reeling. In fact, I spent the majority of the weekend pondering what the lack of response meant. Had they all changed their mind? Were they testing me? Trying to set me up? Was this their way of getting rid of me?

A million questions had bounced around in my head and I'd had answers to none of them.

Needless to say, it hadn't been a good weekend.

Well, other than when Kristen and I had grabbed breakfast on Sunday morning. Of course, I hadn't shared any of the sexy details of my office encounters, opting to keep that to myself for the time being. As it was, Kristen had the ability to read me like a book, so I think she had figured something out, but thankfully, she hadn't called me on it. It wasn't every day that a woman was propositioned by her four bosses and said woman found herself craving their attention. I didn't know if Kristen would understand.

"We'll get started once everyone takes their seat."

Justin's deep voice jarred me from my thoughts and I turned to see that I was the only one still standing. Talk about embarrassing.

Forcing a smile, I moved toward the only empty seat available. It was the one between Langston and Justin, the same one I'd sat in last week. I could feel all eyes on me as I moved and I mentally checked my outfit without looking down to see what I was wearing.

Or rather, what I wasn't.

Today I had opted for a long, black maxi skirt, which was sheer, except for the tight mini beneath it. The black and red short-sleeve sweater I'd paired with it had given me a boost this morning. It was formfitting, accentuating my breasts, and long enough to reach the waistband of the skirt, but just barely.

Ben kicked things off by discussing upcoming events taking place, including a meeting he had to discuss ROI with one of his clients. He sounded positive as he explained what he was looking to outline for them. After he finished, Landon went into detail about a phone call he'd had with a new author he was hoping to bring on board. I wasn't paying all that much attention, though, my gaze jumping from one man to another.

I'm not sure what I was expecting, but the fact that no one seemed to be interested in moving this meeting in the same direction as last week's was making me nervous.

"Luci?"

My gaze snapped over to Langston when his warm hand brushed my forearm.

"Yes, sir?"

"Did you have anything you wanted to discuss?"

Remembering that I had been tasked with setting up the quarterly meeting, I decided to launch into an update on that. "I sent out the invites to all the managers, and I reserved a block of rooms at the Hilton. Each manager has been instructed to book their own room and to use the code I provided, which would offer a discount."

"Impressive," Ben said, glancing between all the others. "I didn't even know we could get a discount."

That was what I was here for.

"I've confirmed our reservations for four of the small conference rooms, and I also have a tentative hold on one of the large ballrooms at the convention center. I wanted to confirm how long we needed it for. Since it's close to several restaurants and pubs, I wasn't sure if we wanted to hold a happy hour afterward, which would allow for more personal interaction. Or we could always cater something into the convention center and hold it there."

"Great ideas," Landon noted. "I'd like to talk more about that later, whenever you have time."

"Absolutely, sir." I jotted it down in my notebook. "Other than that, I'm still working to confirm all managers have RSVP'd, and for those who haven't, I'm getting details as to whether they are tentative or if it's a conflict that can't be helped. There is one relatively new manager who tried to back out, but I informed her that it's a crucial engagement that will only help her growth within the organization. She has since confirmed she will attend."

Justin's expression was one of wonder, and I couldn't help but think he was surprised. I only hoped it wasn't in a bad way. I wanted to show them that I was far more than a pretty face who knew how to pour a cup of coffee.

He finally spoke. "Well, I can definitely say that you're handling this far better than the rest of us ever have."

Pride swelled in my chest at his praise.

His hooded gaze roamed over my face momentarily before he said, "Is there anything else you'd like to discuss?"

I peered over at Langston, Landon, then Ben, and finally back to Justin while shaking my head. "I…uh… No. Not that I can think of."

Justin's cocky grin set off something inside me. He obviously knew where my mind was and I think that pleased him.

"Would you like to go over the notes from the last meeting?" Justin inquired.

My eyes widened as I realized I hadn't taken notes. Then again, they were all aware of that fact considering during our last meeting, other things had taken place.

Swallowing hard, I held Justin's stare. "I recall discussions about expectations," I told him, my voice rougher than I'd expected it to be.

"And what else?" Langston prompted. "What took place?"

I turned to look at him.

"The...uh...meeting ended with..." I swallowed again, not sure I could actually speak the words aloud.

"Please continue," Ben urged.

My gaze bounced to him.

Langston's deep voice drew my attention back to him, though. "For future reference, we expect you to be as detailed as possible when speaking of the prior weeks' events."

I nodded, understanding.

"We discussed tests." I lifted the file folder in my hand to show them before setting it back in my lap.

"And then...?"

Obviously Langston wanted real details.

"The meeting ended with Justin using his fingers to...uh..."

"To what?" Justin probed.

Well, hell. They obviously weren't going to let this go and I wasn't about to let them intimidate me. After all, I wanted this. Probably more than they did, so what would it hurt if I blurted it out?

Clearing my throat, I gripped the arms of the chair with both hands. "The meeting ended with Justin making me come with his fingers."

"Details, Luci," Langston stated firmly, his tone leaving no room for argument.

I swallowed hard. "Justin used two fingers, fucking me to orgasm, while the three of you watched."

Landon's raspy gasp did wonders to my ego. Obviously, he remembered what had taken place. I certainly hadn't forgotten about it.

"And just to make sure we're all on the same page, I want to clarify the rules that we all agreed to," Justin added. "Luci, would you mind going over them?"

They were evidently putting me on the spot.

I smiled sweetly. "Test results were to be provided, which they were. I must be on birth control, which I am." I glanced from one man to the next as I spoke. "No one is allowed to have sex with anyone outside of this room. Condoms are not necessary for vaginal or anal sex now that the test results have been provided."

I loved the response my recollection was invoking. Seemed as though my words alone were getting these guys worked up. It left me feeling empowered.

"Do you have any questions?" Langston's inquiry was directed at me.

"No, sir." I understood quite clearly, in fact.

"As you can expect, there will be more rules added as we go along. We'll be sure to let you know so that you're aware. Should they be broken, there will be...consequences."

I nodded my agreement, unable to look away from him.

"Good." His fingers circled my wrist and he tugged gently. "Now come here."

Moving the folder and my notebook to the table, I got to my feet and allowed Langston to pull me closer to him. I wasn't sure exactly what he was looking for, so I allowed him to guide me, which he did. Right into his lap.

I could feel the evidence of his desire beneath my leg as I positioned myself on his lap at a slight angle. He placed one big hand on my bare calf, then inched it higher, slipping beneath the sheer skirt.

"Put your mouth on mine, Luci," he ordered in a deep, gravelly tone.

My eyes dropped to his lips at the same time my heartbeat sped up.

As I cupped his neck with my hand, I noticed how warm his skin was compared to mine. I leaned in and kissed him, keeping the initial contact gentle. More of a tease than anything. I licked his lower lip, then sucked it into my mouth, earning a rough growl from him, which made my pussy throb in earnest.

His hand snaked higher, seeking the heat between my legs. Without thinking, I shifted, giving him better access to what he was looking for. I needed this.

I had honestly thought long and hard about what these four men had proposed, and I still couldn't find a reason to back out. Now that we were resuming the activities that had started last week, it felt perfectly natural for me. It didn't bother me that Justin, Landon, and Ben were all watching either. In fact, the exhibitionist in me liked the idea.

"Don't be selfish, cowboy," Ben grumbled from behind me. "Do what your momma taught you to do and share."

I could feel Langston's smile against my mouth. When he pulled back slightly, I caught a twinkle in his beautiful eyes. I knew there was something dirty rolling around in that big brain of his and I wanted to know what it was.

It didn't take long before I figured it out.

Langston shifted me on his lap, turning me so that my back was against his chest, his arm curling around my waist as his hands resumed their searching, this time beneath my sweater.

"Anyone have any objections to me being the first one to taste her?" Ben asked, his golden eyes darting over to Justin, then Langston and Landon.

I could see Justin's agreement and when Ben got up from his chair, I figured the other two had also given him the go-ahead.

"I think we all agree she's stunning when she's clothed," Landon noted. "I'd like to see how beautiful she is naked."

I barely processed his words before Langston was lifting my sweater up. I raised my hands so he could remove it, shifting my hips when Ben moved to pull my skirt off.

"You take direction very well," Ben said, his tone dripping with approval.

I knew he was referring to the fact that I wasn't wearing panties.

A second later, I was still perched in Langston's lap wearing only my bra, plus the strappy sandals I'd selected that morning. However, the bra was the next to go, but they did leave my shoes on.

I moaned when Langston cupped my breasts, pulling me back against him as he tweaked my nipples between his thumbs and forefingers. My eyes were glued to Ben as he knelt before me, his dark hands pushing my thighs apart, hooking my knees over Langston's legs.

"Pink and pretty," Ben murmured as his fingers drifted to my pussy.

He teased my labia, kneading the bare skin of my mound as he fondled me. I knew he could see how wet I was. Hell, everyone could see.

"Shift forward," he ordered.

Before I could fully understand what he wanted me to do, Langston moved me again, forcing my butt down his thighs, his hands leaving my breasts and hooking beneath my knees to hold me open. It was a slightly awkward position in which I was slouched in Langston's lap. Even more so because my legs were spread wide, my pussy in Ben's face.

I cried out when Ben's mouth descended. His breath was warm, his tongue gentle as he licked me. Slowly, sensually.

"How does she taste?" Justin's deep voice rumbled from a few feet away.

I forced my eyes open and watched him, his eyes raking over my body, dropping to where Ben's head was nestled between my legs.

"Like candy, Mr. Parker," Ben groaned, then resumed his feast.

My eyes shot up to Justin's face and I saw more heat there, only this time, I was pretty sure it was focused on Ben. There had to be something more going on there. Something I wasn't privy to.

Not that I could think about it now. Not with Ben's tongue doing wicked things to my clit.

I curled my hands around Langston's biceps and held on, my fingernails digging into his suit jacket as I ground my hips forward, urging Ben to give me more. Heat rocketed through me, making me tremble. He was teasing, inching me higher and higher only to bring me back down as he slowed his tongue, working me over good.

"You're not ready to come yet, are you?" Langston asked, his words rumbled softly against my ear.

"I am."

Apparently, Ben had other ideas, because he grabbed my hips and jerked my butt closer to him. I was practically folded in half on Langston's lap, my knees up near my shoulders as Langston held me tightly.

Ben's tongue slipped lower, grazing my asshole and making me shudder.

"Oh, God, yes," I hissed.

He continued to brush the sensitive skin with his tongue, then returned to my clit. He alternated, driving me absolutely wild.

My eyes cut over to Justin to see he was still watching as Ben continued to fondle me with his tongue. When our eyes met, he smirked once more.

"One of these days," Justin said gruffly, "we're gonna fill all those sweet holes at one time."

I nodded.

"Imagine that, Luci." Justin's eyes remained locked with mine. "Langston's cock buried in your ass. Ben's cock lodged deep in your pussy while Landon fucks that sweet mouth."

"What will you be doing?" I asked breathlessly, my fingernails digging deeper into Langston's muscles.

"I'll have plenty to do."

"Like what?" I wanted him to continue talking.

Ben's head lifted and I cut my eyes to his.

"He'll be fucking my ass," Ben groaned, then dove back between my legs, his mouth latching on to my clit, his tongue flicking relentlessly.

I was so close.

"Do you want to come, little one?" Langston asked again.

"Yes, sir," I panted.

"Ask very nicely. In your sweetest voice."

I swallowed hard, trying to hold back, scared I was going to come before I had permission. Finally, I found my voice. "Please, sir. Please, please, *please* may I come?"

"You may."

It took less than two seconds for my orgasm to detonate. I wasn't sure if it was Ben's mouth or the thought of Justin fucking Ben's ass while the three of them fucked me. Or maybe it was Langston giving me permission.

Whatever it was, I came harder than I ever had in my life.

My body shook; my muscles clenched tightly as the powerful sensations swarmed me. I cried out, pressing back against Langston, already looking forward to what came next.

SIXTEEN

WEDNESDAY ROLLED AROUND AND I had to admit, I was once again antsy.

After the Monday meeting, things went back to normal. Ben was in and out of the office throughout the day, Justin was off on a two-day business trip, while Landon and Langston spent hours on the phone in their respective offices. From what I could tell, they were gearing up for a book expo in New York. It was apparently something that occurred once a year and a highly coveted event in the publishing industry.

Meanwhile, I was keeping myself busy by scheduling meetings for the four of them, answering emails from their team members, putting together a proposal for one of Landon's prospective clients, and helping Jordan man the phones when they were overloading the circuits. All while I was taking care of the little details for the quarterly meeting. I had to admit, I liked that I had that to work on. Coordinating an event of that magnitude required a significant amount of time and attention to detail. I was happy to contribute both.

Sitting at my desk, I was gearing up to run through a few emails that one of Landon's team members had sent me when Landon's door opened and he peeked out.

"I'd like to see you in my office, Luci."

I smiled, despite the fact that my insides had started to riot instantly. "Of course."

Because I wasn't sure what he needed and I didn't want to be presumptuous, I grabbed a pen and a notepad and made my way into his office.

The place looked the same as the last time I'd been in there. Everything neat and tidy, including his desk. His cell phone and laptop were the only items on the rustic wood top.

"Please, have a seat," he said, motioning toward the chair across from him.

Landon waited until I eased into my chair before he sat down and I recognized the chivalrous move. They were all like that, but admittedly, Langston and Landon more so than the others.

"How're things going?" he prompted, leaning back in his chair.

"Very well," I admitted. "I'm keeping busy."

"Good." His eyes perused my face. "And you're still happy here?"

"Absolutely."

"No regrets?"

I wasn't sure if he was referring to the job or the extracurricular activities. However, my answer was the same for both. "Not at all."

"I'm glad to hear that."

There was a long pause, the lack of sound almost deafening as Landon continued to watch me. I wasn't sure if he was expecting me to say or do something. There were plenty of things I wanted from him, but he had yet to touch me. Nothing more than a kiss. While Justin had already had his fingers inside me and Ben's tongue had done a number on me, Landon and Langston seemed to be holding back. I wasn't sure why that was.

A soft knock sounded on the door behind me. Twisting in my chair, I watched as Langston stepped into the room, closing the door behind him. His eyes, all intense and sexy, instantly found mine.

Turning back to Landon, I saw he was watching me as well.

Warm hands settled on my shoulders and I took a deep breath, loving the way Langston always seemed to touch me. Those big hands cupped my neck and then my head was being tilted back. Langston leaned over and, in his upside-down position, brushed his lips against mine. It was a gentle move, both sexy and sweet, and extremely dominating.

"Do you have plans for dinner tonight?" Landon inquired once Langston let me go.

I peered over at the handsome man still seated behind his desk.

"No, sir," I said softly.

"We'd like to take you to dinner."

We?

Langston moved to stand beside his twin, and I glanced between the two men. I studied them for a moment, trying to figure out what was going on here. I thought we were keeping this to an office affair, but apparently I'd been wrong.

Landon smiled. "I can assure you that the one thing that won't happen tonight is you paying for dinner."

I laughed. "I'd appreciate that."

"So? Dinner?"

I glanced from one to the other, then nodded. "I'd like that."

"Good." Landon looked over his shoulder at his brother and Langston nodded. "Unless you have anything for us," Landon said, once more looking my way, "that'll be all for now."

A little taken aback, I managed a nod as I got to my feet. I'm not sure why I thought something was going to happen, but admittedly, I did. Since I was being dismissed, I felt a little shaken. And not in a good way.

"Luci?"

I paused with my hand on the doorknob, my shoulders tensing from the gruff sound of Landon's voice.

"Yes, sir?" I didn't bother to turn around, not wanting them to see my disappointment.

"We're lookin' forward to dinner."

I nodded.

"A limo will pick you up at your apartment at seven," Langston stated, his voice just a tad deeper than his twin's. "Wear something black."

"And short," Landon added.

"And don't bother with panties," Langston said gruffly.

I swallowed hard, my body tingling.

"Or a bra," he added.

Okay, so that was going to prove challenging.

"Oh, and one more thing." I noticed that Landon's voice was louder, sounding closer.

I turned to find he was standing directly behind me.

"When you get home tonight, I want you to put this in." He handed me a box. "Don't open it until you get home. But I expect you to have it in when we arrive."

"Yes, sir." My voice was rough with the lust coursing through me, my gaze shooting over to Langston briefly. "Sirs," I amended, then with my gift in hand, I opened the door and made my way back to my desk.

•

When five thirty rolled around, I said good-bye to Ben, who was the only one still in the office, before heading toward the front. All the lights had already been shut off and the elevator was waiting. The trip down was uneventful and I couldn't keep from thinking about the box in my purse. I had no idea what was in it, but I was eager to find out.

"Good evening, Miss Wagner," the doorman said when I stepped out of the building.

My car was pulled around and waiting for me as it usually was at this time.

"Good evening, Todd."

"Hope you have a wonderful night."

"Thanks. You, too."

The worst part of my day was the evening traffic. Getting out of downtown took time and patience, and part of me wished that I didn't have to do it daily. Especially today, when I wanted to get home as soon as possible so I could shower and change. I probably would've been fine to go out to dinner wearing the silky pantsuit I'd donned this morning, but I remembered Landon's and Langston's requests. Although I had forgone underwear for work today, it likely didn't have the same impact since I was wearing pants, but still.

However, the pantsuit had earned me an email from Ben, advising that he needed to speak with me. When I met him in his office, he notified me that the only time I was permitted to wear pants was when I had my period. He said it would let them know that sex was off the table and that they could enjoy me in other ways.

The way he had relayed the message didn't come across as sexist or demeaning in any way. It was intensely hot to hear him instruct me on how he wanted it to go. His dominating tone had appealed to me on a level that surprised even me.

And I totally understood. Like I said, the little rules they'd implemented gave me goals to work toward. In turn, they constantly kept me thinking of ways I could please all four of my bosses.

However, I wasn't on my period and tonight I was hoping to get lucky with both Landon and Langston, so freshening up seemed the way to go.

So that was exactly what I did when I got home. Well, not exactly that. First, I ripped open the box in my purse and stared at the contents. There was a small note.

In case you don't know what this is, it's a butt plug. Insert it using the lube included. It will help to stretch you so your body's ready to take both of us at the same time.

I inhaled sharply, heat slamming through me at the thought of Landon and Langston taking me at the same time. I was no dummy. I knew exactly what it meant and I even understood why he wanted me to insert the plug. It would allow my ass to be stretched so that taking one of them wouldn't hurt. Well, I assumed it would still hurt, but maybe not as badly as without.

Now, as for whether or not I could go through with it, that was another story.

•

Although I hadn't wasted a single second, I was scrambling to get my clutch when my phone rang at seven o'clock on the dot.

"Hello?"

"Miss Wagner?"

"Yes."

"This is your driver. We're ready when you are."

"Thank you. I'll be right down."

And now I was ridiculously nervous, but somehow, I managed to make my way to the ground floor, then out into the darkness. Sure enough, there was a stretch limousine idling in front of my building. Better than that, Landon and Langston were both standing outside of it, waiting for me.

I was pretty sure my heart did a little stutter in my chest when I noticed they'd both changed, their suits immaculate and fitted to their impressive bodies. It made me all the more eager to know what they looked like *without* the suits.

"Good evening," Landon greeted when I approached.

"Good evening." I smiled.

"You look stunning," he added as he leaned in and kissed me. His lips were firm against my mouth.

"Thank you," I whispered, slightly breathless from his mouth on mine.

Langston was a little more hands-on. His palms traveled from my wrists up to my neck before his lips lightly brushed mine. "My brother's right. You do look stunning."

I appreciated the way they treated me as though this really was a date and not an extension of our office agreement. Truth be told, I hadn't expected to see any of them outside of the office, so this was a nice surprise.

"Are you ready?" Langston asked, tilting my head back as he leaned in once more and pressed his lips to mine.

When he released me, I nodded. For a brief second, I wondered whether anyone saw us. More accurately, I wondered if anyone saw the fact that I was kissing two men.

I shrugged it off because it didn't bother me. At some point, it might, but right then, I was more worried about spending the evening with the two of them. I couldn't deny that I was nervous. Although I knew them, I didn't really *know* them. Which meant this was going to likely be awkward.

Once the three of us were in the car, the privacy window went up.

"Did you like the gift?" Landon inquired.

Heat infused my face as I became aware once again of the plug currently filling my ass. "I did. Thank you."

"Turn around," Landon instructed, his voice firm.

I frowned, confused about what he meant.

His tone became slightly less insistent when he said, "If you don't mind, I'd like you to bend over and show me the plug."

My face flamed with embarrassment, but strangely enough, my body did as he requested. I turned around, then felt my dress being lifted. Strong hands urged me to lean forward, baring my ass for them.

"Very nice," Landon said approvingly, his hands squeezing my ass cheeks gently.

More heat slammed into me.

When my dress was lowered to cover my butt, I turned around and sat on the seat. I felt the pressure of the plug inside me. I'd thought it would be painful, but it wasn't. Oh, sure, I was completely aware that it was there, but it didn't hurt. Just uncomfortable.

"Are you hungry?" Landon asked.

"Starving." It was no less than the truth. I hadn't eaten since lunch, which seemed so long ago.

"Then we should get you fed," Langston noted.

I smiled at both men, feeling a tad uncomfortable. I mean, I did work for them, so going to dinner wasn't exactly in the job requirements. Then again, much of what had taken place wasn't in the job requirements. At least none that I would've signed on for initially.

"How long have you lived in the area?" Landon prompted.

"All my life." I smiled. "My mother and stepfather live about twenty minutes away in the house I grew up in. When I graduated from high school at seventeen, I moved into dorms for college, desperate to get out of their house."

"You were young when you graduated," he acknowledged.

"My birthday's in June. I turned eighteen shortly after graduation."

"Eager to run off to college, then?"

I chuckled. "More like I was eager to get out of my parents' house."

"Were they difficult to live with?" Landon probed.

"It wasn't so much that as it was I was lonely. My mother wasn't the hands-on type." I forced a smile. I didn't particularly care to talk about my mother. "Needless to say, college was an adventure for me. I had dozens of friends and, truthfully, graduating was the hardest part. I got my degree in three years, having taken summer classes so I didn't have to go home."

"Impressive. What made you decide on an accounting degree?"

"That was my mother's choice. I would've preferred something else." I chuckled again. "Anything else, actually. But I learned early on not to challenge her." My smile wasn't quite so forced as I continued, "Once I was finished, I knew I had to come home. More so because my stepfather asked me to. He wanted me to be close, in case I needed anything. I opted for not *too* close."

"Far enough your mother wouldn't drop in every day?" Landon asked, his smile mischievous.

It was obvious Landon was the one leading the conversation, so I focused my attention on him.

"Exactly." I glanced down at my lap. "Not that she would. I invited her once. She's never even seen the inside of my place although I've lived there for almost three years. We aren't very close. She's very…opinionated. And aside from telling me how she really feels when one of my actions displeases her, my mother was never really there to give me direction." I looked up to see both men watching me.

"Do you feel you need direction?" Landon prodded.

The question threw me. It seemed somewhat strange. "I've never really thought about it, I guess. In some ways, sure. I think I do," I admitted. "Not in everything, of course. I mean, I'm capable of taking care of myself and excelling at what I put my mind to, but I appreciate the direction from time to time. It helps to make me feel grounded. As though I'm…cared for."

I realized just how much of myself I'd revealed and it shocked me. I didn't mean to tell them something so personal. Not this soon. Rather than wait for them to push for more details, I turned the conversation back to them. "And your parents? Do they live close?"

"Relatively," Landon explained, his eyes still studying me. "They live in Texas most of the time, but we keep an apartment for them here so they can visit whenever they want."

"Does this apartment happen to be in the office building?" I remembered that they'd all claimed to have an apartment in the building.

"It is." Landon's grin widened. "Helps that we own the building."

I couldn't help it, I chuckled. "Well, that certainly explains a lot."

Landon lobbed the next question. "Any brothers or sisters?"

"Nope. Only child." Once again, I felt as though this was a two-way conversation between Landon and me, so I kept my eyes on him. "Any siblings?" I smiled. "Besides him."

"One sister. Older," Landon stated. "She lives in Kentucky with her husband and four kids. She drops in once a year at most."

"I'm sorry to hear that. Are you not close with her?"

He shook his head. "She doesn't exactly approve of our parents'...choices."

"I get it. Sometimes we're instilled with a need to rebel," I said lightly.

Landon's smirk was wicked and sexy. "That's one way to put it."

And to conclude the getting-to-know-you part of our evening, the limo came to a stop.

"We've arrived."

I had no idea where they were taking me and I couldn't tell from where I sat, so I waited patiently until both men had exited the vehicle.

I figured now the true test was about to begin.

SEVENTEEN

DINNER WAS LOVELY. THE THREE of us had been seated at a secluded table in the back. I sat between the two of them, and during our conversation, they'd heated me up by placing their hands on my legs. It seemed they wanted to touch me and my body had welcomed them.

The air in the restaurant was cool, which caused my nipples to pebble. Due to the fact I'd been instructed not to wear a bra, I knew the hard little points were visible through my dress, but I chose to ignore them. Sure, it bothered me a little. I was always the type to avoid the headlights if at all possible, wearing bras that would conceal such an incident. However, Landon and Langston seemed quite enthralled, their hands casually grazing my chest frequently as they kept the conversation going.

It wasn't like I didn't know what they were doing. I welcomed the interaction, the teasing. I was not used to first dates being quite so…intimate. On the other hand, I found I didn't mind it one bit.

We had continued the conversation we'd started in the car. Again, it had mostly been between Landon and me; however, I could tell Langston was engaged, even if he didn't say much. Although words didn't come out of his mouth, his eyes spoke volumes. He was certainly paying close attention to every word I said. I could see the interest there, the promise of more to come.

Needless to say, by the time the meal was finished, my body was humming.

After declining dessert and coffee, the three of us returned to the limo and I was slightly disappointed when Langston advised the driver to return to my apartment. I spent the short drive wondering if I'd said or done something wrong. Neither man spoke, not even to each other, and it left me feeling insecure and awkward, yet I had no idea what to say or how to engage them in conversation.

That changed when we arrived at my apartment building and both men exited the limo before helping me out. This time they walked me in. My mind began to wander, thinking about what my apartment would look like to a stranger. I was pretty sure I'd left my clothes on the floor, my towel hanging on the door, a couple of dirty dishes in the sink, and, of course, the package the plug had come in was on my kitchen table.

Maybe they wouldn't want to come in.

"Thank you for dinner," I told them as we took the elevator up to my floor. "It was lovely."

"Our pleasure," Landon said. "We enjoyed it as well."

The elevator jerked to a stop, rocking me on my heels, and Langston placed his hand on my back to steady me. When the doors opened, we stepped out onto my floor and headed down the hallway, Langston's warm hand remaining on my back.

"Luci?" I stopped when the door across from mine opened.

"Hi, Mrs. Idlemann." I smiled at the elderly woman.

"I thought that was you." Her eyes slowly scanned Landon and Langston. "Is everything all right?"

"Yes. Of course. I..." I had no idea what to say, how to explain who these men were.

"Good evening, ma'am," Landon greeted. "We were just seein' Luci home."

"You're twins," she said, her expression never changing.

"Yes, ma'am. We are."

She looked at me and a mischievous smirk tilted her mouth. If I had to guess, she had been watching the parking lot from her window and likely saw me leave with them as well as return. Which also meant she'd probably seen me kiss them. *Both* of them.

I felt heat creeping up my neck.

"Well, I hope you have a good evening, dear."

"Thank you, Mrs. Idlemann."

The yapping of a little dog had Mrs. Idlemann turning, then closing the door. I breathed a sigh of relief. I liked my neighbors, but they were definitely nosy. Then again, so was I, so I couldn't fault them, really.

"Invite us inside," Langston stated firmly, his voice low and seductive.

My gaze shot up to his. "Would you like to come in?"

My breath hitched when Landon brushed the backs of his fingers over my left breast, causing my nipple to pebble instantly.

"What do *you* think?"

I knew the question was rhetorical, but when they touched me, I seemed to lose my train of thought.

"You have beautiful tits," Landon said as he palmed my breast. "And yes, we'd like to come inside. Either that or we're going to enjoy you right here in the hallway. Probably not a wise idea since you've got curious neighbors."

No, definitely not a wise idea.

I nodded, then unlocked my door and stepped inside, both men following. My apartment instantly felt smaller when the two large men moved deeper into the space. Landon's gaze traveled the space as he headed into the living room while Langston seemed content to keep his eyes on me.

I was still nervous, my belly fluttering as I set my clutch on the counter. "Thank you again for dinner," I said, speaking to Langston since he was the only one in the room with me.

His eyes slowly perused the length of my body before returning to my face.

"It was our pleasure," Langston replied gruffly, his eyes hooded, his gaze heating me up as it traveled over my face.

Neither of us spoke for a few moments and my anxiety ratcheted up a notch.

"You mentioned in the limo that you liked direction."

It wasn't a question, but I answered anyway. "Yes. I do."

"Good. Because we'll be giving you plenty of that tonight."

My breath hitched in my chest.

"Remove the dress," Langston commanded, his eyes locked with mine. "But not the shoes."

I didn't know what it was about his gruff voice, but I found myself wanting to do exactly as he instructed. And it was true, I did like the direction, the point-blank demand that came from his sensuous lips. I hesitantly unzipped the dress and allowed it to slowly slide to the floor, pooling at my feet. My attention was on his face, watching every expression as he observed me stripping before him.

"Very pretty. I think I like you just like this."

My body heated as he moved closer. He was touching me, but not. I could feel the warmth of his body, the slight brush of his suit jacket against my nipples as we stood there, toe to toe. I tilted my head up and he tilted his head down, his lips hovering just out of reach.

"Are you ready for us, Luci?"

I didn't know exactly what he was referring to, but I assumed he meant sex, so I answered him quickly and honestly. "Yes, sir."

"We're going to fuck you," he stated matter-of-factly, his eyes studying mine.

"Both of you," I clarified, making sure I was on the same page as he was.

"Yes."

"Okay." I found the idea of being with both of them at the same time intensely arousing, and more than a little intimidating.

"And we won't be gentle about it."

I didn't need gentle. I needed whatever this man had in store for me. I just wanted him to touch me, to kiss me, to invade all of my senses.

"Do you understand?"

"Yes, sir," I whispered. "I understand."

Langston cupped my cheek, his lips fanning mine as he whispered, "Very good girl," before he took my hand and led me toward my bedroom. It was the only room in the place with a door, so it wasn't difficult to find. When Landon fell into step behind us, I felt my body flush with heat.

This wasn't a position that I'd ever found myself in.

For one thing, casual sex wasn't something I was used to. Sure, I'd been with men I wasn't in a relationship with, but not many and not often. For another thing, I'd never had sex with a man on the first date. This was out of my realm of experience—double that due to there being two men—but for whatever reason, it felt natural. I wasn't at all put off by the fact that I was completely naked with two men—who happened to be my bosses—in my apartment. In fact, I was turned on more than I'd ever been in my life.

"Undress me," Langston instructed after he turned to face me.

I took my time unbuttoning his shirt. When I slid my palms over the crisp dark hair on his chest, Langston removed the jacket and shirt, placing them on the chair near the door. My fingers trailed over his rock-hard abdomen, sliding between the muscles that gave him the sexy washboard look. The man's body was to be worshipped. I tried to focus on my task, but this was the first time I was seeing so much of him and he truly was a masterpiece. I wanted to stare, I wanted to touch, I wanted to taste. Hell, I wanted everything.

On the other hand, I wasn't sure what he was allowing me to do, and for some reason, I was hesitant to do anything without his permission. So, rather than kiss him the way I wanted, I unbuttoned his slacks, then lowered the zipper as I eased myself onto my knees in front of him.

I could feel his eyes on me as I nudged his pants down his hips, freeing his erection. I couldn't help but admire the thick length of him. His cock was beautiful and I had the sudden urge to take him in my mouth, but I somehow managed to refrain.

Once he was naked, Langston stepped away from me and Landon took his place. Since I was already on my knees, I started with his pants. While I did so, he removed his jacket and shirt, placing them beside his brother's.

Then the three of us were naked, except for the fact I still had my heels on. With me kneeling between them, they flanked me, their beautiful dicks right at eye level.

"Touch us," Langston ordered. "Without using your hands."

That seemed like such an easy thing to do but proved far more difficult than I thought. I moved closer to Landon, who was still standing in front of me, and pressed my mouth to the underside of his cock, which was standing at attention. I brushed my lips over the smooth length of him, then ran my tongue over the vein. Up, down, I continued this motion before taking his balls into my mouth. I didn't apply too much suction, merely caressing them with my lips and tongue.

A deep grumble sounded from above me and I pulled back.

"Now Langston," Landon instructed.

I pivoted and performed the same maneuver on him, my body catching fire when Langston put his hand on my head, his fingers gently tangling in my hair.

"How much of me can you take?" he asked, angling his cock toward my lips.

I opened my mouth as much as I could, then allowed him to dip the wide crest inside. Using my tongue, I caressed him, but he reached down and stopped the movement by gripping my jaw.

Now, I wasn't a big girl. Along with a short stature, I also had a small frame. Next to these men, I felt ridiculously tiny. They overwhelmed me in every way. Not that I was scared of them, but I felt miniscule in comparison. So, to have such a big man wanting to put his large cock deep in my mouth was both daunting and exciting.

"Keep your mouth open," Langston insisted, pushing his cock in deep.

I instantly gagged when he brushed the back of my throat, jerking my head back only to be held in place with his strong grip on my hair.

"Breathe deep and relax your throat," he said, his eyes locked with mine.

Unable to refuse him anything, because I was eager to please him, I did as he said. The next thing I knew, he was pushing his cock into my throat, effectively choking me. He pulled back slowly while I drooled uncontrollably. I was a sputtering mess and I couldn't imagine it was sexy at all.

"Relax, little one. You can do this."

I nodded, tears streaming down my face from gagging.

He repeated the motion over and over until finally I managed to take him deeper than I thought possible. Having his cock push against my throat wasn't a bad feeling, but it was slightly terrifying. It required me to focus, to breathe slow and steady through my nose, allowing him to inch farther into my mouth.

"Now swallow," he said sternly, the head of his cock lodged in my throat.

I tried but failed, once again gagging harshly.

He pulled back, his eyes locked with mine as a smile curved his lips. "We'll work on it, little one. You'll be able to deep-throat me in no time."

I nodded, wanting to please him.

Langston released my hair and Landon helped me to my feet, then pulled my back against his chest. I could feel the thick length of him brushing against my ass. My pussy was so wet, so eager, I silently wished he would put me out of my misery.

I should've known better.

EIGHTEEN

NEITHER MAN SEEMED TO BE in a hurry, which was obvious when Langston moved in close, sandwiching me between them. I leaned my head back against Landon's chest as Langston leaned down and kissed me. It was rough and passionate, fanning the flames already burning inside me.

"Such a sweet girl," he praised. "You're eager to please us, aren't you?"

"Yes, sir." So eager.

A small smile tilted his lips. "We're going to enjoy you."

I wanted them to.

"Have you ever taken two men at one time?" he inquired, sliding his finger down my cheek while his other hand slipped between my thighs.

I could feel Landon's hand move down my side, caressing my hip before cupping my ass.

"No, sir," I whispered. I was intensely aware of so many hands on me.

"You will," Langston said simply. "And you'll crave it."

"I already do," I admitted, my eyes meeting his.

Langston's thumb brushed over my clit and I hissed in a breath as the sensation shocked me.

"Have you ever taken a dick in your ass?" Landon asked, his mouth close to my ear.

"No, sir," I told him, the thought making me tremble.

"So wet," Langston mumbled. "And I'm gonna be the first of us to fuck this sweet little pussy."

The way he said it was as though it was a triumph.

"Where's the lube?" Landon asked, his finger brushing the plug still lodged in my ass.

I assumed he was referring to the lube he had provided with the butt plug. It was in the bathroom, but the idea of him leaving me wasn't a pleasant one, so I referred him to the bottle I kept on hand. "In my nightstand."

Langston stepped away and I instantly missed his warmth. I watched as he opened my nightstand drawer. He chuckled as he pulled out the vibrator I'd nicknamed Big Red, for obvious reasons.

He glanced at me over his shoulder. "New rule. You are no longer allowed to masturbate unless someone instructs you otherwise."

I nodded despite my disappointment.

Langston must have noticed my discontent because he added, "Should you defy my instruction, you will be punished."

That was the third time he'd mentioned punishment or consequences. I wasn't sure I was supposed to be aroused by that, but I was. Granted, this new rule was not one that I was fond of. Big Red and I were close. I was going to miss it.

He tossed the vibrator on the chair with their clothes before pulling out the tiny bottle of lubricant I kept there. I'd never had reason to use it, but I kept it on hand because one never knew when it might be needed.

Like now.

Landon's finger continued to brush against the plug in my ass while his other hand moved to my mound. When his fingers dipped into my wetness, I inhaled sharply, my knees going weak.

"You're so wet, sweetness. Are you needing to be fucked?"

"Yes," I moaned when he pushed one thick finger inside me.

"Good girl."

My eyes drifted closed as he continued to tease me, my body temperature skyrocketing. For several minutes, Landon teased me with his hands. I felt myself relaxing, enjoying the way his fingers made my skin tingle. When Langston returned, I kept my eyes closed, focusing on all four hands as they explored me.

Langston's hands left me again, but I fought the disappointment. I knew he would return eventually.

"Kiss me," Landon ordered.

I glanced back at him over my shoulder and his mouth met mine while his fingers continued to explore and tease. He practically surrounded me with his warmth, his arms wrapped around me, his tongue insistently pushing into my mouth. I moaned softly, loving every second of his attention.

"Come here, little one."

I opened my eyes at Langston's gruff command. Only then did I notice that he was lying on my bed. Although it was a queen, it looked ridiculously small with his large body on top of it.

"Come straddle me and grind your wet pussy on my dick."

Landon released me and I crawled onto the bed, trying to be graceful as I moved over Langston. I couldn't help but admire his decadent body as I straddled his thick thighs. The coarse hair on his legs erotically scraped the insides of my thighs and I felt more wetness pooling between my legs. The man was a god, so incredibly sexy. They both were.

Shifting forward, I planted my hands on Langston's chest as my pussy lips grazed the velvety smooth length of his erection. I used the motion to tease my clit, moaning loudly.

Langston's hands curled around my wrists, pulling me down so that I was resting on top of him.

"My brother wants to be the first to take your ass."

I nodded.

"And I want to be the first to bury my cock in your pussy. Do you want that, little one?"

"God, yes," I moaned as his cock brushed against my clit again.

I hadn't really considered what this entailed until he asked me that question. I mean, it hadn't seemed real until that moment. A fantasy, sure. But now it was reality and I was dangerously close to finding out how it felt to be completely overwhelmed by two men. I couldn't imagine it would be all that comfortable. Then again, I was so worked up, maybe it would. But they were so big and I was...not. As it was, my dildo wasn't as big as Langston, so I couldn't imagine what it would be like to have them both filling me, much less at the same time.

"Are you scared?"

"A little," I admitted.

His eyes never left mine as he commanded, "Put me inside you. Let me feel that sweet little pussy caressing my cock."

I shifted so that I could maneuver my hand between our naked bodies. I curled my fingers around his cock, reveling in how thick he was. I stroked him, enjoying the soft groan that rumbled in his chest as I lined our bodies up. Momentarily, I wanted to amend my previous answer. I was no longer scared, I was eager, desperate.

Then again, I flip-flopped on my answer when I attempted to seat myself atop him. Taking him inside me was much more difficult than I'd anticipated. Especially with the plug still lodged in my ass. He was almost too big. It took several minutes for my body to adjust to the intrusion, but Langston was patient. His muscles tensed as I lowered myself onto him inch by excruciating inch.

"So tight," he growled. "So wet."

There was an intensity in his eyes that riveted me. It was as though he was peering deep into my soul, seeking something.

"Take all of me, Luci."

I took more of him inside me, wondering if he would fit. It was slightly terrifying to think that Landon was going to take my ass. They were the same size, which meant if Langston didn't fit in my pussy, no way would Landon fit in my ass. However, I wasn't scared about the prospect, merely hesitant that there would be more pain than I could endure.

"You'll take both of us," Langston said reassuringly. "I promise." His tone turned harder, rougher. "Now sit on my dick, little one. I want my cock buried all the way in your pussy."

My belly fluttered with sensations as I slowly eased down once more. Langston's hands gripped my hips and he pulled me down on him. I cried out as pain slammed through my insides, quickly morphing into pleasure as my body adapted to his girth.

"That's a good girl," he groaned, keeping my hips still as he rocked his hips, forcing his cock even deeper. "Such a good girl."

I was consumed by overwhelming pleasure as his cock filled me, stretched me. With the plug still inside me, the combination of both was unlike anything I'd ever felt before, one that I didn't want to end. Between the eroticism of having two men focused on me and the way they praised me, I wasn't sure I was going to last all that long.

My shoes slipped from my feet and I heard the *thump-thump* as they landed on the floor. A second later, the bed shifted behind me and I knew Landon was joining us. My body tensed automatically as fear trickled into my veins. I wasn't sure I could handle what these men were asking of me.

"Ride my dick," Langston commanded. "Slowly. Focus on me. Only on me."

I began rocking on his cock, taking him deeper and deeper. I moaned uncontrollably as he brushed sensitive nerve endings over and over again.

There was pressure against my backside, then I felt the plug being shifted, moved, and finally pulled out. I exhaled sharply as the stretching of my ass disappeared completely. However, it didn't last long, because then something cool dribbled over my asshole and I knew it was the lube. Again, I tensed.

"Fuck me, Luci," Langston demanded, his tone rough. "I want to feel your pussy contract on my cock. Squeeze my dick, baby."

His tone was hard, insistent, and I found myself doing as he said. I rode him, lifting and lowering on his cock, my pussy clenching around his shaft. It wouldn't take much to ignite my orgasm, but before I could get to that point, Langston swatted my ass.

"You do not come until I say you can."

I swallowed back a cry of pain. I wasn't sure how I could control my orgasm. It didn't seem possible when I was overwhelmed with sensation so great my skin tingled.

When I dropped back down onto Langston, he grabbed my hips and held me there. He shifted his pelvis, grinding upward, his cock punching into me. Shallow thrusts had me moaning his name over and over.

I felt something breach my ass and I realized it was Landon's finger. While I sat on Langston's cock, Landon fingered my ass. The sensation was foreign but not at all unpleasant. It was far more exciting than the plug had been, that was for sure.

"Relax, sweetness," Landon urged from over my shoulder. "It's gonna feel good."

I wasn't sure that was true.

"Is this what you want?" Langston asked when Landon pushed two fingers in my ass.

I grunted from the sensations warring inside. "Yes. I want this." Despite my reservations, I desperately wanted this.

Landon continued to tease my ass, working two fingers inside. He was stretching me slowly, working my virgin asshole open.

Moaning, I tried to rock between them, needing more stimulation.

"Tell me," Langston demanded. "Tell me exactly what you want us to do to you."

"I want Landon to fuck my ass while you fuck my pussy," I blurted, my body trembling with need.

Langston nodded, his eyes darting over my shoulder, and I knew he was giving Landon the go-ahead. A second later, the blunt head of Landon's cock brushed against my asshole and I tensed.

"Relax," Langston whispered, his voice softer, not quite so demanding.

He pulled me down so that my breasts were crushed against his chest. His lips pressed to mine and his tongue dipped into my mouth. The kiss was ferocious. It should've been enough to distract me from the discomfort that ignited when Landon's cock continued to prod my ass, but it wasn't.

Warm hands traveled over my back. "We'll get there, sweetness," Landon crooned. "No need to rush. I want this sweet ass to swallow my dick."

I groaned as pain consumed me, the head of his cock working its way inside me. It wasn't at all what I'd expected. My ass burned as he stretched me open, his cock pushing slowly deeper. He was so much bigger than that plug. So. Much. Bigger.

"Be a good girl, Luci," Langston crooned. "Let us take care of you."

A vulnerability unlike anything I'd ever experienced consumed me. I was at the mercy of these two men and I loved every second of it. The pain didn't matter; it was the pleasure I was focused on. Not my own, though. I wanted to please them. I didn't know why that was, but I couldn't deny it. I wanted to be their play toy, for them to use me however they wanted.

That thought shocked me. I had no idea where it'd come from, but I ran with it, giving up my own needs in an effort to meet theirs.

Landon's cock pushed in deeper, stretching my ass painfully. I whimpered, not sure my body could handle any more.

"I've got you, little one," Langston said softly. "I promise. I've got you."

Those words were a balm to my soul. My emotions were running rampant, despite the fact that my brain was well aware of what this was. Still, when Langston said that, I noticed the gentleness in his tone. It was as though he meant it in more than the sexual sense and my body heated with the knowledge.

"Do you feel both of us?" Langston asked. "Filling you? Stretching you? God, your pussy's so tight."

I nodded, my teeth clenched, pain slamming into me as Landon lodged himself deeper in my ass.

"Look at me," Langston demanded.

I met his eyes.

"Now we're gonna fuck you, Luci."

I nodded again.

"We're gonna fuck you hard."

I didn't expect anything less.

"You have my permission to come. I want to feel your pussy come all over my dick."

I nearly came from his words alone.

My body was shocked into submission when Landon pulled out of my ass at the same time Langston's hips punched forward. Then Langston pulled back and Landon drove into my ass. Over and over, they kept a leisurely pace at first, but then their thrusts intensified in both speed and velocity until they were alternately fucking me, rocking my body between them.

"Now we're gonna fuck you at the same time," Langston said, his hands cupping my face. "I want you to come for us, Luci."

This time, when Landon pushed in, Langston's cock remained inside me. Then they both retreated and slammed into me.

I cried out.

It was too much. I felt too full, as though my body was going to be ripped apart. I whimpered and moaned, trying to get away, but Langston held me tighter.

"Relax, little one. Let it feel good."

I wanted to. I even tried, but it didn't make the pain dissipate.

"Do you want this?"

Again, I nodded.

"Then let us make you feel good. Let us give you what you need. Focus on how we feel inside you."

Inhaling deeply, I nodded once more as they began fucking me again. Slowly at first, then more intensely, until they were once again impaling me. Only this time, the pain wasn't as intense. No, the pleasure overrode it, the slow grind of their cocks inside me, the friction against sensitive nerve endings. Small waves of electricity started in my core.

They fucked me hard, almost brutally, filling me at the same time. I felt stretched beyond capacity. My skin tightened as Langston's cock brushed against my G-spot. They didn't go slow this time, grunting in unison as they both speared me.

My orgasm slammed into me, shocking my senses with its onslaught. I hadn't expected it, but I welcomed the release, the wave of ecstasy that I rode as it washed over me.

"That's a good girl," Langston grunted, holding my hips still as he fucked up into me at the same time Landon drove into my ass.

"Now it's our turn," Langston advised. "I'm gonna fill your pussy with my cum."

His words triggered another orgasm and my pussy gripped the cock filling me.

Langston groaned, slamming into me harder and faster until every sensation morphed into one giant explosion. It was as though a tsunami had overcome me, racking my body as another orgasm, this one far more intense than anything I'd ever experienced, rocketed through my body.

"Fuck, yes," Landon groaned from behind me. "I'm coming, Luci. Fuck...oh, fuck. Filling your tight little ass."

Langston's body stilled and I could feel both cocks pulsing inside me as they came. An aftershock vibrated through my core and Langston chuckled as I slumped onto him.

"So beautiful," Langston whispered as my eyes drifted closed and I let the blackness consume me. "So *fucking* beautiful."

NINETEEN

BOSS MEETING

BEN

WHEN MR. PARKER ASKED ME to schedule a Friday afternoon meeting to discuss the events of the week, I didn't hesitate. I sent an invite to Landon and Langston for two o'clock, ensuring that Luci and Jordan were gone for the day. I had realized early on that the plan was to keep these impromptu meetings off the radar so as not to worry Luci.

Not only did I schedule the meeting because my master asked me to, but I was also curious as to how things had gone with Landon and Langston on Wednesday night. I hadn't been able to decipher based on the way either of them had acted yesterday, so I was looking forward to hearing it from them directly.

Evidently, Mr. Parker was just as interested based on the question he launched the moment Langston had closed the door.

"How'd things go with Luci?"

"Very well," Landon said, leaning back and casually regarding the rest of us.

"Care to go into detail?"

Langston smirked. "We can. Or you can wait until the Monday meeting and we'll have her go into detail."

Mr. Parker seemed amused by that idea.

"Which do you prefer, pup?"

Personally, I would rather have Luci relay the details. That girl fascinated me. She made me want things I'd put on the back burner for so long. I was eager for the first time I could get her alone, for the day I got to dominate her the way I wanted to.

Then again, the idea of hearing Landon's and Langston's point of view on it was equally rewarding. I could admit that I was a voyeur and the next best thing to getting to watch the action firsthand was hearing it relayed.

"I'd like them to give a high level," I answered.

Landon grinned. "Just as we said we would, we took her to dinner. The conversation was relatively light."

"Relatively?" Mr. Parker seemed confused by that revelation.

Landon sighed. "From what I can tell, Luci doesn't have a good relationship with her mother. And because of that, I think she feels isolated somewhat."

"But you said she's friends with Kristen?" I asked. "Are they close? Do they interact often?" I didn't like the idea of Luci not having someone she could confide in. Especially when she was enduring the four of us in such an intimate way. It was important for a submissive—although she wasn't technically a submissive yet—to have a good network of friends.

"Not too close," Landon admitted. "Although they hang out from time to time."

"She seems to be getting closer to Jordan," Mr. Parker said.

"True," Landon acknowledged. "They've hit it off. Which is a plus all around. They work really well together."

I completely agreed with that assessment. "They do."

"So, after dinner…" Mr. Parker prompted.

"We took her back to her apartment," Langston stated. "As for details, you'll have to get them from her. I'm not willing to sit here and assess her abilities."

That didn't surprise me one bit. None of us were really the kiss-and-tell kind.

"Did you spend the night?" Mr. Parker asked.

Langston frowned. "What'd you think we were gonna do? Fuck her and run?"

"It's happened before," Mr. Parker noted, his tone flat.

"We spent the night," Landon confirmed, obviously wanting to keep the two of them from going at it.

Mr. Parker and Langston tended to knock heads from time to time. I figured it had a lot to do with the fact that they were both the alpha, both needing to be in control of every aspect of their lives. When you put two of those personalities together, it was inevitable that one or the other was going to try to come out on top.

"Any other plans before next week?" Mr. Parker asked Landon directly.

"No," Landon stated firmly. "But in the event that changes, we'll be sure to let you know."

"Fine. That's all I've got," Mr. Parker stated firmly.

Obviously, Landon and Langston didn't have to be told twice, because they both got up and left the room immediately.

"Come here, pup," Mr. Parker ordered when we were alone.

I got up from my desk chair and moved around to stand in front of him. He remained sitting as his fingers hooked into the waistband of my slacks.

Those mesmerizing blue eyes peered up at me and I couldn't look away.

"I missed you this week," he said softly.

I didn't respond because I knew it wasn't necessary. He already knew that I missed him, and Mr. Parker wasn't the type to need to hear the words. That didn't mean I didn't tell him often, but I tended to do that when I wasn't prompted, so he knew that I meant it.

Mr. Parker's hands dropped to his lap and he regarded me inquisitively. "Take your cock out. I want to admire it for a minute."

Without hesitation, I freed my cock from my slacks, fisting the base. The man made me hard with little more than a look, and I'd been anticipating his return from his trip for this very reason. Well, not necessarily because I wanted him to admire my cock, although I did enjoy that immensely. The man made sure to show me just how hot I made him.

"Who does that monster cock belong to?" he asked, peering up at my face.

"You, Master. It belongs to you."

"Did you jack off while I was away?"

I shook my head. "No, Master." I knew better than that.

Mr. Parker leaned forward. "Feed me your cock, pup."

The damn thing throbbed from his words alone and I did as instructed, brushing the thick, swollen head over his lips. I loved watching Mr. Parker tease me. I'd loved it from the day we met all those years ago. Back when neither of us really knew what we wanted, but we were both willing to experiment.

Mr. Parker's wicked tongue laved my shaft before he took as much as he could in his mouth. I knew better than to force my cock to go deeper. This man controlled both our pleasure and that was something I needed. Although we were equals here in the office, at least as far as everyone else was concerned, this man owned me. Heart, body, and soul.

When he pulled back, I was breathing hard, gripping the edge of the desk.

"Did you wear your plug while I was away?"

"Yes, Master."

"Did it make you think of me? Of the way I enjoy burying my dick in that tight hole?"

Heat slammed through me at his words. "Yes, Master."

"Did you think about Luci? About what you wanted from her?"

"I did." I'd thought about her endlessly since the first day I met her.

"Tell me while I suck your cock." Mr. Parker practically growled the words.

When he wrapped his lips around my dick, I jerked, the pleasure overwhelming me.

Although my words were raspy and interspersed with moans, I proceeded to tell him. "I fantasized about you fucking her. Fuck, that feels good. I thought about you fucking her. On your desk." I hissed when he sucked me harder, deeper. "While I watch. I want to see you fuck her pussy, to make her come on your cock while I watch. Fuck…"

I white-knuckled the edge of the desk, trying to hold on as my cock tunneled in and out of Mr. Parker's mouth. The man was always content to take his pleasure from me, but he never failed to give in return. And give he did.

I was on the verge of coming down his throat when he pulled back and got to his feet.

"Strip and move over to the couch."

Primed and eager, I maintained as much of my sanity as I could while I removed my clothes, tossing them over the arm of the sofa.

"On your knees," he commanded. "With your chest against the back cushions."

I got into position while Mr. Parker lubed his cock, then placed one knee on the sofa between my calves. He put his other foot flat, which meant he fully intended to fuck me hard.

"Do you want a submissive of your own?" Mr. Parker questioned as he aligned his cock, then pushed in roughly.

I hissed as he filled me. "I do, Master. I want a submissive of my own."

Mr. Parker's teeth nipped my earlobe and I turned my head. His lips met mine and I gave myself over to the kiss as he began thrusting shallowly into my ass.

"God, I missed you," he moaned. "I fucking need you, Ben. So fucking much."

It was words like those that did crazy things to me. I'd never thought we would ever have a real relationship, both of us quite content with the D/s relationship we did have, but somewhere along the way it had morphed into something more, something intense.

"Push back against me, pup," he whispered into my ear. "Because I'm gonna fuck you so goddamn hard."

I groaned because I was desperate for it.

"Is that what you need?" he asked.

"Yes. I fucking need it."

"Ask me nicely," he insisted.

"Please fuck me hard, Master. I need you to unleash on me."

"God, I love hearing that. And I promise, pup, that's exactly what I'm going to do."

Mr. Parker made good on his promise.

TWENTY

AFTER THE EVENTS OF LAST Wednesday night, after having been fucked into a mindless oblivion by Landon and Langston, I had expected things to be different at the office. They weren't. Again.

I don't know what it was about these men where they thought of these encounters as so casual, but it irked me. And fine. I knew they were casual, but that didn't mean I wasn't hoping for more. More time with them, more of their attention, more...sex.

There, I said it.

I was hoping for more sex.

Did that make me a nympho? Perhaps. Did I care? Not even a little bit.

So, yes, I could admit to my disappointment when everything remained the same. Which was the very reason I decided to treat them just as casually as they were treating me. No way was I going to let them think that I expected more.

So, every day, I went in to work, did my regular duties, focused mostly on the quarterly meeting that was coming up in a couple of weeks, and met with all four men to give them updates before heading out for the evening. Nothing changed. Well, nothing except for my outlook. I now saw Langston and Landon in an entirely different light. A super-sexy, rock-my-world kind of light.

And as I did every Monday morning, I went into the conference room a few minutes before ten and started the coffee, despite the fact that my bosses all drank way too much coffee if you asked me. While it percolated, I didn't get comfortable, choosing rather to wait for them by the coffee station so I could greet them when they arrived. My overall objective was still to maintain my professionalism, even if I was hoping for the opportunity to jump one of them at any second.

Ben and Justin were the first to arrive, followed closely by Landon and Langston. They all offered a round of pleasant good mornings before we took our seats.

Landon was the first to provide an update, letting everyone know that he would be out of town the following day. That, too, was par for the course. At least one, if not more, of my bosses were generally out of the office one to two days a week. That was something else I was getting used to.

I jotted down notes while Ben gave an update on a client, followed by Justin sharing the details of his brief trip the week before. Apparently, it had gone off without a hitch. It made me wonder just how a meeting with a sex toy developer went. It had to be awkward, right? A bunch of people sitting around discussing a dildo and the cool new features? Yeah. Awkward.

"Do you have any updates, Luci?" Justin prompted as he wrote something down on his notepad.

"Not that I can think of." I didn't have any news on the quarterly meeting, although it was coming along nicely. I was getting rather good at keeping them abreast of the situation prior to them leaving each day.

Justin lifted his head, his eyes meeting mine. "Care to share with us what happened last week?"

"Last week?" For the life of me I couldn't think of what might've happened that he needed me to provide an update on.

"Your outing with Landon and Langston."

Heat infused my cheeks instantly and I glanced over to Landon. He offered a knowing smirk. And I took that to mean he was not going to help me out here.

"Explicit detail," Langston urged. "That's the rule."

Technically...I didn't think it was a written rule, but I knew better than to argue with Langston. Especially when he had that wicked gleam in his eye.

"Explicit?" I glanced from Langston to Justin, then to Ben. They were all evidently waiting for me to share *that* news. Great.

Good news was, I had actually thought about that night quite often over the past few days. Enough that I remembered all of the *explicit* details as though it had happened yesterday.

Taking a deep breath, I pretended this was just any other presentation.

"Landon and Langston picked me up at seven o'clock," I explained. "I was instructed to wear something black and to forego panties and a bra. They took me to a really nice restaurant, where we carried on a casual conversation while they teased me relentlessly."

"Is that what you called that?" Landon joked.

I knew my cheeks were bright red, but I managed to continue. "Then we returned to my apartment and I invited them in, where they proceeded to…to…" Okay, it was much easier to think it than to say it aloud.

"Please continue," Justin encouraged. "I'm enjoying it so far."

I sighed heavily, letting them know just how much this cost me. I could talk about plenty of topics, but explaining the dirty details wasn't something I was good at. Nor did I really want to become good at it.

"I was requested to undress them, which I did. Then I was instructed to touch them…their…uh…cocks without using my hands." I glanced over at Langston. "That's far more difficult than it looks, by the way."

"I'd say you did a phenomenal job," he praised.

"Thank you," I said cheekily before glancing back at Justin and Ben. They were the ones I was telling the story to, after all, since Landon and Langston had been there. "Oh, and Landon had gifted me with a butt plug. He's so generous." I cast a smile his way, then turned back. "Which I was told to insert prior to their arrival. It was my first time having handled one of those things. I managed, with only minimal difficulty."

I should definitely get an A for this presentation.

Unable to help myself, I looked at Landon and Langston. "After they teased me, I was immersed into a world of pleasure I'd never experienced before." I sounded breathless, but I couldn't help it. They were watching me as though I was the most fascinating woman they'd ever met.

Swallowing hard, I forced myself to continue, knowing this was where the explicit detail came in. "Langston reclined on my bed and ordered me to straddle him. I did, then proceeded to rub my wet pussy along his thick shaft." I was purposely laying on the adjectives. "It took some effort, but I managed to impale myself on his cock. He fucked me for several minutes before Landon joined us. Once the plug was removed"—my eyes darted over to Landon again—"he took my anal virginity."

Okay, there.

I did it.

"Anything else?" Justin probed.

"After they fucked me into oblivion, I passed out. I can only assume they took care to clean me before they fell asleep in my bed with me."

I still remembered waking up and finding them there. I honestly hadn't expected it and it had warmed me in ways I'd never expected.

"They did leave before sunrise, allowing me plenty of time to get ready for work."

"Very nice," Landon praised. "I recall that night very fondly as well."

Glancing over at Justin and Ben, I noticed that they were eyeing Landon and Langston. Truthfully, I was a little surprised that they hadn't been told the story already. It made me feel good to know that Landon and Langston hadn't shared that night with them. Although I did relay the details, knowing that they didn't sit around and talk about me behind my back made me feel immensely better.

"Thank you for sharing that," Justin said, his gaze returning to me before darting to the others, a smile forming. "And with that, I say we can conclude today's meeting."

And just like that, things went back to normal.

Although I wasn't sure normal in this office resembled anything close to the definition in the dictionary.

TWENTY-ONE

IT WASN'T UNTIL THE NEXT morning when Justin called me into his office that I felt the shift in the air. Something was going to happen today and my body could tell. It took a tremendous amount of willpower to remain calm and aloof. That certainly wasn't in my nature, but I was learning.

"Shut the door, please," Justin instructed when I entered his office.

I gently closed the door, enforcing a sense of tranquility over myself and wiping the smile from my face.

When I turned back to face him, Justin's blue eyes were perusing me from head to toe. He didn't speak until he met my eyes again.

Both days this week, I had paid close attention to detail, selecting outfits I hadn't worn yet. Keeping them professional but sexy, in an attempt to catch their attention and to discreetly get them to notice me. Clearly, that hadn't worked the way I'd intended.

Today I felt especially sexy with my black-and-white-plaid skirt and white button-down shirt with a sleeveless V-neck sweater that conformed perfectly to my body. I'd topped it off with a pair of white thigh-highs and Mary Janes. Both sweet and sexy, but still professional. Sure, I might've straddled the line of what was appropriately known as professional, but I didn't care. They noticed me; that was what mattered.

"I've got a conference call in a few minutes," Justin informed me. "I'd like you to be in here for it."

Well, this was a first. I had yet to sit in on any of their individual meetings. I wasn't sure what I was supposed to do, nor had I brought anything with me. "Do I need to get something to write with?"

Justin shook his head. "No, but you can strip."

Heat traveled through every inch of my body as I stared back at him. Okay, so this wasn't going to be a typical conference call, obviously. Then again, I wasn't sure these men knew the definition of typical.

"Now," he commanded, his eyes hot.

I couldn't deny that I was a tad nervous. I had yet to disrobe—at least on my own—so I had to work up the courage. Based on the urgency in Justin's eyes, I had to do it quickly, too.

I nodded, then managed to remove my clothes. I discarded one article of clothing at a time while he watched closely. I was waiting to see if he'd tell me to stop when I got to my bra and my knee-high stockings; however, he did not, so I took those off, too. Then I was standing completely naked in his office.

It was then that I experienced an entirely new sense of vulnerability. It was one thing to get naked for a man when you knew what was about to happen. Perhaps while making out, or even simply when he took you back to your apartment and informed you he was going to fuck you. However, it felt distinctly different to go to your boss's office and have him instruct you to strip for him for a conference call.

Not a bad feeling, just different.

Justin got to his feet and moved over to the couch before holding his hand out to me. I loved the way his eyes roamed over my body appreciatively, the bulge in his slacks broadcasting his approval.

I moved slowly, hoping to appear graceful despite the nerves that racked my entire body.

"You're beautiful, Luci," he whispered softly. "I like seeing you naked in my office."

Chills danced down my spine, his compliment warming me.

Justin kissed me softly, his tongue slipping into my mouth, moving against mine. I sighed, enjoying the gentle way he was treating me. Unfortunately, the kiss ended far too soon.

Justin stepped back, then unbuckled his belt before unbuttoning his slacks and lowering the zipper. He freed his cock, took a seat on the couch, then pointed for me to move between his legs. He tossed one of the throw pillows onto the floor between his feet.

"On your knees, Luci."

Well. Okay, then. This was new.

And hot.

I knelt between his legs, admiring the thick, semi-hard length of his cock. Even in its in-between state, his cock was impressive. This was the first time I was seeing it, and admittedly, a thrill shot through me. The man was very well-endowed. Although he wasn't quite as long as Landon and Langston, what he lacked in length, he certainly made up for in girth. I wondered how he would feel inside me.

He threaded his fingers into my hair and pulled me closer to him. "My conference call will last thirty minutes. I want you to tease my cock with that beautiful mouth, but do not make me come."

I nodded, eager to do as he instructed.

"No matter what, you are not to stop. And you are not to make any noise. Understood?"

"Yes, sir."

Without another word to me, Justin picked up the phone receiver and punched in some numbers. I could hear the faint ringing on the other end.

"Suck me, Luci," he ordered, his eyes meeting mine once more.

Leaning in, I inhaled deeply, enjoying his musky scent and the erotic scrape of his leg hair against my palms. I took the head of his cock into my mouth, tentatively tasting him for the first time. He tasted like clean, healthy male. I imagined myself doing this for him daily, servicing him while he tended to his phone calls.

"Good afternoon, gentlemen," Justin said into the phone. "How are things in your world today?"

There were a few beats of silence while I assumed someone spoke on the other end of the line.

Justin chuckled. "Yes. I can completely understand that. We've got some interesting things going on in our office, too." Another chuckle. "Very well. I'm ready to get started when you are."

Justin's cock thickened, swelling in my mouth until he was steel-hard against my tongue. He didn't seem to be paying me any attention; however, I could tell by the random twitch of his cock that he was enjoying what I was doing to him.

"I totally agree. I'm very interested in understanding how this particular product works."

There was silence for a few minutes and I assumed whoever was on the other end of the call was presenting the new product that Justin was considering. Closing my eyes, I focused all of my attention on Justin's cock, licking, sucking, teasing. I kept my pace slow, heeding his instruction to not make him come.

"I like the idea, Charles. Any chance you'd be willing to do a demonstration for me?"

I glided my tongue along the underside of Justin's shaft, teasing as I moved down. His fingers slipped into my hair when I reached his balls and he tugged me forward. I took that to mean he wanted me to tease his ball sac, so I laved him with my tongue, then sucked each into my mouth, one at a time, then both.

"Actually, I have a willing participant," Justin said, sounding pleased. "I'd like to schedule a meeting at my office. I think my partners would be interested in seeing the demonstration as well."

Justin was absently rubbing my hair as I took his cock in my mouth once again. I lowered my head, taking him to the back of my throat. It reminded me of the other night, when Langston insisted that I take all of him. Figuring now was as good a time as any to practice my deep-throat skills, I worked the head of Justin's cock against my throat. It took patience and willpower to keep from gagging, knowing he'd told me I had to be quiet no matter what.

I pulled back before I gagged, but his hand tightened in my hair. He pulled me back down onto his cock, this time using force to press against the back of my throat. I relaxed as much as I could, remembering to breathe through my nose as he lodged himself into my throat. I swallowed and felt his leg muscles tense. I was pretty sure he enjoyed that, so I did it again before I retreated.

"Absolutely, Charles. She's a good little plaything. It'll be a worthy demonstration."

I knew in that moment that Justin was talking about me. Oddly the fact that he called me a plaything didn't upset me in the least. It had the opposite effect, making my pussy throb and my insides tingle.

"Perfect. She's my secretary. Her name's Luci. Pretty little thing. I'll have her call you back to schedule a good time next week." There was another pause, followed by, "I look forward to it. See you then."

Justin disconnected the call. Rather than get up, he relaxed into the couch, not instructing me to do anything different, so I continued fondling him with my tongue and lips, savoring the taste of him.

His hand returned to my hair, slowly caressing me as though I was a favored pet. It soothed me, made me feel safe for some unknown reason. It didn't matter that I was on my knees, his cock in my mouth, or that we were at work. It was a rush in and of itself to be doing something so naughty while the world continued around us.

"Such a generous mouth," Justin mused.

I thought for a second that he was going to come, but Justin surprised me when he pulled his cock from my mouth. I remained kneeling before him, even when he stood and zipped his pants.

"Let's see how juicy we can make that pussy," he said, motioning for me to follow him.

Justin had me lie on his desk, my feet flat on the surface. He then proceeded to secure my ankles to my thighs with straps he pulled out of his desk drawer, keeping my knees bent. Another strap went over my hips, restraining me to the top of the desk. Once he was satisfied with that, he belted my wrists together, then pulled my arms over my head and secured my arms in that position.

My body heated as I realized I was completely at his mercy, unable to move. Flat on my back, my pussy on display...it was far more arousing than I would've ever thought possible.

His fingers slid over my labia, then between, teasing my entrance and my clit, but never giving me enough.

"Looks like you enjoyed sucking my cock." His eyes lifted to meet mine. "Is that true?"

"Yes, sir." No need to lie about it; the evidence was there.

He reached for his phone, punched a button, then spoke into the receiver. "I need you to join me in my office. Bring Landon and Langston, too."

I assumed he was talking to Ben and my arousal spiked at the thought of all four men doing wicked things to me while I was helpless to resist.

While we waited for the others to join us, Justin absently caressed my pussy, coating my outer lips with my own juices.

"You're so wet, princess. It makes me hard to feel your juices on my fingers."

My breaths were already increasing as the pleasure ignited under my skin. His thick fingers were gentle in their teasing, somehow knowing exactly what I needed to ratchet up my arousal.

A minute later, the door opened. I couldn't see the men walk in, but I could hear them talking softly.

"Oh, this is pretty," Landon said, his head appearing in my line of sight. " *Very* pretty."

"This little princess sucks cock like a dream," Justin said, still stroking my pussy.

"I concur." Langston's deep voice rumbled through me as he leaned down and brushed his mouth against mine. "Practice makes perfect, right, little one?"

I nodded in agreement.

Justin continued to fondle me as he spoke. "One of my clients will be visiting next week to give us a demonstration of a new toy of his."

"That'll be interesting," Ben noted, his fingers sliding over my pebbled nipples.

"I'm thinking our little princess will be the perfect person to demonstrate."

"Is that something you're interested in?" Ben inquired.

It was hard to think, much less speak, but I managed a breathy, "Yes, sir."

Ben then glanced at Justin. "Just out of curiosity, what'd you need us for?"

Justin shook his head as though clearing his thoughts. "Wanted to show off our play toy. She seems to be doing really well here."

Langston's eyes met mine when he said, "She's perfect."

"I wouldn't go that far," Justin said. "Not yet, anyway." His finger pushed inside me. "But she'll get there eventually. Like you said, practice makes perfect."

I tried to buck my hips, wanting Justin to fuck me with his finger. The strap across my hips kept me from moving, which only frustrated me more. My body was desperate for release. The tension was building as all four men continued to fondle me as they looked their fill.

"I've been giving some thought to our new arrangement. I was thinking that maybe we should dedicate certain days for each of us," Justin said. "But then I changed my mind. I like making her guess what we're up to, what each day might entail."

The unknown was highly erotic; I couldn't deny that.

"I agree," Ben said. "I like her vulnerability."

"I do like seeing her naked," Landon tacked on.

Justin added a second finger, thrusting deeper and faster. "Since Thursday's a holiday, pet, and we'll all be out of the office for the rest of the week, I want you to make a note for yourself. When you arrive next Tuesday, I want you to remove your clothes, place them in your desk. I expect you to work like that all day."

Landon chuckled. "The accountants in the building across from us are going to get a kick out of that."

The idea of someone being able to see me walking around naked for my four bosses was strangely stimulating.

"I'll be sure to give them a call on Monday to let them know," Ben stated.

"She likes that," Justin said. "Her pussy *definitely* likes that."

"Is that true?" Langston asked, caressing my cheek with his thumb. "Do you mind if those men see you naked, Luci?"

I shook my head. "No, sir," I whispered. "If you don't mind, I don't mind."

"Good girl." Langston glanced over at Justin. "Now make her come or step out of the way so that I can."

"Fingers or cock?" Justin asked me.

"Cock," I said breathlessly.

Justin freed his cock from his slacks as Langston moved to stand behind my head. Ben remained on my right side and Landon moved to my left. Three pairs of hands began stroking my body while Justin's cock pressed against my entrance.

"Watch me while I fuck you, Luci," Justin instructed.

I met his gaze and held it. He slammed into me without preamble and my lungs momentarily seized up as his cock stretched me.

"She's got a sweet pussy," Justin said, talking about me while maintaining eye contact. "I love the way it flutters over my dick."

"Her ass is the same way," Landon noted. "So tight."

Justin retreated, then slammed into me again. He began fucking me in earnest while Landon and Ben pinched my nipples. My orgasm didn't stand a chance. I felt the electricity radiate out from my core almost instantly. It intensified as Justin pounded into me, fucking me hard and fast. I managed to keep my eyes open, only I wasn't sure how. The pleasure obliterated my mind, stealing my breath as it consumed me.

"I want to hear you scream," Langston said, his warm fingers sliding over the pulse in the side of my neck. "Show respect for the man fucking you and scream his name when you come."

I didn't look away from Justin, remembering his instruction. Seconds later, when my orgasm crested, I screamed loudly, his name tumbling over my tongue again and again.

Justin didn't slow, continuing to impale me on his thick length, reigniting the flames inside me and driving me higher and higher.

"I want another," Justin demanded. "Come for me again, Luci. And when you do, I expect you to say thank you, Mr. Parker."

Ben's hand slipped down to my clit and he pressed his thumb over the sensitive bundle of nerves.

"Oh, God!" I squealed when he shifted his thumb in circles. "Oh, God! Yes!" My body tensed, my muscles locking as I came again. "Thank you, Mr. Parker!"

Justin slammed into me several more times, and when Ben and Landon pinched my nipples, he stilled at the same time my body tensed with another mind-blowing release.

TWENTY-TWO

THANKSGIVING REALLY WASN'T MY FAVORITE HOLIDAY.

In fact, I didn't have a favorite holiday. Valentine's usually sucked big, hairy donkey balls. Since I wasn't Irish, St. Patrick's Day held no appeal for me either. However, Thanksgiving and Christmas were the loneliest as far as I was concerned.

See, my mother didn't celebrate holidays. Not since my father died had she celebrated anything, really. My birthdays weren't big events for her either. Sure, she usually sent me a gift card, but nothing that she'd had to put any thought into. When I called her this morning to see if she and Jim were doing anything for Thanksgiving, she told me she was enjoying a rare day off and she intended to go to bed early.

So, while plenty of people were spending the day with their families, enjoying big feasts, I was sitting at home watching Netflix. I couldn't even get in the right mindset to read. All those books I'd been devouring held very little appeal right now. Mainly because the fantasy wasn't living up to the reality. Which I thought was the opposite of how it usually was, so there was that.

However, I found I missed being at the office. Since all the stores were closed, I had nothing to do but chill at home. Alone.

Then again, a nap sounded just about perfect.

•

At some point, I must've drifted off while the television droned on in the background. I awoke to the sound of my phone buzzing on the coffee table.

With blurry eyes, I fumbled for it, then squinted at the screen.

The number came up as Landon Moore – Boss.

I smiled to myself, wondering what he could possibly want and why he was texting me on a holiday.

Landon: *What interesting things are you doing on Thanksgiving?*

It took me longer than normal to reply because I was going through a million responses in my head. None of them the truth. How could I possibly tell him that I was spending the entire day watching television because I didn't have anyone to spend Thanksgiving with?

I decided to embellish the truth but not lie exactly.

Luci: *Oh, you know. The same thing a lot of people do on Thanksgiving.*

There. That didn't sound terrible. And I didn't lie. I was sure a lot of people spent the day alone at home, enjoying the peace and quiet.

Landon: *So, does that mean you're at your mother's?*

Well, shit.

Not like I could come up with a lie for that one. I'd already admitted that my mother and I had a strained relationship.

Luci: *No. Not at my mom's.*

I stared at the phone, terrified what he would ask me next. I didn't want to lie, but I also didn't want him to think I was some sort of introverted hermit who spent all my time at home alone. That wasn't the case, but I really didn't get out much. That was mostly by choice.

Landon: *Where are you right now?*

Leave it to Landon to ask the tough questions.

Luci: *At home.*

Landon: *Doing?*

Luci: *Nothing, really.*

I certainly wasn't telling him that I'd been napping for most of the day. That really sounded pathetic.

Before he shot off another text, I opted to get in a question of my own.

Luci: *And where are you spending Thanksgiving?*

Landon: Spent the day with the parents. Sister came into town with the nieces and nephews.

Luci: I'm assuming Langston was there?

Landon: He was. And is. We're at the apartment right now.

I remembered that they'd said they kept an apartment for their parents for when they visited. Which likely meant they stayed nearby when their parents were in town.

Luci: Yours or theirs?

Landon: Ours.

Luci: Is anyone else there with you?

Landon: No. Just me and Langston.

Well, at least he wasn't alone.

Figuring he'd texted in an effort to be polite and tell me Happy Thanksgiving, I decided to give him an out on the conversation.

Luci: Well, Happy Thanksgiving. I hope you have a great day with your family.

Landon: We're not done here, sweetness. Not by a long shot.

Luci: Oh.

Landon: It's not polite to dismiss someone.

Luci: I'm sorry.

Landon: I think it's only fair if you make it up to me.

Luci: And how do I do that?

I couldn't imagine what he would come up with. My bosses were anything but predictable.

Landon: Do you trust me, Luci?

That was easy.

Luci: Yes. I trust you.

Landon: Prove it.

Luci: How do I do that?

Landon: I want you to put the phone down. Go into your bedroom and find the sexiest bra and panty set you have. Put them on. Just those. No other clothes.

That seemed like a strange request, but considering I was now eager to see where this might lead, I typed back a quick *okay*, then headed for my bedroom. I rummaged through my underwear drawer until I found a black-lace set. It wasn't exactly taboo, but it was nice.

I quickly shed my clothes, then put on the bra and panties before returning to my phone.

Luci: *Okay. I changed.*

Landon: *What color are they?*

Luci: *Black.*

Landon: *Nice. But boring. Try again.*

Luci: *Try again?*

Landon: *Yes. Go back into your bedroom, find something different, and change.*

Luci: *Okay.*

I could admit that I was enjoying this game. I hopped up off the couch and ran to my bedroom. I scrounged around until I found another set. This one was nude. It was demure yet sexy. I changed, then went back to the living room.

Luci: *I changed.*

Landon: *Color?*

Luci: *Nude.*

Landon: *Nope. Try again.*

Okay, so this could easily become a pain in the ass. Wondering if he had a specific color in mind, I decided to ask.

Luci: *Is there a certain color you would prefer me to wear?*

Landon: *Thank you for asking, sweetness. And yes, I'd like you to put on something blue.*

Well, at least it wasn't a wild color. I did have blue. Several shades, in fact. Since he liked that I'd asked, I questioned on which shade he would prefer: navy, light blue, royal blue, or turquoise.

Landon: *Navy.*

I hurried to change again. I was actually quite fond of this set. The bralette was see-thru lace and hooked around the back of my neck and had a thin band that went over my ribs. Due to the color, it hid my nipples fairly well. The panties were high-cut in the same see-thru lace, with thin bands on the sides.

Luci: *Okay. I changed again.*
Landon: *Prove it.*
Luci: *How do I do that?*
Landon: *Take a picture and send it to me.*
Holy shit.

Now, that was not something I'd ever done. Pictures weren't private.

Landon: *You said you trusted me, sweetness. Prove it.*
Damn it.

He had me there.

I'd taken millions of selfies over the years. Some even in my bathing suit. Surely this wasn't much different than that. I padded to the bathroom, then looked at myself in the mirror. In case it came down to showing him a full view of myself, I quickly pulled my hair up, wanting to look somewhat decent. I wasn't wearing makeup, but that wasn't a big deal. At least not to me.

Choosing to keep my face out of the image for now, I quickly snapped a picture, then sent it to Landon.

Landon: *Very nice. But I'm not fond of the pose.*

Knowing this could go nowhere fast, I decided I would ask him.

Luci: *Is there a specific pose you would prefer?*
Landon: *There is.*

I waited patiently, wanting him to tell me, yet worried that he would ask for more than I was comfortable giving. However, I had told him that I trusted him.

Landon: *What room are you in?*
Luci: *Living room.*
Landon: *I want you to lie back on the couch, propping yourself against the armrest.*

I did as he requested, getting comfortable, my legs out straight and crossed at the ankles.

Luci: *Done.*
Landon: *Send me a picture.*

Swallowing hard, I snapped a selfie, once again, keeping my face out of the shot.

Landon: *I definitely approve of your underwear choice.*

Luci: Thank you.

Landon: Now slip your hand beneath your panties, put your fingers on your clit. Send me a pic.

Oh, shit.

I knew he wasn't going to go easy on me.

It took me a few minutes to work up the courage, but I finally did as he instructed.

Landon: Mmm. I like to think about what you're doing to yourself beneath those panties.

My body temperature shot up at least ten degrees as I read his text.

Landon: Just remember the rules.

Luci: I remember. I'm not allowed to masturbate without permission.

Admittedly, just the slightest graze of my fingers against my clit was working me up.

Landon: I have another request.

Luci: Okay.

Landon: This one is going to prove how much you trust me.

Aww, crap.

Landon: Now pay close attention.

Luci: Okay.

Landon: You have two options. First, you can record yourself teasing your pussy. It will require you to give me an unobstructed view of your fingers on your cunt. I also require that you expose your tits for my pleasure. Keep in mind, you are NOT allowed to come.

I swallowed hard. That did not sound like fun. Not only was I terrified about recording myself doing something like that, I knew it would be futile if I couldn't come. Hell, he had me so worked up and I had yet to do much more than put on the underwear he preferred.

Landon: *Your second option is: You can Facetime me, then I will instruct you what I want you to do while we're on the phone. Langston will be present to watch. And before I disconnect the call, I will allow you to come. Your choice. But you only have one minute to decide.*

One minute? Holy hell. How was I supposed to make that decision? Record myself masturbating, but never being allowed to come? Or having him and Langston watch as I follow his instructions? The first one seemed easier for the simple fact that I was recording myself. Less pressure. The second sounded far more pleasurable on my part.

Landon: *Fifteen seconds. Make a decision.*

Luci: *I prefer… to Facetime you.*

Landon: *Good answer, sweetness. I'll be waiting for your call. You have one minute.*

Oh, damn.

I was starting to sweat and my hands were trembling, but I pulled up his contact information and hit the button to make the live-video call.

I instantly saw my face on my screen, and a few seconds later, he answered. Landon's beautiful face appeared and I couldn't help but smile.

"Hello, sweet girl."

"Hi."

"Are you ready?"

I wasn't, but I nodded anyway.

"Good. Now, I want you to prop up your phone so that I have a good view of your entire body."

I sat up, then positioned a cushion on the end of the sofa near my feet. Another went on top of it and I managed to prop my phone up.

"Is that good?" I asked.

"So far. I'll let you know if I need you to change it. Now lie back."

I did, continuing to watch the screen so I could see his face. The image shifted and then there were two faces on the screen.

"Hello, little one," Langston greeted.

"Hi."

"You sound eager," Landon stated.

"I am." It was true. "Also nervous."

"No need to be nervous."

Easy for you to say.

"Okay, sweet girl. I want you to slip your hand beneath those sexy little panties once more."

I did. When my finger grazed my clit, I jerked.

Landon smiled.

"Gonna go off like a rocket, huh?"

I smiled shyly. "It's possible."

"In that case, you do not have permission to come until I give you specific instructions. Do you understand?"

"I understand." Whether I could do as he said was still to be determined.

"Good. Now tease your pussy with your fingers. Keep your panties covering your hand."

That wasn't so bad. I mean, I'd never masturbated over the phone, but at least I was covered, for the most part.

I watched my hand as it shifted and moved beneath my panties, my middle finger teasing my clit, then slipping down and dipping inside me. I was soaked, my juices free flowing as I worked myself up in front of my phone audience.

"Show us one of your tits," Landon commanded. "Just a hint of it."

I tugged the stretchy fabric of my bra down, allowing my nipple to peek out above the lace.

"Pinch your nipple for us."

I did.

"Now close your eyes, Luci."

That seemed like an odd request, but I did that, too.

"Continue to finger your pussy, stroking your clit ever so softly. But keep teasing your nipple."

With my eyes closed, this was far more erotic. I couldn't see his face and his voice coming out of the phone speaker was strange but pleasurable at the same time.

"Now slip those panties over so we can see how wet your pussy is."

As my chest heaved from my rapid breaths, I shifted the fabric out of the way with two fingers, holding it back before I rubbed my clit with one finger.

"We need a better view," Langston stated.

"Hold on for a second, sweet girl. I want you to move the phone so that the camera is between your legs. Keep it at an angle so we can see your pussy, but also have a view of your gorgeous face."

It took a minute for me to get the phone positioned so that they had the view they requested. It felt strange having to pause and reposition, but it also gave me a moment to get myself under control.

Once I was lying back on the cushion, I glanced down to ensure the phone was still in place before I closed my eyes once again and resumed teasing myself.

"Fucking beautiful, sweet girl. Let us see your pretty pussy."

Making sure my panties were out of the way, I continued to play with myself. It was getting easier with every passing second because I was horny as hell.

"Show us both of your tits. Raise your bra up. We want to see those hard little nipples."

His words were spurring me on, making me wetter.

"Imagine those are our hands on you. What would you want us to do to you? How hard would we be fingering you? Pinching your nipples?"

I moaned as I kept my eyes closed, imagining my hands were theirs. I shoved two fingers into my pussy and thrust deep.

"Damn, baby. You know how bad I want to put my mouth on your clit? To nip you with my teeth? To make you cry out, begging for us to let you come?"

Unable to hold back, I was moaning in earnest, continuing to plow my pussy with my fingers. My other hand released my breast, moving to my clit. I frigged myself wildly.

"That's it, little one. Show us how you like it."

Their deep voices caressed my skin as though they were in the same room with me, as though their hands and mouths were taking me to heights I'd never known.

"Don't you dare come," Landon bellowed. "Not until I tell you."

"I'm trying," I cried out. "I need to come."

"Not just yet," Langston said. "Keep pumping those fingers into your cunt. It's such a nice sight. I only wish this was being recorded so I could watch it again later."

"We'll have to work her up to that," Landon said. "But you'll get there, sweet girl. You'll be ready and willing to give us everything we ask for."

I was already willing.

I whimpered, unable to stop fucking my fingers deeper, fondling my clit roughly.

"Okay, sweet girl. Pull your fingers out of your pussy and put them in your mouth."

I shoved two fingers into my mouth.

"Now make yourself come by rubbing your clit only."

That was easy. My clit was so sensitive, and the more I thought of them watching what I was doing, the closer I was getting to release.

"That's it," Langston crooned. "Just a little more, Luci."

That did it.

My back bowed and my fingers stilled, my clit pulsing beneath them as I came.

"Ahh, yes. Such a pretty sight."

They let me drift back down to earth, and when my breaths had evened out, Landon told me to grab the phone, so I did. I stared at the screen and he smiled back at me.

"I enjoyed that very much," he said. "Thank you for trusting me."

"You're welcome, sir," I whispered.

"We'll talk to you later."

I nodded, then disconnected the phone.

Lying on the sofa, I stared up at the ceiling.

Only then did I realize I was smiling.

I had to admit, this Thanksgiving hadn't been all that bad.

TWENTY-THREE

I PRACTICALLY RACED TO THE office on Monday morning.

Having had five days off with very little to do was more than I could handle. I needed to be around people, needed to have some direct interaction with someone other than my own reflection.

I arrived a few minutes early, so I didn't see Jordan on my way in. As was my usual routine, I headed back to my desk, got the coffee prepared to start, then sat down at my desk. I perused the calendar, noting the Monday meeting at ten before I settled in to go through my emails.

There were exactly two weeks before the quarterly meeting was to be held. After asking Ben's opinion, I had sent out a survey to all of the managers, requesting input on what they would like to see at the meeting. Since they were being taken away from home for four solid days, I wanted to fill it with events that would keep them interested and eager for more.

The managers had responded positively to the survey, several of them admitting that they appreciated having their input considered. And several of them had come up with some creative ideas for workshops and events to be held during the week. I received an email from one manager elaborating more on their request and I added it to my list, planning to go over it in the Monday meeting.

Plus, I was happy to see that all the managers had been able to rework their schedules so that they could attend. I felt that was a positive response to their bosses and it showed how much they respected them.

Now that I had all of the reservation confirmations, I decided to call the hotel and ensure that they were all taken care of. Each manager had used their own company card to reserve the room; however, I would be handling the payment from our end, confirming that we were getting the discount we'd been offered.

This week I needed to nail down a schedule of events, but first, I had to get my list finalized for my bosses. After the morning meeting, I'd be well on my way to having completed my first big task.

•

"So, aside from individual roundtables with each of your teams, as well as a couple with the entire group, those are the suggestions that I have as well as those that I received from your managers," I explained to my four bosses as we sat in the Monday meeting.

"I'll admit," I continued, "I think it's a good idea to give some insight into each of your clients and the range of products that you all represent. That seemed to be the consensus amongst the managers as well. They're interested in learning and this is the perfect opportunity to provide them with training in a manner that doesn't feel like they're being lectured."

They all four glanced between each other for a moment, then back at me.

"What?" They were looking at me as though I had two heads.

"So, I think I speak on behalf of everyone in this room," Justin said with a grin. "Our quarterly meetings haven't been nearly this engaging. In fact, we've often wondered why we bother because it isn't long before boredom sets in and everyone's ready to head back home. We've had full days when our managers have sat in the conference room, spending the entire day on their laptops."

That didn't sound like fun at all.

I looked at each man in turn. "Am I doing it wrong? I mean, I'm thinking that this is a huge opportunity to have all of the managers together in one place. They can take the information back to their own teams and share the wealth of knowledge that we supply them with. Aside from renting the convention center rooms and catering in food, we have a lot of the presenters volunteering their time because they want to get in front of you and your teams."

Justin waved his hand. "Oh, no, you're not doing anything wrong. This is just so far off the map of what we're used to...I think it's going to set a precedent."

I smiled. "I've tried to put myself in their shoes. If I had to travel for business for a four-day conference, I wouldn't look forward to spending time in my hotel room or having dinner alone or not having the opportunity to get in front of my boss."

"You're going about this the right way," Landon assured me. "The simple fact that you're engaging the managers ahead of time adds a sense of responsibility on their part. They get to contribute." He grinned. "I'm looking forward to it."

"Thank you." I was looking forward to it, too. "And I'm going to nix the few ideas you didn't like," I told the four of them. "I'll come up with a few additional options and get your input. I won't be able to wait until next Monday since that'll only give me a week. But I will present them as soon as I have a solid plan. Does that work?"

"It does," Justin replied. "Now moving on to this week's travel."

While the four of them discussed the trips they had planned for the week, I couldn't help smiling to myself. It felt good that they liked what I was doing and that they weren't afraid to tell me as much. After our extracurricular activities had begun, I had briefly wondered if they wouldn't see me for the potential that I had, but merely for the fun I could offer.

It wasn't like that and I was especially grateful. While I wanted to enjoy my bosses, I also wanted to prove my worth in a business sense. The fact that they could keep the two separate, allowing both sides to coexist in the same work environment, helped to ease some of my worry.

"Is there anything else you'd like to go over?" Justin asked, his question directed at no one in particular.

"I'd like to know how Luci feels about how things are going so far," Ben said.

My attention jerked to him as he put me on the spot.

"In what regard?" I asked, wanting to ensure we were talking about the same thing.

His smile brightened up his entire face. "Your interactions with the four of us. Do you feel you're getting enough of our time? Is there something you'd like to do differently?"

I instantly shook my head.

"What is it, little one?" Langston questioned.

It figured he would be the one to pick up on the fact that I wasn't telling the truth.

"Is something bothering you? Something we're doing wrong?" Justin asked as all four men turned their full attention on me.

"No," I blurted. They weren't doing anything wrong. They were just… I sighed. "I just want to ensure that you know that I'm here if you need anything at all."

Landon smirked. "Are you saying you want *more* of our attention?"

My cheeks heated, but I managed to nod. "I guess, yeah. That's what I'm saying."

"We don't want to wear you out," Justin said, his eyes scanning my face.

"You won't." I grinned, my insides trembling. "I'm young. I think I can handle it."

That caused Landon and Langston to chuckle.

"What's so funny?" I asked them directly.

"Be careful what you wish for, pet," Langston said, his tone deep and grumbly.

I didn't respond, but I didn't look away from him either.

"If no one has anything else, then I say we adjourn," Justin stated, moving to the edge of his seat. "And Luci?"

"Hmm?" I looked over at him.

"Do you remember the rules for tomorrow?"

I frowned, trying to think of what he might be referring to.

My eyes widened as I remembered his request from last week.

"I'm to work naked tomorrow," I said, my eyes bouncing from one man to the next.

"All day," Justin confirmed.

"God, I can't wait for tomorrow," Landon said as he got to his feet.

Everyone chuckled and I was left staring after them.

Naked.

While working.

God, I wasn't sure I was ready for tomorrow.

•

A few hours later, I was wondering if I was going to make it through today, let alone be ready for tomorrow.

At two thirty, Justin opened his office door and peered out at me. "Please join me."

I was staring after him as he slipped back into his office. I managed to call Jordan to let him know I'd be away from my desk for a few minutes, then hurried after my boss. When I turned to close the door behind me, he waved me off.

"Leave it open."

I frowned.

He turned to face me. "You mentioned you wanted more attention."

My eyes widened as I stared at him. I managed a nod.

He smiled. "I'm happy to hear that. We've all been holding back. The truth is, I could fuck you a couple of times a day. Every day."

I swallowed hard, my body heating from his words.

"But your health is of the utmost importance to us."

Okay, just when I thought this was going one way, it seemed to be going another.

"However, your request this morning tells me that you're equipped to handle our demands. Is that true?"

"Yes, sir." I couldn't help it, I was trembling. Not from fear but from anticipation. I wasn't sure which way Justin was going with this, but I was hoping it would result in him doing something wicked right here in his office.

He walked around to one of the chairs sitting in front of his desk and he patted the leather. "Come here, princess."

I moved closer, coming to stand directly in front of him. He reached for my hand, then guided it to his cock, which was currently tenting his slacks.

"You feel that?"

"I do," I whispered roughly, unable to look away from his face.

"That's what you do to me. You make me hard. You make me ache. I think about fucking that sweet little pussy all damn day."

My pussy clenched, my body trembling as the need inside me rose.

Justin moved around behind me, then guided me forward.

"Bend over the chair. Let me see that pretty little ass."

Planting my hands on the seat of the chair, I bent over the back of it, leaning forward with my feet still on the ground. Cool air washed over my butt when he lifted my skirt. Warm hands began kneading my ass and I couldn't resist squirming against the pressure, urging him to continue, letting him know I welcomed whatever he had in mind.

"Is this what you need, princess? You need us to order you into our offices so we can bury our cocks in that tight snatch of yours?"

"Yes, sir." I didn't even care how that made me sound. It was exactly what I wanted. I spent so much time wishing and hoping that my inhibitions were long since buried beneath my desperation.

I heard the clink of his belt buckle being freed, then the distinct sound of his zipper being lowered.

"Hold that thought."

I glanced over my shoulder as Justin strolled out of the room. I frowned, confused about what was happening. He returned less than a minute later.

"I brought my pup with me. He's been eager to watch me pound your little pussy again. Isn't that true?"

"Yes, Mr. Parker," Ben confirmed.

"Would you like a taste of her before I begin?"

"I would love to taste her."

Now my legs were trembling as I held myself over the chair, my ass facing the door. I felt the warmth of Ben's hands as he moved behind me. They trailed over my backside, down my thighs when he kneeled on the floor.

"He's got a wicked tongue, don't you think, princess?"

That wicked tongue took a long swipe between my legs, caressing my clit and my entrance.

"Very wicked," I confirmed as I moaned.

"Make that pussy come for me, pup. I want her ready to take my cock."

Ben was relentless in driving me right to the edge. He didn't hold back, tormenting my clit with precise flicks of his tongue. I cried out as I came, my body trembling. Before I could catch my breath, Justin was behind me, driving his cock inside me in a single, punishing thrust. I gripped the armrests of the chair, pushing back against him.

"Tell me you want my cock, princess."

"I want your cock. Please fuck me. Oh, God!" I moaned and whimpered as he gave me exactly what I asked for, exactly what I needed.

His hands gripped my hips as he slammed forward, retreated, then slammed into me again. For a second, I wondered if the chair would give way beneath me considering how hard he was driving into me.

"Oh, fuck, princess," he groaned, his fingers digging into my flesh. "Fuck yes. Squeeze my dick with that tight cunt. Squeeze me."

My inner muscles locked on to him as the waves of another orgasm churned inside me.

"Beg me for my cum, princess."

"Please come inside me, Justin. I need to feel you come."

And when he did, he triggered my release, causing me to cry out his name again and again.

TWENTY-FOUR

I HAD TO ADMIT THAT working in an office naked was not something I'd ever imagined myself doing. However, the following morning when I arrived, I instantly did as Justin instructed. I removed my boots first, placing them under my desk before discarding my sweater and my skirt, then taking off my bra. I'd been diligent about not wearing panties ever since Ben instructed me not to.

Once I was completely naked, I made quick work of getting the coffee started, then took a seat at my desk. It wasn't quite so bad when I was sitting down. It shielded most of my private parts. Sure, my breasts were exposed, but that wasn't too bad. I mean, there were topless beaches and all. Plenty of women walked around without shirts on. Granted, they probably didn't do it at work. Well, unless they were strippers, but that was a different story altogether.

Still, it took some effort to get used to. I didn't wander around my apartment naked, so it was definitely a new experience for me. The fact that someone was going to see me…well, that was titillating. I guess that officially made me an exhibitionist?

"Good morning, Luci," Ben greeted.

My head jerked up in surprise. I hadn't heard him coming and my nipples instantly hardened as his gaze raked over me approvingly.

"Good morning, sir."

He opened his office door. "When you get a moment, please bring me some coffee."

"Yes, sir."

I waited until he was in his office before I stood. Not like it was really going to matter. I would be naked in front of him in a few minutes, but I was grateful for the extra moment. Then again, my mind drifted back to last week, when I'd been naked and strapped down to Justin's desk. My pussy gushed with enthusiasm. That day had been a particularly good day.

Couldn't forget Thanksgiving either. Definitely a holiday for the record books.

And yesterday...mmm. I could go on and on about yesterday.

Once I added the requisite Sweet 'n Low to Ben's coffee, I carefully picked up the cup and carried it to his office. He was sitting at his desk, so I placed it in front of him.

I was just about to retreat when he said, "Hold on, please."

He finished reading something on his computer before turning to face me. His smile was slow and sensual. "I do like seeing you naked while you work. Mr. Parker's going to be disappointed that he missed this."

I blushed. "Thank you."

He inched his chair closer, his big hands cupping my breasts gently. He squeezed lightly before leaning in and kissing each of my nipples. "I do like your nipples. Small and pink. They'll be very pretty with clamps on them."

My pussy throbbed at the thought, even though I had no experience with nipple clamps. The thought of him using them was quite stimulating.

A soft moan escaped me when Ben leaned in again and sucked my left breast into his mouth, teasing my nipple with his tongue. He then did the same to my right breast before releasing me.

"That's all for now, Luci," he said, his attention turning back to his desk. "And thank you for the coffee."

"You're welcome, sir."

I managed to walk out of his office although my legs were trembling. He had teased me and now my body needed a moment to recover.

"Leave the door open, please," he said.

"Yes, sir."

I returned to my desk and pulled up the calendar. I briefly scanned to see what was on each of their agendas. Landon and Langston had a conference call at ten and then Landon had another at two. Langston had a lunch meeting with one of his team members at one. Ben had two meetings, one at nine thirty and another at three thirty, both in the front conference room. I was sad to see that Justin would be leaving town at noon and not returning until sometime on Thursday.

After calling to confirm that Justin's hotel room was taken care of, I ended up taking several calls before Landon and Langston arrived a few minutes before ten. As soon as I hung up, I called Landon's phone.

"Yes, Luci?"

"Would you like coffee, sir?"

"I would like you to come ask me in person," he said, then disconnected the call.

I should've known they wouldn't let me get away with staying behind my desk all day. I hesitantly got to my feet, then walked to Landon's office, well aware of the way Ben watched from his desk. I could also feel the warmth of the sun shining in through the window and I knew my nakedness was highlighted for the men in the building across from us. I didn't have the nerve to look to see if anyone was watching. I honestly didn't want to know.

I stopped at Landon's office door. "Would you like some coffee, sir?"

"I would. Thank you."

Figuring I could kill two birds with one stone, I walked to Langston's door. Unfortunately, he was on the phone, so I didn't interrupt. Instead, I returned to the coffeepot and poured the coffee into a mug, then carried it back to Landon's office.

As I set the mug on the desk, Landon opened his desk drawer and pulled something out.

"I bought you something," he said.

My heart fluttered because of the sweet gesture.

He pushed the small box toward me.

I picked it up and admired the gold box with the delicate silver and gold bow. My heartbeat accelerated, the generosity of the action filling me with both comfort and desire. These men had been so good to me since I started and I found that I was looking forward to every second I spent with them.

"Thank you, sir," I whispered.

"Open it," he insisted, smiling up at me.

The last time he'd given me a box like this, it had contained a butt plug. I could only imagine what was inside. I hesitated for another minute, staring back at him. The man was ridiculously handsome. Rugged, sexy. The glasses gave him a studious appeal that made me hot. It was interesting how those glasses made him and Langston look different, although without them they were identical.

I pulled the lid off the small box and peered inside.

There, nestled in white tissue paper, was a small bullet vibrator. Strange that Landon had bought me a vibrator when Langston had stolen mine.

"Please, have a seat," Landon said, motioning toward the chair across from him.

I sat on the edge, still admiring the toy. My body had already heated several degrees as I thought about all the things he might want me to do with this toy. He was obviously creative, having turned our relatively innocent text conversation into a full-blown live masturbation show. I still got hot thinking about it.

"Get comfortable, Luci," Landon said.

As I shifted on the chair, I heard footsteps behind me. I turned to see Langston coming into the room, carrying a cup of coffee.

"Ah. I see you gave her your gift."

"I did. And now, while we take this call, I want her to demonstrate how she uses it."

My eyes widened.

"Fantastic idea." Langston's heated gaze traveled over me as he perched on the corner of Landon's desk. "You cleaned it first, I hope."

"Of course. It's all ready for her."

"Sir?" I asked, looking at Landon and waiting for more instruction.

"I want to watch you play with yourself, Luci." His grin turned wicked. "I've decided to make it a hobby of mine. After the other day…"

Oh, yeah. I remembered.

"But you aren't allowed to come," Langston noted.

I glanced up to see him smirking. He was obviously enjoying this.

Taking the toy out of the tissue paper, I turned it over in my hand a couple of times. I twisted the end, causing it to come to life. The vibration was subtle, which I was grateful for.

With one hand, I started moving the toy toward my clit, but Landon cleared his throat.

"Spread yourself open for us," he instructed. "We want an unobstructed view of that pretty pussy."

My belly fluttered again and my pussy gushed with enthusiasm from his words alone. My hesitance wasn't feigned by any means. This was new, exciting, but nerve-racking at the same time.

"Hold that thought." Langston stood tall and headed for the bathroom, returning with a small hand towel.

He motioned for me to stand, then placed the towel on the chair.

Although his gesture was thoughtful, I was embarrassed by the notion that he was worried I would make a mess on the chair. Granted, he was probably right, but still.

I looked up and realized both men were waiting for me.

"Please hurry," Landon said with a hint of irritation in his voice. "I need to get the call underway."

It took me a second, but I managed to find a comfortable position in the leather chair. I placed my feet flat on the seat, my ankles pressed against my butt, my knees pointed outward. I couldn't be any more on display than that.

It was impossible to look either man in the eye as I placed the toy gently on my clit, not applying too much pressure for fear I would come simply from having them watch me.

"Very nice," Langston said approvingly. "This time, show us how you masturbate with a toy."

Landon put the phone on speaker and dialed the number. After he punched in more numbers, the call finally connected.

"Who just joined the call?" a woman asked.

"This is Landon and Langston Moore."

"Thank you for joining."

Neither man said anything and I wondered if anyone could hear the vibration from the toy. If they could, no one said anything.

"We're going to launch right into our presentation, but first I'll introduce you all to the team," the woman on the other end of the line explained. "There are four of us here, along with the author you represent. Mary? Are you still there?"

"I am, yes."

"Great."

While I continued to tease my clit with the vibrations, I felt my pussy growing wetter. It wasn't helping that Landon and Langston were watching me intently while they listened to the woman on the phone introduce them to the team. From what I could ascertain, they were speaking to a publisher.

I briefly wondered what they would think if they could see into this room. I was fairly certain they wouldn't be droning on and on. Then again, they would likely hang up the phone and not be talking at all. This was far from conventional when it came to conference calls.

As the minutes ticked by and the conversation continued, my body caught fire from the sensual heat the vibrator was causing. Neither man seemed to be in a hurry, and it was evident they were listening in on the call, asking random questions from time to time. All while continuing to watch me.

A few times I had to move the vibrator off my clit, sliding it down to my entrance, then over my labia, trying to stave off my impending orgasm. I could tell they were not going to be happy with me if I came, which was both frustrating and highly erotic. I liked that they were somehow controlling my pleasure, despite the fact that I was the one wielding the vibrator.

Half an hour later, the call disconnected, but then Landon was immediately dialing the phone once more.

When a woman answered, Landon said, "Mary?"

"Yes. I'm here."

"So, what did you think?" Landon probed.

"I like their plan. I think it's good that they'll be working to get visibility of the book prior to the release. They've obviously put a lot of thought and effort into getting the book the most publicity possible."

"I agree," Landon told her. "And we'll be launching our own marketing plan alongside theirs in order to give you double the visibility. I thought it was a good idea to let them lead though. However, keep in mind, we are here for you in anything that you need. Any questions you might have, feel free to call. I'll also be glad to converse with them directly if you need me to."

"I'll do that. And thank you both. This is the first book release that will have this much publicity going into release day."

"Which is a good thing."

"It definitely is," Mary said.

"Oh, and Mary? Have you spoken with our secretary yet?"

"I have not."

"She's here with us. Her name is Luci."

Landon motioned toward me, as though he wanted me to speak. I removed the vibrator, but Langston instantly shook his head.

Pushing it back against my clit, I cleared my throat, terrified that I would moan if I attempted to speak.

"It's nice to meet you, Luci," Mary greeted.

"I...uh..." My body hummed with arousal. "It's nice to meet you, too, Mary," I managed to squeak out.

"Sorry, Mary. She's been working on something else for us, so she's multitasking at the moment."

Mary chuckled. "I completely understand that. I constantly find myself working on one thing while my brain has moved on to something else."

Yeah, well. If only it were that easy.

"I considered it a good presentation," Landon said, his hand hovering over the button to disconnect the call. "If you need anything at all, just let us know."

"I will," Mary reassured them. "Thank you again. And it was nice to meet you, Luci."

"You, too," I forced out breathlessly.

Landon disconnected the call, his heated gaze dropping to where I was still teasing my clit with the vibrator.

"You may stop now," Landon told me.

Stop? They wanted me to stop? A twitch of anger ignited at the thought of spending the rest of the day sexually frustrated. Why would they do that?

Langston got to his feet. "I've got a lunch meeting, but I'll be back in the office later this afternoon."

Landon met my eyes. "This afternoon, I want you to use the vibrator in exactly the same way. Tease yourself for ten minutes, but you are not allowed to come."

"I…uh…" I glanced around the room. "Where would you like me to do this?"

"At your desk," he said matter-of-factly. "Once at one thirty and again at four."

I nodded, responding through clenched teeth. "Yes, sir."

I couldn't believe they were tormenting me like this.

"Thanks for sitting in on that one," Landon told Langston. "I didn't necessarily need you here, but I thought you'd be interested in the topic."

"I was and I am." Langston's fingers brushed over my shoulder before he leaned down and pressed his lips to mine. "I look forward to seeing you this afternoon."

I nodded, my body tense from the sexual frustration. Between Ben's teasing earlier and then me having to tease myself for the past half hour, I was ready to shatter. And it wasn't a good feeling.

Landon's phone rang. He glanced down and then hit the button.

"Could you please send Luci to my office?" Justin asked.

"Absolutely." Landon disconnected the call, then cocked an eyebrow at me.

When I got to my feet, he held out his hand.

I frowned.

"I'll take the vibrator for now. We don't want you to have too much fun, now do we? But feel free to come get it out of my desk as needed."

I swallowed hard but managed to pass the silver bullet over to him. When I turned, he reached for my wrist, then spun me back around. His lips met mine in a sweet kiss that didn't do a damn thing to stave off the frustration taking over my body.

"Remember," he said softly. "One thirty and four. Don't let me find out that you disregarded my direct order."

When he released me, I went right for the door.

This time, as I made my exit, I knew I lacked any sort of grace.

But I couldn't bring myself to care.

TWENTY-FIVE

BY THE TIME FIVE O'CLOCK rolled around and I was gearing up to head home, I was ready to crawl right out of my skin.

Not only had Ben teased me that morning, I had also spent half an hour entertaining Landon and Langston with the vibrator, only to have Justin request me to file a huge stack of paperwork he'd apparently saved up for, like, maybe two years.

Did I mention that the filing cabinets lined the hallway that led out of my office? Well, they did.

And that meant I spent the better part of the afternoon bending over and putting papers into drawers. While I was naked. Oh, and that didn't even count the two times I had masturbated at my desk.

Not only were my private parts on display for Landon, Langston, and Ben while I was filing *and* teasing myself—which they all seemed to really enjoy—but I kept freaking myself out thinking that Jordan was going to come down the hall at any moment and witness my nakedness.

Thankfully, Jordan didn't come down the hall. I only assumed my bosses had a hand in keeping him at the front for the entire day. Needless to say, by the time I was finished filing, I was at my wits' end.

"Luci, I'd like to see you in my office please," Ben called as I was getting ready to pull my clothes out of my desk drawer.

Swallowing hard, I composed myself as best as I could—not an easy feat when naked—then walked into his office.

The sun was already setting low in the sky due to the time of year and I knew for a fact that anyone in the building adjacent to ours could see inside Ben's office. He'd obviously left the blinds open and turned all of the lights on for a reason.

"Yes, sir?" I asked when I stepped into the room.

"Come here, gumdrop," he said softly, patting the top of his desk. "Have a seat."

I was surprised by the pet name he used. It was different, and oddly sweet. I walked over to him and positioned myself on top of his desk when he rolled his chair out of the way.

"Put your feet up here," he instructed, taking my ankles and helping to position my feet on the armrests of his chair.

This, of course, put his head right between my thighs.

My breath caught in my chest when he teased my nipples with his fingertips.

"I've thought about these pretty nipples all day." He met my gaze. "How they'd feel against my tongue when they're hard and aching."

Rather than help alleviate some of the sexual frustration by doing as he mentioned, Ben stopped, then retrieved something out of his desk. When he looked up at me, he was smiling.

Although I genuinely liked these guys, I was starting to hold a grudge. It was one thing to play with me, but to forbid me to climax seemed like unnecessary torture.

"I have something for you."

I wasn't sure I could handle another gift from any of these men. I didn't even have to guess at what he'd gotten me. A second later, he held up a gold chain with clamps on each end.

"Hold your breasts up for me, Luci," he crooned softly.

I drew in a deep breath, then lifted my breasts in my hands. I was once again robbed of air when his warm breath fanned my left nipple. His tongue followed, then he sucked me into his mouth completely, teasing my nipple until it hardened beneath his tongue.

When he pulled back, he focused on connecting the clamp. There was a circular piece that closed around my nipple and he then turned something that tightened it. It hurt. Badly.

"Breathe deeply," he ordered when I hissed. "It's not so much painful as it is uncomfortable."

Apparently, he'd never put clamps on then, because the pain was excruciating, shooting from my nipple out through my scalp.

"Is that too much?"

I nodded. He tightened once more and I was on the verge of tears.

"Breathe, baby," he repeated. "Deep breaths. Don't fight the pain, Luci. Breathe."

I did as he instructed, and a few seconds later, the worst of the pain abated, leaving a dull throb. It wasn't terrible, but it certainly wasn't something I wanted to relive.

Unfortunately, he repeated the same process on my other nipple.

"Very pretty," he said when the nipple clamps were in place. He tugged on the chain that dangled between them and a bolt of heat shot from my nipples to my clit. I had no idea how so much pain could translate into arousal, but somehow it did.

"Now lean back on your hands so I can taste that sweet pussy."

Finally.

I needed relief more than I needed him to remove the clamps.

Ben forced my legs wider and pulled my butt closer to the edge of his desk. His eyes darted from my face to my pussy, then back again. I held my breath in anticipation.

"You cannot come until I say so."

Damn it.

I managed a nod, but an embarrassingly needy moan escaped me when his tongue slid over my clit.

"You taste good, gumdrop." His eyes met mine again. "Do not come."

I wasn't sure why he kept saying that, but a couple of minutes later when I was trembling and on the verge of imploding, I completely understood. The man's mouth was wicked. I remembered the first time he'd eaten me out in the back conference room. Clearly, he'd been holding back that day. He did not hold back now, ruthlessly flicking my clit, then thrusting his tongue into my pussy. I couldn't resist trying to grind against his face all while I prayed I didn't come.

"I could do this all night long," he said, his voice rough with what I hoped was need.

The sight of his dark head between my pale thighs turned me on like nothing else. There was a stark contrast in our skin color, which somehow seemed to heighten the pleasure. Then again, it could've been merely Ben's sex appeal that did it for me. He was a beautiful man.

"Please...oh, God...please," I pleaded as he leisurely tongued my clit.

Ben sat up and smiled. I watched as he stood, as his hands dropped to his trousers. He unbuttoned his pants, then freed his massive cock. And I mean, this thing was ginormous. I couldn't help it, my eyes widened as I took in all of him. The man had a monster cock. It was easily as big as my forearm, probably thicker.

Oh, God.

"I've waited all day for this, Luci," he said, tilting my head up and forcing me to look in his eyes. "Hell, I've waited all *month* for this. I've longed to get my hands on you, to feel that sweet pussy wrapped tightly around my cock."

Holy shit, his words were going to make me come.

"Are you ready to be fucked?"

Despite the intimidation factor of having that monster cock inside me, I nodded. After all, I was primed for explosion, so the thought of him fucking me was a welcome relief.

"Beg me."

"Please, Ben. *Please* fuck me. I need to feel you inside me."

"Mr. Snowden," he corrected. "Call me Mr. Snowden."

I wasn't faking it when I whimpered, "Please, please, *please* fuck me, Mr. Snowden."

That seemed to please him because he helped me down from his desk. Holding my hand, he led me over to the window.

"Put both palms on the glass."

I did as he instructed.

He positioned my feet so that my legs were spread wide, maybe a foot away from the window, and I was leaning forward.

"Put your nipples on the glass."

The window pane was cold against my throbbing nipples. The metal clamps scraped lightly, applying pressure and ultimately intensifying the pain. I didn't like it one bit, but the need to be fucked was too great for me to focus on it.

He leaned in, his lips sliding sensually over my neck. I inhaled deeply, enjoying his delicious scent. It was an intoxicating mixture of cologne and Ben.

I hadn't spent a whole lot of time with him, not compared to the time I'd spent with Landon and Langston, so I was grateful to be with him, to have his attention focused on me. Of the four of them, Ben was the most open, always talking, sharing small details of his life. It made me want to know more about him.

"Stay right there. Don't move."

The heat of his body left me, but I didn't move. Due to the darkness outside, I could see his reflection in the glass. I watched as he walked over to his desk and picked up the phone.

"The show starts now."

My eyes instantly shot to the building directly adjacent to ours and that was when I noticed a room full of men sitting at a conference table. All the chairs turned, eyes focused on me. I looked from one stranger to the next as my breathing ramped up. It wasn't until I saw Landon and Langston that my heart did a double tap in my chest. I didn't understand why it made me hot to know that they were sitting over there watching as Ben fucked me, but it did.

Ben's warm hands returned and he shifted my hips again. I felt his cock as it pressed against my entrance. He slicked himself with my juices before inching his way inside.

"Langston and Mr. Parker were right, you have such a tight little pussy."

I moaned loudly as he filled me. His cock was bigger than any I'd ever had. But it wasn't painful as he slowly slid inside me.

"How does it feel?" he asked, his voice rough.

"So good."

His hands tightened on my hips.

"Now be a good girl and don't move. I'm going to fuck you hard and fast. Feel free to come as many times as you'd like."

Before I could agree, Ben pulled out, then slammed into me.

I threw my head back and cried out as the pleasure jolted my entire body. His cock was so big, so thick I wasn't sure how my pussy could take the intrusion. Although it seemed impossible, it clearly wasn't, because Ben began fucking me harder, bottoming out deep within me.

My breasts were flattened against the glass, the metal clamps sending shards of pain pinging through my insides with every punishing plunge of his cock inside me. It wasn't enough to detract from the overwhelming pleasure though.

Ben hadn't been lying. He fucked me hard and fast. He was brutal with his thrusts, pounding me so roughly my entire body shook and my feet came off the ground. He kept his hands on my hips, not letting me move too far. I had to focus on not slamming my face into the glass, but I didn't care. I'd never been fucked like that before.

Minutes felt like an eternity as I came in a monstrous wave, only to have another orgasm crash into me. It felt like one continuous orgasm, but I knew it couldn't be. No way could my body maintain that level of ecstasy for that long.

"Goddamn, you're so sweet, Luci," Ben roared. "Come for me one more time so I can come all over your beautiful tits."

While he continued to thrust, I dared a look over at the men in the conference room. I met Langston's eyes first, then Landon's, alternately holding their stares. Something inside me broke open, filling me with warmth. There was something about those men that drew me in and held me there. Even while another man was fucking me.

Ben impaled me again and again, and when he shouted for me to come, I did. I don't know how it happened, but my body listened to him. When he spun me around, my knees gave out, but he helped me to the floor. I knelt with my ass against the window while he jerked his giant cock before spurting all over my chest.

I watched his face as he came, and something warm erupted inside me. The look on his face was not of a man who was fucking his secretary. There was something more there, something that melted my heart a little bit. Perhaps it was a connection. I wasn't entirely sure.

When his cock stopped jerking, he slid the backs of his fingers down my cheek, his eyes meeting mine.

"Thank you for this, gumdrop."

"My pleasure," I responded, feeling grateful but having no idea why that was.

"Now come on." He held out his hand and helped me to my feet. "Let's get you washed up before you head home."

And on that note, I got to spend the next half hour being fucked again in the shower in Ben's office. This time without the audience.

TWENTY - SIX

BOSS MEETING

LANGSTON

FOR THE LIFE OF ME, I couldn't stop thinking about watching Ben fucking Luci in his office only two days ago.

Sure, I'd enjoyed it immensely; however, there had been something distinctly possessive that took root as I watched the scene. Probably a good thing I'd been in another building at the time.

Now it was a few minutes after six and I was walking into the restaurant I'd agreed to meet my partners in. Not only did the four of us work together, we were also close friends. Had been for a long time and these dinners were generally our time to relax without the weight of work on us. I usually looked forward to these days, only I wasn't sure relaxed was going to be the atmosphere surrounding us tonight. Considering everything that was taking place in the office, tensions were running a little high. Mine especially.

"I ordered you a drink," my brother informed me when I joined the three of them at a table in the back of the restaurant.

"Thanks." I took my seat. "That call lasted longer than I'd expected."

"Who was it?" Justin inquired, clearly trying to make small talk.

"One of my managers is attempting to onboard an author who's currently riding quite the high from her recent success."

Landon smiled knowingly. "Tough sell, huh?"

That seemed to be the case these days. With the rise of self-publishing, independent authors were making big waves and their success was great. As with the traditional publishers, publicists were having to go the distance in proving that they still had a lot to offer. We were no exception. However, we *did* have a lot to offer. For those who wanted to get their names out past Facebook, it required an industry professional who knew something about reaching readers. That was my life.

The waitress delivered our drinks and I grabbed the glass and took a sip. "I'd prefer not to discuss it."

I tried not to take work home with me. I worked a lot of hours as it was. Although I didn't necessarily arrive at the office at the ass-crack of dawn, I did work late into the evenings, most of the time on conference calls or looking over presentations.

Not that I was complaining. Business was good and the money was great, so I had nothing to bitch about.

"How'd Luci seem to you today?" Landon asked me directly.

I gave a brief shrug. "I didn't see much of her. Why?"

He shrugged also.

Ben grinned. "She seemed far less…frustrated than she did on Tuesday. I think we did a number on her."

I grinned as I took another sip of my scotch. We'd purposely worked Luci into a frenzy on Tuesday, and apparently, we'd achieved our goal. It hadn't been with cruel intentions, mind you. We simply wanted to see how far we could push her before she snapped. I was happy to say the woman had far more patience than most people.

"I'm just glad you took the edge off," Justin said to Ben, leaning back in his chair.

"Took the edge off?" Ben chuckled. "I think I did more than that."

Justin grinned, but his attention was on his drink. "I wish I could've been there to see it."

"She was far more relaxed today," Landon noted. "But I think she's expecting more from us."

I couldn't keep from asking, "More how?"

"More attention," Justin supplied. "I don't think she was kidding when she made her request."

"Sexual attention?" I frowned. "More than we've given her this week?"

"Yes."

I glanced at my partners. "I'm more than happy to provide that, but I don't want to hurt her." Nor did I want her to think we were simply in it for sex. Granted, the sex was intensely satisfying, but even I knew we needed to get to know her as we progressed. When it came to Domination and submission, it was far more than sexual. There was an intimacy that would forge a bond. That was my overall objective where Luci was concerned.

Not that I was opposed to riding her hard and often. As it was, I wanted far more than I was getting.

"She's definitely a feisty one," Landon noted with a grin. "I think she's gonna give us all a run for our money."

"She didn't even bat an eyelash when I called her into my office Monday afternoon and fucked her over the back of the chair." Justin grabbed his menu as the waitress arrived.

That was something I didn't want to think long and hard about. I didn't have any claims to the girl, but truthfully, I wanted more of her time, more of her attention. For myself. And my brother.

Several minutes later we had ordered dinner and more drinks were delivered. While my partners talked about…whatever, my mind was elsewhere. On Luci, to be more specific.

I couldn't seem to get her out of my head, which was new for me. I'd been a sexual Dominant since I was old enough to know what it meant. I'd never had an issue with women, never gone without sex unless it was my choice. Yet when I thought about Luci, I wasn't merely thinking about sex.

And that fucking bothered me.

I liked the girl. I liked how fucking hot she was when she came. But I also liked her smile, the way she laughed so easily, and the way she treated people. She was getting under my skin in a way I wasn't comfortable with.

Glancing over at Landon, I wondered what he thought of her. We hadn't had much discussion about Luci. Perhaps that was because we both knew she was more than what we'd originally bargained for. Hell, I'd learned that before we even offered her the office arrangement.

"What's on your mind, Moore?"

Justin's question pulled me from my thoughts.

"Just tryin' to relax," I told him, once again reaching for my drink.

"Or you're plotting what to do with our feisty little secretary tomorrow," Justin countered.

I cocked one eyebrow. "Are you saying it's my turn again?"

He waved me off. "We aren't taking turns."

No, technically, we weren't. We were letting things play out naturally.

Sort of.

I was trying to be cognizant of everyone's time with Luci. I knew myself, knew if I were to unleash on her, I would dominate not only her body but also her time. It was a part of me that I was attempting to keep reined in.

Unfortunately, if instances such as what played out between Ben and Luci on Tuesday night happened too much more, I wasn't sure I would be able to control myself.

And that, I knew, was a recipe for disaster.

TWENTY-SEVEN

THE REMAINDER OF THE WEEK was relatively quiet. With Justin away on business for most of the week and the other three busy handling client issues and concerns, I was able to get everything nailed down for the upcoming quarterly meeting. I was stoked about the opportunity and pleased when my bosses informed me that I would be leading it from beginning to end.

Sure, this was new for me, but not something I wasn't capable of mastering. Although my messy apartment might not show it, I was quite organized, especially when it came to work. I'd spent my time there implementing some structure that would make things easier for everyone. I had rules set up in my inbox, which highlighted emails from my bosses, flagged those that had key words in them so I would look at them first. I had reminders set up so I didn't forget anything.

For those things I couldn't keep on my computer, such as the special requests from my bosses, I set up reminders on my phone. I knew how to be discreet and I was making a concerted effort. So, on Friday afternoon, just a few minutes shy of one o'clock, when I was supposed to go home, I knew when Langston requested me to come into his office that I hadn't forgotten anything.

Ben had already left for the day and Justin was meeting with a local client, so it was just Landon, Langston, and me.

I grabbed my notepad and a pen, then headed for Langston's office. Before I reached the door, Landon was joining me.

"I thought you'd be heading home," Landon said casually as he opened the door for me.

"I was about to," I admitted. "But Langston requested my presence."

Landon's smile was flirty yet devious.

It was obvious he already knew that.

Stepping into Langston's office, I glanced around, not seeing him at first. My gaze came to rest on him lying on one of the sofas. Not in all the time I'd been working there had I ever seen him so relaxed. It was a good look for him, one I wished I could see more of.

"You wanted to see me, sir?"

Langston's eyes tracked me as I moved closer.

"I did." He motioned for me to join him. "Are you finished for the day?"

"Yes, sir. I was about to go home."

"I need one more thing before you go," he said, his eyes locked on my face.

"Anything, sir." My belly fluttered with anticipation. I could see by the wicked gleam in his eyes that they were going to give me a proper send-off for the weekend.

"Put your notepad down," he instructed. "Then remove your shoes, your sweater, and your bra."

I wasn't sure if they knew it or not, but their simple instructions were foreplay for me. The idea of stripping for them, having them watch every move I made caused delicious tingles to stir deep in my core. It didn't seem to matter where we were or what we were doing, I loved the commanding tones of their directives.

Since he didn't request that I remove my skirt, I left it on.

"Now come kneel between my legs."

Langston was lying on the sofa, his head on one cushioned armrest, his feet at the opposite end. He was a ridiculously tall man and he took up the entire length of the sofa.

I crowded onto the cushion between his legs, watching him as I did.

"I want you to demonstrate your impressive oral skills on me," he stated. "And while you do that, Landon's going to fuck you. All three of us must orgasm, but how you get to that outcome will be your choice. You can direct things to your liking."

As I knelt between his legs, watching him speak, I felt both elation and trepidation. I was thrilled about the idea of pleasuring them and being pleasured in return. However, I wasn't all that interested in directing things. I liked that they took control. I enjoyed them guiding me on what they wanted me to do.

"Is there a problem, pet?"

"No, sir," I said, forcing a smile. "I'm just thinking."

"Well, take your time," Langston said, grinning wickedly.

I glanced behind me at Landon. He was standing there, waiting patiently for me to give them direction.

"Would you please take off your shirts?" I said, turning back to Langston as I spoke.

The rustle of fabric was music to my ears as both men removed their dress shirts, laying them neatly on the coffee table.

That was the only request I truly had, but then it dawned on me. They'd given me the opportunity to direct things as I saw fit. And what I wanted was...

"Now, I'd like to hand the control back to both of you," I said sweetly.

Langston seemed quite pleased by the request.

"Very well. Come here and kiss me."

That was an order I could certainly get behind.

Lying over him, my mouth hovering close to his, I felt the temperature in the room increase by several degrees. More so when his big hand ran down my back, over my butt, then beneath my skirt.

Pressing my lips to Langston's, I moaned when he squeezed my ass, his erection pressing right between my legs where I needed him most.

I loved kissing this man. He wasn't a sloppy kisser by any means and that turned me on the most. Although he had told me to kiss him, there was no doubt who was in charge. While our tongues dueled, he ground his erection between my legs, making me moan and writhe against him. And when we both pulled back for air, he nodded toward his erection.

"Free my cock, little one. Let me feel those soft hands on my dick."

I shifted back, once again kneeling between his legs. While I worked to unbuckle and unbutton him, I felt Landon's hands on my ass, pushing my skirt up.

"Lean forward, sweet girl. I wanna see that pretty pussy."

I did as he instructed. And since I was kneeling and bent over, I knew he had a perfect view. I was already wet and desperate for them.

Once I had Langston's steely cock released from his pants, I stroked him slowly, looking up to him for guidance.

"Show me what you've learned about deep-throating. And remember, be careful because Landon might not be gentle. It's been a while for both of us."

Oh, God. A pulse of desire started between my legs and radiated out through my limbs. His words alone were enough to make me feel the pressing urge for release.

There was a stinging slap on my ass and I jumped, giggling.

"I hope you're ready, sweet girl. Because this pussy belongs to me now," Landon said, his tone rough with lust.

"I'm ready," I assured him as I leaned forward and began teasing Langston's cock with my tongue.

I worked him over for a few minutes, slicking him with my lips and tongue while I used my hands to knead his balls. It wasn't until I fully engulfed him in my mouth that I felt Landon's cock press into me. He had one knee on the sofa, his thigh pressed up against mine as he pushed the wide head inside me.

Moaning, I continued to use my mouth to pleasure Langston.

I realized I was holding back when Langston's hand was in my hair and he was forcing himself deeper. I hadn't meant to. I was merely savoring this moment, enjoying the time I had with both of them.

"Show me," he commanded. "I want to see how deep you can take me."

It wasn't easy to focus with Landon gently rocking his hips forward, fucking me in a rhythmic motion that had my pussy clutching him, desperate for more. I could tell he wasn't trying to push me over the edge.

The hand in my hair tightened. "Focus, pet. Your full attention should be on my cock. I'm the one who gave you instruction."

Curling my hand around the base of his cock, I took him into my mouth. My attention remained riveted on him and I fought to ignore the sweet friction of Landon fucking me from behind.

"All the way," Langston directed, guiding my head down as his cock pushed into my throat.

I gagged and pulled back.

"Luci?"

Wiping the slobber from my mouth, I lifted my head and met his gaze.

"Show me what that sweet mouth of yours can do."

I nodded, then took a deep breath.

A few seconds later, I was doing as he requested, focused on pleasuring him and only him. I forced everything else out of my head except taking him all the way into my throat. I breathed through my nose and worked my lips around his wide shaft. It didn't take long before he was guiding me up and down, pulling his cock head from my throat and pushing it back in. Over and over, he fucked my mouth and I was lost to the sensations.

While Landon fucked me from behind and Langston impaled my throat, I let their momentum guide me. Their combined grunts and groans echoed in the room, making my body tingle. I was high on them, loving every second of what they were doing. They were using my body, but I wanted it as much as they did and I think they knew that.

"Your mouth…" Langston groaned. "So fucking sweet. Just like that, Luci. Take all of me."

Langston's gruff words seemed to spur all of us on. Landon's hips began to slam into me, driving his cock deeper as I concentrated on taking Langston's thick length to the back of my throat and holding it there.

Suddenly, there were firm hands on my hips and on my head as both men fucked me. One in my mouth, the other in my pussy. Langston's cock was no longer thrusting into my throat but merely tunneling in and out of my mouth.

"I'm gonna come," Langston growled. "Swallow, Luci."

I moaned my affirmation and was rewarded as his cock began twitching and jerking. I swallowed every drop and only did I release him when he pulled free of my mouth.

"Stay just like that," he commanded, his hands circling around my wrists as I held myself up. "I want to watch you come."

I let my head drop back as Landon slammed into me over and over, his fingertips digging into my flesh as he grunted and growled. His sounds were so damn sexy I couldn't hold back. I was catapulted to the edge of release when Langston cupped my face with his hand and he forced me to look him in the eye.

"So *fucking* beautiful," he whispered reverently.

I came, never looking away, my insides coiling tighter and tighter, pushing me into another orgasm as Landon brutally slammed into me, holding my hips against him as he came in a feverish rush.

With my body wrung out completely, I collapsed onto Langston, my eyes closing as his hands curled around my head, holding me gently, sweetly.

It was then that I knew these two men were going to own me.

And not just my body but also my heart and soul.

TWENTY-EIGHT

I SPENT ALL OF SATURDAY resting after the intense fucking Landon and Langston had given me. I even skipped yoga, because my body was sore in ways I'd never experienced before. Admittedly, I loved it. Knowing that they had wanted me like that did something strange to my insides. In fact, knowing that all four of those men were centrally focused on me was a boost to my ego that I would've never expected.

However, I knew I couldn't spend all my time waiting for them to make their next move. Although I'd been working for them for two months now, I knew the weekends were my own. For the most part, they only made their demands during the workday; therefore, as long as I remained within the parameters of the agreement—no sex with anyone other than them—I could do as I pleased.

As much as I wanted to hang out with Kristen, to tell her everything that was going on, I decided to wait a little while longer. When she called to invite me to lunch on Sunday, I lied and said I had other plans. She said she understood, but then I felt guilty for not being truthful.

Which was how I found myself having breakfast with my mother and stepfather on Sunday morning. It alleviated the guilt and made my initial lie the truth. Although I would've preferred to have lunch with Kristen, I actually missed my mother. We had been avoiding each other for too long as it was. Although our relationship was strained and I often felt as though I owed her nothing, I had diligently paid her back for the clothing with my second paycheck. She had seemed somewhat surprised, but she didn't question me.

In fact, she never questioned me. Nor did she call to check up on me. The only time I received calls or texts from her was when she wanted to let me know she was leaving town on the rare occasions that she did.

If it were up to her, my mother and I would only see each other on birthdays. Well, on her birthday, since she didn't make much of an effort for mine. Like I said, she wasn't the most nurturing woman in the world and the way she belittled me wasn't something I looked forward to. When I was younger, she called it tough love. Now, it felt more like disdain.

But she was still my mother and I loved her, no matter how much she pushed me away. I tried to pretend otherwise most of the time, but the truth was, I did miss her. So, I had to give in sometime and it was usually easier to deal with her when my stepfather was there. Since today was one of his rare days off, I jumped at the opportunity.

"You look good, Luci," my stepfather said when I joined them at the kitchen table. "You look happy."

"I am," I admitted, taking my seat and placing the mimosa in front of me. I couldn't spend much time with my mother without a little alcohol to dull my senses.

My mother passed me an empty plate.

"I take it the new job's going well?" My stepfather moved a plate of pancakes toward me.

Jim Wagner had been married to my mother since I was five years old, and since my father had died, he adopted me when I was six because he wanted to ensure that I was legally taken care of in the event it was necessary. I don't remember my life without him, and for all intents and purposes, he was my father. I didn't refer to him that way although I shared his last name, but I think he knew deep down that I loved him as though he was my biological parent.

However, he had always made it well known that he supported my mother in every way. Since she chose not to be close to me, he respected her wishes. It bothered me more than it should, but I'd acclimated to their lack of family values as I got older. It was one of the reasons I kept most people at arm's length, choosing not to get too close for fear they would simply push me away.

"It is," I answered. "Really well. I'm getting ramped up and they're having me do more things."

"Have you made any friends at the office?" my mother probed, looking at me from beneath her lashes.

I nodded. "Jordan and I usually go to lunch together every day. There's a small sandwich shop downstairs."

"Jordan?" My mother continued to cut her pancakes, only her eyes lifting to look my way. "Is this a man or a woman?"

Leave it to my mother to care about that specific detail. "Man."

Her eyes narrowed, but she didn't say anything. I hadn't expected her to. My mother did not believe that men and women could merely be friends. I didn't bother to tell her that Jordan was gay and that he was happily in a relationship. She wouldn't believe me.

"So, what is it that you're doing there?" my stepfather inquired, taking a sip of his orange juice. "It's a public relations firm, correct?"

"It is," I said with a nod. "They have me answering phones, filing, scheduling appointments, hosting meetings. That sort of thing. I get to interact with their team members, who are all remote and work all over the world."

I could feel my face heat as I thought about all the other things I was doing, but I wasn't about to share that information with anyone, let alone my parents.

"Well, as long as you're happy, that's all that matters," Jim added, his eyes darting over to my mother briefly before he turned his attention back to his plate.

"She could be making significantly more money," my mother said, her gaze lifting to me. "After all, that degree didn't come cheap."

I put all of my attention into eating, pretending not to hear the contempt in her tone. This was the breakfast segment I was familiar with, the one that I dreaded.

And the very reason I tended to keep as much distance between us as I could. I needed to remember these moments when I started missing her. No matter how much I wished otherwise, I seriously doubted there was any salvaging things with her.

•

By the time I got back to my apartment, it was four o'clock. I had spent the remainder of the morning listening to my mother's numerous concerns with my inability to keep a job. She insisted that it was because I should've followed the accounting route. According to her, if I had, I would've been better off.

Financially, maybe. However, I certainly couldn't complain. Since my car was paid for, the only thing I had to pay was rent and utilities, as well as the few other things that came with being a single woman. Cell phone, groceries, yoga, the occasional girls' night out. And of course, my routine trips to the spa. I was happy to say that I was finally back on my feet, no longer worried about how I'd pay my bills. Sure, I was still living paycheck to paycheck, but I had some money left over. It was freeing to say the least.

My mother believed that being able to live comfortably meant having a hefty savings account.

Sure, she had a lot more life experience than I did, and I was sure I'd eventually agree, but at this point in my life, I did not. Not that that ever stopped her from telling me exactly how she felt.

So, after listening to that, I managed to extricate myself from her grasp and opted to stop for a mani-pedi, needing something to relax me. It worked, and with a coat of Raspberry Red Bourbon on my fingernails and toenails, I headed back to my apartment.

After stepping off the elevator, I was digging in my purse to find my key when I heard someone clear their throat. I jumped, startled. My gaze shot up and that was when I noticed the sexy man standing in the hallway, just outside my door.

"Langston." His name came out in a breathless whisper.

"Little one," he greeted with a smile.

He pushed off the wall, tucked his phone into his pocket, then took a step closer.

I wasn't used to seeing him in anything but a suit. So to see him wearing a white long-sleeved Henley with Wranglers and boots had me doing a double take. Although I absolutely loved seeing him in a suit, this was a very good look for him.

As I ogled him, I seemed to be rooted to the spot, unable to move. Even when his warm hand cupped my cheek and he leaned down and pressed his lips to mine.

I sighed.

"This is…a surprise," I whispered when he pulled back.

"Good surprise or bad?"

"Definitely good." I still hadn't moved. "Why're you here?"

I could see the confusion on his face before he offered a small smile. "I couldn't stay away."

Swoon!

"Invite me in, little one."

I jerked, as though kicked into motion. "Right. Let's go inside."

I had no clue what we were going to do once we got in there, but hey, I definitely wasn't interested in doing anything in the hallway. As it was, Mrs. Idlemann had attempted to engage me in conversation on multiple occasions, wanting to know more about the handsome twins I was keeping company with. Her words. I definitely didn't need to add any more fuel to that fire.

After putting my purse down, I offered Langston a drink. He accepted and I managed to scrounge up a bottle of scotch that I'd hidden in the top cabinet. I used to have friends who would raid my liquor cabinet on the rare occasions they came over, and I had learned early on only to keep the cheap stuff within their grasp and it was something I'd never changed. I didn't drink it, but I tried to keep a few varieties on hand.

I poured his drink, grabbed a bottle of water for myself, then joined him in the living room.

Before I sat down, Langston grabbed my hand, then tugged me closer. I stopped directly in front of him. His free hand slid over my ass, then the back of my thigh. His hazel eyes remained on my face while his hand squeezed and teased me through my yoga pants. I could tell he was battling something in his head, so I didn't move.

"Remove your clothes, Luci."

I swallowed hard, my body already trembling with the tremendous need to please him. When I started to move, he tugged on my wrist.

"Right here. So I can watch."

The rich, deep baritone of his voice was so sexy it made my insides quiver. And the way he watched me—as though he liked what he saw—gave me the courage to continue.

Once I was naked, he patted the spot beside him.

"You're stunning no matter how you look at it, but I prefer you naked," he informed me, his finger trailing over the top of my thigh.

Again, his words warmed me.

I still had no clue why he was there. Well, unless it was for sex. That seemed like a logical conclusion, but it proved to be incorrect when he said, "What do you normally do on a Sunday afternoon?"

I shrugged. "Most of the time I go to a yoga class, then grab an early dinner. That or I veg on the couch and watch movies."

"And your plans for this evening?"

"Movies," I said with a grin.

"Sounds like a great time to me."

Langston settled back into the couch while I got up and found the remote. I could feel his eyes on me as I moved around the room.

I clicked on the TV and returned to the couch.

Langston pulled me against him as I flipped through the channels. We ended up watching *The Transporter* followed by *The Fast and the Furious*. My guest didn't say anything throughout either movie, just remained on the couch with me curled up against him. He seemed quite content just to sit there, his arm around me, my hand resting on his chiseled chest.

It was quite possibly the best Sunday I'd had in a long time.

Unfortunately, day turned to night and I was greatly disappointed when Langston got up to go. I thought for sure he would want sex, but again, I was foolish in my thinking. He kissed me—a long, deep kiss that made my body buzz with arousal—then told me he looked forward to seeing me in the morning before he slipped out of my apartment.

The whole interaction left me reeling. He'd insisted that I was naked, but not once had he touched me sexually. His actions made my head spin as I tried to rationalize why he wouldn't want me after all that.

Needless to say, I was in desperate need of my vibrator.

I went right to my bedroom and yanked open the nightstand drawer only to find it empty. I remembered then that Langston had stolen my vibrator that first night he and Landon had come over. He'd said I wasn't allowed to masturbate.

"Shit."

I was in the process of considering taking a bath and taking advantage of the water sprayer when my phone buzzed. It was a text message.

Langston: If you even think about masturbating, I will put you over my knee in front of the entire office.

Damn it.

This so wasn't fair.

TWENTY-NINE

ON MONDAY MORNING, I ARRIVED at the office at seven thirty-five. Jordan was already there, which didn't surprise me. I was running a few minutes late. The smile he greeted me with was nice, so I assumed he didn't hold it against me. Usually I was the first person there these days and walking in was fairly lonely.

"Good morning, gorgeous!" he said cheerfully.

"Hi."

"You look...stressed," he noted with a frown.

I *was* stressed. Well, more like sexually frustrated, but whatever. It was weird to think that Langston's visit could've worked me up that much considering he hadn't really touched me, but still. That was where my head was.

"You wanna grab lunch today? My treat."

I instantly shook my head. "Probably not. I've got so much to do. But tomorrow? *My* treat."

"You're on, sista."

Feeling slightly better, I headed for my desk. I didn't like having to turn Jordan down, but since I had no idea how the Monday meeting would go, it wasn't like I could really make plans. I mean, if any or all of my bosses had their wicked way with me, I wouldn't be in any shape to sit down for lunch.

When I got to my desk, I put down my purse and started the coffee. This had become second nature to me. I logged on to my computer, then skimmed my email to see if anyone had sent me anything over the weekend.

I immediately noticed an email from Landon. It was short and sweet, telling me I needed to look in the top drawer of my desk.

Hesitantly, I opened the drawer and found an envelope with my name scrolled across the front. I opened it and pulled out a note.

Good morning, sweet girl.

We're looking forward to this morning's meeting. Although we won't be in the office until shortly before it starts, there are a few things we would like for you to do to get ready for the meeting.

1.   Go to the back conference room promptly at 9:45.
2.   Leave the blinds closed.
3.   Remove all of your clothing and lay it neatly on the counter.
4.   Put on all of the items that you will find in the top drawer of the coffee station.
5.   Once you've properly adorned yourself, lie on the table and secure yourself to the cuffs you will find there. Both legs and both wrists.
6.   Wait patiently for our arrival.

By the time I had finished reading the instructions, my heart was beating erratically.

One thing became crystal clear though. Obviously, they'd had a reason in mind when they chose that particular table for that room. It was low to the ground, which meant, should I be laid out on it, I would be at the perfect height for them to...watch me? Touch me? Who knew.

There was a smile on my face that I couldn't hide, but there was also a tremor that raced just under my skin. I could easily get behind just about anything they instructed me to do, but the idea of securing myself to the table...

I wasn't sure that was something I could follow through with. It meant that I would be completely alone and unable to free myself. What if they didn't show up? How was I going to get out of there? Would I have to wait until Jordan found me? Or maybe the cleaning staff?

Holy shit. I could imagine the horror of having someone find me naked and restrained to the table.

Thinking about it didn't help, so I decided to focus on my email. Luckily there were several that needed to be addressed. I got to work.

•

At 9:44, I got to my feet and took a deep breath. I focused on my task, carrying the note from Landon with me so that I didn't forget anything they'd asked me to do.

Once I was in the conference room, I followed the instructions to the letter. I left the blinds closed, removed all of my clothing, and set it in a pile on the counter. Then I moved over to the coffee station. For a brief second, I wondered if I was supposed to start the coffee as I normally did. Figuring it couldn't hurt, I hopped to the task, then opened the top drawer and pulled out a gold box. It was slightly larger than the ones Landon had previously given me.

Swallowing hard, I removed the lid and smiled when I saw the first item inside.

The nipple clamps Ben had used on me were included. Attached to them was a small note. *Put these on yourself, and make sure they aren't too tight, but not too loose either. I will be checking your work.*

Great.

I pulled them out and set them on the counter before glancing down again. There was a pink vibrator contraption. The note attached read: *This is known as a Venus Butterfly. The vibrator should be positioned directly over your clit. Put this on.*

I didn't know who was responsible for that one, and I didn't have time to figure it out. I set that down beside the nipple clamps.

There was no mistaking the next item that I located. It was clearly the silicone butt plug that Landon had ordered me to wear the night of our date, and my heart skipped a beat at the idea of inserting that inside myself again. I glanced at the note: *I can't tell you how much I enjoy seeing you wear this.*

The last item was...

My heart slammed against my sternum when I noticed the ball gag. Admittedly, of all four of the items, that was the one I was dreading the most. More so than even the butt plug. If you'd ever had your mouth stuffed full of something—for example, at the dentist—then you knew that it caused unusual amounts of drooling. I was not looking forward to that.

A quick look at the clock told me I only had a couple of minutes before the meeting officially began, so I got to work, quickly donning all the items. The butt plug took the longest time to insert, and for a few seconds, I didn't think I was going to be able to do it. Somehow, I managed to ignore my shame and put it inside me. Just like the first time, the damn thing wasn't comfortable in the least.

The nipple clamps were challenging, but I managed to accomplish the goal. The butterfly vibrator was pretty self-explanatory, so I put it on, securing it with the straps that held it around my waist and my legs.

I then grabbed the ball gag and headed for the table.

"Here goes nothing."

●

I had no idea how long I lay there, secured to the table and wearing a multitude of sex toys, but it couldn't have been too long.

All four men arrived at the same time.

Langston was the first to approach, his gaze assessing me as it slowly inched over me.

"Straighten your spine," he instructed.

I did.

"Being laid out like that is for our pleasure, little one. It's your duty to ensure you present yourself in the most pleasing, graceful manner. Adjust yourself accordingly."

Heat infused me as a sense of shame washed over me. I had inadvertently thought that, simply by lying on the table as instructed, I would please them. To hear the discord in Langston's tone told me I was incorrect in my thinking.

Wanting to please them, I adjusted my position, thrusting my breasts out and straightening my limbs. I tried to picture what I looked like, desperate to prove to them that I wanted this as much as they did.

"Very nice," Langston said with approval.

A second later, I heard more footsteps moving closer.

"Oh, fuck, that's pretty," Justin growled softly when my other bosses came over to stand beside me.

My eyes met each man's in turn and I could see a tremendous amount of heat in each of their gazes. I wouldn't say that it diminished all of my humiliation, but it helped.

"And our little plaything made coffee," Ben noted. "She's definitely a keeper."

While I lay there, waiting for someone to do something, I watched as the four of them retreated to the coffee station. They mumbled softly to one another as they got their drinks prepared. All the while my body heated.

The restraints made it nearly impossible for me to do anything at all. The leg cuffs were attached to the table legs that faced the door. Putting them on hadn't been difficult, but I'd immediately noticed that they left me completely exposed to anyone who came in, my legs spread wide, my knees bent, feet flat on the floor.

The cuffs for my arms were attached to the opposite legs. They had slightly more give than the leg cuffs, which had allowed me to put them both on myself, although freeing myself would be impossible. It allowed very little movement and I wasn't able to sit up. Due to the fact that they had locked on to my ankles and wrists, even if I could get my hands to work together, I wasn't able to free myself without a key. I could admit, that had been the terrifying part.

"Let's see how well you know each of us, little one," Landon said when he appeared above me. "Look directly at the man you believe is responsible when I name the toy."

I nodded my head in understanding, the ball gag hindering my ability to speak.

"The nipple clamps."

My eyes cut to Ben.

"That one was easy," Ben said, grinning. He leaned down and tugged on one side, then the other. "Impressive, young lady. I'm proud of you for doing as I asked."

"Okay, maybe this one'll be a little harder," Landon continued. "The butt plug?"

I heard the sarcasm in his tone. He knew I was well aware of who that one came from.

I kept my eyes locked with Landon's.

"Aww, my sweet. You do know me well, don't you?" His smile was wicked. "I do love that little ass of yours."

Heat coursed through me at his words.

"Okay, how about the clit vibrator. Who do you think is responsible for that one?"

I'd been giving each of the items some thought while I'd been immobilized and I could only come up with one person for that one. The only way I'd come to a conclusion was by reasonable deduction. Since I figured Justin was responsible for the ball gag, the clit vibrator had to have been...

I looked at Langston.

His eyes smiled back at me, but he didn't speak.

"Very good, sweet girl," Landon praised.

"And that means the ball gag came from...?"

I looked at Justin. His blue eyes practically scorched me with their intensity.

"Unfortunately, the gag's gonna have to go," Landon noted, glancing over at Justin. "She can't be an active participant in the meeting with it on."

"Such a shame," Justin said, but he went to his knees beside me and gently removed it.

I was eternally grateful when he wiped the drool from my mouth before leaning down and kissing me tenderly.

The four men took their seats in the chairs that circled the table. They obviously intended to leave me where I was. Fortunately, it wasn't terribly uncomfortable, despite the hard surface.

"Remember," Langston stated firmly. "For our pleasure, not your own. Keep that in mind at all times."

I nodded, then mentally reviewed my position, ensuring the lines of my body were long and even. I wanted them to enjoy looking at me.

"So, let's go through what took place last week," Justin said, kicking off the meeting.

Each man took a turn going through his list of clients he'd interacted with. They talked as though I wasn't even there, which was oddly arousing in its own strange way. I could feel their eyes roam over me from time to time, but for the most part, they simply ignored me.

At least until they wanted to discuss the quarterly meeting, which would take place next week. Talking about work while being naked and restrained to a table was the most awkward situation I'd ever found myself in. However, I did a decent job on my talking points. They seemed pleased by the update.

"What's next on the agenda?" Justin asked as he jotted something down in his notebook.

"I'd like to hear about the individual interactions with our lovely secretary," Ben suggested.

"You want to start?" Justin asked Ben.

"I will. Last Tuesday was the highlight of my week. Having the opportunity to observe our sweet secretary as she moved about completely naked was quite a treat."

"Agreed," Langston said, his voice rough. "Definitely a treat."

THIRTY

I WAS GETTING RATHER USED to lying on the table, listening to them speak, when I felt a sudden vibration against my clit. It started slowly, but then quickly spiked. Since I hadn't turned it on, it had to be controlled by a remote.

A startled groan escaped me as my back bowed.

"Be mindful of your position, pretty girl," Langston insisted. "This is a common request from a Dom."

Dom? Who said anything about a Dom? Was Langston referring to them? Were they my Doms? Sure, I'd read plenty of books at that point, but they were romantic fiction. Did that mean he wanted me to be a submissive?

Those were questions I would have to ask at a later date, because all four of them were watching me closely, apparently waiting for me to respond. Remaining in an attractive position for their viewing pleasure wasn't easy. The fact that the vibrator was resting directly on my clit, causing the tiny bundle of nerves to sing out with delight, made it nearly impossible. It meant I was required to block out the sensation in order to focus on my position.

Not an easy thing to do.

"You are not allowed to come until I say so," Langston commanded, his tone dripping with authority.

I was trying to figure out how I was going to manage that when the vibration suddenly shut off completely. I was breathing hard, my chest heaving as the sensations slowly faded.

"You're an evil man, Langston," Ben told him, laughing.

"I'd like to see Luci working naked on a regular basis," Langston said, picking up the conversation as though nothing had happened.

"Once a week?" Justin asked, genuinely interested in the idea.

"Once or twice. I'm not picky."

Justin continued to write.

"I had the pleasure of watching her masturbate while I was on a conference call," Landon informed them. "Highly impressed with her ability to participate in the call while playing with her pretty pussy."

My pussy gushed at the praise and the nipple clamps tightened more as my nipples pebbled. And just as suddenly, the butterfly came to life over my clit, making me squeal in satisfaction as it rocketed me to near orgasm. I expected it to shut off immediately, but it didn't. I was moaning, writhing against the onslaught as I fought off the release that was threatening to shatter me.

"Position," Langston reminded me.

With my chest heaving, I swallowed hard, once again paying attention to how I was displayed while the vibrator ratcheted up my arousal inch by excruciating inch.

"Not yet, little one," Langston said, smiling at me. It was a wicked smirk and I knew he was enjoying himself.

The vibration instantly shut off.

"I enjoyed that one as well." Langston then glanced over at Ben. "However, I have to admit that the show was damn intriguing. I know our accounting team won't be expecting a Christmas gift after that."

Heat swamped me as I remembered the men watching as Ben fucked me against the window. My pussy throbbed with the need to be filled.

"I'm sorry I had to miss the show," Justin said, his eyes slowly caressing my body.

"Well, I'm happy to say that her deep-throat skills have improved significantly," Langston stated. He could've been talking about the weather for as little inflection was in his voice.

"I'll have to check that out," Justin noted. "And I'm eagerly awaiting my client's arrival to show us the new toy." He glanced at his phone. "According to the calendar, that'll take place on Wednesday at one thirty."

I'd forgotten all about that, although I was the one who'd scheduled the meeting.

The vibrations started again. Rather than spike to high speed, they maintained a low, steady hum. I wasn't sure which was worse, the constant tingling on my clit that had my blood heating to a simmer or the full boil that would eventually take place.

"We do need to keep in mind that Jordan has asked for Thursday off," Landon stated, seemingly ignoring my whimpers as my clit was stimulated to the point of near insanity. "That means Luci'll be responsible for answering the phones that day. Either playtime will be limited or someone will have to come up with a creative idea."

"It might be a good thing," Ben said. "She may need the break."

"How do you feel about that, princess?" Justin asked, his eyes locking on my face. "Are you still requesting more time with us? Or have we pushed your limits?"

My voice trembled when I spoke. "More time. Please."

"Like I said, she's a feisty one," Landon said, his tone reflecting his approval of the situation.

"That she is," Langston noted, glancing over at Justin. "I expect this'll be a hands-on demonstration with your client."

"That's the plan," Justin confirmed.

"How do you feel about that, Luci? Are you a willing participant?" Langston was once again looking at me for a response.

"I am"—I moaned as the vibration kicked up a notch—"very willing."

"Glad to hear it."

"Anyone have anything else?" Landon asked.

There was a chorus of responses, all basically stating that they had nothing else.

"I only have one more item on *my* list," Justin declared, glancing down at his notepad.

"What's that?" Langston asked as the rest of us watched Justin.

"I'd like my pup to get a few minutes of Luci's time. I think it would be a waste not to enjoy her while she's laid out so sweetly."

"What did you have in mind?"

Yeah, what Langston said.

"Ben has a meeting at eleven thirty, so if no one has any objections, I'd like for him to sample her oral skills."

"I'm fine with that," Landon said, waving his hand at me as though encouraging Ben to continue.

Ben walked around to the opposite side of the table as he unbuttoned his slacks and freed his monstrous cock. My mouth watered with the desire to taste him.

"Be careful with her, Snowden," Landon warned, chuckling. "She's just a tiny little thing."

Ben smiled down at me from his position above my head. "Always."

He gently moved me so that my head was hanging off the edge of the table, which put my face upside down. Different, sure. I instantly knew what he was going to do as he dropped to his knees and brushed his cock against my lips.

I continued to hear Langston's warnings in my head, reminding me to focus on my position.

"I want to feel that sweet mouth on me. I've thought about it all weekend." Ben tapped my chin. "Open wide."

My neck ached thanks to the angle, but I managed to open my mouth wide as he pushed the thick head inside. I ignored the pain and focused solely on pleasuring Ben as best I could. I didn't have any control because of the restraints, which left him with free reign over his strokes. He surprised me with how gentle he was, slowly fucking my mouth, but not being aggressive about it.

While he pumped his hips, his hands trailed over my chest, then slid to my nipples. He tugged on the chain that connected the clamps and I moaned, the pain heightening my arousal. Then the vibrator came to life and I was humming, trying to hold back. I felt like a total slut having my mouth fucked and my body on display for my bosses, but I couldn't hide the fact that it turned me on.

I felt Ben's hands shift to my neck, but he didn't apply pressure. Not enough to cut off my airflow anyway. He simply massaged my neck in time with his thrusts.

"I like watching my dick go down your throat. Open wider."

I tried, but it wasn't working.

"Come on, gumdrop. You can do it."

My lips stretched painfully wide as they wrapped around his thick shaft. He was too big, but that didn't stop Ben from pushing in deeper, his cock shocking me as the head brushed the back of my throat. It took a tremendous amount of focus to keep from gagging, but I somehow managed. Tears streamed from my eyes as he lightly fucked my throat. I was on the verge of panic when he pulled out of my mouth, then fixed my position so that my head was once again on the table.

"Turn up the vibration," Ben ordered.

The butterfly intensified.

"Come for us, gumdrop."

Yeah. It didn't take long.

My back bowed off the table and I cried out as my orgasm erupted, sending shockwaves of pleasure coursing through me.

Ben leaned down and kissed me. "Thank you, gumdrop. That's enough for now. But I'd like you to come see me this afternoon when you have a few minutes. I'd like to return the favor."

I nodded, still gasping. I managed a breathy, "Yes, sir."

He kissed me again, then got to his feet and fixed his pants.

I heard Ben leave as Justin was getting to his feet. "As much as I'd like to play for a bit, I have some things to take care of. But I promise, princess, I'll be checking in with you quite frequently this week."

"I'm looking forward to it, sir," I whispered.

Justin leaned down and tugged on the chain attached to the nipple clamps. I groaned as pain shot through my nipples and went straight to my clit.

That was when I realized the vibration had stopped.

"I'm sorry, but I also have to go. I've got a call I need to prepare for," Landon said.

He leaned down and kissed me tenderly before leaving the room.

My eyes shot over to Langston, who was sitting in the chair, watching me. I had absolutely no idea what he was thinking, but I was hoping he wasn't intending to leave me there.

When he finally spoke, it was while he leaned over me.

"I'm very impressed."

"Thank you," I whispered.

"You do seem to enjoy the restraints, yes?"

I nodded.

"That pleases me greatly."

I could tell by the way he was looking at me that it did.

"I'm going to remove the clamps first," he informed me, his hand brushing the underside of my breast. "Although they're quite pretty on you, we can't keep them on for too long. I'm sure you know this won't be pleasant."

I'd learned that when Ben had removed them last week. I hadn't expected the pain to be quite so intense even though he had also warned me.

"Take a deep breath, little one," he whispered roughly. "Breathe out...*now.*"

I did as instructed while he removed the first clamp. The blood rushed back into my nipple. I moaned as the pain nearly overwhelmed me. His mouth was on my breast almost instantly and a moan of a different sort came out. This one fueled by intense pleasure, the warm rasp of his tongue taking my mind off the ache.

It didn't last long enough though. Langston then removed the other clamp, repeating his instructions. I welcomed the heated suction of his mouth. It somehow made it bearable.

I thought for sure that Langston was going to do something more, but my disappointment was great when he merely released me from the restraints, then massaged my arms and legs to help with circulation. I did my best not to overthink it, but I couldn't help but wonder why he didn't want me. I mean, he'd come over yesterday and watched movies, yet left with nothing more than a kiss.

"Why the frown, little one?" Langston asked when he helped me to my feet.

I shook my head and dropped my eyes.

He tilted my chin up so I was forced to look at him.

"Talk to me. Without open communication, this will never work."

I wasn't even sure what *this* was. I got the feeling that they were taking things to the next level, whatever that might be.

I studied his face for a moment, then blurted out my insecurities. "Do you not want me?"

His eyes narrowed slightly. "What would give you that idea?"

I shrugged. "I...I don't know. I just thought..."

"What, Luci?"

"I thought when you came over yesterday that we might..."

He smirked. "You wanted me to fuck you?"

I nodded, slightly ashamed to admit it.

"Trust me, little one. I want that more than anything."

I frowned again, completely confused.

He cupped my face. "One thing you need to understand. Although you've stated that you want more time, the control still remains in our hands. Not yours. We've taken your request into consideration, even obliged you somewhat. However, that doesn't mean we'll bend to your will. In the end, it's about control. Ours. Not yours."

I nodded. "I understand that, sir." And I truly did. I didn't want to be in control. I liked the way they handled things. If I had come across otherwise, I hadn't intended to.

He leaned in and pressed his lips to mine. "In due time, pet. All in due time."

Langston stepped away from me, his eyes dropping to the butterfly vibrator. "I want you to keep that on all day. And the plug stays in as well. You are not to remove either, no matter what. I'll make sure the others know."

I swallowed hard.

"You can remove them when you get home, but remember you are not allowed to masturbate without explicit instruction. And tomorrow morning, when you arrive in the office, I want you to strip immediately. You'll spend the entire day naked."

I nodded, unsure why he was torturing me.

"I've got several meetings tomorrow, but I want you to be in my office at three o'clock. I want you to kneel on the floor beside my desk and wait for me to arrive. Understood?"

I nodded again. "Yes, sir."

"Good girl." He leaned in and pressed his lips to mine. "And I want you to think about me until then, Luci." His voice dropped an octave or ten. "I want you to think about me fucking you until you're screaming my name."

Langston stood tall once more, his fingers gliding over my cheek.

"Because that's what I'll be thinking about," he said. "That's all I seem to be able to think about."

With that, he turned and left the room.

And for some stupid reason, my heart turned over as I replayed his words in my head again and again.

THIRTY-ONE

BECAUSE OF LANGSTON'S INSTRUCTIONS FOR the next day, I went back on my original request and invited Jordan to go to lunch that day instead. He seemed thrilled that I'd changed my mind. Personally, I was quite happy with my decision because I looked forward to spending time with my new friend.

Plus, it seemed the best choice as far as I was concerned. For one, I was allowed to wear clothing today, so that was a good thing. On the other hand, I was intensely aware of the butt plug and the vibrator hidden beneath. It took a tremendous amount of focus not to think about them while I was having lunch with my friend.

"I see they're keeping you busy," Jordan said absently when we sat down at one of the empty tables in the sandwich shop. "Are you at least enjoying yourself?"

I nodded, unable to look him in the eyes.

"Well, I heard Langston and Landon talking and they seem rather impressed with you."

My eyes shot up to his face. "Really?"

He nodded, a huge grin making his cheeks puff out. "Oh, yeah." He opened his chips. "I also heard Justin telling someone on the phone that he was going to be limiting his travel for a while. He said he had something he needed to focus on in the office."

My cheeks heated.

"I'm wondering if that has something to do with you."

I had no idea how much Jordan knew about what was going on during the day. I knew he was curious, and I was almost positive he suspected something. How could he not when he'd seen so many secretaries come and go during his tenure with the company?

"One day, you'll trust me enough to spill the beans," he finally said when I didn't respond. Surprisingly, he didn't sound disappointed that I wasn't laying it all out for him, which alleviated some of my guilt.

I shoved a chip into my mouth, not wanting to reveal all the details to my newfound friend.

His hand touched mine. "You won't get any judgement from me, Luci. I promise. And I won't push you either. But if you ever need someone to talk to, just know that I'm here."

I nodded again. I really liked Jordan. He was so sweet to me.

"So...did you do anything interesting this weekend?" he asked, changing the subject.

This time I smiled, relaxing somewhat. "I did." Groaning, I added, "I had breakfast with my parents."

"Oooh. That sounds fun. Tell me all about it."

So I did.

Unfortunately, that was the exact same moment that damn vibrator came to life.

•

The first lull in my day happened at four o'clock, so I went into Ben's office to see if I could get him anything. Since he had asked me to stop by, I wanted to make sure I gave him the time he deserved.

He was typing furiously on his computer, but he motioned for me to come in.

His gaze darted up to me briefly, then back to his computer screen.

"Strip for me, gumdrop."

For the second time that day, I removed my clothes and neatly placed them in one of the chairs across from his desk.

"Come over here," he said, patting the top of his desk. "Give me another minute and I'll be finished."

I stood beside his chair, mindful of how I presented myself, and waited until he was through typing. He then placed his laptop on one of the shelves behind his desk and turned to face me.

"Lift your chin slightly," he instructed. "But keep it at a respectful angle. When your presence is requested by a Dom, you need to keep in mind that you're here for my pleasure, so you want to present yourself in the most pleasing manner."

"Is that what this is?" I asked, unable to hold the question back.

He smiled, his eyes softening. "Honestly, I don't know what this is, but I'm following Langston's lead. He's evidently trying to teach you something and I want to help you out."

I nodded, adjusting my stance. I wasn't sure I would ever get used to this, but I did notice I was paying more attention to my posture throughout the day now.

"Just like that. Very nice." His big hands curled around my hips as he pulled me closer to him. "I've been thinking about you all day."

I had no idea what to say to that.

"I was thinking about how generous you were this morning."

"But you didn't come," I blurted.

His smile was slow and sexy as he looked up at me. "It's not always about me, Luci. Sometimes it's about…pleasing someone else. Does that make sense?"

"Sort of." But not really.

"Just like you, I take commands from someone else. And when that happens, it's my sole objective to please that person. Does that help?"

It didn't, but I nodded anyway. I guess that made me selfish, because in my experience, sex had the potential to be satisfying and I was generally focused on my own pleasure, rather than my partner's. Which, now that I thought about it, really did make me selfish. That wasn't something I wanted to acknowledge aloud.

"You'll get there. I promise. Just focus on what we're asking of you. You follow instructions rather well."

Huh. I wondered whether that was the lesson they were trying to teach me. Follow instructions and please others. Like Ben had said, it wasn't always about me.

"All right, gumdrop. Enough of the lessons. Right now is all about you, so have a seat." Ben patted the top of his desk before rolling his chair back out of the way. "Put your feet on the arms of my chair."

Once again, I was in the same position I'd been in when he had introduced me to the nipple clamps.

"Spread your knees wide."

Leaning back on my hands, I opened my legs while Ben sat there, his face inches away from my pussy. He inhaled deeply as embarrassment coursed through me. I figured I should've been used to this by now, but I wasn't.

His fingers grazed over my mound, shifting the butterfly vibrator out of the way, then sliding against my clit.

"I enjoy how wet you get," he said absently, still teasing me with his fingers. "And I definitely like the plug." He nudged it slightly, and I was once again reminded that my ass was filled. It wasn't terribly uncomfortable, although it had been that morning. I'd gotten used to it at some point during the day, only really noticing when I got up from my chair or sat down.

"I'm going to feast on your pretty pussy now. Feel free to come as many times as you'd like."

When his mouth descended, I sucked in a sharp breath. He explored me with his skillful tongue for what felt like hours, lapping at my clit, stroking my outer lips, then delving into me. He grabbed my hips and jerked me closer to him as he buried his face in my cunt.

My skin tingled as he continued to drive me out of my mind. I tried to hold back, but my efforts proved futile a short time later when I came in a maddening rush, crying out his name over and over. He slowed only briefly while I tried to catch my breath. My clit was too sensitive and he seemed to know that. Instead of tormenting me, he focused on fucking me with his tongue. Eventually he resumed flicking my clit until I was flying high once again.

Ben made me come two more times with his mouth, then used his fingers to shatter me. By the time he stopped, I was trembling.

"Such a good girl," he whispered as he got to his feet. His big hand curled behind my neck as he pulled me closer.

Ben's kiss was demanding yet gentle. I could taste myself on his lips and that in itself renewed my arousal. I was desperate for him to fuck me again.

As though he could read my mind, Ben pulled back, his golden eyes focusing on my face.

"Not this time, gumdrop."

Ben adjusted the butterfly vibrator so that it was back in place, resting against my overstimulated clit. I groaned at the gentle pressure. Langston had made the thing come to life numerous times throughout the day and I could only hope that he would hold off for a little while. Although I was still horny, my clit did need a little time to recover.

I frowned when Ben's comment sank in. "Are you denying yourself?"

He seemed pleased that I'd caught on. "Like I said, you're not the only one who takes instruction."

I could only assume that Justin had instructed him not to come. It made complete sense. And it certainly explained why Ben referred to Justin as Mr. Parker. Ever since Langston had mentioned Doms that morning, I had given it a little thought. I assumed Ben was Justin's submissive. Although, that didn't make sense at all, considering how demanding Ben was with me.

Regardless, the thought of him denying me *and* himself didn't help my renewed frustration at all.

Someone cleared their throat and I jerked my head toward the sound to see Justin standing in the doorway. He was watching us intently. My gaze dropped and I noticed the hard ridge of his erection tenting his pants.

The sexy blond moved into the room, leaving the door open.

"I'm proud of you, Ben," Justin said approvingly as he moved over to lean against the back of the sofa.

"Thank you, Mr. Parker," Ben said gruffly.

I had no idea what was about to happen, but I figured it had to be something since Ben helped me down from his desk, steadying me on my feet.

"As a reward for not coming, I'm going to let you suck me until I come down your throat."

Wait.

Ben's reward was to make Justin come? I didn't understand. Wouldn't Justin want Ben to come?

I glanced over at Ben, noticing the glazed look in his eyes as though the thought of making Justin come was pleasure in and of itself.

Justin snapped his fingers and pointed to the spot directly in front of him.

I watched in awe as Ben walked toward him. He did not look like a man who took commands from others, but he did exactly as Justin instructed. Being that Ben was several years older than Justin only added to the surreal experience. Granted, it didn't lessen how intensely erotic it was.

But this seemed intimate between the two of them, and I wasn't sure what I was supposed to do.

"Put me in your mouth," Justin commanded Ben, his focus solely on the man in front of him.

I couldn't have looked away if I'd wanted to. I watched as Ben freed Justin's cock from his slacks, stroking him lovingly. I found I enjoyed watching the way Ben's dark hand caressed Justin's cock, making him harder by the second.

Justin then clicked his tongue and Ben took him fully into his mouth.

"Oh, yeah," Justin groaned. "I love your mouth." Justin's eyes shot to me. "Come here, princess." He motioned for me to join them. "I want you to see how well he can take my cock all the way down his throat. It requires finesse and focus and a genuine desire to please. My pup has all of those things."

Swallowing hard, I moved closer.

"I think he's jealous that you're wearing a plug today and he's not," Justin mused while Ben lovingly sucked him from root to tip. "Isn't that right, pup?"

Ben nodded but didn't stop his ministrations.

"Have you ever watched two men together, Luci?"

"No, sir."

"Not even in porn?"

"No, sir."

"Hmm. Well, one of these days I'll have to let you watch while I slide my cock deep inside his tight ass."

Ben moaned, as though pleased by that statement.

"Take me all the way, pup," Justin ordered roughly.

Ben's mouth widened and he shifted down so that his face was buried in Justin's pubic hair.

"Such a good boy," Justin said, his tone gentle, loving. "I love to fuck your throat."

A few seconds passed before Justin pulled his hips back slightly, then thrust forward. Ben seemed to be anticipating the movement, because he didn't flinch, simply allowed Justin to thrust deep in his mouth.

Justin reached out and pulled me closer to him. "Shift that vibrator out of the way."

I did and then his hand delved between my thighs, his fingers separating my lips and finding my slick entrance. He shoved two fingers inside me and I groaned.

"This makes you wet."

"Yes, sir." I was ridiculously turned on by watching Ben suck Justin's cock.

"That pleases me," he said as he removed his fingers from my pussy.

Heat swamped me. For whatever reason, I liked the praise these men gave me. I'd never experienced anything like this before.

Justin's hips continued to punch forward, driving his cock deeper into Ben's throat. I had no idea how the man could sit there like that.

Finally, Justin pulled back.

"I want you to make me come," he ordered Ben. "And I want you to swallow."

Ben nodded. "It'd be my pleasure, Mr. Parker."

Justin's hands curled around Ben's bald head and he jerked him forward, impaling the man's mouth with his cock. He began fucking Ben's face in earnest while Ben moaned loudly.

"Such a good boy," Justin growled. "I want you to teach Luci how to deep-throat the way that you do. *No one* takes my cock like you do. God, that feels good."

Ben's head jerked in a subtle nod while Justin continued to slam his hips forward, fucking him roughly.

"Suck hard," Justin commanded.

I watched as Ben's cheeks hollowed out, his lips wrapped around Justin's thick cock.

"Fuck yes," Justin hissed. "Swallow every bit."

I never thought I'd be turned on by watching two men. However, I most certainly was.

In fact, I was now just as turned on as I'd been when I walked into Ben's office a short time ago. And once again, I found I was sexually frustrated.

This seemed to be a no-win situation for me.

THIRTY-TWO

AFTER JUSTIN AND BEN DISAPPEARED into the bathroom, I pulled my clothing on in Ben's office, then returned to my desk to grab my purse and head out for the evening. It was five forty-five and I was eager to get home so I could guzzle a bottle of wine. I needed something to take the edge off this day, and I was hoping that was going to do it.

Before I made it halfway down the hallway, I heard someone calling my name. I glanced over my shoulder to see Landon strolling toward me.

"You heading out, too?" I slowed my pace and smiled.

"I was thinkin' I'd take you to dinner."

That made me stop in my tracks and turn to face him. "Me?"

Landon chuckled. "Since you're the only other person in the hallway…"

A grin broke out on my mouth. "I'm sorry. It's just…I didn't expect that."

"No?"

I shook my head.

"So my brother can hang out and watch movies, but you find it strange that I want to take you to dinner?"

As a matter of fact, I found both odd.

I blushed. "When you put it that way…"

"How about I follow you to your apartment, then we'll go in my truck. That way you don't have to drive home too late."

That was such a gentlemanly thing to do. I couldn't help but smile wider. "That sounds great."

With Landon standing much closer than he normally did, we headed toward the elevator. The entire time, I was trying to figure out if he was going to work me into a frenzy and leave me hanging, too.

I was pretty sure I might not be able to hold back my scathing words if that were to happen.

However, I could do nothing but wait and see.

•

It took about an hour for us to get back to my apartment and then to the restaurant he'd decided on. It was a nice little Italian place not far from where I lived.

"Do you come here often?" I asked in an effort to make small talk once we were seated.

Landon glanced around. "Can't say that I've been here before. But it has good ratings."

"You checked the ratings?"

He appeared somewhat shy when he said, "Of course. I check ratings for every restaurant I go to."

I chuckled. "That doesn't surprise me."

"No?" His eyebrow lifted in question.

I reached for the napkin and placed it in my lap. "It's a testament to your control. You want to know as much as you can about the situation you're in."

"I've never looked at it like that, but yeah. That's a good way to put it."

I grinned and glanced down at the menu. "It's a great place, actually. Kristen and I come here from time to time to get our lasagna fix."

"So you're recommending the lasagna?"

"That or the ravioli. Both are fantastic." And I had no idea why I was talking about food.

Here I was with Landon and the topic of conversation was related to the menu. But he didn't seem to be bothered by it, so I didn't let it bother me too much.

"May I get you something to dr—"

I peered up at the waitress at the same time her words came to an abrupt halt. There was recognition on her face as she stared at Landon.

"Master Moore?" the pretty young woman greeted Landon.

Master? What in the hell was going on? Doms and Masters? It sounded far too much like the books I'd been reading.

"Good evenin', Mandy," he replied coolly.

Something passed in the woman's eyes, but I hadn't the faintest clue what it was.

She cleared her throat.

"Can I get you something to drink?"

Landon looked at me and cocked an eyebrow.

"I'll have white wine," I informed her, not looking away from Landon.

"Same for me," he answered, his gaze darting to her briefly before locking with mine.

When she disappeared, I couldn't keep from asking, "You know her?"

"She's a su—uh…a member of the club I go to."

"The same club Kristen goes to?"

His eyes widened. "Actually, yes. Has she told you about it?"

I shook my head slightly and dropped my gaze. "No. Just that that was how she knew you."

I really needed to ask her about this mysterious club. It appeared it was a real thing. I wanted to know more about it, but I wasn't sure I wanted to ask Landon. I could very easily probe Kristen for the details later.

Which I would.

Maybe.

"What're you havin'?" Landon questioned.

"I'm going to be predictable tonight," I said with a smirk.

"Lasagna?"

"Yes." I did love their pasta.

"Perfect."

When I looked up, Landon was smiling at me as though I was the only woman in the room. Certainly not like a man who'd just seen a woman he knew, a woman who happened to be staring at him intently from across the room. I wasn't sure if I should be jealous or merely curious. Or neither. It wasn't like this was a date.

Or was it?

"Here's your wine, Master Moore," Mandy said when she returned, her smile bright, her attention focused solely on Landon.

It didn't go unnoticed that she hadn't brought mine.

That didn't seem to make Landon happy at all.

"Mandy?"

"Yes, Master Moore?" she said breathlessly, her eyes wide as though it meant something that he had acknowledged her.

"Please bring another glass," Landon said as he passed his wine over to me. "And remember your manners. It doesn't matter where you are, it's unbecoming not to be respectful."

I couldn't stop staring at him. I could tell he was doing his best not to look at her. Which could only mean one thing. He knew her intimately.

I wanted to slap myself for the sour taste that filled my mouth at the knowledge.

"Yes, Sir. Of course, Sir. I'll be right back."

When she sauntered off, Landon frowned. "I apologize."

"No, please. Don't apologize." For some stupid reason, I reached over and touched his hand. "It's not your fault."

Rather than pull away from me the way I thought he would, Landon's hand turned over and he clasped my fingers with his. He continued to hold my stare. I could tell something was going on in his head, but I didn't know what. And I didn't want to ask for fear of breaking the spell.

It took a few minutes, but Mandy finally returned with Landon's wine and she managed to take both of our orders, which Landon relayed to her directly. When she was gone again, his attention was once again focused solely on me.

"So, tell me something about yourself," he urged. "Something I don't already know."

When I went to retrieve my hand, he held firmly.

"Don't pull away from me," he ordered softly.

I swallowed hard, continuing to maintain eye contact although I wanted to look at anything except him.

"I'm not sure what you don't know." That wasn't the truth. There were a lot of things about me he didn't know, but I was suddenly uncomfortable with the intimate conversation.

"All right. Tell me about your parents. Did you not see them for Thanksgiving? When I talked to you, you were at home."

Okay, I probably should've led with something related to yoga. I definitely had no desire to talk about my parents. I sighed. "No. I didn't. My mother doesn't celebrate Thanksgiving."

"And you have no other family?"

I shook my head. "Jim's parents died when he was young. My mother's parents live in Wisconsin and we haven't visited them in years. My dad's grandmother died when I was twelve. The year before was the last time we celebrated any holiday and that was only because she had insisted."

"What're your plans for Christmas?"

I forced a smile and shrugged. "I'm not sure just yet."

That was another lie. I already knew what I'd be doing on Christmas. The same thing I did last year. Nothing.

Not that it mattered. Christmas was still a ways away and I honestly didn't want to think about it right now.

"All right," Landon said with a grin. "Fair enough. We can talk about anything else as long as it doesn't pertain to work."

I smiled because I was okay with that. I was sure I could think of plenty to talk about that didn't have anything to do with work or parents or…

Actually, I didn't know *what* we would talk about.

Landon seemed to realize my dilemma because he chuckled. "Or…we could play Never Have I Ever."

This time my smile was genuine. "I like that." I took a sip of my wine. "I like that a lot."

•

Dinner turned out far better than I'd expected despite the fact that Mandy seemed to trip all over herself every time she got near Landon. Luckily, Landon pretended not to notice. Or, more importantly, he focused all his attention on me throughout dinner.

We managed to talk about the do's and don'ts of holiday decorations, especially at the mall. He asked me if I was one of those people who would put reindeer antlers on my car. For the record, I was not. Nor was he.

It was nice and after two glasses of wine I had managed to relax.

However, the effects of the wine had worn off now that we were back in his truck and heading to my apartment. I was already trying to figure out what would happen next. Was I supposed to invite him in? Would he merely drop me at the curb? Did I want him to come in?

Well, the last question was dumb. Of course I wanted him to come in. Hell, I wanted him to come in and never leave.

Not that I could tell him that though.

Unfortunately, I found out all the answers to the questions a short time later when he walked me into the building but paused at the elevator.

"Thank you for having dinner with me," he said softly, his hands cupping my face.

"I had a good time," I admitted.

"So did I."

He seemed to be searching my eyes for something.

"Would you...uh...like to come up?"

He instantly shook his head, but he smiled. "That's the only thing I want, Luci. However, I can't. Not tonight."

I nodded, acting as though I understood.

I didn't.

Not really.

Landon's thumb brushed over my cheek as he leaned down. His mouth found mine, our lips fusing together as what started out as a sweet kiss turned into something fueled by pent-up lust and a tremendous amount of heat.

"God, Luce," he moaned into my mouth. "You taste so damn good."

Not wanting to let him go, I pulled his mouth back to mine and let the conflagration consume us both. My back found the wall beside the elevator, Landon's knee pressing between my thighs. Only then did I realize I still had that damn butterfly vibrator on.

I moaned against his mouth, desperate for him to do something to ease the emptiness that consumed me.

"Do you need to come, sweetness?" he asked, his words mumbled against my lips.

"Yes."

"Tell me how you want me to make you come. Keep in mind, it must be right here and not with my cock."

Well, that was disappointing. Not the part about the hallway, because it was empty for the moment.

"Tell me, Luci," he demanded, his lips brushing along my jaw. "What would you like me to do?"

I moaned again, the heat churning inside me.

"You've got ten seconds. If you don't tell me, I'll send you up to your apartment alone, where you'll spend the rest of the night wishing you'd been bold enough because you'll be aching to come."

"With your fingers," I said on a rush of air.

"Good girl."

Landon steered me backward, slipping into a small alcove behind the elevator. His mouth found mine again and I wrapped my arms around his neck, wanting to keep him close.

His hand traveled between my legs, forcing me to open them wider. He then hooked his arm beneath my left knee, lifting my leg as his fingers probed my slick entrance, deftly maneuvering around that damn vibrator.

"You're so wet," he whispered.

I didn't respond because words were unnecessary. However, I moaned loudly when he pushed two fingers inside me. Thanks to his thick fingers and the plug in my ass, the pressure was intense, making me feel filled to overflowing.

He began fingering me slowly. I was writhing against his hand, moaning softly, when I heard the door open and a brisk wind rushed into the small area. Landon pulled back and stared into my eyes, his fingers never leaving me.

"No, Simone, I'm not saying that," a male voice said from around the corner. "Yes. I get it. You're not happy with me, but I don't care."

Landon began fucking me faster, deeper. I dropped my head back against the wall.

"Yes. I hear you. I always hear you." The man huffed. "What do you want from me?"

Landon leaned in, his mouth right against my ear. "I want you to come for me. Come all over my hand."

I swallowed a whimper as my pussy clenched around the intruding digits.

The elevator dinged.

"Right now," Landon commanded, his tone rough, adamant. "Come for me right fucking now."

The man's voice sounded somewhat louder. "Fine, Simone. Whatever you say. I'm so tired of this shit."

Landon pressed against my G-spot and my body tensed as my orgasm ripped through me. He kissed me hard, swallowing my cry as my body exploded in blessed release.

I heard the doors to the elevator closing, the man's voice becoming muffled.

Landon pressed his forehead to mine, his fingers slipping out of me. "You're beautiful when you come."

His compliment made me blush.

It took a couple of minutes for me to catch my breath. I wanted nothing more than to invite him up to my apartment, to ask him to spend the night with me. I didn't want him to leave, hating to even have to let go of him.

However, I said none of that. He'd already told me he couldn't stay, and I wasn't going to make myself any more vulnerable than I already was, so I opted to call it a night.

"Thank you for dinner," I told him. "I enjoyed spending time with you."

"Likewise, sweet girl." He touched his lips to mine once more. "Now go on upstairs. I'll see you in the morning."

"Yes, sir," I whispered, not ready to let him go.

We stood there for a few more seconds before Landon finally pulled back.

"Good night, sweetness."

"Good night."

He steered me around the corner to the elevator, then punched the button. When it arrived, I stepped inside, secretly hoping he would follow, but he didn't.

As the elevator rose to my floor, I touched my lips, remembering his kiss.

That man…

I wasn't sure what it was about him and Langston that made me wish for things that were out of my control, but I did.

I most certainly did.

THIRTY-THREE

TUESDAY PASSED IN A BLUR. Perhaps that was because I'd spent the day walking around naked once again. That or it could've been due to the fact that my bosses were in and out of the office all day, constantly having me call to confirm appointments, reservations, or to make follow-up phone calls.

I didn't mind it one bit. I liked the work, the ability to keep myself busy, which ultimately kept my mind off the fact that I was naked again. On a positive note, at least I didn't have to wear the butterfly vibrator or the butt plug. For that, I was grateful.

I was starting to think that my bosses weren't merely testing me but they were teaching me lessons along the way. Not only how to please them but also things like patience, routine, and even spontaneity. Sort of a contradiction, but still.

That or they simply enjoyed pushing my limits and torturing me in the most sensuous ways.

For example, it was a few minutes after three and I'd been kneeling in Langston's office for the past ten minutes waiting for his arrival. That had been his instruction, so I had informed Jordan that I would be in a meeting and to send all calls to voice mail. Considering Ben, Justin, and Landon were all busy working in their offices, I felt as though I was not pulling my weight.

Had I been with one of my bosses, I would've felt as though I had a reason. However, since I was alone, no one knowing what I was doing or why, it seemed like a big waste of time. I didn't want anyone to think that I was slacking off, so I decided that if Langston didn't arrive in the next ten minutes, I would simply get back to work.

Ten minutes turned into fifteen and I finally gave up. I decided that Langston must've forgotten about me, so I got up and went back to my desk. I was about to call Jordan and let him know he could send the calls my way when Langston came strolling down the hallway, his phone to his ear.

When he saw me, his eyes narrowed and I could tell he wasn't happy.

"I'll have to call you back. I've got something I need to take care of." He disconnected the call, his arm snapping forward, finger pointed directly at me. "You. My office. Right now."

Swallowing hard, I got to my feet and scurried to his office, noticing the disappointment in his voice.

"What did I ask you to do?" He practically barked the words as he followed me inside.

"To wait for you," I said, looking him directly in the eye. "But you didn't show up, so I thought you forgot and I had other things I needed to do."

He kept his eyes on me, the hazel orbs shooting fire. "Did I ask you to make that decision?"

"No, sir."

"Master," he stated roughly.

"What?"

His eyes narrowed. "Do you know what an honorific is?"

I shook my head. I'd never heard the word before.

"An honorific is a way in which a submissive conveys respect using a title selected by her Dom."

Submissive? Dom?

I was so lost.

"From here on out, when we're in the office, in private, or in public, you will call me Master. You will not refer to me as anything else unless specifically instructed."

I'd admit I was completely shocked by this command. I wasn't sure if maybe the guy had fallen and hit his head. There was something distinctly different about him at that moment. Yes, he was certainly the most demanding of all the men in the office. Plus, he presented himself differently, but I'd never suspected him to be quite so…dominant. It was eerily similar to the books that I'd read.

My thoughts inconveniently drifted back to dinner with Landon last night. More specifically, the way the waitress had referred to him as Master Moore.

Oh, hell.

What had I gotten myself into?

"I...uh..."

"It wasn't a request, Luci."

I nodded. "Okay, s...I mean, M-Master."

The word felt strange on my tongue.

Sure, I got that the men in this office found it appealing when I called them sir. It actually made me hot, even. But to directly refer to someone as though that was their name... It felt strange to me. What was worse was the idea of calling someone Master. That seemed a bit over-the-top.

"What is my name?" Langston asked, his gaze boring into me.

"Master."

"When will you refer to me as that?"

I replayed his instructions in my head, then summed it up into one word. "Always."

"Now, what did I ask you to do?" Langston's gaze was hard as steel.

"To kneel by your desk and wait for you."

His gaze cut to the floor beside his desk. It was an obvious command, so I returned to the spot I'd been in a short time ago and knelt on the floor. He moved behind me, then brought me a pillow.

"Get comfortable. Keep your eyes downward," he instructed. "And do not move."

With that, he left the room.

•

Two hours later, I was still kneeling beside Langston's desk. No. Master. He wanted me to refer to him as such; therefore, I decided I would stop thinking about him as Langston, not wanting to do anything to upset him. I could tell that my disobedience had been bothersome to him and for some reason, it hurt to know I was responsible for it.

While I remained with my knees on the pillow, which did very little to cushion me from the hardwood floor—I wasn't lucky enough to be in Ben's office, which was carpeted—my four bosses had continued about their day. Ben had come in to discuss something with Langston (shit, Master), neither man acknowledging me in any way. Then…Master had disappeared for a short while, but I heard him talking with Landon after that.

Finally, Langston—damn it, I feared I was never going to get used to this—returned and he was once again sitting at his desk, his fingers hovering over his keyboard. I did my best to keep my eyes cast downward, but it was difficult. My knees and hips ached something fierce, my feet had long ago fallen asleep under my ass, and my back was throbbing from the position.

It was now after five and I should've been gearing up to head home, but I knew better than to move from where I was.

"I'm heading out," Justin said, stepping into the doorway. "Need anything before I go?"

"No," Langston—or rather, Master—told him. "I'm good."

"All right then. See you both in the morning."

I noticed that Justin did not speak to me directly.

"Actually," Master called out, "is Ben still here?"

"He is," Justin confirmed.

"Would you two mind coming in here for a few minutes?"

He sounded somewhat hesitant when he said, "Not at all. Let me grab him."

Master picked up the phone and dialed someone. "I need you in my office."

A few minutes later, Ben, Justin, and Landon strolled in. I heard their footsteps pause near the door.

"Have a seat on the couch." Although Master didn't phrase it as a question, it came out as a request, not a command.

They did so without saying a word.

I saw Master's shoes appear in front of me, but I didn't move.

"Stand up, pet."

Thankfully, Master offered his hand and assisted me to my feet. My body was in outrage from the position and it took a moment to get my legs sturdy enough to hold me up. Surprisingly, Master didn't rush me; however, I sensed that he wasn't going to be overly patient.

Once I was standing on my own, Master took my hand and led me over to the sofa opposite the other three.

He took a seat and then turned me to face him before pulling me face down over his knee.

"What are you doing?" I squealed, trying to move off him. I mean, I could tolerate a lot, and I was all for the sexual games, but this... No way.

Surprised by the sudden movement, I planted my palms and toes on the floor, holding myself up as best as I could, absolutely shocked that he'd do something like that.

"Be still," he commanded.

I'd never heard his voice so low. It caused me to still instantly.

It took effort, but I reined in my outrage. Although I was highly embarrassed, I was also curious as to what Master had planned for me. Clearly, he hadn't been making idle threats about punishment. I simply wondered how much I was going to like it. I figured it would be hit-or-miss if I based it on the books that I'd read.

Master rested his hand on my butt. It was warm and I silently willed him to move it between my legs. Despite the fact that I was angry with him for making me kneel beside his desk for two hours, I was turned on by his touch.

"Yesterday, I instructed Luci to be in my office at three o'clock this afternoon. I asked that she kneel by my desk and wait for my arrival. When I got here, she was at her desk, not where I instructed her to be. Isn't that correct, pet?"

"Yes, si—I mean, yes, Master."

"Direct disobedience requires punishment." His hand squeezed my ass cheek. "I should go for at least twenty, but we'll start out easy."

Easy? What did he consider easy?

Only then did I realize what his intentions were. It actually made me hot to think about Master spanking me. Seriously. These were sexual games we were playing, so I knew whatever he had in mind was going to be enjoyable. It wasn't like he would intentionally—

Smack.

"Ouch!" I screamed, trying to move off his legs again. That was far from enjoyable.

"Do not move," he growled roughly.

I stilled, my ass smarting from his hand.

"Count for me, pet."

"Count? Count what? I don't—"

Smack.

I screamed when his hand landed on the opposite cheek, fire burning into my skin.

"I didn't hear you."

Then it all made sense. He wanted me to count how many times he spanked me. Talk about humiliating.

"Do you want me to start over?"

I shook my head adamantly and breathed out roughly. Although that was technically the second swat, I started from the beginning. "One."

Smack.

I swallowed hard. "Two."

Smack.

"Three." I sucked in a breath as tears formed in my eyes. The man wasn't holding anything back.

Smack.

"Four." At this point, I was sobbing, the pain so great I thought I would lose it any second.

Smack.

"Five."

Master's hand caressed my ass, making it burn more from his touch. I was crying uncontrollably now. I knew Ben, Justin, and Landon were all watching, but it didn't matter.

"I'm going to give you five more," Master informed me. "You do not need to count."

Five more? There was no way I would survive—

Smack. Smack.

Smack. Smack.

Smack.

Oh. My. God! That hurt so fucking bad I could hardly breathe as the pain pierced my ass.

Sobbing hysterically, I moved when Master shifted me on his lap. My stinging ass pressed against his thighs as he cradled me close to his chest. I didn't even think about it, I simply wrapped my arms around his neck and buried my face in his shoulder, letting the tears fall. His shirt would be wet when this was all over, but I didn't care.

"Thank you for taking the time to be here for that," Master spoke softly to the others.

"No problem," Justin said. "I do have to head out now. But we'll talk more in the morning? It looks to me as though the dynamic has changed."

"Yes," Master confirmed.

I didn't lift my head, but I heard footsteps, which I took to mean everyone was leaving. I managed to stifle my sobs, but just barely.

"Landon, I'd like you to stay."

"I don't think that's necessary," his brother replied. "I'll check in with you in a bit."

I could feel Master nod, then I heard the door open and close.

"Look at me, pet," Master ordered.

I lifted my head and met his eyes.

"Do you understand why I punished you?"

I nodded.

"Tell me why."

"Because I wasn't kneeling when you arrived. I disobeyed your instruction."

"When I ask you to do something, I expect you to follow my orders. I was looking forward to coming in and finding you in my office. It disappointed me to see that you weren't."

My heart ached at that knowledge. Knowing that I had disappointed him was the worst part.

"That's the last thing I want," I told him. "I never want to disappoint you."

"Then I forgive your transgression," he said.

"I really am—"

"It's behind us, Luci. I don't want to hear any more about it. That's what punishment is for. It eradicates the transgression and we can move forward."

I was so confused by what was going on. None of it made sense; however, I couldn't deny that I liked how gentle he was now being with me. Master cupped the back of my head and held me closer to his chest. I sat there for the longest time, trying to ignore the pain in my ass from the spankings while listening to Master breathe.

"Are you better?" he finally asked.

"Yes...Master." It was still difficult to say the word aloud.

"Do you have any questions?"

I had a million, but none that I cared to ask at the moment, so I shook my head and offered a wary, "No."

"Don't lie to me, pet. That's the worst thing you can do."

"I'm being honest," I told him. "I don't have any questions right this minute."

"Fine." He didn't sound as though he believed me, but he was obviously placating me for now. Master shifted, helping me to my feet and turning me to face away from him. "Don't move."

I heard the distinct sound of his belt buckle, and a minute later, he was pulling me back down on his lap, still facing away from him.

I won't lie, sitting down hurt like a bitch.

Master reached around me and rubbed his cock against my pussy while I leaned into him, dropping my head back on his shoulder.

What he was doing was enough of a distraction, making my ass feel a little better.

"Do you want me to fuck you, little one?"

"Yes," I whispered, the need in my voice apparent.

Perhaps I was deranged for wanting to be intimate with him. After he spanked me, embarrassing me in front of my other bosses, I probably should've wanted to hightail it out of the office and never come back.

I didn't.

In fact, I wanted him more now than ever.

"Ask me nicely."

I had no modesty when it came to that. "Please, Master. Will you please fuck me? I want to feel you inside me."

He pressed his lips to the side of my head and mumbled, "I fucking love to hear that."

Master placed the head of his cock at my entrance and maneuvered me so that the blunt tip pressed inside.

"Place your hands on my knees."

I positioned my hands as he pushed me away from him, his fingertips gripping my hips as he slowly pulled me down onto his shaft.

From his position behind me and the way he forced me to lean forward, I knew he could see his cock disappearing inside my pussy. The thought of him watching his cock claim my pussy was sexy. He must've thought so, too, because he continued like that for long minutes, pulling me onto him, pushing me off. It wasn't long before my legs were weak as the pleasure overwhelmed me. I'd waited what felt like forever for him to take me again.

"Put your knees together."

I did as he instructed, closing my legs while his cock was buried deep inside me. It caused the walls of my pussy to tighten, gripping him more firmly.

"Place your hands on my thighs."

I did that, too.

"Now fuck me. Ride my cock."

In that position, it was easier for me to have control, to lift and lower on his cock, and it allowed him to go impossibly deep inside me.

"Faster, pet," he said, his voice rougher than before. "Fuck me like you need me."

"I need you," I whispered, wanting him to know that above all else.

"Show me."

I pushed up, then dropped down onto him, impaling myself on his dick. Over and over, my movements were erratic as the sensations spiraled out of control inside me.

"Come on my cock."

"Oh, God," I groaned, feeling my orgasm as it rushed upon me. It didn't take long before I was crying out.

"Say my name," he ordered.

"Master... Oh, yes!"

Master gripped my hips, holding me still as he fucked me hard from underneath. I could only imagine what it would be like if I was beneath him.

"Again, little one," he insisted. "Come again."

As he pounded into me, another orgasm crested, this one more powerful than the last. It stole my breath and all of my strength. Luckily, Master held me up while he surged deep within me. Seconds later, he jerked me down on him and I felt the pulse of his cock as he came inside me. His lips trailed across my shoulders, his breath warm against my back.

"Luci..."

I sank back into him and he held me close, his arms wrapped around me as his lips grazed my neck.

"Thank you, pet."

I wasn't sure what he was thanking me for, but his words made my heart swell.

THIRTY-FOUR

I LEFT THE OFFICE THAT night feeling confused about everything that had happened. Not only that day but every day leading up to that.

After stopping to grab a taco—my go-to comfort food—I went home and sat on the sofa in the dark, trying to recall everything that had taken place since the day of my interview. That had been almost eight weeks ago. Since that time, I had agreed to be shared by my four bosses, I'd gone on a pseudo-date with two of them, I'd been fucked by all four men, they had adorned me with toys, I'd been taught how to deep-throat, and now I had been publicly spanked.

All while ramping up on my new job. The new job that I sometimes did while naked.

It seemed as though I'd been shoved down the rabbit hole and I was now living in an alternate universe. It hadn't seemed strange in the least until today. Until the change I'd witnessed in Langston.

I had no idea what to think about it all.

While I was sitting there, my arms curled around me, my phone buzzed with a text. I leaned over and picked it up. It was a text from Langston.

Langston: *Little one? How are you doing? Wanted to check in.*

Luci: *I'm okay.*

It was mostly the truth. I was confused, sure, but other than that I was fine.

Langston: *How's your ass? Still hurt?*

Luci: *Not really, no.*

Langston: *If it's still bothersome, put some lotion on it. Something light. I should've done that while you were still in my office.*

Luci: I don't think it's necessary, but okay.
Langston: I need to ask you a question.
Luci: Anything.
Langston: Are you familiar with BDSM? And I'm not just referring to what you've read in fiction?

I frowned. The truth was, until I'd read that first book he loaned me, I'd never even heard about BDSM. Since then I'd devoured numerous others, but that was the gist of my experience. I decided to be honest when I typed my response.

Luci: No. Other than what I've read in romance novels, I'm not very familiar with it.

While I waited, I went into my contacts and changed his name to Master. For whatever reason, I'd started enjoying the way that it sounded. At least in my head. For me it signified a connection between us. I was sure I was overthinking things, but hey. It was all a jumble of chaotic nonsense slipping dangerously through my mind, and I was simply trying to deal.

Master: Search the Internet and read up on it. We'll discuss it more tomorrow, in the office.
Luci: Okay. I can do that.
Master: And Luci, I'll expect you to ask questions. It's not a cut-and-dried lifestyle. You will have questions. Good night, pet.
Luci: Good night, Master.

I pulled up my search browser on my phone, typing in BDSM. The results that came back were shocking. There was so much information, including online groups—more like communities—that lived the lifestyle.

After an hour of reading a variety of blogs and online articles, my eyes were tired and I'd learned more than I'd ever wanted to know on the subject. Sure, it intrigued me, but it also frightened the shit out of me. That was what Master was into? There were so many variations from submissives to slaves, sadists and masochists, even some who were referred to as primals. I read about various honorifics, training programs of all types, punishments. There was a wealth of information available, along with just as many warnings about misunderstandings and people being in it for the wrong reasons.

Finally, I managed to go to sleep, hoping tomorrow Master would enlighten me on this bizarre turn of events.

•

The next morning, I arrived in the office at seven thirty. Not for the first time in the past eight weeks, I felt a little hesitant as I got off the elevator. It was similar to when my bosses had agreed to pursue this unconventional arrangement. Only this time, it was moving in a direction that had me thinking nonstop and not only about sex.

I'd been hoping to see Jordan's smiling face when I arrived, but he wasn't there, so I shuffled back to my desk and started the coffee.

Once that was brewing, I looked at the calendar on my computer for a quick reminder of what my bosses had going on for the day. Then I saw the new toy demonstration, which was scheduled for one thirty, and my heart did a hop, skip, and jump right in my chest.

I managed to move on to my email.

Ben arrived at eight o'clock, Justin strolled in at eight thirty, with Landon only a few minutes behind him. All three men cast curious glances my way, but no one spoke to me. It was weird, but I tried not to think too hard about it as I offered and delivered each man his morning coffee.

I thought for sure they were all ignoring me, but before I could get out of Landon's office, he asked me to return.

"Shut the door and have a seat." His eyes met mine. "Please."

Swallowing hard, I followed his instruction, feeling incredibly shy and more than a little nervous.

"How are you feeling today?"

The question confused me. "I'm…uh…good."

"In comparison to yesterday," he added.

I sighed, managing to relax a little. "I'm fine. Mast...uh...Langston didn't hurt me, if that's what you're wondering."

"I'm glad to hear that, although I hadn't thought he had."

"He spanked me," I declared, narrowing my eyes as I stared at him.

"Did you deserve it?" he countered.

Had I not read so much information last night, I probably would've said no. However, in the realm of BDSM, I had learned that discipline was a necessity.

I nodded. "Yes. I disobeyed him."

"Did he leave any marks?"

"No. Of course not."

"If you have any questions at all, I want you to know that you can ask me or Langston. We'll tell you anything you want to know."

"I know that." And that was the truth. I felt as though I could ask them anything and they'd be honest with me. It was one of the reasons I wasn't freaking out more than I already had.

Landon nodded toward the door. "I won't keep you. You can go back to work."

"Thank you." I got to my feet and hurried back to my desk, wanting something to distract me from all the thinking that they had me doing.

Master showed up a few minutes shy of nine. He nodded to me, then headed right for his office.

My heart sank in my chest.

I wasn't sure why, but I'd been hoping for some sort of greeting from him. At least an acknowledgement. After what had transpired yesterday, I was looking for reassurance that things were okay between us. It was a needy feeling, one that I wasn't familiar with. One I didn't particularly care for either.

Master did accept my offer of coffee, but when I brought it to him, he didn't look up from his computer. As I was walking away, the deep timbre of his voice echoed from behind me.

"Please ask the others to join me in my office."

"Yes…Master," I said hesitantly before slipping out of the room.

I went to Ben's office first.

"Master…uh…Langston would like to see you."

Ben's eyes held something that looked like sympathy as he nodded. I then told Justin and Landon before returning to my desk. A few minutes later, the three men went into Master's office and closed the door.

Once again, my heart sank.

THIRTY-FIVE

BOSS MEETING

JUSTIN

I KNEW WHEN I LEFT the office yesterday that something significant had changed in the dynamic between the five of us. More importantly, between Luci and Langston. Something I wasn't all that happy about, quite frankly. It had become evident when Langston took it upon himself to punish Luci for not obeying his rules.

He had played his hand.

Not that I disagreed with how he had handled it. I would've done the exact same thing had I been in his shoes. Luci actually got off easy with Langston. I would've been much harsher with her, but I was far stricter than Landon and Langston.

Unfortunately, the rest of us could do nothing but sit back and wait to see how things would play out, because the man had practically staked his claim. And when a Dom staked his claim on a submissive, a certain protocol was followed.

The only good thing was the fact that the man had the decency to call a meeting so we could at least discuss it. Granted, it was a little too late, but there was still time for us to talk.

Once we were all settled in Langston's office, we waited patiently for him to speak.

"Get on with it," Landon said roughly.

Okay, maybe patient was the wrong word.

"Care to tell us what happened?" I suggested when it was clear Langston was having a hard time coming up with words.

Langston sighed. "It was time."

I barked a laugh. "Time? Are you fucking kidding me? Time for what? Time to pull the alpha card and take control? Or time to blow everything for the rest of us?"

Yeah. I sounded as angry as I felt. But I didn't care because I was pissed. I'd spent the entire night practically mourning the damn opportunity that Luci had presented for me and Ben.

"Are you planning to collar her?" I asked when no one else spoke up.

"Fuck no," he snapped.

That had the rest of us pretty much flinching.

"What do you mean, no?" Landon questioned, a deep groove marring his forehead.

"It means I have no intention of collaring her."

Again, everyone was speechless.

"Look. I had a moment of weakness."

"Fuck you," Landon hissed, his tone harder than I'd ever heard it. "It's one thing to play with the submissives at the club, Langston. Something else entirely to fuck with a girl who doesn't even understand the world we live in."

For the first time since I walked into the room, Langston actually appeared somewhat remorseful.

"It was a moment of weakness." Langston's eyes went hard. "Now, I'm not apologizin' for what I did, because I don't regret it."

"Personally," Ben said, "I think you handled it rather well."

Langston didn't say anything, but he nodded curtly.

"I agree," I admitted. "But I need you to be clear. You're telling us the rules *haven't* changed?"

"The rules haven't changed."

"Does she know this, *Master?*" Landon snarled at his brother.

Another sigh escaped Langston. He obviously hadn't expected the rest of us to call him on this. He should've known better. Granted, I hadn't seen Landon react quite like this. Not in all the time I'd known him. I'd seen them interact with plenty of submissives at the club, but neither of them had ever developed feelings for any of them. Not that I'd seen, anyway.

And fine, it wasn't like I hadn't suspected what was going on. The four of us kept in contact, and we made certain to share our plans. Maybe not all the details, but we did let one another know when we intended to spend time with Luci. Those two had spent far more time with her than Ben and I had.

However, that girl had become important to all of us. And not merely for sex. Sure, we were probably riding the high of having her eager and available, but that wasn't unexpected. That didn't mean we were willing to walk away. Not anymore.

"I plan to talk to her," Langston finally said. "I asked her to do some research on BDSM. And when the three of you get back to work, I intend to have a lengthy discussion with her."

"Don't you dare lead her on," Landon insisted. "No matter what she says, she's confused. Yes, she's read a little bit of fiction that glamorizes the lifestyle, but she has absolutely no idea what it is you truly want from her."

"I understand that. And I'm not leading her on."

I had to disagree. "You are if you're asking her to call you Master yet you have no intention of collaring her. She doesn't even understand the significance of that term, does she?"

Langston shook his head. "Doubtful. But as we all know, there are no steadfast rules in this lifestyle. We'll implement them as we go along." His gaze cut between each of us. "I have no intention of monopolizing her time or trying to keep her all to myself."

For some reason, I didn't believe him.

Oh, wait.

Maybe that was because he'd gone all territorial on her and insisted that she call him Master.

THIRTY-SIX

THE LONGER MY BOSSES WERE in Langston's office the worse I felt. It wasn't like they'd included me in their ad hoc meetings before, but I knew this was one that involved me. Justin had mentioned that they would discuss the change in dynamic this morning. I assumed that was what the meeting was for. As far as what the change was he had referred to, I had no freaking clue.

Since I had nothing else to do, I decided to continue my lesson on BDSM, scouring the Internet for as much information as I could retain. Truth was, I was fascinated. I found several websites that highlighted the attributes of a submissive. Many of which I could associate with on a level deeper than I expected.

Needless to say, by the time Master's door opened, I was enlightened about a lot of things, including my own feelings. No, I didn't think I'd simply turned into a submissive because Master wished it. I felt as though I *was* submissive on many levels, and truthfully, I was hoping to explore this in depth.

I got the feeling that was what Master wanted as well, but I wondered how the others felt. Most specifically Landon. I had yet to spend much time with him alone—aside from our impromptu dinner two days go—and the idea of not having that opportunity did not make me feel good.

I looked up as Justin approached my desk.

"When you get a moment, please contact Mr. Daniels about today's demonstration. Let him know that the five of us will be in attendance, but any of his assistants will need to remain outside the room."

I frowned.

"He'll understand what I mean."

"Yes, sir."

"Thank you." Justin turned toward his office. "Oh, and once you do that, Langston would like to see you in his office."

My heart instantly felt lighter, so I grabbed the phone as I pulled up Mr. Daniels's contact information, then dialed his number.

I was greeted by his secretary, then the call was sent to him directly.

"Good morning, Miss Wagner," he greeted kindly.

"Good morning, Mr. Daniels. I was calling about today's demonstration scheduled for one thirty. Jus—uh...Mr. Parker asked that I inform you that the five of us will be in attendance today, but he's asked that your assistants not be present in the room."

There was silence for a moment, then I was almost positive I heard a smile in his voice when he said, "I completely understand, and I look forward to it."

"Thank you, sir," I said kindly.

When the call disconnected, I placed the phone receiver in the cradle, then got to my feet. I slid my sweaty palms down the front of my skirt and tugged my sweater down a little before lifting my chin and heading for Master's office.

"Good morning, Master," I greeted formally when I stepped into the room.

"Good morning, pet." His eyes slowly lifted to mine as he got to his feet and moved over to the sofa, motioning for me to follow him.

I stopped in front of him, waiting for his direction.

Master placed a pillow on the floor by his feet and nodded toward it. "Please kneel."

I did so without question.

"Some Doms have their submissive sit in their lap. I prefer mine to kneel before me, touching me in some small way at all times."

I placed my hand on his thigh as he peered down at me. I noticed there were lines around his eyes, as though he hadn't slept well last night. I wondered if that had anything to do with what happened yesterday; however, I didn't ask.

"Were you able to research any information regarding BDSM like I requested?" His eyes locked with mine.

"Yes, Master. After you texted me last night, I got online and researched many sites."

"What were your initial thoughts?"

I considered that for a moment, thinking back on my first gut reaction. "I was intrigued by the idea that there's an entire lifestyle dedicated to Domination and submission. I mean, I've read plenty of romance novels depicting it, but I realize that's romanticized."

"Did what you found frighten you?"

"I would be lying if I said no," I admitted. "However, it also fascinated me."

"How so?"

"I felt as though I connected with many aspects of a submissive."

"I thought you might." His smile was warm and sexy but didn't last long. "I want you to know that reading about it and experiencing it firsthand are vastly different. A lot of people believe their various kinks, such as the desire to be tied up or commanded to do something, will translate into submission. It doesn't. Not by a long shot."

"So how does one know if they're submissive?"

"It's a desire far deeper than merely sexual. It's a deep-seated need to please and to serve their master. Where his needs are more important than their own."

Okay, so I wasn't as certain as I'd thought I was about being a submissive. But I wasn't put off by that explanation. I did have a deep desire to please my bosses. Not only sexually but in the workplace and in the relationships that we were developing.

"In the same sense," he continued, "being a Dom isn't only about control either. It requires the ability to understand what his submissive needs. To know her limits, her desires, as well as push her boundaries. It's not an absolute power exchange, though. There is a give and take."

Well, that made me feel a little better. The thought of not having my concerns considered was bothersome.

"May I ask you a question, Master?"

He nodded.

"Are you a Dominant?"

"I am."

"Do you live this lifestyle?"

"I do."

"Full time?"

"Yes."

"Do the others?"

"They do."

Well, that explained a lot about the dynamic around the office. I noticed that, although Ben was independent in his work, for the most part, he did often take instruction from Justin and not merely when Justin was ordering him to suck his cock. Although, there were those times as well. I'd picked up on the little things but hadn't put two and two together until last night when I was reading.

"Is Ben a submissive?"

"He's a switch."

I'd read that term last night. "That means he's both a Dominant and a submissive?"

"That's correct."

"And he's submissive to Justin?"

"He is. And *only* to Justin. Those are the terms they've agreed upon."

Okay, so at least I was on the right track with my thinking.

I knew my line of questioning was venturing into the personal realm, but I felt compelled to ask. "Are they a couple?"

"I think that's something you'll need to ask them."

Figured he wasn't going to gossip. I should've known better.

Master seemed to be waiting patiently for me to continue asking questions, so I racked my brain for another.

Master chuckled. "You don't have to ask everything right now, pet. But I do expect you to ask questions."

I liked that he referred to me as his pet. It felt special. No one other than him and Landon had called me that. It was similar to the way Justin referred to Ben as *pup*.

"What else intrigued you about what you read?" His eyes narrowed. "Keep in mind, there's a lot of information on the web regarding the lifestyle. A lot of it is sheer and utter bullshit. Some people don't understand the true meaning of a D/s relationship. They merely get off on the power trip they've mistakenly believed is at the root of it."

I nodded. "I read that. I was able to discern some of the...uh...crap."

He seemed pleased by this.

"I think what intrigued me most was the idea of a submissive freely giving her will, trust, and love to her Dom."

"How does that make you feel? The idea of giving so much of yourself?"

"Free, I guess. If it's to the right person. It seems natural in a sense. For me, anyway. That someone would be able to give all of themselves to another, knowing they would keep them safe from harm, yet push their boundaries in an effort to help them grow."

"How is that different than a regular relationship?"

Hmm. That was a good question. I considered it for a moment.

"It's not in many ways. However, a submissive puts her Dom's wants and needs above her own. And she derives pleasure from it."

"Do you derive pleasure from putting our needs above your own?"

"I do." That was the one thing that made the most sense to me.

Master smiled. "You did do your homework. I'm impressed."

My heart soared.

"One thing you need to know is that someone can't simply *claim* to be a Dominant. Just because you have a desire to submit doesn't mean he's earned it. A Dom must prove himself to those he expects to submit to him. Trust is not to be given blindly. It's the reason it has taken us so long to work up to this point."

I thought back to my time in the office, to the way my bosses had treated me. Day after day, week after week, we had established a bond between us. I had come to trust them naturally and I'd never felt as though they had pushed their dominance on me.

"What other questions do you have?"

"They're regarding how things will work here in the office," I admitted.

That was what confused me the most. I'd been hired to do a job. Yes, things had changed and I'd been shared by these four men, but even I knew something was different after last night. I'd been commanded to refer to Langston as Master. I did not want to make assumptions about what that meant though.

"How do you *want* things to work here in the office?" Master asked.

I met and held his gaze. "That's up to you, Master. And the others. I want to do…whatever pleases all of you."

Something sparked in his eyes and I got the sense that was the answer he'd hoped for; however, I don't think he was expecting it.

But it raised another question. "Am I supposed to refer to them differently?"

"I have requested you to call me Master. That's still in effect. As for the others, that will be up to them. Some Doms prefer honorifics, others do not."

"Like Ben and Justin? Ben calls him Mr. Parker because that's what they decided upon?"

"Yes, pet. That's an agreement between them." His hand rested on my head. "For right now, nothing has really changed except for how I prefer you to refer to me."

"I understand, Master."

"The reason we had you contact Mr. Daniels about today's demonstration is because he's a respected Dom in our community. His assistants are not. Nor are they his submissives. Had they been, I would've allowed them to attend. Under normal circumstances, we would not be sharing you with anyone outside of this office. But in this instance, we will allow Mr. Daniels to demonstrate on you as he deems necessary. But as our original agreement states, intercourse is not allowed."

That eased something inside me, but I wasn't sure why.

"May I ask another question, Master?"

"You may."

"Do you have any other submissives?"

"In the past, I have. For the time being, I do not."

His response sent a pain through my chest. I didn't like the idea of Master having another submissive and the way he said it sounded as though he expected to have additional ones in the future.

I didn't realize I'd dropped my gaze to the floor until Master's fingers curled beneath my chin and nudged my head so that I was once again looking at him.

"I'm not looking for any other submissives, pet. I've spent a long time searching...for you."

And that was the moment that I realized I was utterly devoted to this man in every way. Should he ask, I would give him every bit of my submission.

Only, I got the feeling that wasn't exactly what he wanted. Not entirely, anyway.

THIRTY-SEVEN

"LUCI," JORDAN GREETED WHEN I answered the phone. "Mr. Daniels is here for a one thirty appointment."

"Thanks. I'll be right out to get him."

I immediately got to my feet and headed toward the front, not wanting to leave Mr. Daniels waiting. He was a client and it was very clear that my company put their clients first. As it should be. And this was the first time that I had the pleasure of meeting one of their clients, so I wanted to make a good impression.

After my conversation with Master this morning, business had resumed as usual. It was as though nothing had happened and I was beginning to see that my bosses managed the overlap between business and personal much better than I did.

The only thing that had really changed was how I referred to my four bosses. When I typed correspondence, I used Mr. in front of their surnames, including when I sent emails to Master. Something told me that the relationship we'd established—whatever it might be—was not to interfere with work, but I was determined to show a certain level of respect.

And though things in the office hadn't been awkward, I had spent most of the day thinking about this demonstration. I couldn't deny that my emotions were chaotic. I was both nervous and excited.

"Good afternoon, Mr. Daniels," I greeted, holding out my hand to the formidable man in the finely tailored suit.

He appeared older, mid-forties if I had to guess. His jet-black hair was graying at the temples and blended nicely with his salt-and-pepper goatee. He was what I'd consider average height, probably right at six feet with a lean body and big hands.

For some strange reason, he reminded me a lot of Master. Maybe it was his mannerisms or the way he carried himself. There was something distinctly commanding about his presence.

He kindly took my hand, then lifted it to his lips. "It's a pleasure to meet you, Miss Wagner."

I felt Jordan's stare and I glanced over to see his eyes were wide as he took in the scene before him.

"We'll be setting up in the back conference room," I informed him.

Mr. Daniels turned and nodded to two men who were seated in the lounge area. They retrieved several black bags, a couple of hard cases, and a large mirror from the floor, then came to stand behind him. I turned and led the three men down the hall and into the conference room.

"Would you like the blinds open or closed, Mr. Daniels?" I asked, knowing it would be up to him.

"Open, please."

"Yes, sir." I hit the button to raise the blinds. "Is there anything you need before the meeting starts?"

"Just a little privacy." He then held out one small bag. "I'd like you to take this to Mr. Parker and let him know my assistants will notify him when we're ready."

"Yes, sir."

I returned to my desk and found Justin coming out of his office.

"Mr. Daniels is getting set up. He said he'd let you know when they're ready." I held up the bag. "He asked that I give you this."

Justin smiled down at me and nodded toward Master's office door. He led the way and stopped just inside Master's office.

"It's been requested that Luci wear this for the demonstration." Justin turned to me. "Please take Langston the bag."

I carried it over to him and set it on his desk.

Master peeked inside briefly, then lifted his head and nodded to Justin. His expression never changed. "I'll see that she does."

Justin nodded. "Once they're set up, I'll have the assistants return to the lobby and I'll lock the doors until the meeting's over."

"Perfect," Master replied.

Justin left the room. I started to follow.

"Hold up, pet," Master called out. "Please come back."

I returned to his side. He got to his feet and cupped my face. It was just one of the many ways he touched me. I liked that he did it. It made me feel special, as though I meant something to him.

"You and I haven't been over your limits yet. We'll do so tonight over dinner. In the meantime, Justin has offered your assistance in demonstrating one of his client's new toys. You mentioned before that you're willing. I want to make sure that's still the case."

I couldn't deny that the notion scared me. Conversely, my curiosity was getting the best of me. "Do you know what it is, Master?"

"I do, and I can assure you, it will only bring you pleasure. And after discussing with Landon, we've decided that we will not allow Mr. Daniels to touch you during the demonstration. Not in a sexual manner."

I nodded, considering this for a moment. He didn't offer to tell me what the toy was, which meant he didn't want me to know.

His thumb brushed over my cheek. "None of us will allow any harm to come to you, Luci. I assure you of that. I don't believe this will push your limits based on what you've been willing to do thus far. However, at any time, should it begin to be too much for you, you can use your safeword."

I'd read about safewords. It was a word submissives used to stop a scene or situation they weren't comfortable in. If I were to merely say stop, they wouldn't take that as my desire to really quit. Often, during passionate interactions, people used the terms *no* and *stop* when in actuality, they were simply speaking for the sake of speaking aloud. For safety reasons, safewords were used as an automatic stop to all play. Like a failsafe.

"We'll be using *red* as your safeword. Anytime you feel as though you cannot take any more, you will simply call it out. Ensure that you're loud enough to be heard. Under no circumstance will play continue should you use it." He used his thumb on my chin to tilt my head back farther. "Keep in mind, we will be pushing your boundaries at times. That will be our pleasure to take. You have to trust us to know what is right for you."

"I trust you," I whispered.

"I want that to be true, Luci. However, I want to earn that trust. So go with your instincts." Master leaned down and pressed his mouth to mine. It was a gentle kiss that left my lips tingling when he pulled back.

"I will, Master. I promise."

"Very well. And if one of the Doms asks you what your color is…" He tilted my head again, ensuring I was looking him in the eye. "Green means you are fine and you're good to continue. Yellow means you're hesitant and need a moment to collect your thoughts or that you feel as though you can't be pushed any further. If you ever need time to collect yourself, feel free to call out yellow. It will allow us to discuss your hesitations before we continue. Understood?"

"Yes, Master."

Master released me, then turned to the bag on his desk. "Please change into this, then return to your desk. When we're ready for you to join us, someone will call you." He reached out and ran his hand over my hair. "And pull your hair up. We don't want it to get in the way."

Taking a deep breath, I nodded, then watched as Master left his office. He didn't close the door behind him.

I was both nervous and excited about what was to come. This had initially started out as an erotic game, but it seemed to be moving in a much different direction. One that involved rules and structure, something I wasn't at all turned off by. Master helped to make me feel grounded. I liked the feeling.

I pulled out the items in the bag, which included a pair of white knee-high stockings and a white lace bra that wasn't much of a bra at all. It had an underwire, but it did not have cups, which meant my nipples would be exposed. And last but not least, there was a pair of white crotch-less panties. They were frilly and sexy as all get out.

My breath came in rapid pants as I stared at the ensemble. It was definitely sexy, however, it meant I would be basically naked in front of a man I didn't know. It was one thing to be naked in front of my bosses, but this was taking it to an entirely different level.

Glancing at the clock, I noticed that I only had two minutes until the meeting officially started. Without wasting another second, I quickly stripped and changed.

Since they didn't request that I wear shoes, I opted to go without. My booties were cute, but I felt they would detract from the sexy innocence of the outfit—I assumed that was what they were going for—so I left them off and returned to my desk. Taking a seat, I grabbed a couple of clips from my purse, then proceeded to pin my hair up.

I heard Justin's voice, then saw him leading Mr. Daniels's two assistants back to the lobby. No one turned to look at me, but a tingle of awareness shivered down my spine at the thought of them seeing me practically naked.

Rather than stop by my desk to get me, I watched as Justin passed again, returning to the conference room. A second later, my desk phone rang and I answered.

"Please join us in the conference room."

"Yes, sir," I told Justin.

I wondered why he hadn't just told me when he passed, but then I realized as I walked alone to the conference room, wearing the outfit they'd chosen for me, that they'd done it on purpose. Despite the considerable confidence the sexy lingerie gave me, I felt incredibly vulnerable knowing that the five men sat on the other side of the door waiting to do God only knew what to me.

Rather than turn and run, I lifted my chin, keeping it at a respectable angle, squared my shoulders, straightened my spine, cognizant of how pleasing my body would appear, then turned the knob. After all, this was what Master wanted me to do.

And above all else, I wanted to please him.

THIRTY-EIGHT

WHEN I STEPPED INTO THE room, the first thing I noticed was that all five men were sitting in the chairs around the small table. There was something set up on the far side near the windows; however, there was a large black drape covering it, so I couldn't tell what it was. It took a tremendous amount of effort, but I kept myself from staring at it. I would find out what it was eventually.

"You look lovely," Ben said when I turned to face them after closing the door.

My posture remained graceful and pleasing, but not in a manner that said I was looking to attract attention. Or at least that was what I was aiming for.

"You have wicked taste in clothing, Charles," Justin stated.

"I do, don't I?" Mr. Daniels's gaze slid over me from head to toe, warming me more than I already was. "However, I don't know that it's the clothes that make her so stunning. The four of you are very lucky to have such a lovely submissive."

The compliment made me blush.

"Damn lucky," Ben mumbled under his breath.

"We were just talking about you, pet," Master said, motioning me to move farther into the room.

"Yes," Mr. Daniels agreed. "It seems you've made quite the impression on your bosses."

"Thank you, sir."

Mr. Daniels peered over at Master. "Does she have training?"

"Aside from her time here at the office, no. None whatsoever."

Mr. Daniels looked at me once more. "Interesting." He glanced at Master again. "Is it all right with you if I get started?"

"Absolutely." Master's gaze rested on my face, and I could feel the approval coming from him.

When Master's eyes cut over to Landon, I followed, noticing that Landon's eyes were on the floor. He was the only one who hadn't said anything and he looked as though something was bothering him. I couldn't imagine what, and I didn't have a chance to figure it out.

Mr. Daniels got to his feet and moved over to me. He seemed to be assessing me as he circled, his hand leisurely caressing my arm, my hip. His touch was gentle yet firm. I could practically feel the power radiating from him.

"Face me," he commanded when he stopped on my left side.

I turned to face him.

"Mr. Moore, if you wouldn't mind assisting me for a moment."

Landon got to his feet and walked toward us.

"Please touch your submissive; ensure that she's comfortable and ready for the scene."

My eyes lifted to Landon's when he took his position in front of me. His hands were warm as they lightly grazed my arms, his eyes intent as they locked with mine.

The back of his hand brushed my right nipple and I inhaled sharply. The contact was not at all unpleasant. Quite the opposite, in fact. Knowing that everyone in the room was watching as Landon touched me only heightened the experience.

"Very responsive," Mr. Daniels said from beside us.

I never looked away from Landon, completely lost in his gaze.

His hand trailed down between my legs, his finger sliding through my slit. I knew I was wet already and he discovered that also.

"Is she ready?" Mr. Daniels questioned.

Landon didn't look away and I felt the need to assure him that I was okay with this, so I offered a small smile and a slight nod.

"She's ready." Landon's voice was rough.

Mr. Daniels then looked to the others. "This is going to be fun. Thank you for inviting me here." His smile seemed genuine. He spoke to the others when he said, "Now, if you'll join me."

Landon took my hand and led me over to the window where Mr. Daniels had set up, my other three bosses following close behind.

"Now, keep in mind, gentlemen, this will generally be attached to ceiling hooks for play. I intended for it to be a permanent fixture in playrooms. However, I assure you, my temporary setup is secure and it has been tested numerous times."

He removed the drape to reveal a large metal pole secured to a heavy base. The pole arched and at the end hung what appeared to be straps and chains. They dangled freely in one big clump of leather and metal.

"A swing?" Landon questioned, sounding unimpressed.

Mr. Daniels chuckled. "Not just any swing, Mr. Moore. This one is specifically designed for dual penetration."

I watched as Mr. Daniels separated the leather and chains to reveal a thick black dildo that was attached. It had a remarkable resemblance to a real cock, with a thick, bulbous head and veins running down.

"Think of the Sybian machine," he continued. "Only this allows for your interaction as well as your complete control." He turned to face my bosses. "Now which of you will be leading the demonstration?"

"I will," Justin offered.

"Then which do you prefer?" Mr. Daniels probed. "Anal or vaginal entry?"

Justin's eyes trailed over to me and he smiled. "Anal."

"I thought you might. Luci, please join me."

I stepped closer at Mr. Daniels's request.

"Mr. Snowden, would you mind moving the mirror so that you'll also have a view of her from the front."

While Ben situated the mirror, Mr. Daniels had me stand facing away from him. He then took my wrists and cuffed them together with padded leather restraints before lifting them up and attaching the cuffs to the top of the pole. When the mirror shifted in front of me, I could see the other four men behind me, watching as Mr. Daniels positioned me to his liking.

"Comfortable?" Mr. Daniels asked.

"Yes, sir."

"Good." His attention returned to my bosses. "Because it's designed for you to use your submissive in a way that pleases you, you'll be required to strap her in. It is very versatile, as you can see. Since Mr. Parker has decided on anal penetration, I'll have Miss Wagner facing away and the dildo will be inserted vaginally."

"Ben, please do the honors of preparing our submissive," Justin ordered.

"My pleasure, Mr. Parker."

As I stood there with my arms restrained above my head, Ben knelt down before me. He gently nudged my legs apart, then slid his tongue over my clit. And now I knew the real reason for the crotch-less panties.

I moaned.

"I like hearing that," Mr. Daniels said, his voice a mere whisper as he strapped the contraption to my body.

Although they possibly should've been, his words weren't creepy. I could tell he wasn't hitting on me, merely attempting to offer praise and to get me comfortable. Had I been alone with him, the opposite would've been true, but I continued to remember what Master said. They would not allow any harm to come to me.

I was unable to pay attention to what Mr. Daniels was doing because my entire focus was on Ben lapping at my pussy, his tongue pushing inside me, then flicking my clit. It was an exquisite sensation, made even more so since he was obviously not attempting to send me over the edge.

While he suckled my clit, he pushed one thick finger inside me, pulling another desperate moan from me. Unfortunately, he then pulled back, both his mouth and his finger. I swallowed the groan of disappointment.

"She's ready, Mr. Parker," Ben said, getting to his feet.

"Thank you, pup," Justin stated from behind me.

Before he moved away, Ben leaned in and kissed me softly, then placed his finger on my lips. Knowing what he wanted, I sucked my own juices off, grazing him lightly with my teeth.

"Would you like to do the honors, Mr. Parker?" Mr. Daniels asked. "Or shall I?"

"I'd like to."

Justin moved around in front of me, his eyes meeting mine. I could see the heat there and it only intensified my desire. His hands were gentle as he cupped my face, leaning in and kissing me. His tongue stroked its way into my mouth as his hands slid down to my hips, then ventured between my legs.

When he pulled back, he teased my clit with the thick black dildo. I hissed as more pleasure assaulted me.

"You like that?"

I nodded. "Yes, Mr. Parker."

His eyes flashed with yearning.

A second later, he was pushing the dildo inside me. It was a gentle thrust and retreat. He fucked me slowly, teasing me as he inserted it. The silicone toy was quite thick, requiring my muscles to loosen as it inched deeper. My pussy clamped around the intrusion, but I forced myself to relax, to enjoy what he was doing.

Mr. Daniels continued with his spiel. "Normally, when I restrain a submissive, I keep her body taut, but in this instance, the swing is going to be her support so there is no need. You have the ability to move her, shifting her forward and back. We've purposely attached the dildo so that you can use the swing's momentum to intensify her pleasure. However, the toy is removable for cleaning. And I'm working on additional attachments to enhance her pleasure. Aside from the added toy, it does function pretty much as a regular sex swing would."

Mr. Daniels demonstrated this by grabbing the straps above my head and lifting the swing, which brought me to my tiptoes, then allowing it to drop. The sudden momentum caused the strap between my legs to tighten, allowing the dildo to push impossibly deeper, making me cry out as it filled me.

"Color, Luci?" Master called out.

"Green," I said instantly. The toy wasn't painful, not by a long shot.

"Continue," Master instructed.

Mr. Daniels took a step back. "Should you choose to offer her up to another, you can also adjust the swing by shifting the arm restraints and using this strap." He did something that repositioned me so that I was leaning forward, my hands and forearms pulled slightly behind my head while my elbows rested on another strap, which kept my shoulders from bending at an awkward angle. It was different, but not an uncomfortable position. "You can also use the chest strap if you'd prefer not to restrain her arms. It all depends on which position you choose and how creative you want to get. As always, it's about safety and pleasure, not discomfort."

When he adjusted the other strap, I was suspended in the air, my face forward, ass out, with the dildo still penetrating my pussy. I could almost imagine myself using this contraption alone to bring myself pleasure. If my feet were touching the floor, I'd have the ability to rock on the dildo.

"In this position, you have free reign of her mouth and her ass. If she were on her back with the dildo in her ass, her pussy would be available to you. Now we shall enjoy the show."

In my peripheral vision, I noticed Landon move around to my left, while Ben moved to my right. I couldn't see Mr. Daniels or Master, but I knew they were behind me.

Unmoving, I watched as Justin unbuckled his belt, then freed his cock. He was already hard as he caressed my lips with the swollen head.

"Suck," he instructed, his tone gentle.

I opened my mouth and took him inside. I couldn't move, not even my head, which allowed him to fuck my mouth as he saw fit. For several minutes, he played with me, pulling me forward so that his cock pushed deep into my throat, then shifting me back. It was an interesting sensation, to say the least.

I felt warm hands on my ass. Justin was obstructing my view of the mirror, so I wasn't sure if they were Master's or Mr. Daniels's. I could only assume they were Master's since he said they would not be allowing Mr. Daniels to touch me.

While Justin continued to fuck my mouth slow and deep, something cool slid down the crack of my ass and then a thick finger slid inside, teasing me. I was then impaled back and forth. Justin's cock in my mouth, the dildo in my pussy, and the finger in my ass.

I was surprised by how erotic it was.

"Our pet has a very tight ass," Master noted, confirming that he was the one fucking my ass with his finger. "So fucking tight."

He inserted another and I moaned around Justin's cock. They continued to use me, filling all of my holes for several minutes.

And then it all stopped and I was repositioned so that my feet were once again touching the floor and my arms were directly above my head. My breaths were rapid as my arousal intensified. I didn't want them to stop. I could see the men behind me in the mirror and I met Master's heated gaze. He seemed to be enjoying the show.

I was so caught up in looking at him that it shocked me when Justin's cock breached my asshole. The discomfort was significant initially, stealing my breath as his cock filled me. With the dildo inside, it was an overwhelming feeling. Although Master and Landon had fucked me like this before, it had been a while.

"Fuck, she's tight," Justin groaned. "I like the dildo, for sure. I also like that I can move her. I have a swing at home that I've utilized before. I think I like this one better."

Although he sounded clinical in his assessment, there was nothing dispassionate about the way Justin was fucking my ass. The dildo was stuffed inside me, and the angle caused my clit to be pressed against the leather strap between my legs. His hands curled around my thighs and he tilted me so that my feet came off the ground. In that position, he pulled me onto him over and over, fucking me deeper than before.

I moaned, not caring how I sounded. It felt so good I didn't really care.

"There's one more thing I meant to show you," Mr. Daniels said.

The dildo came to life, vibrating inside me.

"Oh, God!" I screamed, the sensation shooting me right to the precipice of a climax that would likely kill me. It was that intense. Up until that point, I hadn't thought about climaxing, but the strength of it launched me straight to the edge.

"You may come, pet," Master growled roughly.

I did.

I came with a scream that I was sure could be heard throughout the building. Seconds later, Justin's hips stopped and I felt him coming in my ass.

"I have to say, Mr. Moore, she's definitely a treat," Mr. Daniels said.

"She certainly is," Master agreed.

The vibration finally shut off and I was still gasping for breath when Justin pulled out. I couldn't move, still restrained.

"While it's my responsibility to handle your aftercare," Justin whispered softly, "I need to meet with my client. Is that okay with you?"

I nodded, meeting his eyes in the mirror. It took effort to hold up my head. Every muscle in my body was lax from the mind-blowing climax.

"Landon, would you please take care of our pet?" Master asked.

Their pet.

Not his.

That distinction was not at all what I had expected to hear, much less dwell on. It made me feel slighted, as though Master wasn't willing to call me his own.

I didn't like that, but I lost track of that thought when Landon wrapped me in his arms and whispered, "It would be my pleasure."

My disappointment instantly faded as I realized one thing. If Master claimed me as his own, I wouldn't have Landon.

And if I was being completely honest with myself, I wasn't willing to give him up. Not even for Master.

THIRTY-NINE

LANDON WAS THE ONE WHO removed the restraints and unhooked me from the swing. My legs were weak, but it didn't matter because Landon easily lifted me into his arms, then carried me out of the room, down the hall, and into his office through the back door.

"Why are there two doors to every office?" I asked because it seemed the appropriate time.

He paused momentarily, then glanced back at the door. He smiled, then turned his attention back to me. "Because we had it reconfigured when we took over this floor. There used to be eight offices here. We only wanted four but we figured it would be a good idea to keep the doors."

"So you could sneak out?" I teased.

"Actually...there have been a couple of secretaries who wanted to know every move we made, so yes. They've been used to sneak out a time or two. Although we haven't felt the need to do that to you. Not yet, anyway."

I chuckled, then leaned against his chest.

Landon didn't put me down until we were in the large shower in his bathroom. After helping me to steady myself, he turned on the water, then stripped us both. He even secured my hair, fixing the few pieces that had fallen out during the demonstration.

He seemed to be taking extra special care of me, which was endearing.

"Did you enjoy the demonstration?" Landon asked as he led me beneath the warmth of the spray. He was careful not to get my hair or my face wet.

"Yes. I did. It was an interesting device."

He grunted, his eyes lifting to my face but then quickly looking away. "You were beautiful."

"Thank you."

His cock was rock hard as he lathered me with soap, cleaning me from neck to toes. The sensation of his hands roaming over me had my body humming, my arousal returning. I enjoyed the way he touched me, how soothing he was.

"May I ask a question, Mr. Moore?"

Landon's smile appeared forced, but he answered easily. "For now, just call me Landon. And yes, you may ask."

"Are you active in the BDSM lifestyle?" I knew that Master had said he was, but I was hoping to get a little more insight into Landon. I wanted to know *him*, to understand *him*, not to have that information relayed to me. With the way things were changing, I wasn't sure if that was something I'd be afforded in the future and the thought upset me.

Although he'd taken me to dinner, I'd been so caught up in the spontaneity of it I hadn't asked many personal questions, and every minute since, I'd wished that I had.

His eyes lifted to meet mine. "I am."

"Do you have a submissive?"

His smile turned sad. "I do not."

"Are you looking for one?"

"You mean besides you?"

I liked that he referred to me as his. "Yes."

"No, I'm not looking for another."

I remained quiet for a moment while he rinsed the soap from my skin.

"May I ask another question?"

He smiled, then nodded.

I glanced down the length of his body, then up to his face. "May I return the favor?"

His eyes flashed with heat. "I'd like that."

He replaced the sprayer and pointed it downward while I grabbed the bottle of body wash. I used it generously, lathering him up, starting at his neck. His shoulders were huge, his muscles deliciously defined. I worked my way down each arm, then over his torso. I briefly stroked his erection with my soapy hands as I went to my knees before venturing lower. Working my way up from his feet, I waited as the water cascaded over his body, rinsing the soap away.

"May I?" I asked, meeting his eyes as I fisted his cock, eager to take him in my mouth.

He was staring down at me, an intensity there I hadn't seen before. When he shook his head, disappointment flooded me. I felt the strange urge to cry. I fought it back.

Landon cupped my face, tilting my head back as he peered down at me. "Although I thoroughly enjoy your mouth, I'd much rather be inside you, sweet girl. Let me slide my cock into your body and fuck your tight little pussy."

My brain was screaming, *Yes, please!* but I controlled my emotions and softly responded with "I would like that" as I got to my feet.

He pressed my back against the tiled wall, his mouth crushing down on mine. I whimpered at his rough touch, enjoying it immensely. Without preamble, Landon lifted my left leg up against his hip as he easily guided his cock inside me. He rammed his hips forward, impaling me.

"Fuck..." He hissed as his hips punched forward. "Luci...damn, baby."

"Oh, God!" I cried out, overwhelmed by the instant sensation of being filled by him. His cock was long and thick, extremely generous in size. It reminded me of when he had fucked my ass. Losing my anal virginity had been overwhelming but not unpleasant.

"Fuck, you feel so good. *So* fucking good," he growled against my neck. "Squeeze my cock, sweet girl."

I tightened my inner muscles around his cock as he pulled back, then impaled me again. He slammed into me hard, over and over again, taking his pleasure from my body.

"I've wanted to fuck you just like this…just me and you."
He pressed against me, our bodies practically one. "I wanted to be
the one fucking your ass," he mumbled. "Only me."

My eyes watered, tears damn near falling, but I held on to
them as tightly as I was holding on to him.

"Fuck, baby. You're so tight."

My inner muscles clamped down on him.

"Aww, baby. Just. Like. That." His hips punched forward
with every word.

I moaned as he pinched my nipple roughly. He wasn't
gentle, but I loved what he was doing to me.

"That night, when I took you to dinner…I wanted to do
this right there in the hallway, with that guy listenin' in. I wanted
to make you scream my name so the entire fucking building knew
who was fucking you."

My breaths slammed in and out of my lungs as he spoke.
I remembered that night so well. I'd wanted the same thing.

"Keep your leg up," he insisted, his hand dropping from
under my knee.

I remained like that, my back against the wall as I kept my
left leg raised, opening myself to him.

Landon gripped my right hip, his fingers digging into my
flesh as his other hand curled under my leg, squeezing my ass. He
bent his knees and changed the angle of his hips, then slammed
into me again, his cock bottoming out. He fucked me roughly, our
combined groans echoing off the tile.

My body burned brighter and hotter until I felt my
impending orgasm. "I'm gonna come… Please let me come, sir."

"Fuck, yes," he growled. "Come all over my dick, sweet
girl."

I shattered, my body reeling, my knees nearly giving out.

Landon held me there, thrusting several more times before
he groaned loudly, his hips banging into mine one last time. He
came, his cock pulsing inside me as I melted against the wall.

That was the first time Landon had fucked me while we
were alone.

The first time he'd been completely in charge.

When I looked up, I noticed Master standing in the doorway, watching us. I couldn't read his expression and I suddenly wondered if I'd ever get this opportunity again.

The thought of never being with Landon again was not something I even wanted to consider. As far as I was concerned, letting him go would never be an option.

FORTY

BOSS MEETING

LANDON

"THIS BETTER BE GOOD," I informed my twin when I walked into his office at four o'clock on the dot. I wasn't happy that he'd called another meeting after the way things had been going for the past couple of days.

Langston didn't bother to answer because Justin and Ben joined us right then.

"What's up?" Justin asked as he took a seat on the opposite couch, unbuttoning his suit jacket. He was clearly getting ready to head out for the day.

"I've invited Luci to my apartment tonight to go over her limits list."

My eyes widened as I glanced over at my brother. "What?"

Langston frowned. "You heard me. I want to go over her limits. I think it's time we move this in the direction we all intended it to go."

"So, it's official?" Justin asked, obviously needing the same clarification I did. "We're training her to be our submissive?"

"Yes," Langston stated flatly.

That was interesting for two reasons. One, we'd never introduced one of our secretaries to that world. Then again, we'd never interacted with one of our secretaries the way we had with Luci. The four of us were much closer to Luci than I think even we had anticipated.

"And why are you the one going over the list with her?" Ben asked, his eyes locked on my brother.

"Because I'm the one who's talked to her about it." Langston glanced at me, then Justin. "If one of you would prefer to do it, feel free. But it needs to be done now."

"Why the rush?" I needed to understand why he was pushing the time table up. We'd all agreed that we would take this slow. Two months, in my opinion, wasn't slow.

"She's interested and eager to learn. By introducing her to the list, she'll have to start thinking about other things, more intimate things."

"I don't have a problem with it," Justin stated. "I agree, on that count. She does need to understand that we'll be introducing her to things she's never heard of before."

I still didn't understand the rush. "Why tonight?"

"Because she experimented with the demonstration. I'm sure she has questions."

"You think you're the best one to give her answers?" My brother was a lot of things, but a teacher he was not.

Then again, I wasn't being completely fair to him. He was a Dom. And that was one position he took very seriously. I knew he wouldn't steer Luci the wrong way.

"You can join us if you'd like," he offered.

I shook my head. "Can't. I have plans."

It was a lie. I didn't have plans, but I certainly needed to put some distance between me and Luci. After what had transpired between us in my office bathroom a short while ago, I knew I needed to get my head on straight. I wanted more from that girl than she could even fathom at this point.

Unfortunately, I knew my brother wasn't on the same page as I was. He wanted Luci, of that I was certain. But he wasn't ready to make the type of commitment that I wanted. And since we'd always known that we would have one submissive between us, I had to give him time to come around to the idea. The idea being Luci was the one.

I knew it.

I think she knew it.

Now, we simply had to wait for Langston to get on board. Which could possibly take far longer than I cared for.

"Once she's filled it out, I'd like a copy," Justin said, leaning forward as though getting ready to stand. "I'm not completely on board with the way you're handling things here. I thought you should know that now. However, I'm capable of backing off to see how things play out."

Langston nodded. "I'll share the list."

"If there's anything I can help clarify for her," Ben offered, "I'll be more than happy to do so. She and I have developed a rapport. I think she trusts me."

That statement got my back up. "I think she trusts all of us," I countered hotly.

Ben's expression softened. "I didn't mean any offense by it. And I agree. I think she trusts all of us. I just know what it's like from her perspective." He cocked one black brow. "Sometimes I think you forget that I'm submissive as well."

"Sorry," I muttered. Ben was right. And I was getting far too defensive.

"Anything else?" Justin asked, getting to his feet.

Langston shook his head. "Not at the moment. However, I would like us to meet on Friday to discuss our plans for her during the conference."

"The daily to-do items?" Ben asked, chuckling. "I like the idea of that. I think it'll help to ease some of her stress."

"I agree," Justin said. "And I want to ensure we assign days. I don't want to overwhelm her too much. She'll have a lot to do."

"Understood."

"See you tomorrow then," Justin said, nodding toward Ben before they exited the office.

I didn't move from my position.

"You want to share what's on your mind?" Langston prompted.

"Not really, no." That was the truth. I did not think my brother needed to know where my head was at right now.

"Well, when you're ready, I'm willin' to listen."

He said that now.

I wasn't so sure that would be the case if I were to tell him that I was ready to make Luci our permanent submissive.

Yeah. I was pretty sure that wouldn't go over well with anyone.

Didn't make it any less true.

FORTY-ONE

"WHAT IS THIS, MASTER?" I asked as Master and I sat at his kitchen table after dinner that night.

I'd spent the remainder of the afternoon working as though nothing had happened that day. Master and Landon had left me to get dressed, and when I came out of Landon's bathroom, I found that all four of my bosses had gone into Langston's office for a meeting.

It wasn't until I was getting ready to leave at five thirty that Master finally emerged. He informed me that we were having dinner in his apartment. I didn't try to argue because I was secretly eager to see their home away from home.

The ride up to the forty-fourth floor was what one would expect after a long day at work. Master was quiet, but so was I. The exhaustion had kicked in and I wanted nothing more than to have dinner, maybe a glass of wine, and to relax for a bit.

When we arrived, a lovely meal consisting of a small salad, a bacon-wrapped filet, and rosemary potatoes had been set out. When I asked if he cooked, Master had informed me that they had a personal chef they used when they were in the city. At home, Landon was apparently the one who cooked most of the time. Master admitted that he preferred to stay out of the kitchen if at all possible.

Dinner was nice, the conversation enjoyable. We talked briefly about the demonstration and he admitted that the swing was interesting but not something he would be outfitting his dungeon with.

"You have a dungeon?"

His smile was sexy as he took a sip of his red wine. "Yes. At the house."

"Do you and Landon both use it?"

"Let's just say we have one. And leave it at that."

That admission opened the conversation to a direction I was curious about. Master gave me a few tidbits of information regarding BDSM, mostly at a high level. Which had led to where we were now, with me staring down at a stack of papers while I once again questioned what I was getting myself into.

"This is a limits list. Keep in mind, there may be various other things that have been left off, although it wasn't intentional. As you can imagine, there are all kinds of kinks and fetishes out there. This is an extensive list though, and I want you to go through it. Take your time and check off the appropriate box for each."

I looked up at him when he paused.

"I want you to give a lot of thought to each one, Luci. There is no right or wrong answer. However, I do want you to have an open mind. If you haven't experienced it, that doesn't mean you should be completely against it."

I nodded.

"As you can see, you'll check off whether or not you've tried it." He pointed to a section that had yes/no. "Then there are five options. *Limit* means you refuse to do it. Those are your hard limits. If it triggers something painful from your past, it will likely be a hard limit. You can select *maybe* for anything that you'd be willing to try with one of the four of us. We would not allow anyone else to do them while you're in our care."

"What does that mean? If I don't select maybe, does that mean you'll let someone else do them?"

Master held my stare. "There could come a time, perhaps at a club, where we would want you to interact with someone else. Maybe with another submissive—male or female. And sometimes if there's a Dom who's mastered a certain area, such as the whip. That's not something the four of us are comfortable with, so if you were interested, we would potentially find someone who you could experiment with."

Okay. So that wasn't exactly what I'd expected him to say.

He continued. "Then you have *curious*, which means you're interested in trying it. Select *okay*, if it's a genuine interest of yours. That means you enjoy it. Or choose *yes, absolutely*, if it's something you are certain you enjoy."

I glanced down at the paper as he read each of the options off. When I looked back up at him, he smiled.

"Just because it's something you enjoy, that doesn't mean we'll necessarily do it. Remember, when it comes to D/s, you are freely giving yourself to your master. For his pleasure. There are many items on that list that I don't find appealing. That doesn't mean you won't experience them."

I wondered if Master realized how he continued to categorize himself as part of a whole. It wasn't whether or not *he* would be doing something, it was *them*. It was as though he was keeping that distance between us. And maybe he was. Maybe he feared I would get attached, which was very possible. Casual sex still wasn't something I was interested in. It was the very reason I'd agreed to this with my bosses. They had explicitly stated they wouldn't be having sex with anyone else, which had given it some exclusivity. Probably the biggest reason I'd agreed.

However, getting to know them on a deeper level was something I craved.

I still loved how I felt when I thought of bringing this man pleasure. It was an intense feeling that I wasn't used to. Then again, I felt the same way with all of my bosses. The thought of making them happy made me happy.

"Do you have any questions?"

"No, Master."

Master left me at the table and I perused the list. My brain was overwhelmed by things that confused me. I had no idea what some of this stuff even was. I decided to go down the list and check off any that I had tried. I found that I ended up only checking a few things, such as anal sex, cuffs, nipple clamps, gags. Basically, the few things they'd introduced me to. Truth was, I didn't have much experience.

Once I'd gone back and selected no for everything else, I decided to add an extra column. I titled it NEED CLARIFICATION. I then proceeded down the list, deciding I would mark off anything I refused to do first. I knew without a doubt that I wasn't interested in anything that had to do with blood play, like needles, cutting, or the like. So not my thing. Nor was I interested in golden showers or scat play. Yuck.

I found that I didn't know what a lot of things were, but there were many that seemed self-explanatory. Role playing, biting, phone sex, voyeurism, being recorded, and the list went on. Although some of those things made me a little nervous, I decided if it wasn't going to cause physical pain, I could likely endure it. Although humiliation and objectification didn't sound fun, at least I figured I would survive.

It all boiled down to how much I trusted my bosses. Many of these things I would've said no to immediately had I not spent the past two months getting to know them. Trust was a huge factor in how I would answer.

I had no idea how long it took for me to fill it out, but when I looked up, I found Master standing at the kitchen island watching me. At some point, he'd ditched the wine and made himself a glass of scotch.

"I'm finished."

"Go through it again," he instructed. "For every single one, I want you to answer as though you hadn't already. If your second answer is different from your first, select *maybe* or *curious.*"

"Yes, Master."

I went through the list again. I found myself changing my answer for several things, including ice play, being recorded, and pussy worship. Up to this point in my life, I had not been with a woman, but...should the situation require it, I was definitely curious. I also changed my answer regarding triple penetration, which I took to mean multiple cocks in the same hole, which, honestly, I wasn't even sure was possible. I had originally selected *maybe* for those and changed my answer to *curious.* However, I did not add any additional hard limits and I didn't waver on anything I'd said *yes, absolutely* to.

This time, when I looked up, Master was not in the kitchen. I got up, taking the stack of papers with me, and headed toward the living room.

I took a moment to admire the apartment. It was significantly larger than mine and had high-end everything. From the travertine floors to the brushed-nickel fixtures, it was relatively modern in style, although there was a rustic twist. The floor-to-ceiling windows overlooked downtown and the view at night was stunning.

"Did you finish?"

I turned away from the window to see Master coming into the room from down the hallway.

"I did."

"Bring it to me."

I stepped around the large area rug and the glass coffee table, taking the papers to him.

He took them and set them on a chair before turning back to me.

When Master cupped my face gently, I stared up into his eyes, my heart swelling inside my chest. I had no idea what it was about this man that called to me on a very base level, but it did. I'd never felt this way for anyone in my life. I'd go so far as to say I'd never even thought I would.

"Thank you for trusting me," Master whispered softly.

His hands slid down to my neck as he leaned in, his lips finding mine. I sighed as he kissed me. It was gentle yet intense at the same time. As though something was passing between us. Maybe it was, I wasn't sure. Whatever the feeling, I liked it. A lot.

When he pulled back, Master once again peered down into my eyes. "As much as I want to fuck you right now, I think your pussy has had enough for one day."

His words alone made my pussy clench. But he was right. Between the demonstration and Landon's rough but exquisite treatment, I was sore.

Master brushed his thumb over my bottom lip. "However, I'm gonna take you home and I'm gonna partake of your lovely mouth before I leave you there to get a good night's rest."

My voice came out raspy when I said, "I would like that, Master. Very much."

FORTY-TWO

MONDAY MORNING ROLLED AROUND AND excitement had been fizzing in my veins from the second I opened my eyes. Needless to say, the snooze button was not necessary this morning. Today was the first day of our four-day quarterly meeting, and I was bound and determined to make this the absolute best meeting they'd had in the history of the company.

I arrived at the office half an hour early, wanting to ensure everything was set up. Since most of the managers would be flying in first thing this morning, I had scheduled for them all to come to the office for a catered brunch. The afternoon sessions would be held at the convention center, along with all sessions after that.

"There she is," Jordan greeted merrily when I stepped off the elevator.

I was so happy to see that he'd arrived early. Plus, the man looked like a million dollars. The suit he wore fit him exceptionally well. In fact, he would give my bosses a run for their money in the *GQ* department.

"You look amazing," I told him.

Jordan tugged on the front of his jacket. "Oh, this old thing?"

Yep, I was definitely glad he would be working alongside me. "Is anyone here yet?"

"Nope. You're good to go."

"Perfect."

"And I'm at your disposal for the next four days," he informed me. "The phones have been set to voice mail so I won't be distracted."

"That's actually the best thing I've heard all day."

Jordan chuckled. "It's early."

"I know."

"So, where do we start?"

"First let me lock my purse in my desk, then I'd like to get the packets set up in the conference room." I'd put together schedules of events, as well as brief bios of each manager in attendance, as well as detailed bios for my bosses.

I had learned while getting everyone scheduled that there were a lot of new managers who weren't aware of everything the company did. Some of them worked in a bubble, reporting only to one person and not realizing the extent of services that the company offered. I felt that was a disservice because even if one manager focused solely on Justin's clientele, that didn't mean they wouldn't run into someone who needed a service that one of the others offered. This was my way of cross-promoting each team.

"You get settled and I'll start getting things laid out," Jordan said, taking his keys and unlocking the conference room.

I rushed to the back, stashing my purse in my desk and glancing at my email to ensure there weren't any issues.

So far, so good.

When I made my way back up front, Jordan had turned on all the lights and set out the packets on the side table. All in all, there were twenty-three managers stationed in the United States. Landon and Langston each had six each, while Ben had seven, and Justin had four. There was a total of seven who were overseas, three for Landon and Langston, three for Ben and one for Justin. That meant we were expecting thirty in total since they had all committed to attending.

We had also invited quite a few clients within the area, providing them the opportunity to meet with the managers, ask questions, and follow up on anything they needed.

That was a lot of people, but I was happy with the plan I had in place. If all went well, there would be very little downtime during the meeting and everyone would leave with a better understanding of their peers as well as some incredible presentations by those who were eager to get information in front of the teams.

Now, we just needed everyone to arrive.

•

There were roughly ten managers there when Landon and Langston arrived at eight forty-five. Ben and Justin came in right at nine along with about seven more managers. Jordan and I greeted everyone officially, introducing ourselves and directing them into the conference room, where the caterers had finished setting up shortly before the first people arrived.

When there was a lull in arrivals, I joined everyone in the conference room, checking in to see how they were doing, how their flights had been. It made me feel good to see everyone smiling and chatting amongst themselves while they feasted on a variety of pastries and several flavors of coffee and tea.

From what I could tell, everyone seemed happy to be there. I had imagined finding a group of people with their noses stuck in their laptops while they waited for it to be over. The good news was there wasn't a laptop in sight.

Landon came to stand beside me, his hand gently touching my back before falling away.

"Would it be possible to see you for a few minutes?" he asked.

"Of course."

When I followed Landon out of the conference room, Langston, Ben, and Justin followed behind.

Landon led the way to their offices.

"We thought we'd take a couple of minutes to check in. Let you know that we're here should you need anything at all."

"Thank you," I said with a wide smile. "So far, I think I have everything under control." I held up my phone. "I've sent the itinerary to each of your phones as well as set up reminders for when you're required to be somewhere. Jordan and I will ensure everything's set up for each of the sessions as well as check in with all of the presenters to ensure they have what they need."

"You've put a lot of effort into this," Langston acknowledged. "We're very impressed."

"Thank you. There's a lot of work left to go, but I think the four of you will find it's laid out in a way that should make it the least stressful for you. That was my goal anyway."

"Speaking of stressful…" Landon's smirk was devious. "We've got a few instructions for you over the next four days."

"Me?" Now I was definitely curious.

"Yes, pet," Langston said, stepping into my personal space. "Your instructions will come in the form of a text message. When you receive one, you will only have a few minutes to do what it is you're asked to do."

"Should you fail," Justin stated, "or choose not to do them, you will be punished."

I didn't like the sound of that. However, it made me want to work harder to meet their demands. And truthfully, I liked the idea of having tasks assigned for me. I didn't even care what they were, just knowing that it would please my bosses was all I needed.

"I won't let you down," I told them all.

"Gumdrop, we don't think you could let us down if you tried." Ben's tone was heavy with approval.

"We're proud of you," Landon added. "This event is going to go smoothly, and it's all thanks to your hard work and dedication."

"Okay, then," Justin stated. "We should get back out there before someone comes looking for us."

"One more thing," Langston growled as he pulled me into him, his mouth finding mine. He was gentle but demanding as his tongue thrust into my mouth. I sighed against him, tension coiling in my core from the contact alone.

"My turn," Ben said as soon as Langston pulled back.

My bosses took their turns kissing me. When they were finished, they all headed back to the lobby while I took a moment to compose myself. I touched up my makeup, noticing the huge grin on my face.

Yeah. This was going to be an epic event.

There was no doubt about it.

•

My first text message came that afternoon when I was sitting at a small table talking to Sharla Simons. She was one of Langston's tenured managers. We'd been discussing several of her clients, who were best-selling authors. I was intrigued by how close she was to her authors, speaking to several of them at least once a week, more when they had a release. It was enlightening to hear her explain her process and her desire to befriend the people she worked for, earning their trust and respect.

Although I wanted to pick her brain, I knew the text couldn't go unanswered. "If you'll excuse me for a moment…"

"Sure, no problem," she said, smiling widely.

Glancing down at my phone, I read the text message three times, feeling a strange flutter in my belly.

Ben: *For your first task, you will need to head to the room where they will be setting up for the three p.m. presentation. Since it's 2:40, I suggest you hurry.*

Keeping my attention on my phone, hoping no one would stop me with any questions, I hurried out of the room we had set up for people to drop by when they needed a break. There were a lot of people in the room because the last session had ended at 2:30 p.m.

"Miss Wagner?" someone called from behind me.

"I'm sorry," I said, being as polite as possible without meeting the man's eyes. "I'll be back in just a few minutes. Jordan's just inside if you have a question."

"Sure."

I walked as fast as my five-inch heels would allow. When I got to the door where a friend of Langston's would be giving an introduction to BDSM in just twenty short minutes, I opened it and stepped inside.

The room was empty.

Luci: *I made it to the room.*

Ben: *Very good. On the table at the front of the room you will find a small box. Open it, then take a seat in the chair beside that table. Take the item and make yourself come. Remember, people will begin arriving soon. You are not to leave that chair until you come. To ensure you're doing as instructed, someone will be stepping into the room shortly. They will let me know whether you succeeded or not.*

Oh, my God.

I couldn't believe Ben was making me do this. Especially since I was trying to coordinate the efforts here at the convention center. With so many people in attendance, I seriously doubted I was going to succeed.

However, I was certainly going to try.

I raced to the front of the room and grabbed the small box. Inside was the small bullet vibrator Landon had given me. I smiled. The damn thing turned up in the strangest places sometimes.

Dropping into the chair, I flipped it on, then snuck it beneath my skirt.

The door opened and I hesitated, waiting to see who had joined me.

There was a man I hadn't been introduced to, so I assumed he was not one of the managers. Because he didn't approach me, merely stood with his arms crossed over his massive chest, his gaze locked on me, I figured he was the one responsible for confirming I did as instructed.

I watched him while I teased my clit with the vibrating toy.

I had to admit that pleasuring myself while looking into the face of a stranger was quite arousing. I would've never expected it to be. It wasn't long before I started to whimper and moan. At that point, I noticed the man was moving closer.

"If you want to be believable, I suggest you scream when you orgasm," he said, the deep rumble of his voice almost as sexy as he was.

"Yes, sir," I whispered, never removing the toy from my clit.

Having an audience made it a little more difficult to give myself over to the sensations, but a few minutes later, I felt the stirrings of my orgasm. I twisted the end of the vibrator, turning it up higher as I held it tightly against my clit, shifting it from side to side.

"Oh, God," I moaned, my eyes drifting shut as the sensations rocked through me. My insides coiled tightly as I relaxed, letting my release consume me.

"Scream for me," the man urged.

Yeah. That did it.

Having a stranger watch while I made myself come was my tipping point. I felt my pussy clench tightly as the imaginary band inside me coiled tighter until it finally snapped. I screamed in ecstasy as I rode wave after wave of intense pleasure.

Sagging against the back of the chair, I took a moment to catch my breath while I watched the man who had moved to the front of the room.

Knowing people would be pouring in any second now, I pushed to my feet, my legs still shaky. I tucked the vibrator back into the box and straightened my skirt.

Before I could head toward the door, the mystery man held out his hand.

"My name's Timothy Triton."

My eyes widened as I shook his hand.

He grinned.

"Most of my friends refer to me as Master Chaos."

Oh, my God.

I had just pleasured myself while Master Chaos—the man who would be leading the BDSM session—stood by and watched.

I could feel my face flame.

"No need to be embarrassed," he said with a genuine smile. "I enjoyed watching."

"Thank you." My voice came out rough, sounding strangled.

He grinned again.

And then the doors opened and people began to stream into the room.

"If you'd like, you can stick around," he said kindly. "I hear you're undergoing training."

Not officially, but I nodded anyway.

"Maybe you'll learn a thing or two."

I wasn't sure if that was a good thing or not.

However, I stayed because...why the hell not?

FORTY-THREE

DAY TWO OF THE CONFERENCE was well on its way to being even better than day one.

That morning, Jordan and I hosted a breakfast in one of the large banquet rooms at the convention center. Rather than buffet style, we had opted for a sit-down meal while my four bosses provided the financials outlook. It took approximately two hours for them to get through the presentation and to take most of the questions. After that, I gave them an hour break so they could relax before they would move into their roundtables with their team members.

It was during that short break that I received a text.

Master: You are looking incredibly fuckable today. So much so that my dick is rock hard every time I so much as think about you. As you can imagine, it's difficult to focus. Which leads me to my request.

My heart was racing already. I had no idea what he was going to ask of me, but I knew without a doubt that I was going to accommodate him in any way that I could.

Master: The roundtables will begin in approximately ten minutes. I need for you to postpone mine. You can ask my team members to sit in during Landon's session. Once you've done that, you will meet me in the room you had scheduled for me. I will then fuck you until I get my fill.

Oh, God. That room was adjacent to Landon's and it was only separated by a partition wall. It wasn't even a real wall. Any noise that I made would likely be heard by every one of their managers.

Master: Eight minutes and counting. Should you not arrive by exactly 11:00, I will be forced to take matters into my own hands. If that happens, you will be punished.

Not only that but I would miss out on having Master fuck me into oblivion.

Knowing the first thing I had to do was to inform all of Langston's managers, I glanced around, looking for each of them. Unfortunately, several of them had already started toward the assigned room and I had to escort them back out and over to Landon's side.

There was still one person missing and I glanced down at my watch. I had two minutes before I had to be there.

Crap.

Glancing at the door, then over to a long table with several pens, blank name tags and a couple of maps on it, I grabbed a pen and a map. I flipped the page to the blank side, then scribbled a note that Master's session was postponed and that all attendees should go next door.

I fastened it to the door with one of the sticker tags, but it wouldn't stay. I grabbed several more and plastered them all around the paper before smacking it onto the wood. That time it stayed and I stepped inside the room just as the clock struck eleven.

Master's eyebrows lifted when he heard me. He was standing at the front of the room, propped against a table. I could feel the intensity of his gaze as he pushed himself to a standing position, then moved closer. From the other side of the wall, I heard Landon speaking to his team members, sounding slightly surprised by the additional people. He welcomed them and I breathed a sigh of relief.

Master approached, his hands instantly slipping beneath my blazer and curling around my hips. He pulled me into him, then lowered his mouth to my ear.

"Did you get everyone situated?" His voice was barely a whisper.

I nodded.

"Are you sure no one will come in?"

Well, I wasn't absolutely sure, but the note on the door would hopefully deter anyone else.

"Yes, Master."

He reached for my hand and placed it against his crotch. His cock was hard, pressing against the confines of his slacks.

"I fucking *ache* for you, Luci," he said roughly, his voice so quiet I barely heard him. "I need your sweet pussy right now."

His words sent a shiver dancing down my spine. I wanted him more than I wanted air.

When he pulled back and took my hand, I followed him across the room. At first I thought he was going to the temporary partition that separated the rooms, but he went into the far corner instead. Granted, that was where the wall retracted from, so there was a small sliver of space where I could see the people in the next room. They were all looking in our direction, although their attention was on Landon.

Master pressed his lips against my ear again. His voice was barely a whisper when he said, "Remember, the slightest sound and they'll hear you. Then they'll look this way."

I swallowed hard.

"Then they'll know I'm fucking you."

Yep, they would.

"I want no one to know."

Aww, hell.

I knew that was a challenge. It meant I was to be completely quiet. It sounded easy, but I knew Master was not going to be gentle.

"Hike up that skirt," he instructed, his words rasped against my cheek.

I did.

"Now free my dick."

I worked open his slacks, then pushed them down a little so that his cock was free.

"Stroke it."

Fisting him, I caressed his cock while staring up into his beautiful eyes. The man looked so intense and I was desperate for him to unleash on me. Knowing someone could see us, or even walk in on us, added an air of danger that turned me on.

His voice was barely above a whisper but laced with what sounded a lot like desperation. "Oh, fuck, Luci…I need you so fucking bad."

Master pushed me into the wall, his mouth crushing down on mine at the same time he lifted my leg and pushed inside me. The forceful move stole my breath and had me wrapping my arms around his neck.

From that point forward, neither of us said anything. The only sound was that of our labored breaths and the conversations taking place in the room next to us. Master fucked me hard, slamming into me again and again as though he would never get enough of me. I felt his energy, his need, as he took what he wanted and I freely gave him everything that I had.

I bit my lip to keep from crying out when he shifted me back, holding my leg up as he slammed into me. It was primal and vicious and so fucking hot my body temperature skyrocketed as I chased the inevitable release.

Master met my eyes and I knew the instant he was going to come. I could feel his body harden, see the intent in his gaze. I knew what he wanted from me and I gave it to him. Dropping my head back against the wall with a thud, my body shattered, my pussy milking him as he slammed into me one last time.

My brain was buzzing with adrenaline by the time we were finished. Surprisingly, he waited to pull out, giving me a minute to catch my breath. Before he did, he leaned down, his mouth once more against my ear.

"Thank you, pet. I look forward to seeing you at dinner tonight."

He was referring to the formal meal we would be attending at a steakhouse around the corner.

"I'm looking forward to it, too," I whispered back.

I felt him press something into my hand.

I looked down and noticed a handkerchief.

It might've seemed crude, but it was actually quite thoughtful. Considering I was hosting this event and we had quite a few people in attendance, it probably wouldn't look good for me to walk around with his essence dripping down my legs.

Definitely thoughtful.

•

Dinner went better than I thought it would.

Considering it was at the end of the day and I knew everyone was exhausted from the meetings and discussions, I thought it would be a little less...festive.

However, the managers proved me wrong, the majority of them talking about how well things had been run and how Jordan and I deserved a raise for all our efforts. I had to admit, Jordan's help had been critical. The man knew how to schmooze like nobody's business. Granted, the two of us probably sounded like a couple of ass kissers when we constantly gave each other praise. But it was true. Things wouldn't have gone as smoothly without his help and I had made sure to let my bosses know.

At Master's request, I ended up sitting between him and Landon for the meal. It was the first time I'd truly seen all four of my bosses completely in their element. The way they spoke so eloquently about their business proved that they were all very proud of their successes. As they should've been.

It was after dinner when everyone decided to go back to the hotel bar for a little while that the first hiccup occurred. I had attempted to leave, telling my bosses that it would be best for me to go home so I could be rested for tomorrow. They had proceeded to talk me into staying, insisting that everyone wanted me there.

Well, it didn't take me long to figure out that not *everyone* was on board with that plan.

There was one manager on Landon's team who had been giving me the stink eye from the beginning. Sure, she was syrupy sweet anytime Landon or Langston was around, but when they weren't, her tone said she believed me to be beneath her.

It hadn't bothered me for the most part because she was just one person in a sea of many and I wasn't there to make friends. And honestly, I hadn't expected everyone to like me. Had they, I probably would've been suspicious.

Still, I did my best to ignore Misty Ballard. I steered clear as best I could, but she somehow managed to corner me at the bar. I could tell she'd had more than a few drinks because she couldn't keep her voice lowered to a reasonable level when she spoke.

"So, how well do you know Landon and Langston?" the older woman asked. I pegged her to be somewhere in her late thirties, but she looked older than that.

I tried to keep my expression masked when I spoke. "I've worked for them for a little over eight weeks now."

"I get that," she huffed. "We all know how long you've been around. The question is, how well do you know them?"

Yes, she sounded hostile.

"I'm not sure I understand the question." It was the truth. I wasn't sure what she was getting at.

Misty rolled her eyes. "God, where did they even find you? What? Were they scouting high schools looking for help?"

Shaking my head, I tried to turn away from her, knowing that this was going nowhere fast. She was acting like an asshole and I didn't deserve her wrath. I had no idea what she had against me, but I was sure she would eventually tell me, and since I didn't particularly care to hear it, I was hoping to make a graceful exit.

Thankfully, Jordan chose that moment to walk up. I could tell his smile was forced, but I played along.

"Hey," I greeted. "Have you met Misty? She's one of Landon's managers."

"Landon *and* Langston," she clarified with a snap in her tone. "I'm the only one who works for both of them."

I wasn't aware they had managers who overlapped, but I wasn't going to argue with her.

"It's a pleasure to meet you," Jordan said, holding out his hand.

Misty picked up her drink, pretending not to notice his hand. It was a dick move.

I turned to Jordan. "You doing okay?"

"I was actually coming to find you. I'm about to head out."

Damn. That wasn't good news. I didn't want to be left alone. However, I completely understood. As it was, I was exhausted and ready to sleep for a solid day.

"Well, I'll see you bright and early in the morning then," I said sweetly, wishing I could slip out with him. Unfortunately, Misty was staring us down.

"Bright and early," he agreed, then nodded to Misty before leaving me there with the wicked witch.

"You probably should head out," she said, tilting her glass to her lips. "It's past your bedtime and your parents are likely worried. Don't want to miss curfew."

Okay, now she just sounded like an idiot.

"You know, we can all see how interested you are in your bosses," Misty said, glaring at me.

I frowned. She was starting to piss me off.

"The way you stare at them."

I vowed to keep my mouth shut.

She leaned in close and I could smell the stench of alcohol on her breath.

"You know they're not interested, right? You're just a baby. Won't matter how short you make those skirts you wear. They wouldn't touch you with a ten-foot pole."

Great.

"Look," she said, her voice dripping with false sweetness, "I just don't want to see you get hurt. The truth is, Landon and Langston are into something that sweet little girls like you know nothing about. I'm close to them and I know things you don't."

Yeah. I could almost guarantee that wasn't the case.

"And tonight, I fully intend to see how far they're willing to go."

My eyes snapped over to her face. "What does that mean?"

"God, you're so naïve. I still have no idea where they found you." She turned to face the bar. "Those two require an experienced woman, honey. Not one who's still wearing training wheels."

"Who *wears* training wheels?" I asked, unable to hide the sarcasm from my tone.

"It's just best you understand now. Sure, my colleagues might pretend you deserve the praise for managing the office and keeping those men in line, but we all know better. It doesn't take much to answer phones and fill in calendars. Once they've sampled the goodies, they'll boot you to the curb."

"I thought you said they weren't interested," I countered. "Why would they sample anything?"

A hand landed on my shoulder and I shifted to see who it was. Another warm body moved behind me and I realized the objects of this woman's affections were standing right behind me and she had absolutely no idea.

"Just like the others, you'll figure it out soon enough. Those two are interested in someone who's got more to offer." Misty took a sip of her drink, staring down at the bar. "Not a lowly secretary."

If she would've looked up even a fraction of an inch, she would've seen Landon and Langston standing there.

"I haven't been able to spend enough time with them, but they know what I want. The same thing they do. And this time I fully intend to show them everything I can offer. See, I'm not the type who'll try to come between them. I actually prefer the two of them at the same—"

Landon cleared his throat.

As if in slow motion, Misty's head swung around, her eyes landing on the two men standing behind me. Her eyes widened and her jaw dropped.

"We didn't mean to interrupt," Landon said, his hand still on my shoulder.

"Oh, you weren't," I assured him. "Misty was just telling me about—"

"You liar!" she yelled before I could even get the words out. Her eyes flew up to Landon. "She was sitting here telling me about how she's been screwing you behind Langston's back. I was just warning—"

Landon held his hand up. "We've been standing here, Misty."

Surprisingly, the woman shut her mouth.

"First thing tomorrow," Langston said, his words directed at her, "we'd like to see you in the office. Seven o'clock. Do not be late."

"I didn't do anything wrong," she insisted.

"We didn't say you did."

No, they hadn't. That was her guilt talking.

Landon took my hand and helped me up from the stool. "I think it's time to call it a night. We'll drive you home."

It took everything in me not to look back at Misty. I had a feeling her tongue was now on the floor.

And yes, I felt a little vindication.

FORTY-FOUR

THE FOLLOWING MORNING, I ARRIVED at the office at eight o'clock per my bosses' instruction. Apparently, they were planning to speak to Misty and wanted to do it in private. Since the first of the sessions would not start until noon today, I would have a little time to catch up on the work I'd put off this week.

Unfortunately, when I arrived, I noticed there were people in the conference room. I couldn't see through the opaque glass, but I figured Misty was probably in there.

Somehow, I managed to keep my feet moving as I headed to my desk. I was surprised to find Ben in his office.

"Good morning," I greeted as I set my purse down. "Would you like me to make you some coffee?"

"No, thanks. I'm good." He crooked his finger at me, silently requesting me to come into his office.

I did.

"Is something wrong?"

He shook his head. "Close the door."

He was acting a little strange, but I closed the door anyway. Before I could turn around, Ben was invading my personal space, pressing me up against the door.

I smiled up at him. "Well, good morning to you."

His answering smile was sexy. "Although your meetings are going well, they're driving me crazy," he said softly, cupping my face. "I'm not getting nearly enough Luci time."

I laughed at his admission. Truth was, I knew exactly how he felt. The meetings were going well and I enjoyed getting to know the people who worked so hard to make the company what it was, but I did enjoy the day-to-day routine we'd established.

"It's almost over. Only today and half of tomorrow."

He leaned in, his lips brushing against mine. His breath smelled like mint and my mouth suddenly watered to taste him.

"I'm counting down the minutes," he said before gently pressing his lips to mine.

I slid my hands into his jacket, wrapping around his waist and kissing him back. It was sweet, but the underlying tension was palpable. We were both holding back.

"By the way, Master Chaos was rather impressed," Ben said when he pulled back. "Said it was quite a treat to watch you come."

I felt my cheeks heat from the memory of having an unknown man watch me pleasure myself.

"I enjoyed the task," I admitted.

"Next time, I'll be there to watch for myself."

I sure hoped so.

Ben took a deep breath, then stepped back. I was forced to let him go.

"I should pretend to work," he said with a chuckle.

"Pretend?"

"Yeah. I'm too curious as to what the outcome will be from the meeting taking place."

"Are Landon and Langston meeting with Misty?"

Ben nodded. "Mr. Parker's in there, too. You know, in case they needed backup. Someone to dig her claws out of their chests."

I couldn't help myself, I blurted the question before I realized I was going to. "Why do you refer to Justin as Mr. Parker when he's not around?"

Smiling, Ben took another step back.

"I mean, you could simply refer to him as Justin unless you're with him, right?"

Ben pushed his hands into his pockets and regarded me for a few seconds. "I could, sure. However, he means something to me. And when I think about him using the honorific we agreed upon, it makes me feel closer to him."

"I understand that." And I really did. "That's the way I feel when I think about Langston. The fact that he asked me to call him Master… It feels like there's a connection."

Ben's smile was sad, but his words didn't align to his facial reaction. "Then you do understand. And that's why I do it."

"Do you always call him Mr. Parker? Or is there something you call him when you're alone with him?"

"When we're alone, he asks that I call him Master. But it took us some time to build up to that."

It sounded as though he was knocking the fact that Langston had asked me to refer to him as Master. During the conference, I'd been careful to think of him as Langston so that I didn't accidentally say something that would give me away. However, I did like calling him Master.

Not wanting to consider what Ben's response had actually meant, I decided it was time to make my exit. "Well, I should get back to it," I said, my tone too high-pitched to be genuine. "I'll let you get back to…pretending."

"Luci?"

I could tell he wanted to explain, but truthfully, I didn't want to know.

"I'll talk to you later," I replied, then slipped out the door.

•

That day's sessions consisted of several vendors coming in to show off their goods. Things that they wanted the managers to use for their business. There were quite a few technology clients giving away some cool stuff, too. And they'd drawn a lot of attention. I had worked closely with each of my bosses to determine who they wanted there based on the direction they saw things going and it seemed we'd made the right choices.

The response was overwhelming and I found myself wandering around for a little while, watching as everyone grabbed their free gifts and got more information on the products they were curious about.

That was when I got my daily text message.

Landon: Good afternoon, sweet girl. As I watch you walking the halls, I can't help but be intrigued by your sweet mouth. It makes me think of that first night when you so kindly wrapped my cock between those luscious lips. In fact, it makes me want to feel them again.

Holy moly. The man had a way with words.

Landon: With that said, the last of the roundtable sessions starts in twenty minutes. It could last ten minutes, it could last two hours. Regardless, I want you beneath the table when I arrive. I will be sure to take the last chair on the left (your left, when you are beneath the table, facing the chairs). Lucky for you, the tablecloth will provide you with cover. Do you understand?

Luci: Yes, sir.

Landon: Good. Once all four of us are seated, you are to unbutton my slacks and free my cock. For the entirety of the session, I want you to use those pretty lips and that curious little tongue to please me. There are two rules: 1. You cannot let anyone know you're there. 2. You are not permitted to make me come.

Crap.

There wasn't much time before that session started and if I wasn't to allow anyone to know I was there, that meant I had to be beneath that table before anyone arrived in the room.

Clutching my phone in my hand, I hurried to the room, eager for my assignment.

•

I had absolutely no idea how long the session had been underway, but I eventually figured out that Landon was purposely keeping it going. I found it amusing. At first. However, my jaw did eventually start to hurt and since I couldn't move so much as a muscle without risking giving myself away, my legs were starting to cramp.

Still, I focused all my attention on him, laving his thick erection with my lips and tongue, working him over good. Every now and then, his hand would slip beneath the table and he would caress my head, urging me to continue.

I feared that he was going to grab my head and force his cock into my throat. If he did that, it was possible that I would gag and the whole room would know what was taking place right under their noses. So, I lived with that constant fear trickling in my veins as I continued to pleasure him.

A whimper nearly escaped at one point as my legs cramped up painfully. I squeezed Landon's thigh gently, hoping he would understand.

He must've realized my intent because another fifteen minutes or so passed and then the session wrapped up. While everyone was leaving, Landon remained where he was, as did my other bosses. Since Landon's instruction had been that no one could know I was there, I assumed that also meant them, so I didn't dare move.

After a few minutes, Justin and Ben left and I heard the door close behind them.

The conversation resumed and I realized one of the managers was still in the room, speaking to two of my bosses. Another few minutes passed before Master's legs disappeared from beneath the table and I heard the door open and close again.

"Come on out here, sweet girl," Landon said, moving his chair back.

I crawled out from beneath the table, my legs aching from the prolonged position.

He helped me to my feet, then pressed his lips to mine, kissing me roughly as he twined his fist in my hair.

"That is the sweetest mouth I've ever known," he growled, the vibrations of his words reverberating against my breasts because of the closeness of our bodies.

"Now I think it's only fair for me to return the favor."

That time I did whimper.

My ass met the edge of the table and Landon picked me up and set me on it, forcing me backward before he pulled the chair back to the table and took a seat. He massaged my thighs and knees for several minutes before his mouth descended between my legs, his tongue rasping against my clit.

"Mmm. Are you wet from sucking my dick?"

"Yes, sir," I moaned. It was true.

"That pleases me."

I would do anything to please this man.

"Now I want you to come all over my face, sweet girl."

It didn't take long for me to do just that.

FORTY-FIVE

BY THURSDAY MORNING, I WAS eager for the quarterly meeting to wind down. Sure, I'd had a good time throughout, but it was hard work keeping up with all the managers as well as anticipating the sexy requests from my bosses.

Thankfully, today was the last day and we were all meeting in the office for the official closing ceremony. Not that it was a ceremony, but it sounded good.

I purposely arrived at seven so that I could get a few things taken care of, including verifying all the flights for the managers I had yet to check on. Plus, I had put together a packet for the managers to take back with them, which had the information on what had taken place as well as the vendors who had attended for those who needed the details.

When I arrived, I was surprised to see Justin was already in the office.

"Would you like me to start some coffee?" I asked when he peeked out his door.

"That would be great, princess," he said before going back to typing away on his laptop.

I got the coffee started, and while it brewed, I started down the list of managers, checking them off as I confirmed their flights. I also scheduled for a shuttle to arrive at the office to take them to the airport at noon. I figured it would be easier than each of them trying to catch a cab on their own.

As I was delivering Justin his coffee, his phone rang.

"Yeah?"

Whoever it was, he didn't sound pleased to hear from them.

His eyes shot up to me and I could tell he wanted privacy for his call so I hurried out of the room and closed the door behind me. Before I could get two feet away, I heard him raise his voice, his tone reflecting his unhappiness.

I would hate to be whoever was on the other end of that call.

Rather than wait around to see what happened, I went to the front in time to catch Jordan coming off the elevator. He was once again wearing a suit and I grinned.

"Just so you know," he said, walking toward me, "I only dress like this for you."

"I'm honored. But you look amazing. I'm sure your man would be quite pleased to see you like this from time to time."

Jordan chuckled. "My man is pleased because I say he has to be."

I didn't even bother trying to decipher his cryptic message.

"When does everyone arrive?" he asked as he unlocked his desk drawer.

"The caterers should be here by eight and the managers will be here at nine."

"So, how do you think it's been so far?" he asked, perching on the edge of his desk.

I shrugged. "I'd like to say it's been successful. There have been very few issues." At least that I knew of.

"I agree." His grinned widened. "And only one manager was fired."

My eyes widened as I stared at him in shock. "Someone got fired?"

He shook his head slightly as though he couldn't believe I didn't know. "Yeah. Misty? Remember the meeting they had?"

"Oh, my God. Why'd they fire her?"

"Because she was harassing you," he said with a silent but implied *duh.*

"She was drinking," I countered. "I don't think she deserved to be fired for that."

"Trust me, it wasn't because she was drinking. As it turns out, she was actually the reason for a couple of your predecessors to quit."

"Really?"

"Yep. Apparently, she was vying for Landon's and Langston's attention, so she was sabotaging the secretaries. I think they figured it out once they overheard her conversation with you."

"Holy shit." That was...surprising. I mean, sure, Misty wasn't a very likable woman and, yeah, I knew she'd been belittling me, but I hadn't been bothered by it. Well, other than wanting to get away from the hate she spewed. But to fire her? Wow.

"Honestly, I think they were relieved that they finally had a valid reason to let her go. Plus, one of her direct reports will be stepping up to take her position. The guy's been working circles around her and they've been wanting to promote him."

Part of me wondered how Jordan knew all of this when I didn't. Then again, he'd been around longer, so he had probably established a good rapport with most of the managers. Which meant they likely shared information with him.

The elevator dinged and we both turned to see who had arrived.

"Good morning, Mr. Snowden," I greeted Ben when he stepped off the elevator.

His eyes swung from me to Jordan, then back. He didn't look happy. I wondered if it had to do with the phone call Justin had taken. Not that I got to find out, because he nodded his head briefly before disappearing down the hall.

"Well, we better get the conference room ready. They'll be here before you know it," Jordan suggested.

Yep. They would. So we got to work.

•

By the time noon hit, I was exhausted. Both physically and mentally. It had been a fantastic few days, but I was desperate to get back to a normal routine.

With so much going on that morning, there was one thing that didn't happen.

No text.

Based on the way it had played out, the text should've come from Justin, but it never came. It wasn't until everyone was out the door and I was back at my desk that I realized he had left for the day. No note, no email. Nothing.

Justin had simply vanished.

In an attempt to mind my own business, I got to work, checking emails and answering the few calls that came in. Finally, my curiosity got the best of me and I knocked on Ben's door.

"Come in!"

I opened the door slowly and peeked inside. He was sitting at his desk.

"What's up, Luci?" He sounded slightly perturbed by the intrusion and I suddenly felt guilty.

"Never mind."

I turned to leave, but he called me back.

"I was…uh…just wondering if Justin's all right. I noticed he was gone."

Ben's eyes remained fixed on my face for what felt like minutes but was likely only seconds before he finally answered. "He's dealing with some personal issues."

"Oh. Okay." That was all I needed to know, so I turned and left the office, closing the door behind me.

It wasn't that I was being selfish and wondering why Justin hadn't texted me or why he hadn't bothered to email me. I was simply worried about him. I could tell by his response to his call earlier that something had happened. I merely wanted to check in, to see if there was anything that I could do.

I didn't. Check in, that was. I decided not to bother him. If he wanted me to know what was going on, I was sure he would tell me.

So, I pushed it all aside and got back to work.

About an hour later, Landon stuck his head out of his office and told me I should go home early.

"I'm all right," I informed him, not sure why he wanted to send me away.

"You worked your ass off this week," he said with a smile. "Take a break. It'll all be here in the morning."

Clearly, he wanted me to go, so I wasn't going to be petulant and argue with him. When he slipped back into his office, I grabbed my purse and my phone, then headed out. I was surprised to see that Jordan's desk was empty. I figured they had sent him home as well. Hopefully that was the case, because he had worked as hard as I had making everything as perfect as possible.

Of course, I spent the rest of the afternoon fretting over what happened to Justin until finally I caved and texted him.

Luci: Hey, it's me. I don't mean to be a bother, but I wanted to check in. Make sure you're all right. I've been worried.

I probably should've expected my text message to go unanswered. If he was dealing with a personal matter like Ben had said, then he was probably busy. However, I felt better knowing that I had at least checked.

I knew how it felt to be ignored. My mother ignored me as much as she could. In fact, I hadn't heard from her since the last time I'd gone over there for breakfast. Then again, I didn't make much of an effort either.

Of course, I probably shouldn't spend too much time dwelling on emotional issues. I knew exactly what my problem was. My period was about to start, which was expected but inconvenient at the same time. And that whole bitchy/emotional thing that went along with PMS? Well, I got it in spades.

Deciding a hot bath was in order, I took my phone, grabbed a wineglass and a bottle of wine, then headed for the bathroom.

Twenty minutes later, as I was immersed in the warm water, bubbles surrounding me, I received a text message.

Justin: Thank you for thinking of me, princess. I'm fine. I'm sorry I left without letting you know. Look forward to seeing you on Monday morning.

And just like that, my mind was put at ease.

That was all I'd needed.

Well, that and maybe the sexy text I'd been promised.

But I wasn't going to be greedy. Not today, anyway.

FORTY-SIX

BOSS MEETING

BEN

A MEETING WITHOUT MR. PARKER wasn't the same, as far as I was concerned. Then again, it was hard to have a meeting with the man when he was out of town taking care of his personal business. I had offered to go with him, but he'd told me that he needed me to stay in the office for now.

Although the two of us had forged a bond over the years, even I recognized that it was difficult for him to open up to me. He felt as though he was burdening me, or so he'd said. Didn't matter that I had informed him that was part of a relationship, he still held himself back.

"What're your thoughts on the quarterly meeting outcome?" Landon prompted as we sat in his office at one thirty on Friday afternoon.

"I was highly impressed," I admitted, pulling my attention back to the task at hand. "Luci and Jordan went above and beyond. I think she's the brains behind the operation, but she utilized the tools necessary to make it successful. I'm glad to see that she works so well with Jordan."

"They definitely work well together," Landon noted. "And my managers are highly impressed with her."

"As are mine." Which was no small feat, as far as I was concerned. Being in the tech industry was far different than the publishing industry, yet Luci had managed to bring them all together without any issues.

"Any suggestions for the next one?" Langston asked.

"Other than we give Luci free rein to handle it as she sees fit?" I chuckled. "As long as she's at the helm, I think it'll be fine."

"She mentioned wanting to send out a survey to the attendees."

Seriously, I was impressed with the girl. She was remarkable. "I think that's a great idea. And I can tell you, they appreciate being included."

"Any news from Justin?" Landon prompted.

I shook my head. "Nothing much. But he assured me he'd be back on Monday."

I wasn't sure how much information Justin had shared with them, so I didn't want to overstep.

"If he needs anything..." Landon held my gaze for a second. "Let him know we're here to help him. I know he hates asking for help, but that's what we're here for."

It was true, Mr. Parker did not like asking anyone for anything. He'd been that way since the day that I met him. In fact, it was one of the reasons he retreated from everyone from time to time. He could've very easily sought comfort from me and Luci; however, he'd opted to vanish. It bothered me, but I had learned not to question him. The man was nothing if not stubborn.

"Any plans for the weekend?" Landon apparently was looking to lighten the mood.

"I've got some stuff to catch up on," I admitted. "So, I'll probably be here in the office."

"You want us to come in? We haven't worked a Saturday in a while. I can call Luci, get her to help out."

That was the last thing I wanted. Not because I didn't want to see Luci, because a little time with her would be just what the doctor ordered. However, I really did think she needed the break. She'd worked her little ass off this week. "No. I'm good. The quiet will help me to stay focused."

"All right. But the same goes for you," Landon said, staring at me. "If you need anything, just holler."

I grinned. "I'm not sure I've ever *hollered* in my life."

That made them both laugh and for the first time in the last two days, I felt myself relax somewhat.

FORTY-SEVEN

I HATED BEING ON MY PERIOD.

It sucked.

Then again, I doubted there was a woman out there who got excited when her monthly cycle hit.

And now, here I was sitting with my four bosses at the Monday meeting while wearing a pair of slacks. I knew they all recognized what was going on and not a one of them had said anything.

Not about that, anyway.

"Okay, now that we've got a list of the points we want to change for the next quarterly meeting, I think you have something to go on," Justin stated as I glanced down at my notes.

"I do," I agreed, lifting my gaze and looking at him.

"Perfect." He then glanced at the others. "If there's nothing else, I'd like to spend a little time with Luci."

"Very well," Master stated as he got to his feet. "I'll be out of the office this afternoon."

He looked my way and I felt something stirring in my belly. It was as though he wanted to say something, but his mouth didn't open.

Justin nodded, then glanced over at Ben. "Please stay."

"Of course, Mr. Parker."

Master and Landon left the room, closing the door behind them. I turned my attention to the two of them.

"I take it you're on your period?" Justin asked point-blank.

Never in my life had I met a group of men who spoke their minds the way my bosses did. They had absolutely no shame.

I nodded. "Yes, sir. I am."

He smiled. "Just wanted to ensure you weren't breaking the rules."

I couldn't help but smile at that. "No, sir. I try my best to follow them."

"I know. And I'm very impressed." His dark blue eyes leveled on mine for several long seconds. "I've missed you, Luci."

My heart turned over in my chest.

Admittedly, I wasn't as close to Ben or Justin as I'd thought I would be. Sure, we spent some time together, but it wasn't the same. It felt almost as though they were keeping their distance, trying not to form a connection. I couldn't complain, because I'd already started to have feelings for Landon and Master and although I knew it wasn't the logical outcome, all things considered, I couldn't change the way I felt.

However, when I was with Justin and Ben, I did my absolute best to focus only on them. They were important to me and I'd come to care about them as well. Although these opportunities were few and far between, I welcomed them.

"I've missed you, too, sir."

"I wanted to thank you for checking up on me. I hadn't expected that." Justin glanced over at Ben. "My pup informed me that you were asking about me."

I nodded. "I wasn't trying to be nosy. I was...I...uh...I was just worried about you."

"God, you're sweet." He motioned for me to get up.

I stood, then allowed him to pull me toward him. I sat on his lap and he pressed his lips to mine. His hands curled around my cheek as his tongue dipped into my mouth.

When he pulled back, I could see the intense lust burning in his gaze.

"As much as I want to indulge in you right now, I know I can't."

I smiled. "No, but I could indulge in you."

"Is that right?"

I glanced at Ben, then back to Justin. "We both could."

He leaned back and rested his hand on my thigh. "And how would you do that?"

I nodded toward the floor. "May I get down on my knees?"

"You may."

I got down on my knees, thankful for the soft rug covering the tile, then looked at Ben. "Will you join me?"

"It'd be my pleasure," he said before getting down on the floor beside me. I turned back to Justin. "Would you mind if we pleasure you, sir?"

His eyes remained locked on mine. "Under one condition."

I waited for him to continue.

"You mentioned you'd never seen two men fuck."

Whew. Those few simple words had heat billowing in my belly.

"That's true." I hadn't. However, I had thought about the two of them together on many occasions and it made me hot.

"Then once you pleasure me, I want you to watch while I fuck my submissive."

"I'd like that." Granted, I wasn't sure how I'd survive it knowing that I would get no pleasure in return. Then again, as Ben had taught me, it wasn't always about me.

"Free my cock, princess."

I worked Justin's slacks open and freed his cock. It was long and thick, eager for attention.

For several minutes, Ben and I worked him up using our mouths and our hands, alternately sucking and fondling him as he moaned his pleasure. Justin's hands rested on the tops of our heads as he watched.

Admittedly, I liked this part. Being able to focus all of my attention on him, listening to his grunts and groans, knowing that he was enjoying what we were doing to him. I enjoyed it immensely, realizing that it really didn't have to be about me all the time.

"Do not make me come," Justin ordered roughly, his cock twitching.

Ben and I pulled back slightly, doing our best to continue to pleasure him without forcing his orgasm. Justin allowed it for a few more minutes before ordering us both to our feet.

Justin's tone was raspy with restrained lust when he bellowed his next command. "Undress him."

"It would be my pleasure," I said, using Ben's words.

I slowly undressed Ben, laying his clothes neatly over one of the chairs while I pressed kisses over his smooth, warm skin. His breaths were coming in deep and shallow, which only spurred me on. Not to mention, the man had a body that made women drool. He was solid muscle, a testament to how well he took care of himself.

Justin got to his feet and stepped behind Ben, placing his hand on his back. While I stood at Ben's front, pressing my lips against his chest, Justin's mouth glided over Ben's neck.

"I missed you, pup," Justin whispered. "I needed you."

There were moments like this when Justin's vulnerability was palpable. It was obvious he only allowed himself to be when he was with Ben.

"I missed you, too, Master," Ben whispered, tilting his head and giving Justin better access to his neck.

I took a step back and watched them, in awe of what I felt transpiring between them.

"Do you want to feel my cock?" Justin asked. "Want me to fuck you while Luci watches?"

"Yes, Master," Ben hissed when Justin nipped him with his teeth.

"Lean over and press your palms to the table."

Ben took up the position as Justin ordered me to come stand beside him. He handed me a small packet of lube.

"Slick my cock."

I greased him up, my body humming as I thought about what they were about to do. I liked being a part of it, eager to watch the interaction between the two of them.

Justin lubed two fingers, then inserted them into Ben's ass, fucking him slowly while I continued to stroke Justin's cock.

"Hand me one of the wipes in the drawer," Justin stated as he continued to prod Ben's ass with his fingers.

I went to the coffee station and grabbed the box of hand wipes I'd seen there. I handed one to Justin and used one to clean the lube from my hands.

"Have a seat, princess."

Not wanting to miss a thing, I took a seat in Ben's chair so I had the best view.

"I missed you, pup," Justin whispered again as he leaned over Ben. His lips pressed along Ben's spine. "I fucking missed you so much."

Ben moaned. "I missed you too, Master."

I felt the emotional connection between the two of them, and not for the first time, I felt like a complete voyeur. On the outside, looking in. It was so erotic but sweet at the same time.

"Are you ready for my cock?"

"Yes, Master."

I swallowed hard, watching as Justin aligned his cock with Ben's ass. Seconds later, his erection disappeared inside him and Ben groaned loudly.

Justin's voice was far more powerful when he said, "Did you masturbate while I was gone, pup?"

"No, Master," Ben growled.

"Good boy."

Justin retreated until only the head of his cock was inside Ben's ass. He drove back in.

Ben moaned loudly.

"I'm going to fuck you hard," Justin informed Ben. "I do not want you to come. If you can manage to refrain, I'll allow our sweet princess to suck your cock."

My body trembled. I wanted that. I wanted to give to Ben in the one way I knew I could.

"I won't come, Master," Ben said, his tone full of self-assurance.

"I'll hold you to that."

Justin slammed into Ben over and over, his fingers digging into his hips as he fucked him roughly. It was a unique experience to see them like this.

"Who does your ass belong to?" Justin snarled.

Ben moaned. "You, Master."

"Who's the only man who has ever fucked this ass?"

"You, Master."

"Who's the only man who will *ever* fuck this ass?" Justin's tone was definitely possessive.

"You, Master. Only you."

"Fuck…" Justin continued to slam into Ben over and over. "I'm going to come, pup."

Justin impaled him several more times before he stilled, his hips jerking against Ben as he came. When he finally caught his breath, he pulled out of Ben and motioned toward me. "Please my pup, Luci. Make him come in your mouth."

"My pleasure, sir."

Ben stood up and moved over in front of me. I leaned forward and took his monster cock in my mouth. I sucked him furiously, desperate to make him come, wanting to bring him as much pleasure as I could.

His big hands curled around my head as he drove into my mouth.

"Such a sweet girl," Ben mumbled. "Thank you, gumdrop. Your mouth feels so good."

It only took a couple of minutes before Ben was crying out, his cock lodged deep in my throat as he came in a furious rush.

And a few minutes later, after we had all cleaned up and Ben had gotten dressed, I thanked them both for including me, letting them know I considered it an honor to be part of the experience.

FORTY-EIGHT

TWO DAYS LATER, ON WEDNESDAY, I came into work feeling anxious and deprived. Having spent the past five days on my period, my body was in desperate need of attention. I was one of those unlucky women who suffered heavy and lengthy periods, even on birth control, which, quite frankly, sucked.

I was secretly looking forward to someone giving me something to sate this overzealous craving for human touch. Granted, I knew that wasn't my decision to make; however, I hoped that by wearing a skirt, one of them would take notice.

After greeting Jordan and listening to his lively story about his boyfriend having loved the surprise dinner I'd suggested Jordan do for his birthday, I went back to my desk and started a pot of coffee.

When Ben and Justin arrived shortly after eight, they disappeared into Justin's office. The sounds that emanated from that room told me they did not want to be interrupted. I secretly listened from my desk, wishing they'd left the door open. Yes, that made me a voyeur, but so what. It wasn't like I was innocent in any other way at this point.

Master was the next to arrive and I immediately offered him coffee and then delivered it while he was removing his suit jacket and rolling up his sleeves.

"Thank you, pet."

"You're very welcome, Master."

Calling him Master was now second nature. In fact, the name suited him. I never even thought of him as Langston much anymore. Sure, I was mindful of our audience before I said anything. When his team members were around, I was diligent in referring to him as Langston or Mr. Moore.

As I was turning to leave, he called me back.

"Yes, Master?"

"Please remove your clothes for the remainder of the day."

I didn't even bat an eyelash when I said, "If it pleases you, Master."

I could see the approval in his eyes and I went to work removing my clothing in front of him. I neatly folded each item and placed them on the chair. When I was completely naked, I picked them up to carry them to my desk.

"You may leave them there, pet."

"Thank you, Master."

"We'll be attending a dinner tonight," he continued, "with one of my authors. It's a small gathering to celebrate the release of his next book."

"Yes, Master. I'll add that to your calendar. And by we, I assume you mean Landon will be attending with you."

"No, pet," he said with a smirk. "*You* will be attending with me."

My stomach fluttered at the idea of going to such an event with Master. Sure, I'd gone to dinner with him and Landon, but that had been a long time ago and things between us had changed drastically since. I wasn't sure how I was supposed to act.

"Don't worry, little one. I'll provide you with instructions prior to our arrival. I'll pick you up at your apartment at seven, but you'll need to prepare an overnight bag. You'll be staying with me tonight."

I swallowed hard. "Yes, Master."

The idea of spending the night with him gave me chills. The kind that tingled from my scalp to my toes and made my belly flutter with anticipation. It felt like a step in the right direction, as though maybe he was accepting me as his. I wasn't going to get my hopes up, but... Oh, who was I kidding? I was totally getting my hopes up.

Realizing he was finished speaking to me, I left his office and went right to my desk. When I passed Justin's office, I noticed his door was open and Ben was walking out.

His gaze roamed over me approvingly. "Lovely way to start the day," he said with a smile.

I wasn't sure if he meant because he was seeing me naked or because of what Justin had just done to him behind closed doors. Not that it mattered. I offered him coffee, which he accepted.

After delivering Ben's coffee, I went back to my desk and got to work. There was an email from Mr. Daniels asking me to provide feedback about the new toy he had demonstrated a couple of weeks ago. I quickly replied that I would have it to him by the end of the day, then got to work writing something I hoped would be impressive.

A short time later, Master asked me to join him in his office.

I instantly noticed the pillow beside his chair, so I went over and knelt beside his desk. He finished typing before turning his chair and retrieving something from the bookshelf behind him. He then swiveled to face me.

"Spread your knees apart," he instructed.

I shifted, widening them.

"Place your hands on your thighs, palms up, straighten your spine, and lift your chest."

His instructions basically changed my entire position. It felt as though I was offering myself up to him.

"That's the way you will kneel going forward. You'll also keep your eyes downturned. But not now."

I nodded.

"I have a client who has asked me to provide her with some feedback on her latest manuscript. It has yet to be published and she's having concerns about a couple of scenes."

I kept my eyes on his face as he spoke, unsure what this had to do with me.

"I'd like for you to read it and tell me what you think."

I frowned. "Okay, Master."

He held the bound papers out for me. I glanced down and noticed the title: *Her Total Submission.*

"Is this fictional, Master?" I assumed it was, but I asked anyway.

"It is. She's renowned in her genre and it's because she's very particular about her scenes."

I met his gaze again. "I'd be honored to read it."

"I'll give you until we return from the holiday. Then I'll plan to have you act out the two scenes in question to ensure feasibility. After that, you can provide detailed feedback that I will pass along to her."

"Yes, Master."

"That's all for now, pet."

Part of me wished that Master would've asked for something more from me—because I longed for his touch—but he didn't and I didn't linger in his office. I knew he had a plan for me, and I trusted that he knew what was best. It seemed with every passing minute, every new day, I trusted him more, seeking his guidance. I had no idea how the transformation had happened, but I wasn't questioning it either.

Ever since he had asked me to research BDSM, I found myself craving more details. I'd read everything I could possibly find, including numerous blogs written by both Dominants and submissives. I was versed enough now that I could tell the difference between an experienced Dominant and a wanna-be. It wasn't like there was a subtle difference. A true Dominant did not glorify himself the way a wanna-be did and he had a distinct way of articulating. I found it fascinating.

And truthfully, the information I had stumbled upon was informative. I found an online community dedicated to the lifestyle. I joined so that I could get a better understanding of the various relationships. In fact, last weekend, I found myself reading a conversation regarding a bratty submissive. It seemed the submissive had boasted about her interactions with her master and how she'd been able to garner his attention by acting out.

It seemed there was a difference when it came to brats. They were a real thing, I learned. Some Doms appreciated having a bratty submissive because they kept things lively, but their reasons for being a brat didn't come from seeking attention in a negative manner. It took me a while to understand the difference.

This particular submissive's actions, as well as her pride in them, had seemed rather childish to me, but I'd read all the comments. Most of them were from Dominants stating that her behavior was uncalled for and that she needed to step back and take a mental review of her life. They had stated that if she had to act out in order to get attention, then she was obviously missing something in her life or in her relationship. They had suggested she have a conversation with her master.

It was fascinating to see the interactions and to witness the care and devotion that were the underlying strength of this community. It seemed because of the negative connotation that was placed on the D/s relationship by people who didn't understand the true dynamic, there were both submissives and Dominants who went into it for the wrong reasons. Those who were truly dedicated to the lifestyle were focused on teaching and sharing best practices.

The fact that I had no preconceived notions made me thirst for more information. Plus, I had an ulterior motive.

I wanted to please my bosses.

•

Master arrived at my apartment promptly at seven o'clock. Before I left the office, he had handed me a wrapped box, with the instruction that I was not to open it until I got home.

I somehow managed to make the drive without defying his instruction. But the moment I stepped inside my apartment, I tore into the package. Inside the box was one of the sexiest little black dresses I'd ever seen and a black lace thong. Because of the backless, spaghetti-strap design of the simple silk dress, I wasn't able to wear a bra. That wasn't a terrible inconvenience, because my breasts weren't all that big to begin with.

Knowing I didn't have much time, I managed to shower, then dried my hair and worked it into a sexy updo, leaving some strands hanging around my face and curling them for effect. I opted for my favorite strappy black heels.

And the moment Master's eyes slid over me, I knew he liked what he saw.

"You look stunning, pet," he whispered when he greeted me, his hand cupping my cheek. "You're lucky I don't strip that off you and ravish you right here on your table."

I forced a smile and kept from blurting out that I'd be more than happy for him to do that.

"Do you have a coat?"

Crap. I hadn't been thinking about the fact that it was cold outside and what I was wearing certainly wasn't appropriate for the weather. I mentally ran through all the clothes in my closet and smiled.

"I do have one. I'll be right back."

I returned a minute later with the faux-fur black wrap that I'd bought on sale a couple of years back. I liked the way it looked on me although I hadn't had the opportunity to wear it. Until now.

"Very nice," he said as he placed it over my shoulders. "Did you pack a bag?"

"Yes, Master." I reached for my small duffel, but he took it from me and then led me out of the apartment and down to the parking lot.

There was no limousine waiting for us this time.

Master walked over to a sleek red sports car and opened the passenger door.

Once we were on the road, I turned to him, my curiosity getting the best of me. "Can you share with me the name of the author we're meeting tonight?"

Master cast a quick look my way, then reached down and took my hand, linking our fingers together.

"TJ Arlington."

Well, holy crap. My eyes widened. "*The* TJ Arlington?"

Master chuckled. "I'm sure he doesn't include *the* when introducing himself. Then again, he's rather eccentric, so maybe he does."

I had been introduced to TJ Arlington's work by Master. However, it hadn't taken long for me to figure out that he was one of the most highly anticipated BDSM authors because of his accurate depiction of the lifestyle. "He's highly respected in the BDSM circles."

"That he is," Master confirmed.

"Sir, do all of your clients write BDSM?"

"Most of them, yes. Several don't have labels for their particular style, but it all revolves around kink and various fetishes."

Well, that made sense considering he was into the lifestyle.

"Do they all...uh...are they?"

"Participants in the lifestyle?" He chuckled again. "No. They are not. However, TJ is and you'll find that he's rather strict when it comes to his parties."

Eccentric *and* strict. Interesting combination.

I swallowed hard, my nerves getting the best of me. I had no idea how I was supposed to act. There was something I'd read about high protocol, but I had no clue what that really meant. I'd read tons of information about how submissives were to act with their Doms. Some were very extreme while others were more lax. I had no idea what Master wanted from me and the last thing I wanted to do was disappoint him.

Master squeezed my hand. "You'll be fine, pet. I have complete faith in you."

I was glad someone did.

"Can you tell me what your expectations are?" I asked, jumping right in with both feet.

"Once we're inside the house, you will not be allowed to speak."

"Like, at all?"

"Not at all."

Okay, I wasn't sure I liked that.

"You'll remain with me throughout, so you won't have to worry about being on your own. However, should you go to the restroom or anywhere by yourself, you have to remember, you are not allowed to speak. It doesn't matter what you see or who tries to engage you in conversation. Do not talk."

"Yes, Sir. No speaking." I understood that part.

"You are also not to make eye contact with anyone."

I inhaled sharply.

"From the moment we step inside, keep your eyes on the floor. I will introduce you as my pet, but I will not use your name. At this dinner, you are merely arm candy."

The idea of that was horrifying. Hadn't women spent decades trying to fight this exact thing?

Master pulled the car to a stop at a red light. He turned to face me, curling his hand around my neck.

"This is the way TJ wants it. And while we're in his home, we will respect his wishes."

"What if I accidently look at someone?"

He smiled. "Don't. You are there as my pet. Consider yourself an ornament for the evening."

An ornament?

My jaw dropped open and I stared at him in shock. To be honest, I would rather be a fuck toy than an ornament. And wasn't that just all kinds of fucked up?

"This is me allowing you to get a real glimpse of what it truly means to be submissive. You said you understood, but I don't think you do. However, by the time the night is over, you'll get a good understanding of what dedicated submissives will do for their masters."

"But an ornament?"

"An ornament, pet. It's a couple of hours."

"Am I not supposed to eat dinner?"

He shook his head. "I will feed you."

By this point, I was trembling. I'd read a lot of things about this lifestyle, but I guess I hadn't actually believed that something like this really took place.

The light turned green and Master put his foot on the gas. A few minutes later, we arrived at our destination, where a valet met us outside and took the keys to Master's car. While the place could've been misconstrued as an elaborate hotel, it was actually a house. Well, a mansion, to be exact, complete with a circle drive with a lavish waterfall in the middle of it. Apparently, TJ Arlington sold a lot of books.

Although I was dressed for the part, I felt completely out of my element. These people clearly had money to go along with their kink.

Rather than walking up to the porch, Master stood next to his car after helping me out. He curled his finger beneath my chin and leaned in close to speak.

"Remember, pet, it's an honor for you to be here with me. You're here because I want you here. And in order to please me, you will do as I've asked."

I dropped my gaze to his chest and nodded. That was what he wanted, right?

"Look at me." His command was low and rough.

I lifted my eyes to his.

His voice was deep and rough when he spoke. "From the moment I met you, Luci, I knew you would be mine. Tonight, I want you to prove to me and to everyone else that I was right."

His?

Until tonight, I'd never gotten the impression that he wanted me for himself. He did seem content to bestow his wisdom, to train me, I guess you could say. But for him to declare that...

I was speechless.

I took a deep breath and stood up straight.

Master *was* right. It was an honor for me to be here with him. He didn't have to invite me, but he had. And now that I was here, it was my honor and duty to please him. He was highly respected in these circles and I would not do anything to damage his reputation.

"As long as it pleases you," I choked out.

He brushed his thumb over my bottom lip, then leaned down to kiss me. "It most certainly does. And tonight, once we're back at my apartment, I'll reward you for being a good girl."

I was fairly certain sparks ignited beneath my skin from those words alone.

"And if you aren't a good girl," he said, keeping his tone low, "I will punish you."

My heart sank as I remembered the spanking he'd given me. The worst part had been knowing how I'd failed him by not doing as he'd instructed. I refused to allow that to happen again.

"I won't disappoint you, Master."

He kissed me lightly again. "Not on purpose, I know. Now, let's go enjoy the evening."

Enjoy seemed like a stretch, but what did I know.

FORTY-NINE

DO NOT SPEAK.
Do not look at anyone.
Those seemed like relatively easy instructions to follow.

However, the moment the door opened and we were greeted by the host, I found it nearly impossible to do anything Master had asked me to do. It took all my willpower not to look around, not to admire my surroundings. That was the core of who I was. I was curious. I'd go so far as to say I was even nosy.

Not a good quality to possess under these circumstances.

Master removed my wrap, then his coat, passing them over to an attendant before taking a few steps forward.

"Master Moore, what an honor to have you here tonight." The man who spoke had a raspy, elegant voice and black shoes. Since I wasn't permitted to look up, I couldn't tell what the rest of him looked like.

"Thank you, Master Arlington. It's an honor to be here."

"And who did you bring with you?"

"This is my pet," Master informed him.

Yep. That's me! Just an ornament!

"I'm glad to see you have one," TJ said. "It's been a long time."

Hmm. I wondered how long.

"It has," Master confirmed.

I kept my eyes on the elaborate marble floor, reminding myself over and over again that I was not allowed to look at anyone and I was not allowed to speak. This was, by far, the hardest thing I'd ever had to do. Harder than walking around the office naked, even.

Everything I'd learned in my life about being courteous and being polite was all lost on this moment. It seemed that the exact opposite was what was respectful in this house and I wasn't sure how I would be successful.

You will please your master. That's the only thing that matters.

"Please mingle. Dinner will be served in half an hour."

Master guided me through the foyer and into a large, open room.

"From this point forward, you will remain one foot behind me on my right at all times unless I request otherwise."

My heart sank in my chest. The thought of being pushed to the side was even worse than being told not to talk. Needless to say, I didn't like it and I suspected Master had known, hence the reason he didn't inform me until now. Disregarding my hurt feelings, I managed to nod and didn't move until Master was a foot in front of me. I kept my eyes down, focused on the floor just to the right of his feet.

When he stopped, I stopped. When he walked, I walked. Quite frankly, I felt like a dog heeling at my Master's side. I didn't like it.

However, I did enjoy listening to him. He spoke at length with several people, both men and women. I could only assume that the women he conversed with were Dommes. I'd learned through my research that there were both male and female Dominants, as well as male and female submissives.

Regardless, no one seemed to pay any attention to me whatsoever. The conversations took place as though I wasn't there. Aside from Master Arlington, no one even asked about me. It was as though I was invisible.

An ornament.

I felt as though I was doing fairly well until we ventured farther into the room. Master stopped near a table. This wasn't just any table. This one was adorned with a naked woman covered in food. Thanks to the items that had already been snacked on, her nipples were showing. I subtly swept my gaze down her body, noticing that her nether region was still partially covered. I wondered if people really ate food that had been resting on her pussy. As I thought it, a man picked up a piece of fruit from her mound.

Yep, they ate it.

Glancing at the woman's face, I noticed she was solely focused on the ceiling. Her eyes never moved, even when another man's fingers grazed her nipple as he took a slice of cheese. She played her role as a platter quite perfectly.

Okay, so it appeared that all the things I'd thought were merely rumors were true. Objectification was really a thing.

Thankfully, we didn't stay near the naked food-woman for long. Master meandered around the room, speaking to nearly everyone. He was very popular, it appeared. Not that I'd expected any less. The PR firm hadn't made it as far as they had by huddling on the sidelines. He spoke eloquently and at length about a variety of things, most of which were not work related. It was the first time I'd gotten a glimpse of this side of him.

I was impressed and perhaps a little love-struck. Despite, you know, being an ornament and all.

Half an hour into it, I learned that there *was* something more disturbing than following Master around the room and keeping my eyes down and my mouth shut. That happened when we sat down for dinner. Once I was settled in my chair, my gaze traveled the length of the table. I was awestruck to see the other submissives who were sitting silently, as though they weren't even there.

"Eyes down," Master commanded from beside me.

Shit.

I dropped my gaze to my lap.

My stomach rumbled dangerously loud and I felt heat infuse my face.

No one seemed to notice. And if they did, no one said anything.

Someone clinked a fork against a glass. My first instinct was to look up, but I fought the urge, squeezing my eyes closed and keeping my head tilted down.

"I want to thank you all for coming tonight. It's an honor to be embraced by this community," Master Arlington noted. "I'm continuously humbled by the support and I'm beyond excited about the new release. I took some liberties with this one, I must admit. In my modest opinion, I think it's my best yet."

He chuckled softly.

"However, tonight I'm not going to boast about my accomplishments."

Several people laughed.

"But I am going to say"—he paused for effect—"Master Moore, I'm expecting the same great things out of you as I've always received."

"You won't be disappointed," Master said, a smile in his voice.

"I know I won't. Now, let's eat. And after dinner, you're welcome to visit my dungeon. It's quite elaborate, for those of you who haven't been here before. You're invited to participate should the need arise."

More laughter ensued.

Apparently, these were all inside jokes, because I didn't get it.

Conversations around us resumed, and Master was instantly engrossed in a discussion about book release expectations and the notoriety that Master Arlington had garnered thanks to the efforts of Master's firm. Someone delivered a salad and set it directly in front of Master. I received nothing.

The next thing I knew, he was bringing the fork to my mouth. Not wanting to be rude, I opened, feeling rather foolish for being fed by my Master. This continued, both the conversation and the eating/being fed. Finally, the main course was brought out. I didn't even bother to look to see what it was. At that point, I didn't care. I was ready to go home.

While they talked, again ignoring me completely, I kept my eyes down, waiting for whatever I was supposed to do next. Obviously, I wasn't going to say anything. I was merely an ornament. A freaking ornament.

Master must've sensed my frustration because he leaned over, cupping my face and pressing his lips close to my ear. "I'm proud of you, pet. Don't think I don't notice how hard this is for you."

He leaned down and kissed my neck, just below my ear, before returning his attention to the other guests.

His words warmed my heart and the fact that he was acknowledging me, even without acknowledging me, made me feel marginally better. I had to remember that this was his time to shine. Not mine. And I wanted to be here with him, to share this moment. Even if it meant I had to endure…being an ornament.

I guess there could be worse things.

At least I wasn't a platter.

•

The party turned out to be a humbling experience for me. Granted, Master did not visit Master Arlington's dungeon, which was a little disappointing. I was immensely curious as to what a dungeon looked like. However, we did cut out rather early, which I didn't mind one bit.

The drive home was silent. Master didn't say anything, nor did I. I wasn't even sure what to say. I doubted he wanted to hear all the questions I had regarding the evening. Why were the submissives treated like objects at Master Arlington's house? Was it always like that? Was it popular for women to be platters? Did he ever intend to make me into one?

No, I seriously doubted he wanted to go through that tonight, so I opted to watch out the window as we drove.

When we arrived back at Master's apartment, he led me inside, then down a narrow hallway. He paused at one door but appeared to change his mind and kept going. The next door he stopped at, he opened and pulled me into the room.

I followed obediently. I could tell that something was bothering him and I knew it had to have been something I did. It had been impossible to keep my eyes down at all times. And at one point, I had gasped at something someone said. I knew I'd made the mistakes, but I had quickly corrected my actions, doing the best that I could.

The room that we entered had a bed, but I could tell it wasn't Master's bedroom. It was too sterile, too void of anything remotely personal. It had to be a guest room. Which made me wonder where Landon's room was. More accurately, where Landon was. Was he there in the apartment? Would I see him if he was? Would he join us?

"Remove your clothing and put it on the bed," Master instructed, then left the room.

I twirled in a circle, wondering what he intended to do to me in this room. Was he going to punish me by making me sleep alone in his apartment? I hoped not because I didn't want to be away from him. Although I'd been at his side all night, I felt so far away.

Still, I managed to slip off my heels, the dress, and my panties, placing everything neatly on the bed. Well, except for the shoes. I left them on the floor.

Master returned carrying something in his hand. It had a long handle and dozens of leather strands dangling from it. The ends of some of the strands appeared to be knotted.

"What is that?" I blurted.

His eyes lifted to mine. "It's a flogger. And until I ask you to speak, I expect you to remain silent."

A flogger? I'd read about them but had yet to see one for myself. I also remembered that it was a tool that could be used for punishment.

Okay, so I was in serious trouble here. If he was going to punish me with that…that…implement of torture, I knew this thing between us wasn't going to work out. I couldn't stand the thought of being beaten with an object, regardless of whether he considered it fitting punishment.

Master removed his jacket, then his tie, and finally his shirt. He was bare chested and I couldn't look away from the magnificent sight. The way his wide chest arrowed down to lean hips, the crisp, dark hair that trailed down beneath his slacks. The way his muscles shifted and bunched as he moved. And yes, I'd seen him naked before, but I was still dumbstruck by how incredible he looked shirtless.

I didn't stop ogling him until he held up the flogger. At that point, I flinched.

"This is a suede flogger," he informed me. "It's one of the softer ones and offers a slight sting. It's not an instrument to only be used to inflict pain. It can be, yes. But those who understand it understand the pleasure that it can bring. Do you have any questions?"

"Yes, Master." My gaze darted down to the flogger. "Are you going to punish me with that?"

"No. I'm going to use it on you."

Okay, now I was sincerely confused.

"Your punishment is that you are not allowed to come, pet. Do you know why you're being punished?"

"Because I failed to keep my eyes down and my mouth shut during the party."

"You did. Considering it was your first outing, I *am* impressed with how well you did, but you disobeyed my orders. Therefore, you will be punished, and next time, you'll do even better. So, your punishment is that you cannot come during our scene together."

"I'm sure I can manage that." That didn't seem too harsh. I did not see how a flogger—I didn't care *how* soft he said it was— was going to make me want to orgasm in the first place.

A smile tugged at Master's lips. "Don't underestimate me, pet. I know what I'm doing and my objective is to make you come."

"But you said I can't."

"No, I said you're *not allowed* to come. If you do, I *will* punish you for that infraction."

Wow. It seemed to be a never-ending cycle.

"From this point forward, you are not to speak unless I ask you a direct question, or unless you need to use your safeword. Do you remember what it is?"

"Red, Master."

"Very good."

Master moved toward the corner and that was the first time I noticed there were chains connected to the ceiling. They were adjustable apparently, because Master pulled them lower, putting the padded leather cuffs on the ends within my reach. Sort of.

"Stand on your toes," he instructed.

I did and he lifted my arms above my head and restrained me with the cuffs. They were high enough that I had to remain on my toes so that I didn't dangle freely in the air. The position was uncomfortable, but not so much that it bothered me. Not yet anyway.

"Do not come, pet."

Yeah. That wasn't going to be a problem.

The strands of the flogger slid down my spine, then lower, over my ass. The leather was cool against my skin.

"I do like this sweet little ass," he said, then swatted me with the flogger.

It didn't hurt.

The leather strands went lower, on the backs of my legs, behind my knees, over my calves.

"You should always be required to wear heels. Especially with legs as nice as these."

The sensations along with the uplifting words made me tremble.

Master caressed my entire body with the strands of the flogger, paying the most attention to my breasts and my ass. The leather was soothing as it slid over my back, my shoulders, my neck.

"I'm going to warm up your back now. This should not hurt."

I had no idea what that meant, but then the leather left my skin, only to return with a gentle thud over my shoulder blades. Master was right. It didn't hurt. He continued, moving slowly from my shoulders to my ass. Up, down, again and again. The rhythm was so consistent I felt myself drifting into a strange state of bliss.

I could admit it was slightly arousing, but I seriously doubted I could come like this.

Then the slaps became more intense, leaving a slight sting on my skin. It wasn't so much painful as it was making me aware that it was there. Still, it was bearable, and before I knew it, I was once again lingering in a state of mindless ecstasy. It was enjoyable.

When he changed the motion, I floated back to earth, once again feeling the sting, only this time, there was something intensely erotic about his movements. I felt my body warming, my insides tingling.

Then he paused, moving around so that he was in front of me.

"Color, little one?"

"Green," I sang out. "Definitely green."

He chuckled as his hand slipped between my thighs, his finger sliding inside me without warning. Instantly my arousal spiked as he fingered me leisurely. I moaned as the ache inside me began to build.

"Have you ever experienced subspace?"

I shook my head. I had absolutely no idea what that even was.

Master pushed two fingers in, gently fucking me.

"Get ready to fly, little one."

I frowned, trying to grasp what he was telling me, but it was hard to ignore the methodical fucking of his fingers. I needed more, but he was keeping my orgasm just out of reach.

Fortunately, since I wasn't allowed to come, Master removed his hand, then moved out of my line of sight. The flogger's tails picked up their rhythm, a little harder than before. This time, I felt the gentle stings across my body, as though my skin was tingling from the inside out. My nipples pebbled as a sense of euphoria consumed me.

As my mind floated, I moaned softly, enjoying the feel of the leather against my skin. It was a strange sensation, almost like a high. Not something I could really explain.

"Come back to me, pet."

Master's voice wrapped around me, tugging me back to reality. My body still tingled delightfully and I was hesitant to let go of that feeling.

His hand brushed over my cheek. "Let me see those beautiful eyes, little one."

When I was able to focus, I realized I was no longer cuffed to the chains, but rather lying on the bed with Master beside me. He was as naked as I was and I couldn't resist curling in closer to him, feeling his warmth, the soft rasp of his chest hair against my palms. He smelled so good.

"I probably should've anticipated you drifting into subspace so easily," he mumbled softly.

I frowned. I had absolutely no idea what he'd just said.

Then my eyes widened. "Did I come?"

He laughed, a hearty sound that made my heart swell in my chest. "No, pet. Not yet, anyway."

"Thank God," I whispered harshly. The thought of being punished for an orgasm was absolutely horrifying. And though I hadn't thought it was possible before he started flogging me, I certainly could see how it could happen.

"So, what did you think of the flogger?"

"I liked it…more than I thought I would."

Master chuckled again, his fingers brushing the stray strands of hair back from my face. He leaned down and his lips met mine.

I gently pulled back so I could look in his eyes. "May I touch you, Master?"

"You may touch me," he whispered softly. "In fact, I command you to."

Leaning into him again, I got lost in his kiss. It started out slow and sweet but soon morphed into something intensely erotic. While I slid my hands over his chest, his back, his neck, I pressed myself as close to him as I could get. This was the first time I'd had him all to myself when we weren't in the office. It felt ridiculously intimate.

"Ahh, pet, I'm going to enjoy this immensely."

I wreathed my arms around Master's neck as he shifted positions, moving over me. The warm weight of him pushed me into the mattress as his hips settled between my thighs. I clung to him, wanting him to remain as close to me as possible. He never stopped kissing me, even when he reached between us to guide his cock inside me.

A deep, rumbling moan escaped me as he surged inside, his hips stilling when he was lodged to the hilt.

"I've been looking forward to this," he whispered. "To sinking deep inside you, having you all to myself."

His words were like a balm to my soul, and I'd never felt as cherished as I felt with him in that moment.

"Master," I whispered, rocking my hips in time with his. His thrusts were shallow, filling me to overflowing, his lips gentle as he continued to kiss me. Time seemed to stand still as we made love, my body giving in to the pleasure.

"Come for me, little one."

Seconds after his command, my body relented and I came. It was a beautiful orgasm, not an overwhelming tidal wave but a gentle rolling as it consumed me.

"Such a good girl," he praised as he continued to thrust inside me, building the momentum again.

I found myself riding another wave, only this one was more powerful. His thrusts became more demanding, as though his body was urging mine. Master lifted my right leg, draping it over his arm as he held himself above me while he pivoted his hips, changing the angle. He surged inside me again and this time I cried out as the pleasure rocked me to the core.

"Look at me, pet," he commanded. "I want you looking in my eyes when I make you come."

My eyes locked with his as I tried to hold on, not ready to give up this incredible feeling just yet. Master seemed to be aware of what I was doing and his eyes narrowed.

"Don't hold back. Come for me, Luci. Let that pussy come all over my cock."

I screamed his name as the eroticism of his words mixed with the overwhelming friction of his cock sent me spiraling. My orgasm shook me to my core.

Seconds later, Master came with a muffled roar, his eyes still locked with mine.

It was the most intense thing I'd ever experienced.

And I knew in that moment, I could so easily fall in love with this man.

FIFTY

"I'VE GOT A MEETING THIS MORNIN'."

I heard the words being whispered in my ear but it took a moment to realize where I was and whose resonant voice was pulling me out of a deep sleep.

"Good morning, Master." It wasn't easy to force my eyes open, but I managed, smiling up at him. It should be a damn crime to look that good first thing in the morning.

"Good mornin', pet." He brushed my hair back from my face.

"What time is it?"

"Six o'clock."

I lazily stretched, loving the soreness I felt after an incredible night spent with—

I jerked to a sitting position.

"Did you say six?" Yep, that was my voice sounding slightly shrill.

I started to dart off the bed but didn't get far before Master pulled me back to him, his big arm curling around my waist and tugging me backward.

It was too late to hide the panic. "I have to get ready. I have to be at work at seven thirty."

"You've got plenty of time. Remember? No commute."

Right. No commute. I was at his apartment, which would save me at least thirty minutes. I had a little time.

I sighed, relaxing into the pillow as I stared up at the most handsome man on the face of the planet. Well, except for maybe Landon, who happened to be my master's identical twin. I secretly wished that Landon had been there last night. Although, I wasn't going to share that detail with anyone.

"Which means I've got plenty of time to take you before you have to get in the shower."

I moaned softly as he shifted me onto my stomach. While his lips trailed over my shoulder, his hand snaked between my thighs. I opened my legs, urging him closer. When his fingers teased my entrance, I sighed again. This was one hell of a way to be woken up.

"You're already wet for me," he groaned against my ear.

"Always."

Master moved over me, positioning himself between my legs before pulling my hips back. Within seconds he was plunging deep inside me. My pussy tightened, clamping down on his cock, which had him groaning again. I loved that sound. Knowing that I could give this man pleasure was euphoric in its own right.

"Remember, you have to get to work, pet. So don't hold back." Master retreated slowly. "I'm certainly not going to."

He drove his hips forward, sliding in as deep as possible. He didn't stop, fucking me hard, pushing me closer and closer to the headboard with the strength of his thrusts. It didn't take long before I was flying high, riding the waves of my orgasm.

"That's a good girl," he praised seconds before he roared his release.

•

"So what put that huge grin on your pretty face? I must know."

A heated blush infused my face when I stepped off the elevator to find Jordan sitting at his desk, his eyes glued to me.

"I don't know what you're talking about," I teased.

"Did you have a late night?"

I frowned. "Of course not. And I slept like a baby."

It wasn't a complete lie. I did sleep like a baby with Master in bed with me. It didn't even bother me that we had remained in the guest room rather than him taking me to his bed. Although, I did wonder why he'd done that. Part of me thought he'd done it in an effort to keep his distance. To make it less intimate than if we'd been in his bed, maybe. The other part of me didn't want to think about that too hard because it kind of hurt.

"I just bet you did." Jordan chuckled again. "So, you want to go to lunch today?"

"Absolutely." I needed some Jordan time. It had been far too long since I'd spent any real time with a true friend.

That reminded me, I needed to call Kristen. She had left me two messages and if I didn't call her back she was going to freak out. Since I had no one else to talk to about all that was going on, Kristen would be the one who would listen and not judge me for this...unconventional life I was living. At least I hoped she wouldn't. The thought of her turning on me was what kept me not sharing all the new details of my life.

Still, I would send her a text to let her know I was busy. That should pacify her for a little while and maybe I'd be ready to share all the juicy details with her by the weekend.

Until then, I would get to spend time with my newest friend.

"Perfect. Meet you back here at one," Jordan said, reaching for the phone.

I smiled, then headed to my desk. I started a pot of coffee, then skimmed the calendar for the day. I noticed that Justin had canceled an out-of-town trip, which I took to mean he would be in the office. The calendar was actually free for the most part, aside from one conference call Ben had at three.

Once I'd familiarized myself with the plan for the day, I skimmed my email. The first thing that caught my attention was a meeting request from Landon. He instructed me to schedule it for eleven thirty and to invite Ben, Justin, and Master.

I quickly added it to the calendar and sent the invite just as Master and Justin were walking in at the same time. They must've received the meeting notification on their phones because they both checked them simultaneously.

Justin stopped outside his office door, his gaze sliding my way. "What's this meeting for?"

"Landon didn't say. Just that I needed to schedule it for eleven thirty."

Justin shot a questionable look at Master before they both disappeared into their respective offices. I instantly got to my feet, offering each of them coffee. Surprisingly, Master declined and asked me to shut his door.

When I delivered Justin's coffee to him, his eyes tracked me. I felt a blush heat my cheeks, but I wasn't sure why. Perhaps it was because I'd spent the night with Master last night.

"Have a seat, Luci," Justin stated—more of a command than a request—before I could slip out of the room.

"Yes, sir."

I eased into the chair across from him.

"How're things going with you?"

"Very well."

"I heard you attended a party with Langston last night. Did you enjoy yourself?"

I wouldn't go so far as to say I enjoyed the party. It was an experience, sure. However, I kept those thoughts to myself. I wanted to talk to Master at length about what had happened, how things had transpired, and what his expectations were from here on out. It felt wrong to share any of my feelings with someone else first.

"I did," I said confidently. "It was…interesting."

"I can only imagine. TJ Arlington is an interesting man."

I nodded.

Justin continued to watch me, as though he expected me to say something.

"Luci, are things progressing the way you expected them to?"

"I'm not sure what you mean."

"Here in the office. Based on our…arrangement."

That was a difficult question to answer. I didn't want to lie to Justin, but I also didn't know how to answer it.

"I'm not sure I had any expectations."

He nodded, but I could tell he wasn't buying what I was selling.

"Do you have any questions for me?"

I had plenty of questions, and being that Justin was a Dom, I could probably get all the answers I wanted. Only, I didn't think that was the right way to go about it. I just wasn't sure what Master expected from me, and honestly, I was scared to ask, not sure I was ready to hear the answer.

"If you're not happy, Luci…"

I sat up straight. "I'm happy, sir. Very happy."

"No regrets?"

I shook my head. "Absolutely not."

He smiled for the first time since I'd stepped into the office. "Good. I'm glad to hear that."

I waited for him to say something more, but he didn't. Finally, I got to my feet. "Is there anything else I can get you?"

His dark blue eyes flashed with heat and I felt a chill dance down my spine.

"I'm good for now. Thanks."

I nodded, then returned to my desk feeling even more disoriented than I had that morning.

Something was happening, but I wasn't sure what it was.

•

By the time one o'clock rolled around, I was starving.

I was also greatly concerned about what was going on.

All four of my bosses had been in the back conference room since eleven thirty. They'd had Jordan order in lunch and specifically asked that he deliver it to them. They informed me that they did not want to be bothered for anything else.

My desk phone rang right at one.

"Hello?"

"Come on, hot stuff. Let's go grab some lunch."

I glanced at the hallway. "I'm...not so sure that's a good idea right now."

"It's a perfect idea. They're in a meeting and they won't come out until they're ready. In the meantime, you and I are going to have a sandwich and gossip like we'd planned."

I sighed. I knew Jordan was right. And it wouldn't do any good for me to sit there and wait. I would only drive myself crazy if I did.

"Okay," I reluctantly agreed. "I'm on my way."

After grabbing my purse, I went straight for the lobby, fully expecting one of my bosses to stop me, to tell me what was going on. Unfortunately, the hallway behind me remained silent.

Jordan was waiting for me by the elevator. When I approached, he took my arm.

"The frowny thing... It does nothing for you."

I rolled my eyes and smiled.

"That's better."

It took all of ten minutes to get downstairs, order, pay and find an empty table. The place was practically empty. I figured that had a lot to do with Christmas being right around the corner. If I had to guess, a lot of people took the week off. Unfortunately, our office would be shutting down starting tomorrow. I didn't particularly want the time off, because I had absolutely nothing to do, but it wasn't like I could ask them to work on a holiday.

"All right, Luci. I've been waiting weeks to hear what's going on with you. It's time you spill the beans."

I looked at my friend, a little taken aback by such a dominant statement coming from him.

He chuckled, then added, "Please."

God, what I wouldn't give to tell him everything that was happening. Unfortunately, I couldn't. I knew that our arrangement wasn't something my bosses would want me sharing with anyone. However, this was Jordan. He was my friend. Then again, he worked for them. If he disagreed with anyone's actions, he could possibly sue them, right?

It was too much pressure. I didn't know what to do or who to talk to. I couldn't imagine anyone would understand.

On top of that, I was so confused. After spending last night with Master, I didn't even know what I expected anymore. The things he'd said...telling me that he knew I would belong to him...Was that real? Or had he merely said what he thought I wanted to hear? I was desperate to get someone's take on it, but I knew it wasn't my place to say anything.

"Okay," Jordan said with a huff. "Since you're not going to tell me, I'll just start guessing. You can blink once if I'm right, twice if I'm wrong."

I laughed.

Jordan took a bite of his sandwich and appeared to be thinking about his first question. I, on the other hand, was trying to figure out how much I wanted to tell him. Well, more like how much I was *willing* to tell him. I *wanted* to tell him everything. Hell, I just needed to get it off my chest.

"First, let me sum up what I *do* know," Jordan said with a twinkle in his eye.

"All right."

"You've been working here for what? Two and a half months? Which is longer than any secretary they've had in the past year and a half. I heard rumors that they lay out the requirements of the position after two weeks."

"One month in my case," I informed him.

His smile widened. "Okay, so they laid out the requirements at the one-month point. And you stuck around, even though the requirements aren't...traditional?"

I didn't say anything.

"You're smoking-hot, and I've seen the big boys look at you like they want to eat you up."

I hadn't realized that, but I allowed Jordan to continue.

"Plus, I did catch on to the little game you were playing during the quarterly meeting. Every so often you would disappear. And coincidentally, so would one of the bosses."

Oh, shit. I didn't realize anyone had picked up on that.

"Oh, don't look so worried. I don't think anyone else noticed."

I hoped not.

"So, along with all that, you've captured the attention of four yummy men." He winked. "During the time you've been here, I've heard at least three of them talk about you in a very positive manner. Then there was the sex toy client who came to do a demonstration. I happen to know you were in that demonstration because I tried to call your desk during that time and you didn't answer."

I blushed as the memory of that day flooded back.

"Yep, and the pink in your cheeks confirms it." Jordan chuckled. "Then, this morning, you showed up looking a little starry-eyed after spending the night with one of the bosses."

My eyes widened. "How did you know that?"

His smirk was mischievous. "The elevator came down from the forty-fourth floor."

Oh, my God.

Jordan held up his hand, obviously noticing the panic-stricken look that had taken over my face.

"Don't worry, kiddo. I'm not going to say anything. I'm your friend." His expression turned serious. "And believe it or not, I really am your friend. I like you, Luci. I want to be here if you want to talk. I get it if there're details you don't want to share, but I want you to know I'll listen. I talk to Dale about you all the time and let's just say, if you were a dude, he'd be ten shades of green right about now."

I exhaled slowly. "I don't know what I'm gonna do, Jordan."

"What do you mean?"

"I mean…whatever's going on…it didn't start out this way and I'm not sure which direction it's going to go."

His forehead creased. "Since that's super vague, I'm going to ask you…which way do you want it to go?"

I shrugged.

And that was the biggest problem of all.

I was fairly certain I was falling in love with Master. And Landon.

Yep, that was right. I was falling in love with two of my bosses.

However, anytime I thought about Ben or Justin, my heart sank when I even considered not being able to spend time with them. Something was changing, taking our original arrangement off course, and honestly, I wasn't sure I was ready to veer in that direction. Maybe that made me selfish, or perhaps simply crazy, but I couldn't change how I felt.

Jordan's hand covered mine. "I truly believe that everything works out the way it's supposed to, Luci. So, why don't you sit back, take a breath, and let the cards fall where they may."

My eyes met his and I took a deep breath. I couldn't stop the smile. "When did you get to be so philosophical?"

"I'm the whole package, kiddo. Don't you know?" He said it without arrogance, which was one of the things I loved about Jordan.

"So, when you're ready to share all the dirty deets, I'm here. Until then, I'm going to keep sitting at my desk, wondering what sexy deliciousness is taking place behind those doors."

I huffed out a laugh.

It was all I could do to keep the tears from falling.

FIFTY-ONE

WHEN I GOT BACK TO the office, I found that my bosses were no longer in their meeting; however, they were all four out of the office and it was driving me crazy not to know what was going on. Knowing that answers weren't going to be forthcoming, I focused my attention on work.

At three o'clock, I looked up when I heard the sound of footsteps coming toward me. I noticed that Justin was carrying several bags, as was Ben. They stopped in front of my desk and placed their loot on top.

"What is this?" I noticed tinsel and Christmas lights peeking out of one of the bags and excitement stirred inside me.

"We're decorating for Christmas," Ben informed me.

I glanced around the space unnecessarily. They all knew what I knew. "But we don't have a tree."

Justin's smile was wicked.

About that time, Landon and Langston came in, both carrying a bag, but these were far more discreet than the shopping bags Ben and Justin had been carrying. I was anxious to know what they had, where they'd gotten it from, and more importantly, what they intended to do with them.

Ben began emptying the bags onto my desk, whistling a Christmas tune while he worked. He had to know that I was fascinated by the possibilities, but he gave nothing away.

"Strip," Master instructed, nodding toward me before heading to his office right behind Landon.

While Ben tossed approving glances my way, I hurried to remove my clothing before sitting back down at my desk. Master and Landon disappeared into their offices momentarily, then returned. They had removed their suit jackets, and Justin was doing the same.

"You ready for this, sweet girl?"

I met Landon's heated gaze and smiled. "I don't even know what *this* is, but sure. I'm ready."

Justin disappeared only to return with a small step stool in his hand, which he carried over to the wall.

Landon held out his hand for me and I got to my feet, stepping around my desk into the middle of the area. Landon teased me with subtle brushes of his fingers over my naked skin while Justin brought various items over and handed them to Ben.

I'd never realized until then how incredibly vulnerable I felt when I was the only naked one in the room. All four of my bosses were dressed and I was not. Somehow, they'd easily made that a rule that I tended to follow without question.

"We figured we could all use some Christmas spirit, so we decided we'd decorate *you* today."

"*Me?*" Yep. I giggled, feeling giddy at the prospect. My nipples pebbled as the warmth of Landon's knuckles grazed them.

"Very nice," Landon praised, leaning over and sucking one of my nipples into his mouth.

"Oh, God," I groaned, tipping my head back as sensations erupted throughout my body. His mouth was gentle yet insistent as he steadily worked my nipples into hardened points.

I groaned my disappointment when he pulled back, but he didn't go far. I watched as Master handed over a set of nipple clamps. I wasn't sure where they'd found them, but they were obviously meant to be holiday decorations. There were several charms that dangled from the chain.

He fastened them to my nipples, teasing me relentlessly as he did. The pain was intense, but I blocked most of it out, thrilled by the notion of being their holiday decoration. While Landon was fixing the clamps, Ben began draping my body with the long strands of tinsel, affixing one end to my upper arm by circling it and tying it off. The thin pieces of silver tickled my skin.

Although definitely not traditional, it was intensely erotic.

"Spread your legs wide," Justin instructed, his eyes warm as they caressed my face.

"I'm really the tree, huh?" I grinned.

"You're really the tree. A sexy little tree, might I add."

He then took my arms, raising them above my head and fastening my wrists to a set of cuffs dangling from the ceiling. Obviously, that had been Justin's doing, hence the need for a step stool.

Once I was restrained, all four men continued to adorn me with various items, including long strands of LED lights, a butt plug with some sort of decorative jewel on the end, small bells around my neck and ankles, and a variety of ornaments that they hung on the wire that ran through the tinsel. When they were finished, Ben plugged in the lights and then all four of them stepped back, admiring me with heated stares.

"One more thing." Master stepped up to me, then lowered himself to one knee. I dropped my chin to my chest and watched as his head lowered. He teased my pussy with his fingers, brushing over my clit until I was moaning in earnest.

The moans died a quick and painful death when I felt something clamp onto my clit. I cried out when his fingers disappeared. Whatever he had put on me caused my clit to throb painfully.

"Did you...clamp my clit?" I asked, the words rushing out on a pinch of pain that shot through my entire body.

"Breathe, pet," Master instructed as he got to his feet. "A submissive's goal is to please her masters, remember?"

"I remember." Swallowing hard and trying to ignore the intense sensation, I focused on the four men surrounding me. Or I tried to anyway. Between the clamps on my nipples and the one on my clit, I could hardly breathe.

"Oh, I almost forgot," Landon said, pulling something out of his pocket.

"Please..." I wasn't sure I could take any more.

"You make a stunning tree, sweet girl. But we need a star."

I lifted my eyebrows in question.

He stepped closer, holding what appeared to be a star on a chain. He hooked it to the chain dangling between the nipple clamps. The weight of it had me moaning as the clamps tightened, pain shooting straight to my clit, ratcheting up my arousal and making me hyperaware of every sensual ache.

"Now she's perfect," Landon whispered, brushing his fingers down my cheek. "You bring us all great pleasure."

My body warmed from his praise.

"I have to say, I wish I had a tree like that in my apartment," Ben said, grinning mischievously. "I'd keep it up all year long."

"I think someone needs to inspect her," Landon noted, glancing over at Justin.

"I'm more than willing," Justin replied.

He rolled up his sleeves as he approached. I met his gaze, trying not to smile.

Justin leaned in and kissed me. His lips were warm and soft, his tongue demanding as it pushed into my mouth. He cupped his hand around the back of my head and held me still. I moaned, trying to get closer, wanting him to ease the devastating ache inside me. His kiss only had me desperate for more.

When his hand slipped down between my legs, I held my breath, praying he wouldn't torture me for too long.

He slipped one finger inside me.

I whimpered.

"She's wet," Justin informed the others. "I think she likes this."

I nodded, letting him know that I definitely did.

By the time Justin stepped back, I was moaning and writhing from his intimate finger-fucking. Ben took his place, dipping two fingers inside me and fucking me, giving me a little more than Justin had. He repeatedly brushed my G-spot but didn't give me enough to send me over.

Tears of frustration were falling from my eyes when Master approached. He did the same, fingering me feverishly while he held my gaze.

"I've been waiting for this," he whispered. "To see you like this, restrained and eager."

I was certainly that.

"You can't come yet, little one."

I groaned loudly, even as my body burned hotter, brighter, so close to climax but not quite there. Before he stepped away, Master tugged the chain on the nipple clamps and flicked the clamp on my clit, making me cry out.

Then Landon stepped up.

"Are you ready to come, pet?"

I nodded. "Please. *Please* make me come."

To my utter relief, Landon unfastened his slacks and freed his cock before grabbing my butt and lifting my feet off the floor.

"Put your legs around my waist," he insisted.

I didn't hesitate, wrapping myself around him while he held the brunt of my weight with his arms.

He impaled me on his cock while my wrists remained restrained above my head. Gripping the chain above me, I did my best to hold on, unable to do anything more than accept the torturously slow fucking as he thrust into me again and again. I felt overwhelmingly full thanks to the plug in my ass and the huge cock filling my pussy. I watched Landon's face, every expression that crossed it, and I held out, wanting him to come with me.

Master moved around behind me, his hands gripping my hips as he lifted me slightly, allowing Landon to fuck me harder, deeper.

"Landon! Oh, God!" I couldn't stop moaning as I inched closer and closer to orgasm. "May I come?"

"You may," he growled, slamming into me several more times.

My body shot straight over the precipice, and seconds later, he was coming with me, roaring his release while Master continued to hold me up.

Honestly, it was the most creative Christmas gift anyone had ever given me.

•

After they had removed all the decorations from my body, Landon spent some time with me, cleaning me, then helping me to get dressed. I enjoyed the few minutes we spent together, but then they all returned to their offices, leaving me alone with my thoughts once more.

No one said anything as to why they'd spent so much time holed up in the conference room and I didn't ask. Truth was, I'd been fretting over the fact that Jordan had confirmed my fears. The office would be closed starting tomorrow thru the day after New Year's. I could only assume that their impromptu decoration party was their way of sending me off.

That meant I was going to be spending a significant amount of time twiddling my thumbs.

Initially, I thought I would head over to my mother's, hang out even if she didn't necessarily want me there. However, a few minutes ago, I'd received a text from her letting me know that— *surprise!*—she and Jim would be on a cruise until after the first of the year.

For whatever reason, the news had dampened my spirits even more, although I probably should've seen it coming. After all, they did it every year.

"So, any big plans for your time off?" Ben asked me when he came out of his office to get another cup of afternoon coffee.

"No, actually." I planted a smile on my face and pretended it didn't bother me. "My family doesn't really celebrate. My mom and stepdad are off on a two-week cruise."

Ben frowned. "Really?"

"Really. It's a ritual of theirs. She works hard all year and chooses to shut down her dental practice for a few weeks during the holidays."

"What about your dad?"

"He died when I was three. My mom remarried a couple of years later and they're still together. I have no other close family members."

I definitely didn't want Ben or anyone else to feel sorry for me. I certainly wasn't seeking sympathy. I was extremely content with my life the way that it was. Especially now that I was building relationships with my bosses. Although we were doing some untraditional things, I still enjoyed getting to know these men and letting them show me things I'd never thought possible. Two weeks without that was going to be unbearable.

"What about you?" I prompted, wanting to redirect. "Where will you be spending Christmas?"

Ben smiled. "I'll see my mother on Christmas Eve. She lives close and we make sure to spend that day together every year."

"Will you be spending any time with Justin?" Sure, it was a personal question, but I already knew what their relationship entailed.

"I will," he confirmed with a smile. "At least a couple of days."

"Well, I hope you two have fun."

Ben gave me a mock toast with his coffee mug, then disappeared into his office. I got to work, clearing out my email so that when I came back, I wouldn't feel quite so overwhelmed.

•

I felt slightly shafted when Landon sent me an email at four thirty, telling me that I should go home for the remainder of the day and to have a good holiday. I knew he was simply trying to be nice, not cruelly kicking me out into the cold the way that I felt he was doing, but I couldn't deny I felt dejected.

Knowing I couldn't very well argue and tell him I'd rather stay, I sucked it up and started packing up my things. I wouldn't be back until after the first of the year, so I made sure to grab anything I might need during my time off. Not that I kept a lot of personal effects in the office, but I did have a couple of things in my desk that I might need, such as my compact mirror and a tube of lip gloss I favored.

A few minutes later, the four of them walked out of their respective offices, all eyes landing on me.

"You're headin' out, right?" Landon asked, his eyes warm, his smile firmly in place.

Not one of them realized how hesitant I was to leave. Then again, I didn't really want them to notice either.

"Yes, sir," I answered with a forced amount of cheer in my voice.

I didn't want to go, but it seemed I had no choice. With my purse in hand, I followed them to the lobby, which I found was empty because they had also sent Jordan home.

"We hope you have a good holiday," Landon said, stepping in close to me.

I relaxed my posture and forced a smile. "Thank you."

Landon leaned down and kissed me sweetly before stepping back out of the way. His eyes lingered on my face for a few seconds longer. The pain of loss intensified as reality sank in. I wouldn't see him for at least two weeks.

Ben moved in close, his lips brushing mine. "Merry Christmas, Luci."

"Merry Christmas."

Justin was the next one to kiss me, and although I should've felt better, I didn't.

When Master pulled me into him, I could tell he was trying to read my mind. I purposely put a blank expression on my face because the last thing I wanted was for any of them to pity me. It wasn't their fault I was alone for the holidays. I could've probably spent time with Kristen if I hadn't been avoiding her for the past month or so.

The long, deep kiss with Master was interrupted by the ding of the elevator. Like Landon, Master seemed to be regarding me curiously, so I forced a smile and released a little sigh.

The five of us stepped into the elevator and rode down to the main floor. They offered quick good-byes when I climbed into my car that the valet had pulled around for me.

As I drove out of the parking lot, I felt a sudden overwhelming sense of loss. I wasn't sure what I'd expected, but that certainly hadn't been it. I felt as though they'd shunned me, as though I meant little to them after all we'd experienced recently. Sure, they had all kissed me good-bye, so there wasn't much more for them to do. However, the thought of them off to spend time with their loved ones for the holidays while I was at home alone didn't make me feel good. It was selfish, I knew, but I couldn't help it.

Rather than dwell on it, though, I shoved it all down and drove to Starbucks before heading home. When I got to my apartment, I unpacked the small bag I'd taken to Master's and got settled in. It wasn't surprising that I was instantly restless and opted to head over to the evening yoga class. I was disappointed when Kristen wasn't there, but I figured she was likely spending time with her family for the holidays as well.

It took everything in me to return to my apartment later that night, knowing I would be spending the entire next two weeks alone.

I didn't want to be alone.

I wanted to be with my bosses.

And wasn't that a disturbing thought. All this time I'd gotten used to being with them in the office. Now that we weren't there, I still wanted to be with them.

Only now, I wanted something *outside* of the office.

Unfortunately, that wasn't part of the arrangement.

FIFTY-TWO

BOSS MEETING

LANDON

"OKAY, WHAT DID I MISS?" my brother asked as we stood at the front of the building staring after Luci's car as she pulled away.

At least I wasn't the only one who'd noticed how strangely she was acting.

Something had just happened, but I had no idea what. It was obvious she was disappointed, although I wasn't sure why. Most people were grateful for time off. That certainly didn't seem the be the case where she was concerned.

Then again, even as she drove away, I realized I wasn't ready to let her go. Two weeks without her was going to be hell.

"Did she seem upset to you?" I asked Ben, trying to ensure we'd all noticed the same thing.

He nodded but didn't elaborate.

I glanced at Langston, both of us shrugging.

"Let's grab a drink," Justin suggested. "I think we need to talk."

I frowned. Clearly Justin knew something my brother and I didn't.

Then again, I wasn't going to argue about a drink. I needed one. If for no other reason than Luci had just driven away and the chance to see her for the next couple of weeks was slim to none.

Although the four of us had met this morning to go over in detail everything we had pending in an effort to ensure we all took the time off that the holidays allowed, we would all still be busy with family and other get-togethers that naturally occurred at this time of year.

As, I was sure, Luci would be, too.

I noticed Justin subtly shaking his head as he and Ben turned toward the restaurant.

Once again, I glanced at Langston, wishing my brother could enlighten me. Clearly we'd missed something big. Something that evidently had to do with Luci.

I wasn't sure what it was I was feeling, but I knew for a fact I didn't like it.

Not a fucking bit

♥ ▫ ▫ ▫ ▫ ♥ ▫ ▫ ▫ ▫ ♥

I hope you enjoyed the first part of Luci's story. The 2nd book is available now, so you can pick right up where you left off. Originally, I had intended for this to be one standalone book, however, it came in FAR too long to be a single book. Therefore, there are two books, but I did release them at the same time so you wouldn't have to wait.

Keep reading for the first chapter in the next book:

ONE

BOSS MEETING

LANGSTON

FOR POSSIBLY THE FIRST TIME in my life, I didn't like the holidays one fucking bit.

The thought of not seeing Luci bothered me. Not only the fact that I was thinking about it too much, but also the fact that she would be away from me. I wanted more time with her, not less.

And, fuck, that bothered me, too.

By the time we got a table at a nearby restaurant, I was trying to read minds. I could tell by the look on Ben's face that he knew something that Landon and I didn't. As much as I wanted to grab him by the collar and insist he tell me what it was, I managed to refrain. I was nothing if not controlled. It was what made me a damn good Dom. I couldn't even remember the last time I'd lost control.

Okay, that wasn't true. It was the day I'd come into the office to find Luci at her desk and not naked in my office like I had requested. I'd lost it that day. After I'd spent so much time anticipating having her all to myself, seeing her not where I'd instructed her to be had set me off.

However, I did at least have the common sense to let some time pass before I had punished her for her transgression. I derived absolutely no pleasure from punishment that wasn't associated with playing. However, I would dole it out as it was necessary to maintain the balance between a Dom and a submissive.

"All right," Justin said after we'd received our drinks. "Go ahead and tell them what Luci told you."

I knew it.

Ben glanced at me and Landon. "I asked what her plans were for the holidays. I got the sense that she was not looking forward to them because she would be spending it alone."

"Why would you assume that?" I narrowed my eyes, trying to read him. "What about her parents?"

"She said they went on a cruise," Ben explained. "Won't be back until after the first of the year."

"According to Luci," Landon offered, "she doesn't spend much time with them anyway."

Well, fuck. Why didn't I know that?

"And Kristen?" I asked Landon.

He shrugged. "No idea, but that does explain why she's hesitant to go home when I tell her to."

"She doesn't want to be alone," Ben offered, which was the same conclusion I'd drawn.

"Was anyone planning to spend time with her over the holidays?" Justin asked.

I glanced at Landon. I hadn't spoken to him about it, but I had intended to see her. No way could I go two fucking weeks without seeing her. I'd probably go out of my mind.

And that honestly had nothing to do with the fact that I wouldn't get sex otherwise. Although I was hesitant to act on my attraction to Luci, that didn't mean I could ignore her entirely.

"I was going to call her," Landon admitted. "I haven't nailed down anything at this point, but I was going to see her. Or try, anyway. Take her to dinner or something."

Justin glanced at Ben, then back to me. "Unfortunately, we've got a lot going on. I'm not sure we can see her much until after Christmas."

Ben took a sip of his drink before speaking. "I'm willing to change some things around. I'm spending Christmas Eve with my momma, but I'll be available before and after."

As I sipped my drink, an idea came to me. I glanced at my brother and he nodded, as though he had read my mind. Sometimes I thought he could actually do that.

"Let me call our folks," Landon told Justin and Ben. "See if they'd be willin' to do somethin' different."

"Like what?" Justin was obviously curious.

Fortunately, my brother didn't show his hand before he was ready to play it. "Give me until tomorrow mornin'. Then we'll let you know."

"As long as someone's going to take care of Luci," Ben said firmly. "Otherwise, I'll shift what I have to. I don't like the idea of her spending the holidays by herself."

I didn't like the idea either, but if it came down to it, I would rather be the one to spend time with her. Well, Landon and I. That was my possessive streak coming out, though.

"She won't be spending them alone," I assured them.

No matter what my brother and I came up with, Luci would not be spending the holidays by herself.

I would make damn sure of that.

INTRIGUED out of the OFFICE is available now!

♥ ▫ ▫ ▫ ♥ ▫ ▫ ▫ ♥

Want to see some fun stuff related to the Office Intrigue Duet, you can find extras on my website. Or how about what's coming next? Find more at: www.NicoleEdwardsAuthor.com

If you're interested in keeping up to date on any of my series, as well as receiving updates on all that I'm working on, you can sign up for my monthly newsletter.

Want a simple, *fast* way to get updates on new releases? You can also sign up for text messaging. If you are in the U.S. simply text NICOLE to 64600 or sign up on my website. I promise not to spam your phone. This is just my way of letting you know what's happening because I know you're busy, but if you're anything like me, you always have your phone on you.

And last but certainly not least, if you want to see what's going on with me each week, sign up for my weekly Hot Sheet! It's a short, entertaining weekly update of things going on in my life and that of the team that supports me. We're a little crazy at times and this is a firsthand account of our antics.

Acknowledgments

First and always, I have to thank my wonderfully patient husband who puts up with me every single day. If it wasn't for him and his belief that I could (and can) do this, I wouldn't be writing this today. He has been my backbone, my rock, the very reason I continue to believe in myself. I love you for that, babe.

Chancy Powley – This was a tough one, I know. It tested our friendship and I hope you know that you mean the world to me. I thank you for everything you do for me, all the wonderful suggestions and ideas, and especially for letting me bounce mine off you.

Allison Holzapfel – Our friendship has grown stronger the past few months and I'm so glad that I have you. This book tested all of us, but I thank you for the time and dedication you put into reading it and giving me your input. The book is better because of it.

Amber Willis – You don't particularly care for BDSM romance, but you dug in and powered through. I thank you for all you do for me, and for being my friend.

Karen DiGaetano – You're probably the fastest reader I've ever met, and I thank you for taking the time to read through this book – twice – and for giving me your input. Thanks to you, I decided to elaborate some and add a few more perspectives. The book is certainly better because of it.

Wander Aguiar and Andrey Bahia – You two are class acts in every way. Thank you SO much for giving my characters life. Working with you is a true pleasure and I look forward to what the future has in store for us.

Thank you to my proofreaders. Jenna Underwood, Annette Elens, Theresa Martin, and Sara Gross. Not only do you catch my blunders, you are my friends and it is an honor to call you that.

I also have to thank my street team – Naughty (and nice) Girls – Your unwavering support is something I will never take for granted. So, thank you Traci Hyland, Maureen Ames, Erin Lewis, Jackie Wright, Chris Geier, Kara Hildebrand, Shannon Thompson, Tracy Barbour, Nadine Hunter, Toni Thompson, and Rachelle Newham.

I can't forget my copyeditor, Amy at Blue Otter Editing. Thank goodness I've got you to catch all my punctuation, grammar, and tense errors.

Nicole Nation 2.0 for the constant support and love. You've been there for me from almost the beginning. This group of ladies has kept me going for so long, I'm not sure I'd know what to do without them.

And, of course, YOU, the reader. Your emails, messages, posts, comments, tweets… they mean more to me than you can imagine. I thrive on hearing from you, knowing that my characters and my stories have touched you in some way keeps me going. I've been known to shed a tear or two when reading an email because you simply bring so much joy to my life with your support. I thank you for that.

About Nicole Edwards

New York Times and *USA Today* bestselling author Nicole Edwards lives in Austin, Texas with her husband, their three kids, and four rambunctious dogs. When she's not writing about sexy alpha males, Nicole can often be found with a book in hand or making an attempt to keep the dogs happy. You can find her hanging out on Facebook and interacting with her readers - even when she's supposed to be writing.

By Nicole Edwards

The Alluring Indulgence Series
Kaleb
Zane
Travis
Holidays with the Walker Brothers
Ethan
Braydon
Sawyer
Brendon

The Austin Arrows Series
The SEASON: Rush
The SEASON: Kaufman

The Bad Boys of Sports Series
Bad Reputation
Bad Business

The Caine Cousins Series
Hard to Hold
Hard to Handle

The Club Destiny Series
Conviction
Temptation
Addicted
Seduction
Infatuation
Captivated
Devotion
Perception
Entrusted
Adored
Distraction

The Coyote Ridge Series
Curtis
Jared

BECAUSE NAUGHTY CAN BE OH SO NICE®

NE LTD

CPSIA information can be obtained
at www.ICGtesting.com
Printed in the USA
LVHW05s0313270718
585041LV00013B/1083/P

9 781939 786838